Hostage
Of
Diplomacy

Anne-Marie Price

Copyright © 2015 Anne-Marie Price

ISBN: 09942761-1-7
ISBN-13: 978-0-9942761-1-7

DEDICATION

To Margaret and Laurence Price,
who fight the black dog with me
each and every day.

.

ACKNOWLEDGMENTS

My sincere thanks to Wendy Stackhouse
for her expertise and technical support
in getting this book finally published.

To save the reader from trying to locate
Kathou and Pangani on a map
I would like to state that the country
is entirely fictional.

FRIDAY

The New Ambassador

By lunchtime the new internal steel re-enforced security walls were in place and the door with a keypad lock would soon be following. Throughout all the offices, workmen were finishing the installation of the new alarm system. That they were nearly finished was the good news. The bad news was that the workmen still had a habit of leaving their empty packaging and tools lying around on the floor. The Australian Embassy staff had to walk around very carefully so as to not fall over anything and break their necks. Realising that it was useless to ask the workmen yet again to clean up, and that the Diplomats were extremely busy with the present crisis, Sarah Trent, the Embassy Secretary decided that she would have to do the job herself.

She didn't have an office; her desk was situated in the corridor, beside the Ambassador's office. Sarah was small in stature but buxom, her pretty face was usually unadorned by excessive makeup and her blonde hair was pulled back into a plait that ran down past her waist. At twenty-five, this was Sarah's first posting in the diplomatic corps and she had been enjoying it immensely. *Well I had been enjoying myself until a fortnight ago*, she mused.

With a sigh, she began to collect up the tools that were strewn across her desk and on the floor. There were footsteps behind her and presuming it was Con Zuco, the Public Affairs Officer, since she would have seen if one of the other diplomats had come out of their rooms, she dumped the tools into the man's arms without looking up into his face.

'Will you get rid of these, please Con?' Sarah asked, 'And warn the workers that the next tool I pick up goes into the bin with the rest of their rubbish!'

'Certainly, but tell me, do I have the honour of addressing Miss Sarah Trent?' At the sound of an unfamiliar but amused male voice Sarah's head snapped up, her eyes filled with disbelief.

'M...M...Mr. Ambassador! We weren't expecting you till next week!' Horror and embarrassment reflected in Sarah's voice.

Laughter filled James Greene's eyes as he swept a brief glance around at the mess and disorder of the construction around them, 'Obviously not.' Sarah tried valiantly to take the tools from him, but the Ambassador refused to relinquish them. 'I'll deal with the workers, Sarah,' he added, 'while you round up the rest of the Diplomats.' Without waiting for an answer Ambassador Greene headed downstairs with the armload of tools.

Sarah made her way swiftly to Marianne Davis' door and upon her knock being answered, entered the room. Marianne, the Political Attaché, looked up from where she sat behind her desk and smiled warmly. 'The new Ambassador has already arrived!' stated Sarah.

Marianne rose calmly to her feet, smoothing down her ankle length skirt. She knew how to disguise her physical imperfections with great dress sense. She was 46, a divorcee with four grown children in Australia. 'What's he like?' Her tone was quite casual but she was as curious as hell. It was all anyone in the Embassy could think about for the past two weeks, as no one had previously met James Greene. Sarah frowned for a moment as she thought about it.

'Nearly fifty, tall with light brown hair, tinged with a little grey. A handsome man and a sense of humour, thank goodness!'

Marianne laughed as Sarah explained her first encounter with James Greene. Soon afterwards Sarah knocked on the Ambassador's door after having gathered up the male members of the Embassy and followed the diplomats inside.

James Greene turned from where he stood looking out the French doors. The view was quite beautiful. The Embassy driveway wove through a colourful tropical garden that bloomed and blossomed in the humidity of the summer. Through the trees, the Ambassador's residence could just be seen. Sarah introduced each of the Diplomats before quietly closing the door behind her and returning to her own work area. Sitting down behind his new desk, the Ambassador surveyed his staff as they were invited to pull up a chair. He insisted that they call him James rather than his official title.

'My assignment to Pangani was so sudden that I've not had the time to be properly briefed about not only the situation here but also what happened to my predecessor.' Just as the Embassy staff had been curious about their new Ambassador, so was he curious about the reason behind his sudden transfer. The significant glance exchanged between the diplomats, filled James with foreboding.

It was Major Gary Winters, 35, the Military Advisor for the past five years, who finally spoke in a quiet, matter of fact, unemotional manner, 'Nearly two weeks ago Ambassador Lucas ignored my advice about delivering much needed medical supplies to a hospital in the north of the country. At present there is a revolt with a faction of the fanatic Muslim community rebelling against the Emir. They wish to form their own extremist government. The Rebels weren't impressed by Lucas' mission of mercy and sent him back to us in a pine box. The night after that, the American Embassy was bombed. Although no one was injured, all their un-essential personnel were on the next flight home. Prince Kahlee, the Emir's eldest son, has already arranged new temporary facilities, with added security for the American Embassy. We've warned our Nationals that if they can't leave, then they're to be extra careful. There is currently a curfew after sunset.'

'Good God!' James Greene took a deep breath before continuing, 'Thus the additional security measures that were being installed when I arrived?'

'Yes Sir! These precautions were suggested by Nasseur.' The Ambassador's eyebrows rose in an obvious question. 'That is Colonel Joseph Nasseur,' Gary quickly added, 'There isn't much going on here in Pangani that he doesn't know about. One of his many tasks is to ensure the safety of foreigners in this country and that Islamic law and codes of behaviour are upheld and respected by residents and visitors. If you have any doubts, Ambassador, then consult Sarah, as she's not only conversant in Islamic customs but also speaks and reads Arabic.'

'What's this? Brains and a pretty face?'

Gary's face remained an unemotional mask as he rose to his feet. 'Please excuse me; I have an appointment with the Colonel in a few minutes.' He came to attention and saluted before leaving the office.

When the door had closed, James looked to Marianne for enlightenment as he had hoped to break the Major's rigidity but he failed. 'Is the Major always so serious?'

'You see it was Gary and Sarah who found Lucas' body. When he said a pine box, he didn't mean a coffin. The Rebels had… they had chopped Lucas up and put him in a packing crate. The Major feels responsible for not stopping Lucas going north.'

'Oh my God!' A look of acute pain crossed James' face, 'That is definitely something that I was not briefed on!' After a moment he added, 'I left my bags downstairs, not knowing how matters would be with the Residency.'

Con Zuco, the Public Affairs Officer, rose immediately to his feet. He was 29, single, good looking with an over-exaggerated sense of his own worth. 'I'll see to that James. I suspect that you have many questions that Kevin and Marianne are more suitable to answer.' He fled from the room, pleased with the ease of his escape.

There was a frown on the Ambassador's brow as he thought deeply for a moment. 'I'm wondering if it is such a good idea for Crystal to be joining me here,' he finally said.

Kevin Shaw, the Cultural Attaché, was 42, in his second marriage to a much younger woman and seriously regretting it. He asked politely, 'Your wife?'

James shook his head and sighed. 'No, my wife died three years ago. Crystal's my youngest daughter. She has just divorced her cheating husband and wants the chance to see something of the world. Marianne do you think it will be too difficult for her here?'

There was a pause before she answered, 'If Crystal is a timid sort of woman then it might be rather frightening for her. Neither Sarah nor I intend to leave the mission unless it's made absolutely necessary. She must also abide by the strict guidelines that are in place for visitors.'

'That's all right then,' with a sigh of relief, James smiled. 'Crystal's quite capable of taking care of herself. She must be just a few years older than Sarah. If there's any trouble I can send her straight home.'

Kevin and Marianne exchanged a silent look of concern but if the new Ambassador had made his mind up, there was nothing they could do to change it.

Con's Attentions

While James Greene had been assessing his staff, Sarah had continued cleaning up after the workmen. They had finally finished their work and been escorted out of the Embassy by Abu, the Panganian Office Manager who was in charge of all the locals who worked in the Embassy. Sarah shut the new security door that now locked off the top floor. She had just dropped the last of the rubbish into her waste paper basket when, with her back to the security door, she felt a breeze waft gently across the nape of her neck. *The security door should be locked and Abu never comes upstairs without first announcing himself over the intercom.*

As Sarah spun around, her heart was racing, *I know that there can't possibly be anyone there, but Lucas' death has made me nervous.* Leaning against the shut door, Colonel Joseph Nasseur, Head of Panganian Security stood, his arms folded across his chest as he watched Sarah, his face completely unreadable. She gave a slight start, mainly from relief.

'Oh Colonel, how you startled me!' She uttered a nervous laugh, her hand rising to press against her racing heart.

'My apologies, Miss Trent,' Joseph pushed himself off the door and approached to take her hand. 'You were working so industriously that I did not wish to disturb you.' With great finesse, echoing of a distant time, he raised her hand to his lips. For a brief moment Sarah could only stare at him. Not that this was a distasteful activity. A muscular build filled the Colonel's military uniform. He was 33, very handsome with an olive complexion, black hair and his eyes were almost as black. It was unusual to be a full Colonel at such a young age but not only was Joseph an exceptional warrior but he was also Prince Kahlee's best friend. That actually meant that he had to work even harder for any promotions to prevent any suggestion of favouritism.

Sarah pulled herself together, taking a step backwards from Joseph. Feeling more comfortable by putting her desk between them, she asked, 'Colonel Nasseur, how did you get in? I'm certain that door was locked when I shut it.'

'Now Miss Trent,' His eyes were filled with amusement. 'Would you ask the magician to reveal how he performs his tricks?'

Sarah wasn't forced to answer by the emergence of Gary Winters from the Ambassador's office, which was just as well as she didn't know how she was supposed to demand that the Colonel answered her question.

'My apologies, Colonel, for keeping you waiting,' Gary shook hands with Joseph before leading him down the corridor to his office. Sarah sank into her chair, a little shaken. *In all the times that I'd had to deal with Joseph Nasseur, I'd never been able to be completely at ease with him. There is a mysterious air about him, something beneath the surface that seems unfathomable.* Yet Sarah wondered, *Is there something more than mere gallantry in his behaviour towards me? I'm certain that he isn't flirting with me, yet I find him unlike any other man I've ever met.*

A pair of hands suddenly descended over Sarah's eyes making her jump startled out of her reflections. Con Zuco had scared her more than she wanted to admit and she shrugged him off in annoyance.

'Don't you have work to do?' she demanded, a little more firmly than her usual tone.

Con sat down on the edge of Sarah's desk and placing one of his hands under her chin; he forced her to look up at him. 'No work is important enough to keep me from admiring you.'

Sarah burst into laughter, 'Do your facetious lines ever really work in picking up women?'

'Of course they do! On normal women that is! Come on Sarah, where's the harm in a little fun together?' He attempted to kiss her but Sarah pushed hard against Con, causing him to fall off the end of her desk and on to the floor. Neither of them saw or heard the figure that suddenly appeared behind him as a hand clasped down upon the back of Con's neck, and dragged him painfully to his feet.

'Your attentions are obviously unwanted and offensive Mr. Zuco! Do not force me to hurt you!' Joseph let Con go before turning to Sarah, who was looking at him in surprise.

'Thank you Colonel, but I did have the situation under control,' she stated.

'Not from where I was standing! Perhaps you should consider Major Winters' offer to teach you self-defence, Miss Trent,' suggested Joseph as Con vanished down the stairs to deal with the Ambassador's luggage.

'How do you know about that?' Sarah looked up at Joseph even more surprised.

The Colonel smiled, and she had to admit that he had a very nice smile. 'I suggested it to him!'

Gary foresaw an awkward confrontation about why he'd been discussing Sarah's problems with an outsider and he rushed into explanation, 'I thought it would be appropriate to introduce the Colonel to Ambassador Greene.' He opened the Ambassador's door for Joseph, but before he followed him, Gary glanced back at Sarah, 'I'll explain everything later!'

'You'd better!'

Gary sighed, *that is one conversation I'm not looking forward to having in the near future.*

Joseph's Concerns

Colonel Nasseur was well known to all the Embassy staff and was warmly welcomed by Marianne and Kevin. James came round from behind his desk with his hand extended towards Joseph. It was accepted and firmly grasped.

'Welcome to Kathou, our capital city of Pangani, Ambassador Greene. I am only sorry that you find our country in sad upheaval at the present.'

'A revolt is never a happy event, Colonel.' James Greene sighed. 'I promise before heading anywhere in Pangani, I will get your advice first.'

Joseph inclined his head in acknowledgment, but his face was serious. 'Since I had only just returned from the conflict in the north, the information that Ambassador Lucas was given was the latest. If he chose to ignore us both, then Lucas' death falls upon his own head. Sorry, no pun intended. I must ask you to remember, Ambassador Greene that this is not down town Sydney!'

'My apologies, Colonel,' James looked suitably chastised. 'That's the second time today I've attempted humour and failed miserably.'

'I'm afraid it has been some time since many of us have been able to appreciate a good laugh.' Joseph's mouth relaxed into a charming smile. 'It is customary for a new Ambassador to seek an audience with the Emir.'

James looked worried, 'Are there certain protocols that I should be aware of?' His concern made Marianne chuckle.

'We won't let you make a fool of yourself. Sarah will have a complete list of protocols for visiting the Emir.' Marianne glanced across to Joseph Nasseur. 'Will you be coming to Ambassador Greene's first official function Sunday evening? Or must you return to the conflict in the north?'

The Colonel shook his head. 'Matters have settled down a little since Lucas' unfortunate death. A little bloodletting sometimes cools the tempers. Unless an emergency arises, I am stationed in Kathou for the next few weeks, so I am sure I can find something suitable to wear to an official function.' This was Joseph's attempt at humour as he never appeared anywhere out of uniform. A beeping of his mobile phone interrupted his words. The Colonel glanced at it as he switched it off. 'My apologies, Ambassador Greene, duty calls. Heed the advice of your staff and you will enjoy your stay in Pangani.' He glanced significantly across at Gary, who nodded and walked across to open the door. 'Until Sunday night then,' added Joseph.

Gary followed him out of the Ambassador's office and after Joseph had said farewell to Sarah, accompanied him down to the front door. The Major had understood that his friend had something private he wished to say. Abu, the Panganian Office Manager, came forward to open the outer Embassy door, but Gary waved him away.

'What is it Sir?' asked Gary as they stepped out into the sunshine.

Joseph waited until Abu had disappeared before speaking, 'Does that happen often, Gary? Con Zuco, I mean!'

'His attentions have always been over familiar but never before has he gone beyond the line of what was acceptable.' Gary scowled as his gaze rested on Con standing by the front gate talking to Ahkman, the Security Guard as they had a cigarette. 'That is one of the reasons I want to teach Sarah to defend herself.'

The Colonel considered this, 'Make sure that Con is not permitted the opportunity to be alone with her.'

Gary nodded as the driver opened the back door of the Colonel's car. 'Perhaps it is time for you to tell Sarah how you feel about her.'

'I doubt it very much, Gary!' Joseph sighed, 'I cannot ask for Miss Trent's heart when I cannot ask for her hand as well.'

Major Winters waited silently until the Colonel had driven away from the Australian Embassy, wondering *how do I tell Sarah why Nasseur is concerned for her well-being without revealing the truth?*

General Inspection

Kevin headed back to his office while Marianne, as the senior diplomat, showed James around the compound. The Australian Embassy was an old colonial style building which consisted of two floors, the ground floor being used for meetings, official dinners and entertaining. On the top floor, there was the Ambassador's office with its balcony looking out across the gardens, a tearoom, a secured document room as well as an office for each of the diplomats. They went over the top floor and its offices, down the stairs to look over the lower floor with its extensive entertaining area, before they headed across to the Residency.

As she followed James inside the house, Marianne heard the happy yapping of all three dogs playing in the garden. Yisi, the native house servant was a little nervous about meeting the new Ambassador as she stammered and kept curtsying.

'It's all right, Yisi, I shan't bite. Why don't you collect all the other staff so that I can say a brief hello?' Yisi departed as James and Marianne looked around the Residency before returning to the living room.

The other Residency staff members were just as nervous as Yisi. They giggled at James' humour, which was a fairly good sign. James only laughed, he was an easy going man and he was happy to allow the staff time to get used to him. As they stepped back out onto the verandah Simon let out a joyous bark and thumped his tail excitedly upon seeing Marianne.

'Hello little man. Have you been playing with your siblings?' Marianne bent down to pat the excited puppy. James squatted down beside the German shepherd three month old pup with a plaster cast on his back leg and slowly offered his hand, which was enthusiastically licked.

'Is he another victim of the riots?'

'Oh not at all.' Marianne chuckled, 'When Sarah went with Gary to pick up Jeb and Ash, a couple of guard dogs, from the breeder; she was the only one Simon would let get close enough to examine him and diagnose his defect. The vet said the operation should make him as good as new but he's no good for breeding or as a guard dog.'

'How on earth did you find a vet to treat a dog? I thought the only vets in the Middle East treated falcons and other birds of prey?'

'Prince Kahlee, the Emir's eldest son, attended university in England and became very fond of dogs and has all the royal residences guarded by dogs from this particular breeder.'

James laughed as Simon enthusiastically greeted him, 'He appears more likely to lick someone to death!'

'Be careful what you say James, Simon nearly took off Abu's finger when he tried to escort Sarah back to the main building. He's very protective of Sarah.'

'I'll keep that in mind.'

'Also Gary is licensed to carry a gun in this country.'

'Whoa there!' James threw his hands up in defeat, 'What on earth have I said to warrant this? My youngest daughter is older than Sarah!'

Marianne gave a guilty laugh. 'Sorry, Sarah and I have become like a foster family. It was obvious from your earlier comment that you find Sarah very attractive, so I thought it better to get a few things straight before you got into trouble.'

'You're over protective for another reason though,' Straightening, James scratched his head thoughtfully. 'Something happened before my arrival or is it simply due to finding your Boss chopped into little pieces?'

Marianne hesitated before she replied, 'It was necessary to report Con Zuco for sexual harassment. He stopped for a while, but he does seem to fancy he's in love with her.'

'He could be transferred.'

'We have enough trouble getting staff and we have to use local people more than we should do. I mean he's not a bad kid, I just wish he could get his libido under control.'

'Well I might be tempted to tease her, but if it makes her uncomfortable, I'll control the urge. Everyone should be given compliments, and praise should be given where it is due. A happy worker is a good worker.' James laughed.

They left Simon and strolled through the compound grounds, pausing by the swimming pool and outdoor entertaining area. Jeb and Ash, the older siblings to Simon the German shepherd puppy, followed them for a brief time before a noise in the shrubs attracted their attention and they went running off to investigate.

'Do you really believe in that?' Marianne referred to his previous comment.

'What? About praise? Of course! It has to be honest though. False praise is poisonous and deadly. I've been thinking about how to put some distance between Con and Sarah, and I may have a solution. It really depends upon what we're allowed to do with the main building.'

They sat down in the shade, watching the way the sun sparkled across the water in the pool as he continued, 'Sarah's too cramped up where she is. I want her to have Con's office. He doesn't need to be in the secure area, he can have one of the empty offices downstairs.'

'He won't like that,' she stated quietly.

'Tough!'

'Sarah needs to be easily accessible not only to the Ambassador but also other diplomats and arriving visitors.'

'I've thought of that,' James stretched his legs out in front of him. 'We knock down the two interior walls of Con's office, opening up the area. What we need to discover is if those walls are load bearing, and therefore can't be removed, or if these buildings are heritage listed. Then we couldn't make any structural changes. What do you think of the idea, if we overcome those two hurdles?'

'That's absolutely brilliant!' Marianne stared at him stunned. 'I can't think why we never thought of it before now. It would be perfect. It would bring more natural light into the passage way as well as take away that boxed in feeling that the office sometimes gives.'

'A few inquiries will have to be made. Planning department, a structural engineer and convincing Con to move. A little bit ambitious for my first day,' James' eyes twinkled wickedly.

'Too true,' she solemnly agreed, 'That's at least a day two ambition!'

The Current Crisis

They both started laughing, and although they were in the shade, the heat and humidity drove them back into the air conditioned main building to seek some relief from the oppressive weather. They found Sarah setting up a tray of ice-cold glasses and a carafe of cold lemon squash upon the Ambassador's desk. She smiled as they walked in.

'I've just been down to see Simon, and Yisi told me that you had gone for a walk around the compound. I thought you'd be in need of cold refreshment when you returned,' she explained, gesturing to the tray.

'You are an angel!' Sarah blushed, not knowing what to say.

Marianne beamed at her in fond pride. 'In a short period of time, she'll have you so organised that you'll wonder how you ever managed before.'

'Please Marianne,' Sarah blushed, uncomfortable with praise. 'You'll give Mr. Greene a false impression of me.'

James fell into his chair as he uttered a groan. 'What have I let myself in for? Working in such close proximity of two beautiful women who are also as smart as whips?'

'Well your Excellency,' said Sarah. 'There's always a cold shower.'

Both Marianne and James started to laugh. Sarah had looked completely innocent when describing a cruel remedy to dampen James' attempt to flirt with them.

'You'd better leave before I'm tempted to indulge in too many fantasies about showers. Thank you for the cool drink. I'm certainly feeling parched; and I'm not quite sure that it is all to do with the weather.'

Sarah smiled shyly as he winked at her and she closed the door behind her as she left.

Looking impressed, Marianne poured them both a drink before sitting down opposite James. 'Now if Con had said any of those things, I'd be itching to slap his face and Sarah would have shuddered in revulsion.'

'My daughter Crystal says I get away with it because women know I'm harmless.' James took a sip of the drink and approved of its tangy flavour. 'I don't want an unhappy work environment. No matter how tough the mission is I hope to add some light heartedness to ease the tension.'

'It has been a trying time,' Marianne sighed. 'Even before Lucas' death, there was an atmosphere of tension, mistrust, and a sense that a storm was about to break over our heads. We've been so serious for so long that we've forgotten how to find time for relaxation or a bit of fun.'

He chuckled. 'Crystal will change that! She's not shy or reserved like Sarah seems. Actually they'd probably be good for each other.' For a moment James pondered further upon that thought. When he leant forward, his expression had changed from dreamy to business like. 'Right then, what exactly are we up against here?' It was time to get down to brass tacks.

'Where to begin,' she mused, 'well the Emir is a well-educated and very enlightened man. His predecessor, his uncle, was a cruel and hard man, who did not really care about improving the standard of living of his people. The present Emir has been on the throne for nearly twenty years, and is very much into creating a better way of life for all. Better schools, hospitals, housing and sanitary facilities. Life for women has also improved. Although it is necessary for all women to wear in public a Hijab which is the headscarf, it is optional for Muslim women to wear the Niqab which is the veil that covers the nose and mouth, they no longer have to wear the black Burqa, that's when their entire face is covered too. It is also possible for women to get work and no longer remain at home. There is a pension for the elderly so that they aren't a complete burden to the family or simply drop dead working. The Emir is a very strong family man. He encourages family unity, looking after each other.' Marianne paused for thought. 'Despite all this, the Emir isn't short of enemies. Therefore as we very strongly support the Emir, his enemies are ours.'

'So who are causing the Emir a headache?'

Marianne took another sip of her drink. 'Firstly there are the Fundamentalists. They are happy enough to have an Emir, but want stricter Islamic laws. The second group can be labelled loosely as Communists. We tend to refer to them as the Commune. They have abandoned their Islamic heritage and live a kind of hippy existence. They want a government freely elected, with religious freedom for all, more equal opportunities for those not conforming to Islamic law. Jobs for every person, free education, free medicines, and basically the Utopia described by Karl Marx. A very charismatic man leads the Commune. He is known as Caracal.'

James' eyebrows rose. 'Which means what?'

'It's the type of Lynx cat that exists in this area. Anyway, the Commune is also against foreign interference, but not foreign nationals. Live and let live, but keep your Western ideas out of Pangani! Definitely peace, free love and grow your own dope!'

Rising to her feet, she moved over to one of the French doors and looked out across the grounds. In the distance she saw Jeb and Ash sitting in the shade not far from the main gate where Ahkman Amed, the Panganian Embassy Guard, sat on duty. Beside him Con stood smoking and chatting.

'Finally there are the Rebels. Extremists! When the Fundamentalists and the Commune protest it is usually a peaceful affair. The Rebels are responsible for most of the violence, riots and they want to remove the Emir, have all women to wear the black Burqa, harsher punishments for breaking laws, no tolerance to other religions and naturally the removal of foreign nationals, interference, trade and aid.'

"When you say Rebels do you mean ...'

Marianne would not let him finish, 'That is not a word or initials we use around here. It is much safer to refer to them as Rebels although they prefer to think of themselves as Freedom Fighters.'

'Does anyone want us here?' With a heavy sigh James leant back in his chair.

Marianne smiled. 'The Emir, businesses we trade with, the local people we employ, the charities we support and other foreign Embassies. It's impossible to keep out foreign trade, companies and nationals. It's essential for any economy.'

'What exactly are we involved in here? Companies, charities, facilities, and that sort of thing?'

'Sarah will be able to provide you with all that detail.' Marianne turned away from the window. 'She also has a protocol file of do's and don'ts. Especially useful for when you meet the Emir.'

As Marianne opened the door, Sarah was about to knock upon it. She entered with a pile of papers. James breathed a sigh of relief when Sarah handed half of these to Marianne. The other half she placed on his desk.

'The protocol file,' she explained.

'Can you also provide James with our current interests in Pangani?' asked Marianne.

'Of course, I'll print it immediately.' Sarah departed again.

'I'll leave you to try and absorb all this information.' Marianne would have also left, but James stopped her.

'What are you doing this evening?'

She looked surprised. 'Not much.'

'Good, I'd like you to have dinner with me at the Residency. I'm sure to have a hundred and one questions to ask you after I've been through this lot. Is that convenient for you?'

'Of course Sir.'

Sarah re-entered with some more papers. 'An appointment has been made for you to see the Emir tomorrow at 10 a.m. and Freddy, Mr. Fredericks, the cook at the Residency also asked if you have any particular food preferences or dislikes?' As Marianne slid out of the room, Sarah wondered, *Have I interrupted something important, as there is a slight tense atmosphere in the air?*

'I can't think of anything at the moment, but I'll put my brain to it and jot down a few suggestions. Is there anything else?'

'No,' Sarah shook her head, 'except a suggestion, if you want peace and quiet, you might want to take your reading to the Residency.'

'I hadn't thought it was particularly noisy here.' Just at that moment the air was pierced by the sound of an electric drill. 'What on earth?' James demanded, surprised.

'They're re-enforcing the front door. It could take an hour.'

'I'll be at the Residency if anyone wants me.' James collected up the papers he needed to peruse and rose swiftly to his feet.

Sarah smiled as he hurried away and wished that she too could escape the head pounding noise.

Night Curfew

That evening James and Marianne dined alone, Freddy preparing a meal that was a favourite of Marianne's, and James whole-heartedly approved. She was always conscious of her weight and the usual fare for Embassy functions tended to be very rich and fattening, so Marianne tried to avoid these types of meals when she cooked for herself. Aware of this, Freddy presented them with an absolutely delicious but healthy meal, Marianne apologized that James' first dinner wasn't more spectacular. James waved away her apology.

'I agree that diplomats eat too much and especially drink too much. I'm looking forward to more simple meals like the one we've just eaten, especially if the company is just as enchanting.'

With a cup of coffee, they moved from the dining room out onto the verandah where a cool breeze had sprung up and was dancing through the garden around them. Their conversation turned towards their own personal histories. They had mutual friends in the Diplomatic Corps and spent an enjoyable evening discovering what old friends were up to, as well as the latest gossip.

So engrossed were they in conversation that by the time James glanced at his watch, it was indeed very late. With a sunset curfew still in place, James asked Yisi to make up the spare bed, which was a relief for Marianne. *I like the new Ambassador, he is amusing, intelligent and handsome, but we've only just met and I'm not someone who rushes into relationships or into someone's bed.* Something of her concern must have shown on her face because James leant forward and laid his hand lightly on her arm, a twinkle in his eyes.

'Not on the first date!' he murmured. They both laughed and the tension passed as they retired for the night to separate rooms.

SATURDAY

Another Working Day

It was already hot when James woke but by the time he had a cool shower and a full breakfast, he was feeling a lot better. Marianne had already eaten, showered and was watching the early morning edition of the news on the television. She greeted James before turning back to the broadcast. Completing his breakfast, James joined Marianne in the living room.

'Anything of interest?' he asked.

'Not really.' Rubbing a hand across her eyes, Marianne sighed. 'After Lucas was found nearly two weeks ago, the north of Kathou was a riot zone day and night. Now, although there are protestors outside various Embassies during the day, there's only rioting at night. We've been lucky so far, being south of all the fighting. Not a very welcoming start for you, I'm afraid.'

James shrugged his shoulders. 'It's because of these events that I'm here in the first place. I hardly expected it to be a picnic. Although from what you've just told me I'm surprised that the Embassy staff hasn't moved in to the Residency for security.'

'We did move in together for the first week,' Marianne rose to turn off the television, 'but once Colonel Nasseur had provided us with a guard for each of our homes, we were able to go back to our own places.' Picking up her napkin she brushed crumbs off the front of her dress before saying, 'I'm just going home to change into something more suitable for your meeting with the Emir this morning and then I'll back to pick you up.' Marianne looked towards the window as she heard a car drive into the compound. 'That will be Sarah and Gary arriving. If you have any problems or questions don't hesitate to contact us.'

'But its Saturday isn't it?'

Marianne smiled wearily, 'during the crisis we have been working throughout the weekend.'

James saw Marianne out the front door before he settled down to read once more the instructions regarding meeting the Emir, as well as the situation that had brought him to his new posting.

A Good Old Barbie

After a successful meeting with the Emir, James arranged a barbecue later that evening by the Embassy pool for all the staff so that he could get to know his team in a social surrounding. Looking around from where he sat on the edge of the pool, James felt *that although we are relaxed and sociable, there is an underlying tension. There is talking, laughing and joking but there is also silence. A silence that speaks volumes about the stress and worries that they have been under lately.* The new Ambassador pondered upon *what problems this continuing stress will have upon our mission, and how or when my team will buckle under the pressure.* They weren't pleasant thoughts, but necessary, if James was to be prepared for any difficulties. *The more I can do to prevent the crisis, the better we will all be in the end.*

SUNDAY

Party Preparations

Sarah and Marianne were busy in the Embassy's entertainment area in preparation for the new Ambassador's first official function that evening. Native staff cleaned and polished the room; tables were set up that would that evening be laden with a delicious array of food, as well as a variety of drinks. A great number of beverages were to be non-alcoholic. Many of the invited guests, other than dignitaries from other Embassies, would be Pangani elite, and being Muslim, they did not consume alcohol.

The preparations for the function appeared to be numerous to James, and although he had seen the written procedure for arranging a function, he still was over whelmed by the amount of organizing that Sarah and Marianne seemed to take in their stride. *To try to arrange this function I would've worked myself into a nervous breakdown. I wonder if Crystal will be able to cope? From what I've seen of Sarah, I'm certain that she will guide my daughter through the duties of hostess to the diplomats. The only difficulty that I can foresee is the unpredictable nature of my daughter's personality. Her divorce had shaken some of her self-confidence and this chance of freedom means that Crystal could possibly act a little unconventional. I hope that Sarah will be a sobering influence upon Crystal. Then again,* as James watched the serious, organized secretary, *I secretly hope that my lively daughter will in fact have a positive influence upon Sarah and bring her out of her rigid shell a little.* He smiled at the thought. *There are interesting times ahead for us all.*

Attack In The Market

During the afternoon, as the caterers worked extremely diligently in the Embassy function kitchen, Sarah and Marianne went down to the markets to do their weekly shopping. It was the first time in two weeks that they had been permitted to go out in public without being accompanied. The two women were well known to the stall owners and were greeted with pleasure and respect. Both women were appropriately dressed and wore a colourful scarf over their hair.

Although the markets were out in the streets, a material shade extending between the buildings and running the length of the street kept the area protected from the heat and the rain. A couple of times Marianne glanced behind them. Nothing looked out of the ordinary so the older woman put it down to nerves but by the time she had looked around three times, Sarah was forced to say, 'Marianne, you're starting to scare me. What's wrong?'

'I just have this feeling that we're being followed.' The older woman tried to laugh. 'Perhaps we should talk to James about increasing personal security.'

Sarah shifted her loaded canvas shopping bag from one hand to the other and gently squeezed Marianne's shoulder with her free hand. 'Surely we're safe enough in the south of Kathou? All the trouble so far has been centred in the north of the city. You're just nervous because of Lucas' death!' The motherly woman accepted this rebuke and resisted the desire to once more glance over her shoulder.

Ben Makita, a well-known spice and herb dealer, warmly greeted them. He was a Panganian in his late forties and always ensured the very best quality in his produce. Ben spoke English but Marianne knew some Arabic and Sarah was fluent. Ben's wife, Karlia, a small woman, bowed her head in a mark of respect, always hesitant to put herself forward but politely answered Sarah's inquires of her and her children's health.

Marianne was negotiating a price on some fresh herbs with Ben when Sarah felt something hard and menacing pressed into her back. She stiffened, her hand automatically grasping tighter upon her handbag.

'If it's money you want, then take it but don't hurt anyone.' Sarah had spoken softly in English but when she was answered by silence she repeated herself in Arabic. The man laughed.

'I don't want your money, Miss Trent! You're more valuable to our cause than your shopping money. Come quietly and no one need get hurt.'

Sarah glanced across to Marianne who was still haggling on a price and she couldn't catch her eye. 'What do you hope to achieve?' She asked calmly as the gunman urged her to walk away from her friend.

'Political Freedom!'

'I see. There's only one problem,' Sarah had managed to get into a clearing away from the mass of mingling people.

'What is that?' The gunman was over confidant and full of conceit.

'Only this!' Sarah suddenly turned around, her full shopping bag swinging to hit him in the groin. As the gun exploded, she felt a searing pain in her left hand as a pair of arms grabbed her from behind and threw her to the ground. Sarah heard Marianne scream out her name but she couldn't take her eyes off the young man who had leapt out of nowhere to her rescue. He appeared little more than a high school boy but she doubted that was the case as his hand professionally chopped down on the gunman's wrist forcing him to drop the gun. A few well-aimed and calculated blows from the school boy rescuer brought the would-be kidnapper to his knees.

A whistle sounded, announcing the arrival of the Police. The young man looked around him to ensure that there were no further signs of danger. He glanced down at her in concern assuring that she wasn't badly injured before he disappeared. Sarah held out her bleeding hand towards him. 'Please, don't go! What's your name?' But she was too late, as he had already vanished into the crowd.

Marianne ran across, moving people out of the way, to kneel beside Sarah as the Police took charge of the situation. The would-be kidnapper was handcuffed and escorted away. Karlia disappeared into their shop to return with a first aid kit. Sarah's hand was covered with blood, the bullet having sliced across her palm.

'Oh dear girl! What a risk you took! You could've been killed!' Marianne chastised Sarah as she took a bandage from Karlia with a word of thanks and wrapped up Sarah's bleeding hand.

Sarah gave a shaky laugh in embarrassment as Marianne assisted her to her feet, making certain that her scarf was back in place. 'Marianne please don't fuss. Everyone is looking at us.'

Ben Makita offered the Police the use of his shop until Sarah had recovered enough to make a statement. Marianne held on to Sarah's good hand so tightly, it was as if she feared that letting her go, she would lose her. To each of the Police officer's questions, Sarah answered clearly and calmly. She vaguely wondered, *Am I in shock, because I don't feel upset or afraid?*

Statements were taken from eyewitnesses, but it had happened so fast that no one had really known what had been occurring until it was nearly all over. There was absolutely no sign of the youth who had come to Sarah's rescue and no one had seen where he had disappeared to, or could remember anything remarkable to distinguish him from any other Panganian boy.

'You should have that wound seen too immediately Miss Trent,' suggested the Police officer.

'It's nothing more than a scratch.' Sarah adamantly shook her head.

'Miss Trent, even a scratch should be seen by a doctor. The last thing you need is an infection.'

'Don't worry Sergeant; I'll take her straight to the hospital now.' Marianne placed her arm around Sarah's shoulder as they rose to their feet. 'Thank you for all your assistance.'

'No problem, Mrs. Davies.' The Sergeant escorted them through the market and back to Marianne's car. As they drove away Marianne punched in a number on the speed dial on her mobile phone.

'Oh Marianne, don't, please don't!' Marianne ignored the plea and waited for her call to be answered.

'Major Winters!'

'Gary, I'm taking Sarah to the hospital, minor gunshot injury, but I want you to meet us there.' Sarah groaned in defeat, it was obvious that Marianne was extremely upset and nothing she could say would placate her.

Priority One

Sarah was prepared for a long wait at the hospital; *the emergency department of any hospital in any part of the world is always very busy.* She sat down patiently while Marianne filled in the paper work and she was trying to not drip blood all over the floor, as an elderly lady beside her filled Sarah in on what the movie on the television was about. Marianne had barely sat down when they were whisked away to a cubicle where a young intern doctor was perusing Sarah's form. The registration nurse had written in big red letters 'Gunshot wound' and 'Telephoned Priority One'. Marianne wondered *what does the last one mean? But as it seems to have caused us to jump the queue, I'm not going enquire too closely.*

The young doctor looked tired as he un-wrapped the temporary bandage, to examine the wound. He was a quiet, earnest young man, but an attempt by Sarah at humour about the severity of the wound made him smile broadly, admitting the words 'Gunshot wound' had brought a different image to his mind.

Cleansing the wound, the doctor numbed her hand and put in half a dozen stitches. He had instructions for Sarah about keeping the wound clean, dry and sterile then he wrapped up her hand so that the bandage completely covered her fingers. This was only temporary for a few days, to really limit her using the hand. Sarah felt guilty as they re-entered the waiting room where all the people who had been there before her were still waiting.

Pacing the waiting room was Gary Winters; his worried look dissolved as he saw Sarah walking towards him. 'Thank God you're all right! I've just been informed of the details of the attack in the market place.' He led them outside, his hand under Sarah's elbow to support her.

'It's only a scratch, Gary!' Sarah protested as she gently pulled her arm out of his grasp.

'It could have been worse!' retorted Marianne. Gary escorted them to Marianne's car, Sarah was surprised not to see his anywhere nearby.

'How did you get here so fast Gary?' she asked, getting into the back seat.

At that moment two Panganian soldiers appeared and saluted Gary, 'Anything to report to the Colonel, Sir?'

Gary glanced across to Marianne who gave them the exact extent of the wound. They saluted again before disappearing. Sarah groaned in disbelief. *How many people already know about my embarrassing accident?* She thought.

The Major refused to meet Sarah's eyes as he got in behind the wheel with Marianne beside him.

'Why did you call Colonel Nasseur?' demanded Sarah.

'He is the Head of National Security!'

Marianne gave a sudden laugh. 'So that's what 'Telephone Priority One' meant! Then it was Nasseur who called the hospital?'

Gary concentrated upon getting out of the parking lot and joining the chaotic traffic before he answered, 'Actually, no. The Colonel was with Prince Kahlee when I called him. It was the Prince who phoned the hospital.'

'Oh no!' Sarah groaned in disbelief. 'Does everybody know about this incident?' Her head was starting to pound, and her hand was throbbing.

'It's not something that could be kept secret, honey,' reassured Marianne.

'I'm going to look a real Pratt at tonight's function!'

'Nonsense!' argued Gary, 'You'll be a heroine! You took on a gun man and won!'

Marianne glanced back at Sarah in concern. *There is obvious pain etched on her youthful features.* 'We can manage tonight without you.'

'Marianne!' Sarah looked shocked at the suggestion. 'This is our new Ambassador's first function. We must all be there!'

'I'll make sure it's not a late one for you then.' Marianne sighed. *I'm not convinced that Sarah should be going at all but the girl can be as stubborn as a mule.*

Gary changed the topic to get something off his chest. 'Individual security will be organized immediately, but I still think you should know how to defend yourself Sarah.'

Sarah sighed, 'I thought I'd done fairly well, all things considered!' Her headache was getting worse; *I don't feel like arguing about anything at the moment.* 'If you're assigning us individual security I don't see why it's necessary, but to stop a lecture before it starts, if you think I need it, go ahead. Just not right now. My head's about to explode!'

Gary was a tiny bit annoyed that his carefully planned argument was to be wasted, but privately was pleased with such an easy win. They dropped Sarah off at her home. Gary carried in her groceries and Marianne offered to stay with her, but all Sarah wanted to do was take a couple of pain-killers and sleep for a while. So after they had left, Sarah lay down with the puppy Simon curled up beside her. It took about ten minutes to convince him that this was sleeping time, and not playing time. Once he had finally settled down, Sarah breathed a sigh of relief, and closing her eyes, allowed sleep to aid the medication in relieving her pain.

James' First Function

Feeling refreshed and once more composed Sarah stood beside Ambassador Greene in the doorway of the Embassy function area that evening as she introduced to him Pangani's dignitaries and representatives from other Embassies. Sarah wore a floor length white silk skirt that hugged the contours of her body, a short sleeved white silk top that was embroidered with opal flowers and covered by a shapely long sleeved white jacket, done up at the waist by a single clasp of opal. Her hair hung loose down her back, an insistence of Marianne's, who had also done Sarah's make up.

Marianne was stylishly dressed, preferring darker colours and less figure hugging design. She had finally bowed to Sarah's pressure and had taken off her wedding ring. Her divorce had been finalised over a year ago but she had been unable to take the final step in removing the ring she had worn for over twenty years. Marianne felt naked and exposed without such protection but soon relaxed when she realized that no one had really noticed.

James Greene had just been introduced to Pangani's Foreign Minister, Amwar Beodan, when Colonel Nasseur entered the room in formal military uniform. It wasn't his imposing presence though that caused the assembled group to suddenly fall silent, but his companion. A great honour had been bestowed upon the new Australian Ambassador, as Prince Kahlee, the eldest son of the Emir, had arrived at James' first official function. Sarah kept her eyes respectfully lowered as she curtsied and introduced the Ambassador. Prince Kahlee gently took Sarah's bandaged hand between his own.

'My apologies, Miss Trent, that you have suffered such an insult from one of my countrymen,' he said. Sarah's cheeks flamed as she managed to thank him, her eyes remaining lowered. The Prince placed his other hand under her chin and persuaded her to raise her head. 'It is not a sin to look at me, Miss Trent, and you have such lovely eyes.'

'Please your Highness!' Sarah looked up, feeling her colour deepen as she tried to protest.

The Prince laughed in delight, 'Such modesty! I do envy the man who finally wins your heart.' With a few words to the Ambassador, Prince Kahlee moved through the room, chatting to friends and acquaintances.

Public Insult

Sarah managed to escape into the ladies' toilets until her cheeks had returned to a more normal colour. Once more composed, she rejoined the party. Getting herself a glass of fruit punch and taking a couple of pain killers as her head began to throb, Sarah stood back and watched the people that mingled around her. She managed a sympathetic smile as she watched James Greene struggling to follow the conversation with Minister Beodan. *The Minister is a well-known windbag, loud, corpulent and gross. His hands are known to wander and not just with the girls.* Beodan glanced over at Sarah, his smile showing his crooked, discoloured and missing teeth, causing Sarah to look away in disgust. The Minister laughed and turned back to James Greene.

'Such a pretty child you have in your employ, Ambassador,' wheezed Beodan, not worried about who heard him and many people did. 'I wouldn't be surprised at all if you tried to bed her. Such a reserved manner, though, one wonders if that conceals a passionate tigress or a frozen popsicle? It's hoped that it's not the latter, but I fear that it must be so!'

Angry tears stung Sarah's eyes as she fought them back, although James reproached the Minister, Sarah felt suddenly very alone and vulnerable. Glancing away from them, her eyes meeting Joseph's, she was surprised to find him watching her so intently and feared that her cheeks were aflame once more. The Colonel smiled reassuringly and raised his glass of punch in a silent toast, which brought a shy, appreciative returning smile from Sarah. Joseph was about to cross the room to her side when Minister Beodan's loud voice arrested his movement.

'So the little Australian mouse has eyes for our dashing Colonel has she? Perhaps there is passion and not ice in her blood after all?'

Everyone in the room had fallen silent, looking from Joseph to Sarah. Her good hand clenched in an angry fist as a rush of whispers swept through the room and she would have stepped towards Beodan if her arm hadn't been grasped to stop her. Sarah looked around to find Prince Kahlee standing beside her, his hand firmly holding her elbow in restraint.

'Don't do it, Miss Trent. He is not worth losing your job over. It is time for me to leave and I would like you to escort me out.' His Highness spoke softly so that only Sarah heard him. He drew her arm through his as they approached James. 'Don't let him have the satisfaction of knowing how much he has hurt you.' Sarah nodded, and found it somewhere in her to remain composed. The Prince ensured that he now spoke loudly enough for those around the Ambassador to hear him. 'It has been a pleasure to make your acquaintance, Ambassador Greene but unfortunately, duty calls and I must depart. No need to see me out, Miss Trent will give me the honour of her company.' With these commanding words, Prince Kahlee left the room with Sarah on his arm.

Outside, in the cool night air, Sarah tried to thank the Prince as he stepped into the back of his car, but he wouldn't have it. 'It is always a pleasure to be a service to you, Miss Trent.' A single tear fell, causing the Prince to brush his thumb against her cheek to wipe it away. 'Don't cry over him. Beodan will know my displeasure over his rudeness.' His lips thinned in his anger.

'Please your Highness; I don't want a fuss made,' Sarah begged.

'But I will not have guests to my country insulted.' Prince Kahlee smiled gently. 'Trust me, Miss Trent and do not return to the party just yet. Let them get such nonsense out of their systems.'

Sarah sighed, *I wish that I didn't have to return at all.* 'Yes. Thank you, your Highness.' She watched as he was driven away and looked up to consider the clear night sky before turning to head back into the Embassy.

Let Me Teach You

Pausing outside the entertainment area, Sarah's hand hesitated before it reached the door handle. The laughter inside the room, not necessarily directed at her, made her turn away and head up the stairs to the offices. She let herself in and headed for the Ambassador's office, disarming the alarm before she opened the French doors. The breeze outside had picked up and Sarah lent against the doorway, letting the air cool her heated cheeks. It wasn't a strong enough breeze, though, to dry her tears. *I know that it's ridiculous to allow Minister Beodan to upset me this way but it had been the icing on a bad day. A bad fortnight!*

The Ambassador's interior door shut with a barely audible click but it was enough to make Sarah look around in surprise.

Colonel Nasseur strode towards her, one hand taking her gently by the chin to compel her to raise her face so that he could see her tears in the moonlight.

'That stupid fool has made you cry! I am sorry for that. But you must not allow his hurtful comment to upset you.'

Sarah managed to draw away from him, moving to the Ambassador's desk to pick up a tissue to wipe her eyes and blow her nose. She struggled to compose herself but was actually trembling inside.

'Colonel Nasseur, how did you get up here? This is supposed to be a secured area. Please, I must ask you to leave,' She tried to sound official but her heart was racing as Joseph approached her.

'Always the perfect diplomat!' He smiled kindly down at her, 'Kevin Shaw is known for his inability to remember anything so the code would have to be something easy for him. Therefore I deduced that the code for the security door would be his birthday. But please don't make me leave, Beodan's words made me realize how vulnerable you are. Gary has informed me that you agreed to take self-defence lessons. Will you allow me to teach you?'

Sarah stared at him dumbfounded; her jaw dropped causing Joseph to groan slightly. Gently he lifted her chin to close her slightly parted lips. 'Please Sarah; don't offer me temptations like that!'

'I don't understand any of this.' She shook her head in bewilderment.

Colonel Nasseur laughed gently, releasing his usually stern expression as he cupped Sarah's face between his hands. His eyes sparkled in a deep emotion that stunned her. 'Delightful child! I am offering to train you. What is to misunderstand about that?'

Sarah was conscious about how close he stood to her, and about the effect he seemed to be having on her legs which were shaking but found that she could not move away from him.

'Do you offer to teach others?'

'No, only you.' He released her face but remained standing close to her.

'Why?'

'Although you won't admit it yourself, you are a very attractive young woman. Men can't help but wish to possess you! Fortunately some of us have more control than Con Zuco and more discretion than Beodan. I want to be able to protect you but I am unsure of how you feel.'

Sarah's eyes scanned his face to see if he was teasing her. 'About what?' she whispered. Her breathing had quickened and her heart was beating wildly as she wondered, *where is this going to lead us?*

'About me!' He gently caressed his finger against her cheek and she felt her knees turn into jelly. He could not have been any plainer about his intentions or his feelings towards her.

Sarah took a deep breath and exhaled slowly. 'I never knew if you were just being friendly, teasing me or that something deeper lay behind your behaviour. I tried not to take it too seriously, not wishing to get hurt,' she confessed, her breath catching in a gasp as Joseph lowered his head towards hers.

'Sarah?' Marianne's voice called out as she entered the top floor of the Embassy and Joseph swore under his breath.

Sarah's hands rose to press against his chest, her eyes pleading, 'Oh please, if you're found here it'll be thought that I breached security!'

He clasped her hands between his own. 'Will you let me teach you?' He asked quickly.

Sarah glanced at the door as it began to open. 'Yes! Oh please just go!' As soon as she had agreed, Joseph had disappeared through the French doors, easily scaling the balcony and dropping noiselessly to the ground, landing like a cat.

Sarah turned as Marianne entered the room.

'I thought I might find you here. Gary is ready to drive you home.' Marianne placed her arm comfortingly around Sarah's shoulder. 'I want to hear all that the Prince had to say to you.'

Sarah locked up the window and reset the alarm. 'I know it wasn't necessary for him to get involved but I was so glad to get out of that room.'

They turned off the lights as they locked up and headed back downstairs. Gary was waiting at the front door and he cast Sarah a searching glance. 'Are you all right?'

She smiled and nodded. 'Yes, thank you Gary, I am now!'

You Need To Be Careful

Marianne saw Sarah into Gary's car before she returned to the ballroom. It was important that she stayed until the end of the function. Con was heading out into the night garden with the French Embassy's Secretary. Kevin continued to circulate but personally would have preferred to be at home in bed.

For quite some time Gary was silent as he drove Sarah home. She lay back in her seat, her eyes closed as her head throbbed. *I am so looking forward to sleep so that hopefully I can stop my thoughts going over again and again the disastrous events of this evening.*

'Sarah?' There was a hesitant note in Gary's voice as he tried to gain her attention.

Turning her head, she opened her eyes to look at him. 'Please Gary, don't scold me! I already feel that I've been very stupid.'

'Stop torturing yourself kiddo. I wasn't about to mention that pig of a man Beodan.' He took one hand off the steering wheel to cover her nearest hand. 'You saw Joseph didn't you?'

Sarah's hand twitched nervously under his. 'Oh Gary, I swear I didn't breach security! Colonel Nasseur guessed our security code.'

'It's all right; that's not what I'm trying to ask you,' Gary shook his head, releasing her hand. 'Did he manage to convince you to take self defence lessons?'

'Yes, he did, but I had already agreed to you teaching me.' Sarah sighed.

'I think Joseph will be the better teacher. Besides which it'll give you time to spend alone together.'

'I don't understand.' Sarah frowned in confusion. 'What are you getting at?'

Gary laughed indulgently. 'Can't you see that the man is madly in love with you?'

'I'm just a little Aussie mouse.' She shook her head in disbelief.

'You really are impossible! Try and shelve your disbelief for a moment. Although what you and Joseph will be doing will be innocent, it's imperative that your lessons are kept secret. Any hint of clandestine behaviour would ruin both your careers, even if they aren't true.'

Smiling as she closed her eyes Sarah replied, 'I'll be as quiet as a mouse.' Gary playfully slapped her hand.

MONDAY

You Got Everyone Talking

Early the next morning, Colonel Joseph Nasseur knocked on the door of an office in the Emirate palace, and entered. Seated behind the desk Prince Kahlee looked up and smiled lopsidedly. 'Well Seph, you look pleased with yourself! I'm surprised since you really made a mess of things last night!'

Joseph threw himself into a chair in a graceless manner. There was no need to stand on ceremony when in the company of such an old friend. 'What did I do, Kah?' They both spoke in their native tongue.

His lifelong friend shook his head in disbelief. 'If I hadn't already suspected your feelings for a certain member of the Australian Embassy, then I would've guessed it last night! You were so obvious! All evening you hardly took your eyes off the girl. I'm only surprised that no one else noticed before Beodan blatantly drew everyone's attention to you. What made you do something so reckless as to toast Miss Trent in such a public place?'

'You didn't see Sarah's eyes.' Joseph frowned as he scrubbed a hand over his chin. 'She had heard Beodan's comments about her and was obviously distressed by them. I was merely offering her a friendly gesture to show that we're not all like Beodan. I might ask what you think will be said about your own actions?'

'I acted in a moment of chivalry!' He hesitated as his friend burst into laughter. 'What? Don't you think that I am capable of chivalry?' A note of hurt entered the Prince's voice but Joseph wasn't fooled for a moment.

'Not at all! I'm merely surprised that you were capable of such quick thinking!'

Kahlee poked his tongue out at his oldest friend, throwing a stapler at Joseph, who easily ducked the missile.

'Not very mature, my son!' The deep, resonating tone of the Emir from the open doorway caused both young men to spring to their feet, the Colonel immediately straightened his uniform and bowed in respect, but the Emir came forward to embrace him.

'What's this I've been hearing about you, Joseph? Have you set up an amusing little flirtation?'

Joseph shook his head, unable to stop the colour rushing across his features. 'Don't believe all that you hear, your Majesty; I'm on friendly terms with the young lady and nothing more.'

The Emir's eyebrows rose in surprise as he laughed. 'There is more to this than you're telling me!' He turned to address his son, 'I know that you've sent for Amwar Beodan, I would like you to keep me informed of his excuses for his behaviour last night. I've been worried about his lack of decency for some time now.'

'Of course, Father!' Prince Kahlee bowed his head in respect.

The Emir left them and Joseph made movements to also leave, but with his hand on the door handle, he said, 'You'll want to see Beodan alone. In the meantime there are a few matters that I must deal with concerning the Rebels.'

'Be careful, Seph!' Prince Kahlee came out from behind his desk to grasp his best friend's hand. 'I want to be the best man at your wedding!'

Joseph smiled as he returned the pressure of the Prince's hand. 'I won't make any promises!'

Sarah's Mystery Rescuer

The young man, who had come to Sarah's rescue in the marketplace, was bent over a filing cabinet, looking for a confidential file in Joseph Nasseur's office as the Colonel entered the room. Neither looked surprised to find the other there. Straightening the young man revealed his pristine uniform as he came to attention and saluted Joseph. Lieutenant Sartan Cadem kept his full attention on his Commander.

'Your actions were indeed timely yesterday in the market place. Tell me Cadem, what took you there?' Joseph's words were quietly spoken, without a hint of anger as he sat behind his desk and gestured to his Lieutenant to sit down opposite. They slipped naturally into their native language.

'Well Sir, with the Ambassador's death, I thought it wise to keep an eye on the other members of the Australian Embassy. I knew that Major Winters was capable of looking after himself, so I set men to watch over Zuco, Shaw and the new Ambassador, while I kept an eye on Mrs. Davis and Miss Trent. I lost them momentarily in the market, as Mrs. Davis was becoming suspicious about the attacker's presence so I'd dropped back. How did you hear of it, Sir?'

'You're not my only source of information!' The Colonel smiled enigmatically as one eyebrow rose mockingly. 'Tell me have there been any further developments in the north and the Rebel infraction?' His thoughts were rarely far from that problem.

'No, Sir, not at present.' Lieutenant Cadem hesitated, considering how to word what he wished to say. Joseph waited patiently for him to speak his mind, and it gave him a chance to survey his quiet and useful assistant.

Cadem had proven himself to be a resourceful and imaginative solider, working his way quickly up the ranks until at 26 he was the right hand man to Colonel Nasseur, Head of

National Security. Sarah had described him perfectly; out of uniform he could easily pass as a high school student. This was a major advantage when having to get around Kathou under cover, but looking so youthful had made it difficult for him to win respect from lower and higher ranks. His fighting skills, though, were exceptional and at Colonel Nasseur's side had exemplified himself many times.

'Colonel, I don't wish to intrude in your personal life, but I must warn you,' Cadem finally said, 'many rumours are already running riot about last night's events at the Australian Embassy. You must tread carefully, Minister Beodan has never liked you and means to cause trouble. For the sake of your career and Miss Trent's reputation, secrecy is essential and I ... I would like you to know that if there is anything I can do to help, you have but to ask.' As he spoke, Cadem had scanned the Colonel's face to determine whether he had stepped over the line. A weary smile was all that Joseph could manage.

'I'm in a dilemma, Cadem, I can't ask Sarah to marry me. We're from two different worlds. I can't easily forsake my heritage, nor do I expect her to give up the freedoms she was born and raised in. The General, my father, was a hard, cold and cruel man. I watched the pain and suffering that he inflicted upon my mother as well as the indifference he showed me and my brothers and sisters. I don't ever want to be like him, I can't allow myself to become like him!'

Cadem shook his head. 'I admit I don't remember General Nasseur, but I do know that you're nothing like him from the stories I have heard. Your men don't cringe or fear for their lives when you issue an order. I was really happy when I transferred to your department for I knew that you were a Commander that I could respect. There's something though that you mightn't have considered, that's how does Miss Trent feel about all of this? I understand that she's not indifferent to you and your resolution to remain single may hurt you both.'

Joseph rose to his feet, doubt fleeing from his face to be replaced by determination. 'I need to go out for an hour or so. If anything urgent arises, contact me.' He slipped his mobile into his pocket.

The door shut firmly behind Joseph's retreating figure so that he didn't see the rare smile that appeared on Cadem's face. *I know that once my boss sets his mind to it, he can solve anything.*

A Royal Summons

It was with considerable surprise that after lunch, Sarah found on her desk three letters without any postage. One was addressed to her in Arabic, one she knew what it would contain and slipped it into her handbag until she felt strong enough to cope with it later and the third, on official royal stationery, was addressed to the Ambassador. Having delivered the latter one, Sarah sat down at her desk to study the first letter. *It isn't the first incidence that I've had to deal with correspondence in a native language, but it had never been addressed to me and held a warning beneath my name.* Still in disbelief, Sarah translated the message on the envelope again.

'Do not open unless alone. Destroy after reading.' Glancing around her, Sarah ensured that she was indeed alone before opening the envelope. The letter was also in Arabic and as she scanned the lines, Sarah slipped on her reading glasses.

'Miss Trent,

My actions last night have placed you in a delicate position. I am sorry; I did not intend that you would suffer further. My offer for lessons still stands but secrecy is imperative for your reputation as much as my own. If you are still willing for lessons to proceed, then tonight at seven, you will find a black car outside your home. If you do not show, then I will understand.

Yours to command,

Joseph Nasseur.'

Sarah read through the letter several times before turning to feed it and the envelope into the shredder that sat behind her desk. She was just coming to terms with the contents when James Greene buzzed her on the intercom. Gathering up her notebook, Sarah knocked on the Ambassador's door before entering. James looked stunned and standing up and approaching Sarah, he sat her down into a chair before placing a letter into her hands. Quickly perusing it, she looked up, slightly flushed, into James' smiling face.

'Unbelievable!' She exclaimed.

James nodded, taking back the letter. 'Indeed, Minister Beodan has not only formally apologized for his behaviour towards you; it seems that Princess Relanna has taken a personal interest in this matter and wishes to meet with you. What did Prince Kahlee say to you last night?'

Sarah pressed her hands to her over heated cheeks as she tried to recall. 'He was displeased with Beodan, and wasn't going to allow his behaviour to go unchecked. Oh Ambassador! What am I to do? I have seen diplomats expelled for insulting a member of the Ministry!'

A frown appeared upon James' brow. 'But you're not in the wrong, Sarah. Otherwise the Minister would've never admitted his fault. You'll have to leave here about three to get to the palace on time. I presume that you don't have anything suitable to wear here?'

'No, I'll have to go home first.' Sarah shook her head. 'I'll make up the time of course!'

Rising to her feet, she was surprised when James said, 'Nonsense! You're a member of this Mission and official visits are a part of your work. Try not to worry!' Sarah smiled slightly but as she left his office all she could do was worry that she was in deep trouble.

Protestors Revenge

At a quarter to four, one of the chauffeur driven Australian Embassy cars pulled up at the closed gates of the royal palace. A large crowd was gathered around the gate protesting in support of the Rebels. The guards at the gates rushed forward to clear access for the car but the crowd had already surged around the vehicle. Sarah ordered the driver to lock all the doors, but the order came too late.

Several pairs of hands reached in and dragged Sarah out. Her full-length skirt hampered any attempt to break free from her captives and make a run for safety. They'd no wish to harm her as Sarah was worth more to them alive than dead. She was jostled through the street, away from the palace guards trying to force their way through the crowd to reach her. The noise of people chanting and screaming political slogans deafened Sarah as she fought against the sea of hands, receiving a number of slaps for her trouble.

Her eyes flew around the mob hoping to find a friendly face within the crowd. Sarah's breath caught in her throat as she saw the young man from the market place, once more in plain clothes, pushing his way through the people towards her. Seeing him as her salvation, Sarah stretched out her un-bandaged hand towards him. Cadem almost had hold of it when the palace guards suddenly opened fire on the crowd. They shot into the air above the mob, but nevertheless this caused a stampede. People ran screaming and swearing, pulling Sarah and Cadem along with them but away from each other.

'No!' Sarah cried out, fighting against the crowd as she tried desperately to reach the man she saw as being her only salvation from this madness.

Cadem was battered around as he forced his way against the flow of people; his face set in a look of grim determination as every movement brought him closer to Sarah. She pushed people aside as she reached out her hand again towards Cadem. Tears of joy began to flow as Sarah's hand was firmly grasped and she was drawn towards the Lieutenant. A big, burly Panganian stood between them carrying a protest sign, this he brought down upon Cadem's outstretched arm. A sickening sound like bone breaking was heard but although he groaned in pain, Cadem didn't release Sarah's hand.

Anger filled every inch of Sarah's body, causing her to swing around and punch the big man in the face, breaking his nose. Blood poured forth as he roared and in retaliation he slapped her across the face backhanded. Sarah was thrown back against Cadem's shoulder; the last thing she heard before she passed out was the cries of anarchy.

Prince Kahlee's Warning

A scream was torn from Sarah as she sat up abruptly on the bed and groaning, she wished that she hadn't moved so fast. With her head pulsating, Sarah gave into the gentle, cool hands that urged her to lie down again. She found herself in an air-conditioned bedroom, so beautifully ornate and luxurious that she immediately knew that it wasn't the hospital.

Turning her head slightly, she watched as a beautiful Pangani woman bathed a cloth in a bowl of water on a bedside table before turning to lay it across her brow. The woman's regal attire and obvious signs of advanced pregnancy informed Sarah that her nurse was none other than Princess Relanna, wife of Prince Kahlee.

'Your Highness, you shouldn't wait upon me!' protested Sarah, trying to sit up again but Relanna urged her to stay lying down.

'Nonsense! You are an extremely brave woman, Miss Trent. Oh, may I call you Sarah? I doubt that I would have been as brave if I had been in your place.' Relanna's voice was soft, well-educated and pleasant to listen to. She was a tall and graceful woman; her luscious black hair was plaited and wrapped about her head which was uncovered as the Princess was in the privacy of her own rooms in the Palace.

Sarah sighed. 'I doubt I could have got out of it had it not been for that young man. That's the second time that he's saved me and I think that bully broke his arm. Oh, your Highness, where is he? I do wish to thank him and to make sure that he's all right.' Her eyes searched the Princess' face but at that moment it was suddenly devoid of expression.

'I am afraid that I am unaware of whom you speak. While you rest, I will make enquiries of my husband.' Relanna kept her eyes lowered until she was out of the room.

With considerable effort, Sarah slowly raised herself into a sitting position again and when her head had stopped spinning, she tentatively rose to her feet. Her shoes, headscarf and jacket had been removed and she padded across the carpet in her stockinged feet to the mirror over the hand basin. Sarah gasped at her reflection.

There was a large bruise and a lump forming on her forehead and an extensive bruise spreading across her cheekbone. Her hair, which had been neatly braided, now hung in loose strands around her face. Opening her handbag, which had miraculously survived, Sarah got out her hairbrush and went about setting some order to her hair.

When Kahlee and Relanna entered the room, Sarah had re-plaited her hair and washed her face free of make-up and dirt. Sarah curtsied but Prince Kahlee took her firmly by the shoulders and sat her back down on the bed before he forced her face up to look at him. Kahlee groaned as he scanned the damage that had been done to Sarah's face.

'These people shall not escape punishment for such an insult!' The Prince's anger was evident in every syllable of his words.

Sarah shook her head and then wished she hadn't as it hurt to move it too much. 'Please Your Highness, it will only make matters worse.'

'Something has to be done, Sarah.' Relanna sat down on the bed and took Sarah's hands between her own cool, reassuring grasp. 'If this matter is allowed to drop then the Rebels will feel that they have the right to harass and abduct anyone. We do not wish this to escalate into war but we don't want the foreign Embassies to be forced into a position where they advise their country to avoid all contact with Pangani.'

'Yes I see what you mean.' Sarah inclined her head in thought. 'I just wish that I wasn't involved.'

'So do we all!' Prince Kahlee nodded in agreement; his handsome features set in an expression of grim determination. 'If you are feeling a little better, Relanna thought you might like to take tea with her.'

Sarah rose to her feet, slipping them back into her shoes and pulled on her jacket. She slipped her scarf into her handbag before looking back at the Prince with a question in her eyes.

'You look fine.' Prince Kahlee held the door open for them and followed the two women out of the bedroom and into the Princess' private parlour. Kahlee and Relanna didn't normally live in the palace but a recent monsoon storm had done severe structural damage to their own mansion and it was necessary for the family to be out of the way while repairs were being undertaken. The Prince had his own apartments in the palace so that although Relanna got on well with her mother-in-law there was the opportunity for Relanna to be alone with her husband and children.

Sarah cast a curious glance around the room as they sat down in large comfortable chairs. The furniture was old fashioned and very expensive but it held a touch of Relanna's quiet charm and Sarah wondered, *Would I ever get used to such opulence and wealth?*

'Miss Trent, Relanna invited you here because we fear for your safety. We do not consider that these attacks against you have been random or by chance. Pangani's link to Australia is an important one. By kidnapping or harming you, the Rebels may be attempting to damage that link and thus destabilize our economy,' Sarah remained respectfully silent and waited patiently for the Prince to continue. 'We believe that the Rebels are targeting you for two reasons, you are female, no offence, and from what I have seen, most Embassies are held together by the competency of the Secretary. Yesterday offered a third reason, one we hope that the Rebels will never be aware of; that is the affection for you held by one of my high ranking officers. If that was ever known…' The Prince broke off as Sarah gave a gasp of fear. 'Never mind all that now, what we have to consider is how best to protect you. So far we have managed with a young Lieutenant of Joseph's keeping an eye on you.'

'Is that the young man who rescued me outside the gates?' Sarah stirred excitedly in her seat, as she was impatient for news of her rescuer. 'How is he? Was he badly hurt? Oh how I wish to thank him!' She rushed into speech.

'Lieutenant Cadem is being taken care of at the hospital.' Her concern impressed the Prince and he smiled at her. 'His arm was only fractured. He will be assigned to you as a constant bodyguard. When you leave your home or the Embassy grounds, Cadem will be your shadow.'

A small sigh escaped from Sarah. 'Perhaps I should apply for a transfer or take my annual leave until things settle down in Pangani. I can't accept a bodyguard, as I don't see why an important military officer should risk his life to protect mine.'

'Miss Trent, you cannot leave!' Princess Relanna reached across to touch Sarah's hand. 'That will only prove to the Rebels that they can do what they like without any hindrance. You must remain in Pangani, but we will not leave you unprotected. Please, if you leave you will be putting your successor at risk.'

Prince Kahlee paused as a servant entered the room with a tea tray. He placed it on the table in front of the Princess and then bowing he left. Relanna poured out the tea as the Prince continued to speak as he rose to his feet. 'I'll leave you to enjoy your tea, as I know Relanna wants to talk privately with you.' He also left the room.

Princess Relanna's Mission

There was a comfortable silence as the Princess didn't speak until she was satisfied that Sarah had a cup of hot, sweet tea in her hands. 'You've been wondering why I really sent for you?' queried the Princess as she laid her hands contently upon her nicely rounded stomach which indicated that Relanna was nearing her full term in her pregnancy. Sarah nodded and Relanna sighed as she continued, 'I wanted to warn you to not get involved with Joseph Nasseur. To save you from heart break as he will never be permitted to marry anyone of whom the family or the Emir does not approve. His mother is forcing him to make an immediate decision about one of the four young women she has selected from Pangani's elite families. I don't want to see you get hurt.'

'Thank you for your concern, your Highness, but I have no intentions of becoming involved with Colonel Nasseur.'

Relanna looked at her blankly. 'But didn't you agree to take self-defence lessons from him?'

'That's not yet decided upon. No amount of lessons could possibly equip me to fight off a mob like the one I faced this afternoon.'

'I understood it was to protect you from the unwanted amorous advances of your colleague.'

Sarah nodded, wondering, *How on earth does the Princess know all of this?* 'Perhaps to begin with, but I don't need this added complication in my life right now. Forgive me, but why are you so concerned about all this?'

'Why?' Once again Relanna laughed, reaching across to press Sarah's hand. 'Because Joseph Nasseur is my brother!'

'Well you don't have to worry, your Highness, I'm not going to take self-defence lessons with your brother, I'm not going to fall madly in love with him, therefore I'm not going to break my heart if I can't marry him! So please reassure your mother that I'm not a whore out to seduce her son and alienate him from his family or his country!' Sarah's voice became tighter as she fought to keep her emotions under control.

Sarah's Admittance

'Why have you been in communication with our mother?' Joseph's voice from the doorway caused both women to jump startled.

'How long have you been standing there?' Relanna demanded of her brother.

'Only long enough to hear that Mother has been causing trouble again!' He strode across the room to sit down opposite the two women. 'Is the interference of my mother and sister the only reason you have against me, or is there something else? Last night in your Ambassador's office I felt that you responded positively towards me.'

'Yesterday was a moment of madness.' Sarah sighed as she rubbed the back of her neck. 'There are too many factors that make a relationship with you impossible.'

'This is a decision that only the two of you can make.' Relanna slowly rose to her feet. 'I'll be in the next room if either of you need me.'

Joseph rose quickly to open the door for his sister to pass through before coming back to sit in the chair beside Sarah.

'So what are these factors? Perhaps we can find a solution for them?'

Sarah reached into her handbag and pulled out the letter she had not wanted to open earlier that day but had forced herself to read before leaving for the palace. The envelope bore handwriting Joseph was all too familiar with.

'You mean apart from this?' She asked, struggling to keep back her tears.

Joseph opened the letter and quickly scanned it. 'You know I don't believe any of these things?' he folded it again but didn't give it back to Sarah.

'It is what many, many other people will think, feel and say. You should be concentrating your time and energy on dealing with the current crisis, not trying to teach me to defend myself which that mob today proved is pretty pointless anyway. How much more hated will I face if it was thought I dared think myself good enough for one of Panganian's elite sons? And then there is Con…'

Joseph held up his hand. 'Hold on, shelve Con for a moment. I want to deal with the issues you have already raised. Firstly I don't care what people will say. It is no one's business but our own. Lessons were suggested as a way for you to deal with creeps like Con but not that mob, no one is that good! It was also a chance for us to get to know one another better, in private. There is always going to be some sort of crisis or dilemma, but does that mean I cannot have a private life at all? I will attempt to shield you from anything nasty people might say to you as much as I can. Now, what about Con?'

'I don't think he could handle it if I was interested in anyone other than him.' Sarah wrung her hands together. 'While I am single, he's playing some sort of seducing game where he thinks that if he keeps it up long enough I'll have to give in some time. By giving him a rival, and one who has succeeded where he has failed, could make him turn nasty. He would be impossible to work with. I'd be forced to leave the Embassy and Pangani.'

'Then I would just have to follow you.' He laid his hands over hers.

'Don't be ridiculous! This is your Life! Your World! Your Destiny!'

He chuckled, 'Quoting my mother's words to make me angry with you won't work. None of this is the key reason that could keep us apart.'

Sarah sighed. 'I assure you, I'm not a man! I assume homosexuality is still illegal in the Islamic faith.'

Again he laughed. 'No witty one that is not what I meant! Do you hate me?'

Sarah dragged in a sharp breath as she saw where this line of questioning was leading. 'No.'

'Are you indifferent to me?'

'No.'

'Do you like me?'

'Yes,' Sarah jumped to her feet and agitatedly paced the room. 'Please don't continue Colonel Nasseur. I like you enough to want to prevent you from making the biggest mistake of your life. I don't think you can be thinking straight. I know I haven't been ever since I found Ambassador Lucas cut up like a jigsaw puzzle and shoved into a crate! Every night for the last two weeks I dream that I'm the one in the box. That I'm screaming for help but no one can hear me. I just can't take any more stress right now. The Embassy is under constant threat from the rebels. Which Embassy is going to be bombed next? Is it safe to stay in our own homes? Is Con going to make my life miserable again today? The knot that builds in my stomach every time I hear you have gone north again to deal with another uprising or another rebel demonstration...'

'Why do you get a knot in your stomach when I go north?' He spoke very quietly.

Sarah stopped pacing to stare at him in disbelief. 'Why? Because I love you!' An absolute silence followed this statement as it slowly sunk in exactly what she had said. As if to take it back she pressed both her hands against her mouth.

'Well…' Joseph started but she wouldn't allow him to finish.

'No, No, No, No, No! I never meant to say that! You must forget that I ever said that!'

Rising to his feet he stepped towards her. 'Oh that is indubitably burned in to my brain and I am not going to be forgetting it any time soon!' He held his hand out to Sarah but shaking her head she moved backwards away from him.

Sarah's Injuries

A sudden noise outside the door caught the Colonel's alert ears. Whipping out the gun from the holster on his hip, he strode towards the door. Sarah backed into a dresser and let out a gasp of pain before she collapsed to the floor, unconscious. Joseph glanced back at her fleetingly, concerned about her collapse, but more worried about who might find them together. He ripped the door open, gun ready and breathed a sigh of relief when Kahlee appeared in the doorway. The Prince's eyebrows rose in surprise at the gun in Joseph's hand.

'It's all right Seph. No one knows about you meeting Miss Trent here.' Kahlee caught sight of Sarah lying inert upon the floor. Joseph put away his gun to kneel down and take Sarah into his arms.

'Would it be impolite to ask what you did to the young lady?'

Ignoring his friend, Joseph glanced up at the table Sarah had backed into before he turned her on her side. Kahlee uttered a protest that went unheeded as Joseph pulled up the back of Sarah's top and undid the button and zipper of her skirt. Just where her back had made contact with the table, there was a huge swelling that was already blue.

The Prince swore. 'That didn't just happen, did it?'

'No. More likely it happened when the crowd swamped her this afternoon.' Joseph scooped Sarah tenderly up into his arms. 'She needs a doctor, Kah, but he can't know about me.'

The Prince rushed forward to lead them out. 'Take her to Relanna's bedroom. I'll deal with the doctor. You won't be mentioned.'

They hurried out of the room and Relanna was surprised when they burst into her bedroom but when it was explained to her, she immediately wanted to help. Kahlee disappeared to call for a doctor while Relanna examined the wound when Joseph had laid Sarah upon her bed.

'We should have sent for a doctor as soon as Sarah had been brought into the palace. She seemed to be all right when she regained consciousness.'

'Don't blame yourself, Sis. Sarah is very good at concealing her pain.' Joseph paused looking down at Sarah as he contemplated a dilemma. 'We need to undress her, don't we?'

Relanna nodded, understanding his problem. 'I'm sorry, Joseph, but I'm in no condition to undress an unconscious woman.'

He exhaled slowly. 'Well, just remain as a chaperone. I don't want any hint of impropriety getting out.' With more expertise than his sister liked, Joseph removed all of Sarah's clothes except her underwear. Relanna laid the clothes over the back of a chair and pulled up the sheet to cover Sarah.

The siblings were silent for a moment, both had seen the number of bruises that covered Sarah's body and wondered why she hadn't said anything. Kahlee re-entered the room with the news that the doctor was on his way and had an icepack in his hands. Relanna took this and placed it against the swelling at the base of Sarah's spine. As if the cold was a stimulant, Sarah began to stir out of her faint.

'Joseph?' She whispered, confused at her change of location and state of undress. The Colonel took her hand into his own as he sat on the edge of the bed.

'It's all right; I'm here. Why didn't you tell us that you were hurt more seriously?'

Sarah lifted the sheet to see the bruising that covered her pale skin. 'I knew I ached, but I didn't think it was that bad. What did I do to black out?'

Joseph shrugged his shoulders. 'I'm no expert, but I believe that when you knocked this bruise you may have trapped a nerve causing you to lose consciousness, or the pain may have been so excruciating.'

Sighing, Sarah closed her eyes. 'I'm not an accident waiting to happen am I? I've never been this much of a problem before.'

Surprising everyone, Relanna lightly slapped Sarah's arm. 'Now you're just being silly! A couple of incidents hardly make you a walking hazard.'

'Just a spot of bad luck, that's all.' The Prince heartily agreed with his wife.

There was a knock at the door, announcing the Doctor's arrival and as Joseph seemed to suddenly vanish, Relanna drew on her headscarf. Kahlee opened the door and politely dismissed the servant who had escorted the doctor to Relanna's chambers.

'We should have called you sooner, Doctor Said, but we had no idea of the severity of the damage Miss Trent had sustained,' explained the Prince as the royal's personal doctor bowed to Kahlee and then to Relanna.

'No matter, your Highness, the important thing is that we do something for the young lady to ease her pain. Perhaps Sir, if you could step outside for a moment so that I may examine Miss Trent.'

Kahlee immediately left the room. Relanna looked a little doubtful as to whether she should also leave. Doctor Said solved this problem for her as he drew back Sarah's sheet.

'There is no need for you to leave, your Highness; I thought Miss Trent would be less embarrassed without any men in the room. Hum!' The doctor's attention turned to Sarah's injuries. When he removed the icepack and gently touched the swollen area, Sarah couldn't help crying out. Deep in thought Doctor Said replaced the icepack and drew the sheet back over her. 'You are going to be very sore for a few days. Massage will aid muscle stiffness and the bruises will go away in time. It is the swelling at the base of your spine that worries me. The icepack is a good idea, but only for 15 minutes and then a compression bandage for two hours. I want to see you tomorrow and at the end of the week. If the swelling does not go down, we may have to run some tests.'

Relanna was concerned, but tried hard for Sarah's sake not to show it. 'Is it anything to worry about, Doctor?'

He smiled, shaking his head. 'No, not really, I'd avoid angry crowds for a while and tomorrow should be spent resting.' Sarah opened her mouth to protest, but Doctor Said held up a warning finger. 'My dear Miss Trent, the Australian Embassy is not going to fall apart if you are away for a day!' Doctor Said headed for the door. 'Call my Receptionist in the morning to make an appointment to come and see me, or if you feel worse, I will come to you. Good evening your Highness.' He bowed again to Relanna before leaving the room. The servant, who was standing just outside, led the Doctor out of the Palace.

Joseph materialized as suddenly as he had disappeared. 'Do you think it would be wiser to find a bed for Sarah in the Palace for the night?' he asked his sister. 'Would the drive home be too much for her back?'

'It's not a problem for us, Seph!'

'Oh no!' Sarah cried out, surprising them both. 'I'm sorry, that sounded rude. I am very grateful for your hospitality, but I can't leave Simon alone all night. He'd be frightened if I didn't come home at all!'

Relanna's features relaxed into a smile. 'Joseph told me you had acquired a puppy. You are correct, of course, you cannot leave him alone. I'll help you to dress, Sarah, while Joseph arranges for a car to take you home.'

The Colonel had no alternative, having been given his orders, but to leave and carry out his commission. He wasn't kept waiting long as Kahlee soon escorted Sarah out to Joseph's car. Sarah had insisted that Relanna shouldn't come out into the cool night wind. Kahlee made certain that Sarah was comfortable before he shut the passenger door. As the car slid out of a back gate, Kahlee pondered the future that was certainly not going to be smooth sailing for the young lovers, before heading back inside to his wife.

My Right To Protect You

Slumping slightly in her seat, Sarah was forced to acknowledge to herself, the pain that she'd been trying to ignore. Her back ached, her wounded hand throbbed and a headache became more persistent. Even so, when Joseph glanced away briefly from the road to look across at her in concern, Sarah lied at his query if she was all right.

'I'm fine,' she said, managing a tired smile.

Joseph chuckled, 'Liar!' He returned without heat. His attention returned to the road. 'I want you to sleep in tomorrow. Kahlee's secretary will contact Ambassador Greene to let him know you won't be at work. She'll also arrange for your doctor's appointment and I'll send someone to take you to it,' Joseph ordered.

'Is all this really necessary?' Sarah sighed deeply. 'I'm not a child!'

'No you're not a child!' His voice was tight with raw emotion. 'You are the most precious thing in my life. If I was to ever lose you...' Joseph found he couldn't complete his sentence; there was an obstruction in his throat.

'I don't really see that being a possibility, Joseph. I mean when all the who-ha about Lucas' death dies down, things will settle back down to normal. The majority of the Panganian people are more than happy under the Emir's reign.' Sarah shyly laid her hand over one of his on the steering wheel. Joseph turned his hand over so that her palm lay in his.

'In the meantime, it's my right to protect you. Please don't deny me that.' He raised her hand to press against his lips.

'I can't deny you anything,' Sarah said breathlessly.

Joseph laughed in delight. 'I'll remind you of that when you're feeling better!'

Despite her pain, Sarah felt a tingling of anticipation for the day that he would keep that promise.

There were several lights on at Sarah's home when they pulled up outside. This was normal as Sarah had lighting on a timer for security reasons. Hamid, the guard, approached their car to determine their identity, but discerning that it was Colonel Nasseur with Sarah, he returned to his rounds of the gardens. She felt very stiff when she got out of the car and wasn't sorry for the arm that Joseph offered her to lean upon. Even before they had got to the front door, they could hear the excited yaps of Simon inside.

As they entered the hallway, the puppy hobbled around them three times at top speed before plonking himself on his bottom in front of Sarah's feet and while she gingerly knelt down to greet the puppy, Joseph entered the living room cautiously, checking that it was empty.

'Come and sit down whilst I check the rest of the house.' Joseph was then forced to acknowledge the puppy's attempts to gain his attention before he could manoeuvre Sarah into a lounge chair. 'Yes Simon, I'm pleased to see you too!'

While Joseph searched the house, Simon jumped up on to Sarah's lap. Twice he pressed his nose into the palm of her hand to get her interested in patting him, but when both attempts failed; he sighed and laid his head across her arm. Sarah's eyes were closed; she really did feel very tired. It wasn't long before the Colonel rejoined her, picked Simon up and placed him on the ground before assisting Sarah to her feet.

'Bedtime Sarah.'

Like a child, half asleep, she allowed herself to be led to her bedroom. When Joseph started to undress her, Sarah found the strength to protest that she would manage and obediently Joseph stepped back, turning his back to her as she slipped out of her clothes and into a nightie.

'Go to sleep. I can see myself out. Does Simon stay with you?'

Sarah shook her head and she lay down; drawing the top sheet over her. 'His bed is in the laundry. Simon's a bit of a bed hog and he wriggles.' With a relieved sigh she closed her eyes. Simon hesitated to leave the bed, but the command in Joseph's voice wasn't one many people could disobey, so he reluctantly went out to his own bed. Returning to the bedroom, Joseph turned out the light and quietly left the room. He had a couple of words with the guard to ensure that no one had been hanging around, before he felt he could leave Sarah to her slumber and head for home.

TUESDAY

Rude Awakening

'Bloody hell!' Sarah wasn't even half awake when she groaned for the first time that morning. The curtains were drawn so it wasn't a shard of light that had disturbed her, but as there was no repeat of what had roused her, she was in so much pain that she just wanted to drift back to sleep. Suddenly there was a clatter of dishes in the kitchen, jerking Sarah into full awareness.

'Simon, is that you?' She called out, attempting to sit up, but sudden stabbing pains assaulted her and she collapsed back on her pillows. Sarah felt stiff and sore, and she wondered, *am I going to have trouble getting out of bed without assistance?*

'Simon?' Sarah tried again to sit up and this time her aching body allowed her to move reluctantly. Footsteps could be heard walking up the passageway. She glanced around the room for a possible weapon. Apart from the clock radio and the lamp, there was nothing close enough that Sarah could reach.

Nervously grasping the base of the lamp, she swallowed hard upon her fear as the footsteps came closer.

'Sarah? I'm sorry, did I wake you?' Marianne quietly opened the bedroom door and entered.

'Oh Marianne, shouldn't you be at work?'

The older woman straightened the bed sheets before she sat down on the edge of the bed. 'My dear, it's not even 8 a.m. yet. I'll be able to cook you breakfast, make sure you have a long bath and rub ointment on your bruises before I have to get to work.'

'Thank you. That is very thoughtful of you.' Sarah was touched by her concern.

'Well actually,' Marianne admitted, 'I received a phone call this morning. Princess Relanna was quite worried that you're here alone, apart from Simon.'

'The Princess is very thoughtful.' Sarah couldn't stop her cheeks from blushing.

'Well you can tell me all about it later.' Marianne rose to her feet. 'I've fed Simon, and I'll start the bath for you, unless you'd like breakfast first?'

Sarah shook her head, throwing back her bed covers. 'No, a bath sounds wonderful, but I don't want you to worry about cooking breakfast. I don't normally have anything but cereal or toast.'

'You shall have both, my dear.' Marianne ordered, leaving the room, and could be heard in the bathroom filling up the bath, before she returned to the kitchen.

Sarah sat for a moment longer, contemplating what a good friend she had in Marianne, before she convinced her stiff legs to swing over the side of the bed and support her sore body into a standing position. Movement was a little slow at first, but by the time Sarah had walked down the passage to the toilet, and then back up to her bedroom for some clothes, and on to the bathroom, her movement had freed up a little.

'May I come in?' Marianne tapped on the bathroom door.

'Of course!' Sarah looked up from adjusting the hot water tap and adding more cold water.

'How badly hurt are you? The Princess said something about a large swelling.' Marianne couldn't keep the concern out of her voice.

Sarah slipped off her nightie and wasn't surprised by Marianne's gasp of horror. The multitude of bruises had developed deeper in colour and when Marianne turned her around, the swollen area was quite a protrusion.

'Oh My God! My poor child! Where on earth is this going to end?'

Sarah turned off the taps, tested the water temperature before she stepped into the bath.

'I'm afraid I don't know, Marianne. I know it's something that is really worrying Prince Kahlee.'

'Hum! Well you relax while I put the kettle on for tea.' Marianne shut the bathroom door as she left. *Although I think that a close association with the Royal family will be a benefit, career wise, I am worried that it makes Sarah even more susceptible to attack. I'll have a word with Gary about this new danger.*

For nearly twenty minutes Sarah lay in the bath with her eyes closed, allowing the healing power of water to lap around her. When she rose out of the bath, and wrapped herself into a large fluffy towel, Sarah already felt less achy all over. She dressed in a light floral dress, suitable for weekend wear, but not for work. Personally Marianne thought, as Sarah entered the kitchen, she should wear such clothes more often. Sarah had brushed her hair, but not pulled it back into its usual plait. She looked years younger, and it suited her.

'I want to see every bite eaten before I leave, or I'll be very angry!'

Sarah laughed at Marianne trying to look severe. 'Only if you sit down and have a cup of tea with me.'

Marianne agreed as she was so full of curiosity about Sarah's evening at the Palace. Between mouthfuls of cereal, Sarah told her everything, except her meeting with Colonel Nasseur. Sarah loved Marianne, and knew that she could trust her with a secret, but she couldn't risk someone else over hearing.

After they washed up the dishes together, Sarah insisted on helping, Marianne forced Sarah to strip off her dress and lie down on her bed. She rubbed a soothing cold ointment all over, being careful about not putting pressure upon the swollen area. Simon bounded in as Sarah was redressing and he frisked happily around the two women. The smell of the ointment, though, saw him just as quickly leave the room again. The two women laughed at his behaviour and rising from the bed, Sarah escorted Marianne out to her car. The older woman gently embraced her before she got behind the wheel.

'Thank you for coming over. It means a lot to me.'

Marianne pressed her hand. 'We've got to look after you my dear. Where am I going to find another daughter out here so easily?'

Sarah was moved, and stood watching the road even after the car had driven out of sight.

'You should return inside, Miss Trent. You should be resting.' Hamid, the guard said, steering her back inside. She went willingly and taking another couple of painkillers before sitting down upon her lounge. Wondering what to do with herself, she caught sight of yesterday's mail, still unopened. Routines are hard to break, and as her fluffy companion flopped down on the rug at her feet, she started to sort her correspondence.

Progress Report

The top floor of the Embassy was eerily deserted when Marianne arrived. With the absence of both Sarah and Gary, who was spending the day in reconnaissance; the silence seemed strange. Kevin had an appointment first thing that morning, so he wasn't coming in until after 10. Con wasn't a great time keeper and didn't always breeze in until about 9.30. So Marianne had fed Jeb and Ash before sitting down to sort the mail and she had the floor to herself and a peace and quiet that was perfect for getting a lot of work done. That was the plan, but as she placed the sorted mail into their appropriate pigeonholes, James Greene let himself into the secure area.

'Good morning Marianne. I need to see you in my office when you've got a minute.' Although it was pleasantly said, there was a look of anxiety in his eyes.

'Of course James,' Marianne completed her task before she followed the Ambassador into his office.

James was impatiently pacing up and down and he waved Marianne into a chair. 'That assault on Sarah outside the Palace made the news last night. Have you spoken to her? Is she all right? I tried to call her last night but it went straight to voice mail. I didn't want to ring this morning in case I woke her.'

She was touched by his obvious concern. 'I went to see Sarah this morning. She's stiff, sore and bruised, but the main concern is some swelling at the base of her spine. I understand that she's seeing Doctor Said today.'

He stopped pacing as his eyebrows rose in surprise. 'Said? Isn't he the Royals' personal physician?'

'Prince Kahlee called him in last night when Sarah collapsed after backing into a table.'

'Poor kid!'

It was Marianne's turn to look surprised. 'Is that how you see her?'

'Please Marianne, she's as cute as a button but she's so young!' James groaned. 'Or is it that I feel so old? Either way, I'm no cradle snatcher. Despite my teasing, Sarah's safe from me.'

'Speaking of safe,' Marianne suddenly changed the subject, 'Did you get a response about your project to knock down a few walls in the Embassy?'

James couldn't help grinning at the mental image of him willy-nilly going around destroying walls. 'It's only two half walls, Marianne. I'm not planning on bulldozing the whole building!'

'My apologies,' she laughed, 'but you didn't answer my question.'

'Strangely enough, they were quite prompt in getting back to me. Neither walls are heritage nor load-bearing so it's just a matter of getting a couple of quotes for the renovations.'

'Also convincing Con to give up his office,' added Marianne.

'Hum! Might need a bit of tact for that!' mused the Ambassador.

'In that case,' she said, rising to her feet, 'You'd better leave it to me.'

James' features took on a hurt look. 'I think I've been insulted.'

'Not really.' Marianne smiled. 'I just know how Con's mind works and what to appeal to. I'm sorry I can't deal with your mail for you like Sarah does, are you going to be all right with it?'

'I'm sure I can remember how to read a letter.' James shook his head sadly. 'All these insults are undermining my confidence.'

'I'm sure you'll survive!'

'Only if you'll have dinner with me tonight!'

Marianne stared at him in surprise. 'Excuse me?'

'I always thought that it was the eyesight that went first and not the hearing. Obviously I was wrong,' murmured James, his eyes twinkling with devilry.

'There's nothing wrong with my hearing, thank you Mr. Grey Beard. I was expressing surprise at a question that appeared to come out of nowhere.'

'My brain works so fast that you can't even see the process it takes from one point to another.' He laughed. 'What about the question, do I get an answer?'

'I was going to drop in and see Sarah this evening.'

The Ambassador waved this suggestion away. 'Don't take this the wrong way, but that girl needs to rest. Any other objections?'

A shaky laugh escaped from Marianne. 'What about I'm washing my hair tonight?'

'Sorry, not good enough.' James shook his head. 'You may as well come over straight after work, there's no need to change. It'll only be me.'

Marianne reached for the door. 'Well since you asked so graciously, how could I refuse?'

'That a girl! Is there anything urgent of Sarah's work that we need to attend to?'

Marianne shook her head, 'Nothing urgent. Just a few letters that need replies typing and I'll handle that.'

'I'm sure you can.' James smiled so broadly that as Marianne headed back to her office, she was unsure if he'd been teasing her or not.

You Should Have Called Me

Con Zuco entered the Embassy still buzzed from a great night and felt that he could conquer the world. He bounced up the stairs, two at a time, and into the secure area ready to tackle a new day. He pulled up short; his witty greeting for Sarah froze upon his lips as he saw Marianne at the Secretary's desk.

'Oh Sarah this crisis is really taking it out of you!'

'Cute!' Although her teeth were clenched, Marianne managed to smile. 'You're in a merry mood. I thought you'd be more upset about Sarah.'

'What's happened to her?' The grin immediately slid off his face. 'My phone battery died about two this morning.'

Marianne came out from behind Sarah's desk. 'She was attacked by the rebel demonstrators outside the palace gates. If it wasn't for one of Colonel Nasseur's men rescuing her we could have had a kidnapping on our hands as well as everything else that's been going on lately!'

Con continued to stand silently staring at her that she began to wonder if he had actually been struck dumb. Unfortunately he soon regained the use of his tongue.

'She shouldn't have been allowed to go alone! Why wasn't someone there to protect her? Why wasn't I there to protect her? Why wasn't I informed of her situation? I should've been the one to drive her home!' His voice rose as he yelled.

'Why weren't you informed?' Marianne blinked in surprise. 'Well if you hadn't taken off early to hit the pub you might've been here when Prince Kahlee called James with the news.'

'Then you should have found me! Why didn't she contact me herself?' Con exploded.

Marianne's eyebrows rose. 'Don't yell at me Con! Why should Sarah have personally called you? Why should James or I have called you at the time it happened? You're not her boss, her mother or even her boyfriend!'

'How Dare You! You know nothing about my relationship with Sarah!' He was envisioning the scene where he was rescuing Sarah from the angry mob. Marianne stared at Con a little more closely and didn't like how small Con's pupils appeared.

'Have you been taking drugs?'

'Mind your own business!'

Marianne spun him around and pushed him in the back. 'For goodness sake take something and sober up before the Ambassador see you! Go and have a swim and pull yourself together.'

Con looked like he was going to argue but glancing out of his window he looked down at the pool. The water looked cool and inviting, so he grabbed his bathers and a towel from his locker before heading down. Marianne ran a hand over her face as she shook her head in disbelief. *As if we don't have enough problems to worry about; now Con is turning up to work high and delusional. What is going to happen next?* She wondered.

Switching Offices

When Con re-entered the secure area some time later, he was a lot cooler and mellower. Certainly mellow enough that upon seeing Marianne hunt frantically through a drawer of Sarah's desk, he asked politely if she'd lost something.

She looked up and sighed. 'I don't know how Sarah manages. I know she's organized and neat, but the lack of room must be a nightmare.'

Con nodded, but he hadn't really given it much thought. 'What Sarah needs is an office of her own. She shouldn't be stuck in a corner of the hall.'

'The problem is where to put her.' Marianne said, 'There's no point moving her to one of the offices downstairs, she needs to be on hand for the Ambassador. Both Gary and I have too much sensitive information that must be in this secure area. Kevin is prepared to move, but his office is right down the other end of the corridor to the Ambassador. Sarah would be running up and down the passage all day.' Marianne held her breath as she almost saw the cogs of Con's brain working.

'There's always my office I suppose,' he finally said. 'I mean my files contain information that has all ready been made public. Nothing sensitive there,' Con added.

She changed her expression to one of concern. 'Would you be willing to give up your office Con? I mean, the ones downstairs are smaller.'

'That doesn't matter. Actually, it would mean less room for me to make a mess in,' he said shrugging his shoulders.

'Of course there are many advantages of a downstairs office. I mean, there'd be no one looking over your shoulder, wanting to know what you were doing or where you were going every time you wanted a smoke or a drink down at the pub. Your movements would be freer,' Marianne paused for a few seconds before adding, 'It's still a lot to give up!'

'It's only an office.' Con laughed in a superior manner. 'Perhaps you should talk to the Ambassador about it.'

'That's very good of you, Con; I'll certainly put the idea to James.' Marianne smiled up at him.

Con started to whistle on his way into his office. *More freedom of movement is only one of the benefits that attracts me. By giving up my office for Sarah, I'm making her obligated to me. Perhaps such generosity will make her look more favourably upon me.* He indulged in this daydream as Marianne informed James to go ahead with his renovations.

Con's Rant

Sarah had fallen asleep but was awoken with a start by Simon's angry barking and a pounding on the front door. She struggled to her feet, not really awake and went into the hall to open the door. Con Zuco stood outside, with the guard trying to force him to leave.

'I'm sorry Miss Trent; Mr. Zuco would not listen to me. Mrs. Davis said you were not to be disturbed.'

Sarah sighed as Con forced his way into the house. 'It's all right, Hamid. Con obviously has something he needs to say.'

The guard still looked worried but Sarah shut the door and went into the living room. She carefully lowered herself onto the lounge and Simon continued to growl at him as Con sat down beside her on the same couch.

'Please Con; I'm not up to visitors at the moment, so what's the matter?'

'Oh my darling, don't you know how you hurt me with your suspicions? Don't you know how worried I've been? I'm here to serve you in your hour of need. But when there is no word from you about the attack, what am I supposed to think?' crooned Con.

Sarah took a deep breath. 'I'm sorry. I don't see how this is any of your business. Prince Kahlee alerted James as to my condition. Princess Relanna looked after me and Colonel Nasseur drove me home. I don't see why you feel it is necessary that you're informed of my whereabouts?'

Con's fingers travelled down her arm but when he tried to take her hand, Sarah picked up his hand and placed it back into his own lap. His lips had thinned at the mention of the Colonel.

'You should've called me to pick you up. You don't want to be seen in the Colonel's company. It would make it look like the rumours about you are true.'

'What rumours?' Sarah's breath caught in her throat.

'That you're the Colonel's whore!' His hand was running up and down her arm again.

Colour flushed instantly across Sarah's cheeks. 'I hope you're telling everyone that's not true?'

His eyebrows rose. 'If it looks like a duck and quacks like a duck...'

'Rumours like that could ruin both our careers!' Annoyed Sarah pushed his hand away from her neck.

'Then I suggest you steer clear of that man! Has he managed to get his leg over?'

'Excuse me?' Sarah moved to an arm chair to get away from Con's roaming hands.

He laughed, 'Come on, you're not that prim and proper are you? Has the Colonel got you into bed yet? Has he fucked you?'

'Don't be crass! That is none of your business!'

'Well what are your criteria for your lovers? Is it only military men? What was Gary like? I mean you spent a week sharing the same bed when we were all forced to stay at the Residency after Lucas' death.'

'I didn't have sex with Gary.' Pity was in her eyes as she looked at Con. 'Marianne teamed me up with the Major to protect me from you!'

'Why? Am I that repulsive?' Con's eyes nearly popped out of his head.

Sighing Sarah ran a hand across her weary eyes. 'You just won't take no for an answer. I Don't Love You! I Don't Want To Have Sex With You! We're not friends; we're colleagues and nothing more!'

Con grabbed Sarah by the arms and dragged her roughly to her feet. His fingers dug painfully into her flesh. 'It's someone else isn't it? Who is he? Is it really Colonel Nasseur?'

'Even if I was in love with someone, it still wouldn't be any of your business!' A spark of defiance emerged, but it didn't last long. Con smacked her across the face and she fell back against the couch. The cushions softened her fall, but Sarah still had to fight to keep from passing out from the pain in her lower back.

'Why would I lie to you?' she demanded.

'Why do all women lie? Because they can't resist! It's second nature!'

Cadem's Warning

The front door burst open and Hamid, the guard followed Lieutenant Cadem into the living room. Cadem grabbed Con and threw him half way across the room before he knelt down in front of Sarah.

'Miss Trent, are you all right?'

Almost instinctively, Sarah reached out to Cadem, and with a sob wrapped her arms around his neck. For a moment he held her in his arms, comforting her.

'It's you! Always you! Whenever I'm in trouble you are there.' Sarah was crying now as she rambled.

Con rose to his feet, shaking off the restraining hand that the guard had upon his arm. 'So you keep me at arm's length, and yet you fall into the arms of this stranger!' He was struggling to get his temper under control.

'Twice Cadem has saved my life.' Sarah wiped her hand across her face to remove her tears. 'He's my guardian angel. I feel safe with him,' she explained.

'Miss Trent has a doctor's appointment, Mr. Zuco.' Cadem rose to his feet and approached Con. 'I suggest you go home and sober up. Any further annoyance experienced by Miss Trent will be dealt with most seriously.'

'You can't touch me, Bud! I have diplomatic immunity!' Con snorted in disgust as he towered over the young Lieutenant.

Cadem's sudden smile sent a shiver down Con's spine. 'If I were to get hold of you, you would not live long enough to evoke your diplomatic immunity! Hamid, see Mr. Zuco out to his car please!'

Con had no choice but to leave. The Lieutenant's threat was a very real one, and not to be taken lightly. Sarah struggled to rise to her feet and Cadem went immediately to her side to assist her.

'Thank you so much Lieutenant. You always show up when I need you the most.'

Colour flushed across Cadem's cheeks. 'I'm just following orders Ma'am. The Colonel is very particular about your protection.'

'I will thank him when I next see him. I'd better change if you're escorting me to Doctor Said's office.'

'We need to get moving, Miss Trent.' Cadem checked his watch.

Sarah pulled on a pair of sandals and picked up her handbag and head scarf from off a chair. 'I just need to powder my nose and I'll be ready.'

Cadem ensured that the doors and windows were locked while Sarah was in the bathroom. She didn't keep him waiting long and they were soon on the road in the Colonel's own car with Sarah still feeling slightly upset by Con's visit, but she had complete faith in her rescuer.

The Doctor's Counsel

Doctor Said kept Sarah waiting only a couple of minutes before he led her into his spacious consultancy room. He asked Sarah to remove her dress and he checked the state of her injuries. Tut-tutting over the state of the swollen area before his keen eyes caught sight of the latest marks left by Con's fingers upon her upper arms.

'These were not here last night,' Doctor Said pointed out the new bruises. 'Can you tell me how they occurred?' As he sat down behind his desk, Sarah was allowed to redress before sitting down opposite him. After a brief hesitation, she told the Doctor about the episode with Con. He listened in silence, occasionally jotting down a note in his file. When she had finished the Doctor's question wasn't one that she was expecting.

'Are you in love with someone?'

'The relationship is very new, unformed as yet.' Sarah could feel the colour rising up her cheeks betraying her. 'Let's just say that I like him more than I do anyone else.'

The Doctor chuckled. 'That's a nice evasive answer Miss Trent. I won't tease you about his identity, but it is pretty obvious from the rumours flying around Kathou after the function Sunday evening.'

'Oh dear!' Sarah could feel her flesh becoming redder in embarrassment.

'Now I'll give you a prescription for some anti-inflamatories. They should bring the swelling down. As well as something for the pain. If you're worried about using too many strong painkillers, intersperse them with aspirin, but don't go without. I assume you'll be back at work tomorrow. If that is the case, you must not lift anything heavy, and limit the amount of time you spend on the computer. If you need exercise, swimming is acceptable.'

Sarah took the prescriptions he handed her and rose to her feet. 'Thank you for seeing me Doctor Said. I know you're a busy man.'

The Doctor smiled as he also stood up. 'I am never too busy for a friend of Prince Kahlee. You take care of yourself Miss Trent, and perhaps soon we can all look forward to your wedding!'

Sarah was surprised. 'It's a little too soon to presume such an event.'

'I know well the man whom desires to claim your heart.' He took one of her hands into his own. 'He is a very determined young man. He usually gets what he wants.'

Sarah shook her head sadly. 'What if it isn't advantageous to his career, or to Pangani?'

'My dear, if it is advantageous to the man, the rest will fall in place.' He sighed at her scepticism. 'Inshallah!'

'And what if it isn't as God wishes?' She removed her hand to open the door.

'Have faith my child; in God and your man.' There was no arguing with that, so Sarah, leaving the office, didn't even try.

Intimate Dining

That evening James and Marianne ate out on the verandah of the Residency. Jeb and Ash lay most of the time in the garden beside them. They didn't discuss work, although James did ask about what was in Kathou to keep his daughter Crystal entertained. Their pleasant evening together was marred only by the nagging guilt Marianne felt for not visiting Sarah. James almost convinced her that Sarah needed rest and quiet.

In any case, the streets weren't safe to be out at night. The demonstrators were out only during the day, even they were scared of the rioters who struck the city once darkness had fallen. The looting, vandalism and destruction had nothing to do with the Fundamentalists who wanted change; not anarchy. That was the domain of the Rebels.

WEDNESDAY

Chauffeur Duties

When Cadem arrived at Sarah's house to pick her up, he was a little surprised when Simon hobbled out also to get into the car, but as both Sarah and the guard saw nothing extraordinary in this, Cadem kept his mouth shut. The Lieutenant saw Sarah safely through the Embassy gate and watched Ahkman, the security guard, escort her, with Jeb and Ash as well as Simon, up to the main building, before he drove away.

Cadem had a strange feeling that he was being watched. So the Lieutenant parked his car just up the street and scouted the boundary of the Embassy. All he discovered was that Jeb and Ash had very keen hearing and his search caused them to follow his progress from within the boundary. They barked only once, as the sound of his voice reassured them. They knew him to be a friend, but kept an ear open for his activity, as it was unusual.

Unable to satisfy his gut instinct, Cadem had to admit defeat and return to his car. Driving away, Cadem hoped that his instincts weren't leading him falsely. They had got him out of several tricky situations in the past, and he disliked having them proven wrong. Cadem would have disliked it even more to know that his instincts were spot on; he just couldn't see where the trouble was hiding.

Business As Usual

For almost an hour, Sarah had absolute peace as she caught up with any work from the day before and then commenced that morning's mail. It wasn't actually completely solitary, as Simon had insisted on accompanying her into the main building rather than across to his basket on the Residency verandah. He stretched out on a large cushion under her desk and had a perfect view of anyone approaching his mistress. As the security door opened, Simon's head rose immediately in interest. Seeing the legs of the Ambassador, the puppy refrained from barking, but he did hobble from around the desk, his tail wagging ecstatically.

'Hello there old boy! I wondered where you were when I didn't see you on the verandah.' James bent down to greet the happy puppy.

'He wouldn't leave me, Ambassador, I'm afraid Simon is over protective today.'

'Don't you ever leave me without a competent Secretary or the delight of feasting my eyes upon you every day?' James straightened.

Sarah laughed. 'None of this was planned, Sir. Believe me if I could have foreseen the assault outside the Palace, I wouldn't have gone.'

'Well then, you disappoint me. I thought it was a part of being a perfect Secretary to have second sight!'

Sarah winced at a stabbing pain from the swollen area of her back and re-adjusted the cushion positioned behind her. 'At times I really wish I could foresee the future. It would've saved me a great deal of pain.'

'Is there anything I can do to help you?'

An impish smile appeared. 'Well the Doctor suggested that if I wanted to exercise, I was allowed to swim.'

'So you want to use the pool here? I don't see any problem. I do have one stipulation, though,'

'And that would be?' Sarah looked a little wary.

A broad grin answered her. 'I expect you to wear a bikini and give me fair warning that you're going down.'

'I don't think you really want that Sir.' She smiled as she shook her head. 'I'm lily white at the best of times, but at the moment I'm black and blue.' She glanced around, shyly, to ensure that there was no one else about as she rose to her feet and removed her shirt.

Surprise was written all over James' face, he hadn't expected her to take her clothes off. His surprise turned to horror at the sight of all the bruises. When he noticed the swelling, James couldn't stop himself from swearing. Sarah pulled her shirt back on.

'Bloody Hell! My dear girl, you're to take as many breaks as you need! In all seriousness, if there's anything you need, please just ask. I hadn't realized it was that serious!'

'At least I'll live, Sir.'

James went quite white. 'We must never become complaisant about security.' Heading for his office he added, 'If there's any time in my diary this morning, slot Gary in for me.'

'Of course,' Sarah didn't even attempt to argue with him.

Where Are My Glasses?

There was plenty of work to be done, they were understaffed by at least five people and made use of local staff more than they were supposed to. Sarah was surprised, but pleasantly so, when James Greene informed her of his plans to alter Con's office to give her more room. *I can see great possibilities for the opening up of the area, but am uncomfortable about feeling beholden to Con for giving up his office.* She thanked Con sincerely enough, but when he tried to take her hand, she immediately stepped away from him. Although his mouth thinned in displeasure, he didn't make a scene. He just had to be patient. He always got what he wanted in the end, so he slipped downstairs for a cigarette, a chat with Ahkman and to dream of rescuing Sarah from some horrible fate.

Knocking first, Sarah entered the Ambassador's office with a large pile of papers in her arms. She was momentarily surprised to find James on his hands and knees on the floor going through the contents of one of his desk drawers, which he had emptied out on to the floor.

'Lost something Sir?' She asked solicitously.

With a sigh, James sat down on the ground. 'I can't lay my hands on my glasses. I could swear I had them earlier, but for the life of me I can't find them now.'

Sarah blinked twice as she stared down at him in disbelief. A look of great concern crossed her features, as his spectacles sat on the top of his head. With one finger, Sarah gently pushed the glasses down so that they rested in their proper place on his nose. James looked shamefaced as he struggled to his feet.

'I'm not going senile! I'm not going senile!'

Sarah wasn't sure if he was trying to convince her or himself, 'Of course not Sir! Today's mail,' she laid the papers into three piles on the Ambassador's desk. Ignoring the mess on the floor, James looked disbelievingly at the mountains of paper.

'Have I got to read all this?'

'Pile 'A' only requires your signature. Pile 'B' I need you to draft a reply to them, and Pile 'C' are invitations to functions.'

James looked at pile 'C' dubiously. 'How do I know what are critical to attend?'

A twinkle entered Sarah's eyes. 'In the right hand corner of the invitation you'll find a pencilled asterisk for the functions I recommend that you have to attend. Below the invitations are draft copies of acceptance and rejection letters for your approval.'

'You are the perfect Secretary!' James collapsed into his chair. 'If I hadn't fallen madly in love with Simon, I'd be marrying you!'

She shook her head adamantly, 'Oh no! Just think how uncomfortable I'd feel having step children older than me!'

His grin disappeared suddenly. 'I totally forgot Crystal is arriving today but I've got a meeting with Dan Proctor.'

'That's all right, you deal with the American Ambassador and I'll pick up Crystal from the airport.'

'You're an angel!' Relaxing again, James sighed. 'If you won't marry me, it'll just have to be an affair then!'

'Perhaps later we can do dictation while I sit on your lap?' Sarah moved out of reach as James made to pat her on the backside.

James laughed in delight. 'You're on, but I think I should be on your lap!'

Sarah knelt down gingerly to pick up the odds and ends that James had strewn over the floor, while searching for his glasses. He watched her for a moment before asking, 'Sarah how is it that you deal so smoothly with my teasing, but you can't deal with Con Zuco?'

Sarah paused for a moment as she considered the question carefully. 'I suppose,' She finally said, 'that I know you're only teasing. I'm not in any danger from you even if you are serious. As for Con...' Sarah paused; her face showed her conflicting emotions. He waited patiently for her to finish. 'I know it sounds pathetic, but he frightens me. Con thinks he can get anything he wants in life, and doesn't care how he goes about getting it. His compliments are insincere, and he doesn't appreciate that No means No!'

James exhaled slowly. 'Well, if he causes you that much headache, I can always have him recalled to Canberra.'

'On what grounds?' She picked up the final few items before rising to her feet, 'Just because he makes me feel uncomfortable? Canberra won't accept that. I'll just have to learn to deal with him.'

'That's not fair!'

Sarah smiled slightly as she headed for the door. 'Sometimes life isn't fair. We just have to play with the cards we're dealt.' She was about to leave but James stopped her.

'How do you know that I'm not serious when I tease you?' A secret little smile played around Sarah's mouth but she wouldn't answer as she closed the door on her way out.

Returning to her desk Sarah walked straight into Gary who was just coming away from her corner.

'I've left that report you wanted on your desk. I appreciate you offering to type it up for me.'

She cast a quick glance at her watch. 'It's my pleasure. I'll do it as soon as I get back from the airport. The Ambassador has double booked himself so I said I'd go and collect his daughter.'

Out of the corner of his eye Gary caught sight of Con lurking around the door of his office.

'Well then,' he suddenly said, 'I'll come with you. Another pair of hands is always useful when it comes to luggage.'

As Sarah grabbed her handbag, Gary stuck his head into Marianne's office to let her know where they were going before leading Sarah down to the second Embassy car.

Big Brother

Gary opted to drive himself instead of using the chauffeur. This suited Sarah, as there was something she wanted to ask him and she wouldn't get an honest answer with someone else listening.

'Okay Gary, what was all that back there really about?'

His eyebrows rose in surprise but he didn't take his eyes off the road as they pulled out of the compound. 'What are you talking about?' He was fencing, and she knew this wasn't going to be easy.

'Why did you really want to come?' Sarah decided to be blunt and up front.

'I didn't think you should be lifting heavy luggage.' His answer came smoothly.

She shook her head. 'Crystal's luggage will be on a trolley and the driver would have put it into the boot. Try again!'

'You're becoming paranoid!'

Sarah smiled at his distracting tactics. 'No I'm not, and don't change the subject. When I'm not at work I'll be under guard at home. In between times I'm chaperoned by Lieutenant Cadem. What more do you want? You don't have this level of security for anyone else, so why me?'

Gary didn't immediately answer. *For one thing the traffic is a little crazy, for another I'm not quite sure how to answer.*

Sarah allowed several more minutes go silently by before she broke it. 'You're not in love with me are you? I'm not being conceited, but I think we need to be honest now.'

Gary exhaled slowly. 'No, I'm not in love with you,' he admitted.

'Good!' At his startled expression she rushed into speech, 'Don't get me wrong, I like you a lot, but more like a brother.'

'I see!' was his non-committal deadpan answer.

Watching his face become expressionless, she shook her head. 'I don't think you do see exactly. My eldest brother, Jack, he's in the Army and is a lot like you. He's quiet, thoughtful, a man of action when necessary. He's slow to anger and fiercely loyal. I suppose being so far away from my family; I've formed a sort of attachment to you and Marianne as a substitute family.'

A smile suddenly appeared on Gary's face. 'Actually, that is exactly how I would describe how I feel about you; a protective older brother.'

'Right then, big brother, perhaps you'll tell me what it is that you're afraid of? It's not just the Rebel activity is it?'

Gary made a tricky turn before he answered, 'It's Con. Ever since Lucas' death he's been acting even more strangely. I'm worried about what he'd do if he ever got you alone again. Your puppy is too young to defend you and your injuries mean self-defence lessons will have to be put on hold.' Gary waited for her to explode and was very surprised when she didn't.

'Do you really think that Con would want to harm me?' Unintentionally, her voice sounded quite small and childlike in disbelief.

'I honestly don't know.' Gary shrugged his shoulders. 'He's desperate to bed you and whether you're willing or not wouldn't disturb him.' *Personally*, he thought, *Con would actually prefer unwilling and would get some perverse enjoyment out of forcing himself on Sarah*. This, though, Gary kept to himself as he saw no need to further frighten Sarah.

'It's not like that there is a shortage of attractive women in Pangani, so why me?'

Gary snorted in disgust. 'You under value your appeal, and how pretty you are. It's not only these attributes that attract Con, but the fact that you refuse to fall on your knees and worship him.'

'Thank you for being so honest. At least now I know from what I'm being sheltered.'

'Don't start worrying. Con is never short of a conquest. I'm hoping he'll get bored chasing after something he can never have.'

Sarah sighed and brushed her hand against her forehead. 'I do hope so!' *I'm so sick of Con and his unwanted and unhealthy attention.*

Crystal's Arrival

Sarah inhaled sharply as Crystal Hammond nee Greene walked through the airport's arrival doors, pushing her luggage trolley. James had shown her a photo of his daughter, but Sarah still wasn't prepared for how beautiful Crystal was in person. Her auburn hair was quite short and just a mass of curls, rumpled slightly as if she had just got out of bed. Crystal wore no make-up, but was one of those women who seemed to have little need for artificial means to make them attractive. Her clothing was sensible for travelling, but there was no hiding the stunning figure they covered. Gary stood, although not quite open-mouthed, but definitely struck dumb.

Sarah stepped forward and asked tentatively, 'Mrs. Hammond?'

A beautiful smile answered her, 'Please, not by that name! Miss Greene if we have to be formal, but I would much prefer you called me Crystal.'

'I'm Sarah Trent and this is Major Gary Winters. We both work at the Embassy,' Sarah explained.

That smile appeared again as Crystal shook hands with them both. 'Wonderful! I can't begin to tell you how glad I am to be out of that aeroplane. I was starting to feel like a sardine.' An understandable statement as Crystal was as tall as Gary, who was now pushing her trolley as they headed for the exit. Sarah handed Crystal a scarf to cover her hair as many disapproving glances were being cast in their direction.

'What you need is a long soak in a hot bath, or a few laps of the pool,' suggested Sarah, nearly having to take two steps to keep up with Crystal's long stride.

'Ooh! That sounds divine! I can hardly wait. Is the car parked very far away?' Crystal looked out at the row after row of cars sitting in the blazing sun. Leaving the airport they were blasted by the sultry heat outside and Crystal took a deep breath of surprise.

'My God! Is that what they mean by heavy weather?'

Sarah smiled sympathetically. 'It took me at least a month to get used to it.'

They followed Gary to the car, which was parked right outside the main doors.

'How on earth did you pull that off without getting towed away?' Crystal asked impressed. Gary was putting the luggage into the boot, as the women got in the back so it was Sarah who answered again, 'Embassy privilege! Gary is also a good friend of the Airport Security Manager.'

Closing the boot, Gary returned the trolley before getting behind the wheel. All this time he hadn't said a word. Studying the back of Gary's neck, as they returned to the Embassy, Crystal leant closer to Sarah to whisper, 'Does he talk at all, or is he just reserved with strangers?'

Sarah giggled, 'I suspect that he's just struck dumb by your beauty.' The Major's ears turned bright red, and Crystal couldn't help laughing.

'My goodness! If either of you think I look good after nearly twenty hours in an aeroplane, then you've either been out in the sun too long, or I must look better half dead than I do alive!'

Sarah sighed wistfully, 'I only wish I normally looked half as good as you do when you're half dead.'

'What a wonderful balm you are to a wounded ego.' Crystal hugged her in delight. 'Oh, I'm going to enjoy changing your perception of yourself.'

Gary cleared his throat. 'Perhaps you can get through to her; no one else has so far succeeded.'

'Thank you big brother!' Sarah poked her tongue out so that Gary could see in his rear vision mirror.

He laughed, but Crystal was confused, 'Are you actually related?'

Sarah shook her head, 'Oh no! But Gary has designated himself my protective older brother.'

'Recent events have meant the need to be more cautious. I wouldn't be doing my job if I didn't keep an eye on you,' retorted Gary.

'All right children,' laughed Crystal, 'Separate corners. You even fight like siblings. I had no idea I was going to enjoy myself so much.' She leant back against the cushions and asked Sarah to point out various important buildings and landmarks as they passed. Crystal's thoughts were only partly upon her surroundings as her fertile brain was flirting with ideas and possibilities for the future.

A Cooling Brief

Gary took the luggage into the Residency as Crystal was introduced to Jeb and Ash before Sarah led her across to the main building and up to the secure floor. Sarah knocked on the Ambassador's door before entering. Crystal stayed outside the office. Dan Proctor was with James Greene, and James actually looked relieved at Sarah's interruption.

'So sorry to disturb you Sir, but I thought you would like to know that your daughter has arrived safely,' explained Sarah, turning to motion to Crystal to follow her inside. James jumped to his feet and came round from behind his desk.

'Crystal! I hope you had a pleasant flight?' James embraced his daughter, and wasn't immediately aware of the effect his beautiful daughter had upon Dan. The American's mouth dropped open, his cigar fell down between his fingers and he couldn't take his eyes off the new arrival.

'This is Dan Proctor, my American counterpart here in Pangani.'

Crystal shook his hand, 'A pleasure. I won't keep you from your meeting, Dad, I'll see you tonight at dinner. Oh, can I borrow Sarah this afternoon please? You know get a bit of the local background while we go for a swim.'

'Yes of course.' James was surprised but hid it well.

Dan's gaze travelled from one young lady to the other. 'Knowing Miss Trent, she's probably so up to date with her work that she has already completed tomorrow's work today.' His smile had turned into a slight sneer.

Although one of her hands clenched tight, Sarah smiled back at him. 'Well then, perhaps I should take tomorrow off.'

'Now then Dan, don't be putting ideas into that girl's head.' James said, shooing the girls towards the door. 'We all know an Embassy will fall apart without a competent Secretary!' There was general, if somewhat forced laughter and James made a face that only the girls could see. He shut the door behind them and tried to wind up his meeting with Dan as quickly as possible.

Coming through the security door Gary stated, 'Have you seen James yet?'

Crystal smiled. 'Yes just then. Thank you for taking my luggage in, I should have done that, but I was caught up meeting those wonderful dogs.'

Gary chuckled, his eyes flicking fleetingly to Sarah. 'If you think they're wonderful, wait until you meet Simon.'

Sarah laughed as he left them, heading into his own office. At Crystal's bemused look; she explained who Simon was. They headed towards the tearoom, as it was time for afternoon tea, they were sure to find the other Embassy staff making coffee. They weren't to be disappointed. Sarah introduced Crystal, and then making a coffee took it to Gary's office. She left Crystal for a moment getting to know the others while she changed into her one piece bathers. Sarah emerged from the change room, wearing a sarong over her bathers and it wasn't long before the two girls were running down the stairs and across to the Residency.

After a quick tour, and meeting the servants, Crystal was soon also changed and dragging Sarah outside again. On the verandah Crystal stopped short at the sight of a funny looking creature approaching them. With his tail wagging furiously, his tongue hanging out and his odd, cast hampered walk, Simon only had eyes for his mistress. He gave sharp yaps of excitement and fairly leapt up into Sarah's arms.

'Ooh! Isn't he adorable! Come on Simon, you can protect us while we're swimming.'

The puppy happily lopped along behind them down to the pool and finding a shady spot, he lay down.

Crystal's Brazenness

Crystal would have dived straight in, but Sarah urged her to put on sunburn cream first. Even though the pool was shaded by a couple of very large palm trees, the wind was so hot that it actually stung when it hit the skin. Sarah put on a tee shirt over her bathers and refused to take it off when Crystal told her not to be shy.

'Come on Sarah, it's just us girls.'

Sarah shook her head. 'It's not that I'm shy, it's just that I'm covered with bruises and it's not a pretty sight,' she explained.

As if she doubted the story, Crystal lifted up Sarah's tee shirt to see for herself. 'What brutes people can be! Even so you'll be cooler without the top and now that I have seen the bruises they can't shock me.'

Obediently, Sarah slipped off her tee shirt and covered the exposed area with sunburn cream. Then slowly entered the water via the steps and gently submerged herself. The plaster covering her bullet-wounded hand was waterproof. Her plait of blonde hair she wrapped into a bun at the nape of her neck. Sarah sat on one of the steps enjoying the feeling of the water lapping gently against her body. Crystal dived straight in and did a couple of hard laps until she was satisfied that she had worked off her cramped muscles and finally joined Sarah. They floated around in companionable silence for a while; both were busy with their own thoughts.

Something glinting in the sun caught Sarah's attention and she looked up towards the main building. Seeing it came from Con's office window, she couldn't stop the groan that escaped her. Crystal glanced up at the window where the sun reflected occasionally off Con's binoculars.

'A bit of a voyeur is he? Well perhaps we should give him something to steam up his lenses!' Before Sarah could ask what Crystal meant to do, she had already stripped off the top of her bikini and thrown it onto the edge of the pool.

'Crystal!' Sarah protested, but Crystal only laughed and lay back on a step so that her breasts sat just out of the water and very clear to see, obviously completely comfortable with her own body. Envious of Crystal's composure, Sarah wondered, *what is Con making of all this? I hope it is simply torture for him.*

Crystal laid back, her hands behind her head, completely relaxed. 'Now tell me about the people I've met today. Don't hold anything back.'

Sarah painted a general picture about each of the staff, trying to be generous when describing Con, but the words seemed to stick in her throat. Crystal threw her a shrewd glance, and her eyes lit up in curiosity.

'So you don't like our voyeur? Been putting the hard word on you has he?'

Sarah blushed, and couldn't stop herself from glancing furtively up at Con's window. 'My Mum always told us that we should never hate anyone. You can like one person more than another, but you should never actually hate people. I have tried, oh so hard not to hate Con, but I can't find any redeeming features in him.'

'You can't legislate how you feel.' Crystal lightly brushed her hand against Sarah's hair. 'If this man is a lecherous creep who makes comments and suggestions that make you uncomfortable, there's no reason why you should like him. You shouldn't feel guilty about not liking someone.'

'It's not easy,' Sarah admitted.

Crystal laughed. 'We'll just have to keep you so busy that you don't have time to think about the voyeur.'

'Don't you think I work hard enough now?' Sarah smiled.

'Not more work, Sweetie, I'm thinking about more playing.' Crystal smiled wickedly. 'You don't enjoy yourself enough.'

'There aren't enough hours in the day.'

'Then we're just going to have to create a new clock.' It was obvious that she wasn't about to take no for an answer.

Modesty Recommended

Simon whimpered and began to thump his tail against the ground. It was a happy noise, so although Sarah looked around, she didn't feel concern. The sight of Joseph Nasseur approaching the pool and squatting down beside the puppy who yipped happily in greeting, brought the rise of colour to Sarah's cheeks. Crystal noticed this and looked up at Joseph in interest.

'I should have known better that I could not get any closer without him noticing,' The Colonel spoke without looking at them. 'I would recommend that you put your top back on Miss Greene. The American Ambassador intends to speak to you before he leaves. Although I'm sure he'd be more than pleased to ogle you half naked, I fear that it won't do his troublesome heart a lot of good, to get so excited.'

Crystal swam over to the edge of the pool where she had thrown her bikini top. 'I must know, did you realize I was topless because you saw me, or because you saw the top on the edge of the pool?' she asked, slipping it back on.

'Neither!' Joseph grinned, 'I was in Major Winters' office when we heard a thud from Con's room. Apparently your state of undress caused him to fall over.'

With Crystal's breasts covered up, Joseph finally looked at the two girls. Sarah now had the chance to introduce him to the Ambassador's daughter.

The sight of Dan Proctor coming from the main building with James in tow, made Sarah feel guilty about enjoying the cool water, and not working at her desk.

'Perhaps I should return to work, Crystal. I…'

'Nonsense!' Crystal said cutting her off, 'You're bringing me up to date with the current political climate as well as what I can or can't do, so I don't offend anyone.'

Joseph nodded, looking serious. 'Very true, something you might not think is wrong at home may send you to prison here. Tourists may be let off with a warning, but members of the Embassy are expected to know and abide by our laws at all times.'

'Wow!' Crystal blinked in surprise. 'There isn't some sort of hand book I can read, is there?'

'Actually there is,' admitted Sarah. 'There is a brief pamphlet for tourists, a more comprehensive document for our Nationals living and working here, and an A to Z file for Embassy staff and one for Pangani Nationals.'

'I'd better start with the one for Australians living here. It'll give me a brief overview before I start on the file.' Crystal smiled up at her father as he and Dan arrived poolside. 'This is great Dad. I feel really relaxed now after that flight. Sarah is just full of useful information about our new home.'

James glanced cautiously at each of them, concerned by how serious they all looked. 'That's wonderful, honey.'

Dan Proctor glared at Joseph who was still patting Simon. 'Now that's not fair, Colonel! Here we had a chance to see this divine creature in all her glory and you make her cover up.'

Joseph's eyebrows rose, 'But what about the lady's modesty, Mr. Ambassador?'

'Any woman who's prepared to strip off isn't very modest, now is she?' Dan shook his head.

'That would depend upon whether she thought she was alone and not being spied upon!'

Unable to answer this accusation, Dan tried to pat the puppy but it backed into the protection of Joseph's leg and growled.

'He doesn't seem to like you Ambassador Proctor,' Joseph said mildly, laying a calming hand upon the animal's back as Dan snatched his hand away.

'We mustn't keep you standing in the sun Ambassador,' said Crystal. 'I'm sure you're much too busy to be wasting time with two silly girls like us.'

There was nothing Dan Proctor could do but reluctantly take his leave and allow James to lead him back to where his car was waiting for him.

Old Fashion Values

With Dan's departure, Simon came out from behind Joseph and his hackles settled down again, especially as the Colonel scratched one of his ears.

Anxiously Crystal chewed upon her bottom lip. 'That wasn't too rude was it? I just couldn't see the old bore leaving otherwise.' Her glance took in both Joseph and Sarah.

'A little abrupt,' said Joseph.

'But diplomatic enough!' reassured Sarah. 'I mean you've just got off a long flight and don't need stupid comments or someone ogling you,' she was disgusted with Con's and Dan's behaviour. *Sure Crystal is extremely beautiful and has a wonderful figure, but that doesn't give them an excuse to walk around with their tongues hanging out,* thought Sarah.

'You are delightful!' Crystal's features relaxed as she suddenly laughed. 'For a moment I saw you properly attired in Victorian dress and it suited you.'

Blushing, Sarah lowered her face as she murmured, 'I suppose I am terribly old fashioned.'

'There is nothing entirely wrong with that Sarah.' Crystal reached out to embrace her. 'You have strong values in a world where many values no longer exist. It would be a great pity if you were to change any of your ideals. We do need though, to put something other than work into your life. You need some fun.'

Joseph sighed as he straightened into a standing position. 'I'm afraid, Miss Greene, that the current climate of unrest in this country has meant much more tension for us all. There has been little time for, probably much needed, fun and frivolity. I must also leave, I'm afraid. Welcome to Pangani and I hope you enjoy your stay with us.'

A Need For Caution

With a friendly nod, he was gone. Simon followed Joseph for a few steps before he hobbled back to his spot by the pool. Sarah swam a couple of laps while Crystal sat on one of the steps deep in thought.

'I said something wrong then with the Colonel, didn't I?' Crystal finally asked.

'Not really.' Sarah floated beside her. 'I think he was trying to stress that your stay here may not exactly be a picnic. It would be great to lighten up, but to be honest; we're on a knife-edge. Civil war could break out at any moment. We must all be so careful. Nowhere is completely safe, and that is a thorn in the Colonel's side as Head of Security. He was the first person Gary called after he and I found Lucas' body.'

'Oh my God!' Crystal's eyes nearly popped out of her head, 'No one told me you were there when the mutilated body was found! Please forgive me talking about having fun and lightening up. It must have been a horrific experience!'

'It wasn't pleasant. I still have the occasional nightmare about it but Gary was so great in dealing with the situation. You're right though, we need to have some more fun and you may be the breath of fresh air that we need.'

Crystal found that she was lost for words. She also suddenly felt very, very tired. *Jet lag*, Sarah thought, *due to time differences and the big flight.* They didn't stay too much longer in the water. Although Crystal scoffed at the idea of going to bed, she did agree to lie down until dinner time. Sarah couldn't help smiling, as no sooner than Crystal's head had touched the pillow she was asleep. Sarah left the Residency with instructions to Yisi not to disturb Crystal and then returned to her desk, cool and very much refreshed.

Téte A Téte

Crystal spent a quiet evening with her father. She whole heartily approved of the healthy meals that Freddy, the cook at the Residency served James, mischievously suggesting that it should inspire him to do more exercise as well. Since it was normally his habit to run five kilometres a day, this glanced off his armour like water off a duck's back. She asked all manner of questions, mainly about the people he had met and worked with. She knew enough to never ask about his work itself unless he volunteered the information first.

An observant daughter, she noticed that James chose his words ever so carefully whenever he mentioned Marianne. A spark of interest lit up in Crystal as she wondered if her father was ready for a new relationship. He hadn't been in anything serious since her mother's death and she was determined to learn more about Marianne, through other sources, of course. She didn't want to make him shy away from the developing friendship or to interfere in his affairs. So as Crystal settled down to her first night in Pangani, she had much to think about.

THURSDAY

Local Attractions

Feeling totally refreshed after a good night's sleep Crystal, as she crossed the Embassy compound, was surprised to see Con standing by the front gate smoking and wondered if he ever did any actual work. The day before, Crystal had been introduced to Abu, the Pangani Office Manager, so as she stepped through the double front doors, she smiled at him.

'Good morning! I'd like to see Sarah. Is it all right if I go up, or do you need to announce me?'

Abu bowed to her. 'Good morning Miss Greene. I'm afraid that until you are given security clearance, it is necessary that I inform Miss Trent of your wish to go upstairs.' He picked up the telephone that connected him with Sarah. Crystal thanked him as she trotted up the stairs.

Waiting at the top with the security door open, stood Sarah smiling a little shyly as Crystal joined her and they entered the top floor.

'What do you suggest I see first in Kathou?' she asked.

'Just a moment,' Sarah went to her desk and came back with a file. She opened it as she sat down beside Crystal in the visitors' chairs. 'Now it depends upon what you are interested in. We have a list for probably nearly every taste.' She read out aloud the list. 'Historical buildings; City tour; parks; gardens and wild life; night clubs and pubs; river or sea cruises; museums; amusement parks; music, culture and the arts; markets; shopping, which is broken up into categories depending upon the sort of money you have to spend, and sporting facilities. It's probably best to stick to chartered tours, only going out during the day and if possible the south of the city. At present you'll have to wear a head scarf and take a bodyguard whenever you leave the Embassy compound.'

Laughing, Crystal found it hard to catch her breath, 'Oh My God! Who compiled all of that information?'

'I did,' Sarah admitted, surprised by the question.

'That's amazing!'

Sarah shook her head. 'Not really, it's called utilising the excellent tourism and information services that we have here. I didn't personally go out and discover all this info.'

'It's still amazing! I must admit that I have a weakness for markets. I suppose I should do a city tour, though, to get to know my surroundings.'

Sarah closed her file. 'Why not take a tour this morning, they're very informative and this afternoon Gary or I could take you to a market or two? On the tour they use headsets that use a variety of languages, but in the markets it would be useful to have someone who speaks a little Arabic.'

'I'm not taking you away too much from your work?' Crystal looked concerned. 'I don't want to be a nuisance.'

Smiling, Sarah rose to her feet. 'You're not! I can't resist markets either, and it's not safe to go on your own. Would you like me to arrange the tour this morning for you?'

'Yes please!'

Shopping Spree

After lunch, and an hour or so spent cooling down in the pool, not only Sarah but also Gary escorted Crystal to the markets. Gary explained, needlessly, that he was coming along to protect them. Crystal couldn't help teasing him that he was actually a secret market junkie, and as the thought sent him as pale as a ghost, she laughed. *It is obvious that there aren't too many things Gary hates more than shopping.* She reassured him that by the end of a couple of hours, she would have taught him the fine art of bargain hunting, and haggling. He thanked her politely enough, but said he would rather keep his attention on looking out for trouble. A secret female smile was exchanged between Sarah and Crystal as they shared the enjoyment of the joke.

At the markets, Crystal glanced around her in delight. There were so many different sights, sounds and smells. She wanted to be everywhere at once, and sympathetically Sarah wandered up and down each aisle several times as Crystal tried to experience everything. Normally the Major would have been bored, but he was focusing on being alert for danger rather than looking at the merchandise on sale.

There was food, raw and cooked, clothing, jewellery, furniture, animals, trinkets, souvenirs, carpets, books and postcards. The two women were swept away by the glory of shopping. Most of the time, Sarah translated any questions Crystal had for a vendor, a few could speak a few words of English, but at times it was easier in Arabic. Following close behind, like a shadow, Gary didn't join in the girls' chatter. At one point he bought himself an apple and munched on it as they walked.

Purchasing several sarongs for Crystal to wear around the Residency was essential and with so many different colours and designs to choose from it took a little while. Ben Makita, the spice seller, enthusiastically hailed Sarah and she cast a questioning glance at Gary. His keen eyes quickly scanned the area for possible danger and seeing a uniformed Police officer a little further up the market, Gary nodded his approval. So Sarah moved away to talk to Ben and his wife, to reassure them that her hand was healing well. Gary turned into the stall where Crystal was admiring jewellery of intricate design and good quality. It held Crystal's attention as the woman, seeing a possible customer, was showing off some of her finer pieces. A wry grin spread reluctantly across Gary's features, he knew only too well the attraction jewellery had upon women, and expected to be here for quite some time.

The woman's name was Hiba and she spoke very good English. Crystal picked up a necklace that was studded by zircons and man-made sapphires. She examined it closely and was more than satisfied with the quality of the stones and the handiwork. Then laid it to one side and picked up a similar necklace, which this time had white and blue zircons interchanged. She turned to show it to Gary.

'Don't you think this would suit Sarah? It's exactly the colour of her eyes.'

Gary was surprised but replied, 'It's very beautiful.'

Crystal handed that necklace and the first one across to Hiba, who laid them in tissue paper as Crystal continued to examine the merchandise.

'For $20 more I have the matching earrings.' Hiba looked for the blue zircon earrings and showed them to Crystal.

Her eyes lit up and she nodded eagerly. 'Do you have matching earrings for the sapphires?'

Hiba searched and eventually came up with exactly what Crystal wanted, in her reserve stock under the table. Realising that this was a customer who knew the value of her jewels, Hiba pulled out a velvet box that she showed only to special customers. A gasp was drawn from both Gary and Crystal as a delicate gold necklace lay within, at the end was a distorted 's' shape from which hung three real diamonds, one under the other in a row.

'How you tempt me,' breathed Crystal, but she kept control of her urges as she asked, 'How much have I already spent?'

Hiba did a quick calculation, '$140. This necklace is a steal at $90.'

Crystal hesitated. She did like the diamond necklace, but it was a little more than she had wanted to spend. Hiba, though, was a clever sales woman, 'Matching earrings, miss. Normally $20 the pair, but for you, I will make it part of the set for $100.'

That was a bargain Crystal could not pass up, 'Done! Oh Hiba, you're a wicked woman!' Hiba looked startled, glancing uncertainly from Crystal to Gary. Crystal hastily added, 'Perhaps I should have said naughty. You know leading me into temptation.'

Hiba's concerned expression dissolved into a smile. 'Ah, but a beautiful lady should have beautiful trinkets. You are very lucky man, Sir.' Hiba cast a shy glance up at Gary as she wrapped the jewellery and placed it into a bag. Sarah was returning to them, causing the Major to smile.

'Very lucky! They're both mine.' Hiba laughed and thanked Crystal as she took the money offered. When she handed the jewellery bag across to Crystal, Hiba pressed into her hand a business card.

'If I can ever interest you in anything else, Miss, please contact me. I am not always at the same market.' Hiba waved happily goodbye to them. She may not have made as much as she possibly could, having discounted on all the earrings; but she had almost certainly guaranteed a return customer who might also recommend Hiba to friends.

A Sticky Situation

Sarah was agog to discover what had kept them at the jewellery stall so long, but Gary warned them against pulling the jewellery out until they were in safer surroundings. So instead, the girls turned their attention to fruit and vegetables. Crystal was eager to sample local produce and Sarah steered her to a reputable stall from whom she bought her own weekly fruit and vegetables. Crystal would've bought one of each of the different fruits she wanted to try, before returning at a later date to buy a larger quantity, but the grocer was well acquainted with Sarah. He drew out his knife and obligingly cut up slices of fruit for Crystal to try there and then. This way, if she liked it, she would probably buy more now. Like Hiba, he was prepared to be amenable to secure a customer and a larger sale. The Major's hand had moved to his side arm at the sight of the knife the grocer had produced but was satisfied that he presented no threat. The two girls laughed as their hands got quite sticky from various fruits, and Gary offered his handkerchief. The grocer, though, took them behind the stall to wash their hands at a tap. It was all about service, and as Crystal bought nearly a full box of fruit and vegetables, he was amply rewarded.

Gary, who had ended up carrying all their purchases, tactfully reminded the girls that they shouldn't exhaust themselves before the function that evening. Both thought he was a party pooper, but agreed to return to his car. There was a promise made between the girls to future shopping trips, which caused Gary to groan. *If that is going to be the case, then I'm going to assign watching duty to Cadem. I've decided I have no patience for shopping.*

A Less Formal Affair

The cocktail party was a less formal affair than the Ambassador's official function. Marianne had designed it to introduce Crystal to the right people about her own age. Representatives from different Embassies were invited, but it was so low keyed that it wasn't expected that the Ambassadors would attend, but send junior staff, which is what Marianne wanted. The younger generation of several of Pangani's prominent families would also be attending to meet the Ambassador's daughter.

As time drew nearer, Crystal became a little nervous. Sarah, though, was an amazing calming influence, looking as cool as a cucumber, with her hair swept up into a French knot and a simple multi-coloured dress that had the hem cut in a jagged fashion so that she looked like a fairy. She looked very pretty, but privately Sarah felt dowdy against Crystal's sparkling cocktail dress of deep blue. It fitted her like a glove, falling to the ground, with a slit up one leg. Crystal looked exquisite. As she put on the diamond earrings and necklace she had bought at the markets Sarah sighed in delight.

'You're so beautiful! If we get any jealous wives, they'll be scratching your eyes out!'

Crystal laughed at what she assumed was a compliment. *I have come to realize that Sarah doesn't say what she thinks you want to hear, but what is truly in her head and heart.* Crystal told Sarah to close her eyes and she placed the white and blue zircon necklace around her neck, turning her towards the mirror before letting her open her eyes. Sarah gasped in surprise as she looked at the sparkling stones around her neck.

'Oh Crystal, it's beautiful, but I can't accept this!'

Crystal's eyebrows rose, 'Why not? I want to show my appreciation for the friendship and guidance you have shown me.'

'But I don't do that for reward.' Sarah reached up to touch the necklace. 'It's my pleasure!'

Crystal laughed. 'And it's my pleasure to buy you a present. It's not an heirloom. I didn't break the bank. Please, I'll be hurt if you don't want it.'

'Of course I want it!' Sarah smiled despite herself. 'I just don't want you to feel that you have to buy me anything.'

Sinking on to her bed, Crystal sighed. 'I'm in a dilemma then. I don't know what to do with the matching earrings!'

Sarah stared at her in surprise, and then started laughing. 'You're spoiling me, you know that don't you?' She began to take out the earrings she was wearing.

'I think you need a little spoiling!' Crystal grinned as she handed her the earring box. Once the earrings were in she turned Sarah back to the mirror. The sparkle of the jewels seemed to echo in her eyes. Impulsively Crystal grabbed Sarah's un-bandaged hand. 'Come on! I'm ready to meet our guests!' Sarah was swept along behind her.

Crystal Is Stunned

It was Marianne's duty to greet the arriving guests and introduce them to Crystal. More often than not, they stared at Crystal for a moment with open-mouthed surprise. It was true that Ambassador Greene was a good-looking man, but his daughter would only be described as breath-takingly beautiful. Besides her looks she also had poise, charm, elegance and a light wit. She could converse on many different levels and was comfortable in the company of either gender.

Sparkling like the diamonds around her throat, she faltered only slightly when she was presented to Prince Kahlee. It was Crystal's turn to be taken back by how he was so handsome. She swept into a low, elegant curtsy and managed to reply sensibly to the question he asked her. Feeling a little breathless and light headed, Crystal joined Sarah once all the guests had arrived.

'You didn't tell me the Prince is so handsome!'

Sarah glanced across the room to where Kahlee was talking to James. 'Perhaps due to the fact he is already married.'

'I thought Muslims can have more than one wife?'

'That is correct, but Princess Relanna is about to have their third child.'

'Does that prevent the Prince from taking another wife?'

'No, but in the current fragile political environment, the Prince could never marry someone of western background. Forgive me if I speak out of turn, but you're only just out of a relationship; are you really ready to look for another?'

'Oh wise one, what truths you speak!' Crystal laughed, not at all insulted. 'I shall have to rein in my raging hormones. I'll see you later.' Moving away to mingle she fell easily into conversation with someone else, stopping Yisi who was offering drinks on a tray and took a champagne glass. Crystal was unaware of the envy that she stirred in Sarah's breast. *I wish that I felt just as comfortable amongst people as I do behind the scenes organizing the action. I don't really resent Crystal for her poise and glamour; I just wish that I had some of her confidence in public.* This was Crystal's night and the spotlight was on her so that Sarah could gratefully slip into a supervising role behind the scene.

We Can't Meet Like This

It was in the kitchen that Gary later found Sarah, assisting Freddy complete the floral decoration on the trays of little deserts and cakes. Gary waited patiently until the decoration was exactly how Freddy wanted it, before he drew her to one side.

'Are you busy at the moment? I need you to come with me.' He sounded so serious that Sarah became worried.

'Is anything wrong? Has something happened?'

Gary shook his head, 'Nothing to worry about. I just think you need some fresh air.'

The Major led Sarah out the back door of the kitchen and down the path, a little away from the Embassy. Jeb and Ash joined them, thinking it might be time for ball play. All the time, he remained silent; his hand under her elbow and his eyes constantly scanning the compound, lit up by the newly installed external lights, for any signs of trouble. To ease the tension as they headed towards the trees behind the main building, Sarah asked lightly, 'Are we, by any chance, eloping?'

Gary chuckled in delight. 'Not quite!' Silently out of the darkness stepped Colonel Nasseur, who also was glancing cautiously around. Gary nodded to Joseph, and whistling for the dogs to follow him, left Sarah alone with the Colonel.

'I'm sorry about the necessity for such secrecy but it was imperative that I saw you Sarah.' Joseph hesitated to hold his hand out to her. *I so want to take Sarah into my arms, but what if someone saw us?*

'Is anything wrong? Is Princess Relanna all right?' Sarah was alarmed by his seriousness.

'My sister is fine. I just had to see you to make certain that you had recovered from Con Zuco's visit to your home on Tuesday.'

'Please Colonel Nasseur; we can't meet secretly like this!' She glanced nervously around. 'If anyone was to see us there is no logical or innocent explanation for our being alone!'

'Sarah, I want you to marry me! I don't give a damn that you're neither Pangani nor Muslim. You are the only woman I have ever felt this way about and I want to spend the rest of my life with you and I don't care who knows it. Do you understand that?'

'Why can't you see that such a relationship is impossible? Especially in the current political climate!'

'Sarah, stop thinking with your head and listen to your heart.' Sighing, she wished it was as easy as that. 'Sarah, oh Sarah, trust me please? I know what I want.'

She found it difficult to argue when he stood so close to her. 'I'm sorry but every fibre of my being says we'll end up getting hurt.'

'Then I will have to convince each and every one of those fibres that I am right!' He lowered his head to kiss her on the lips. It was no mere peck but a soul searching, knee buckling kiss that left Sarah a little light headed as she clung to Joseph for support.

'You don't play fair!' she complained, a little breathless.

Joseph laughed, kissing her again. 'No my dearest one, I play for keeps!'

Intruders

Gary led Sarah back into the Embassy through the kitchen as Joseph made his way to the front door. None of them had been missed from the cocktail party as Crystal, intentionally or not, was the centre of attention. Marianne was opening the French windows to allow the cool evening breeze to sweep through the room. She smiled upon catching sight of Sarah, and made her way through the throng of people to join her.

'So my dear, have you been organizing Freddy or has he been organizing you?'

'A bit of both actually!' she admitted and laughed, a little embarrassed that she could so easily forget her duty. 'Is everything all right?'

Marianne nodded. 'Very little left for us to do now but mingle. I know that's hard for you, so why don't you go round offering food?'

'How well you know me.' Sarah's eyes twinkled and laughing, Marianne shooed her away before going over to talk to the Russian Under Secretary who had just arrived, very late.

A strange feeling came over Sarah, making her feel dizzy as the tray of food in her hands crashed to the ground causing everyone in the room to suddenly fall silent and look at her. The look of abject horror and confusion on her face caused Marianne and Crystal to rush across to her.

'Sarah?' The sound of Gary's voice seemed to snap her back to reality.

'Oh Gary! Something's wrong! Listen, the dogs are barking madly!'

Gary now heard Jeb and Ash barking quite violently outside and pulling out his gun from his shoulder holster he ran out through the French windows.

A knife wielding intruder burst into the Residency, first going towards Sarah before changing his direction to head for the Prince. Surprise should have been the intruder's major weapon, but Colonel Nasseur was prepared for his attack. He brought the butt of his gun down upon the intruder's hand holding the knife, knocking it to the floor before kicking the intruder behind the knees causing him to lose his balance. The intruder lay on the ground with one of the Colonel's hands against his throat as he knelt on his chest.

'For whom are you working?' Prince Kahlee demanded.

The intruder spat at the ground at the Prince's feet. He received a thump against the side of his head from Joseph for his insolence.

The front door flew open again and everyone turned to look as Gary entered dragging a second intruder. Joseph momentarily looked away from his prisoner, giving his captive a split second to manage to grasp his knife, just in reach, and thrust it straight into the Colonel's forearm. One woman screamed at the sight of blood, but Joseph only looked annoyed at being taken unawares and knocked the intruder unconscious with his fist before rising to his feet and pulling the knife out.

Gary threw his captive down on the floor beside his partner before handing Joseph a handkerchief to press against the wound. Marianne hurried off to get a first aid kit while Gary tore the Colonel's shirtsleeve to get better access to the wound. Prince Kahlee had a brief word with Kevin Shaw, which resulted in the Cultural Attaché heading out of the room to call the Police. There was a flurry of activity for a while as Gary wiped away as much blood as he could before binding Joseph's arm.

'How did they get in, Major Winters?' asked Prince Kahlee, curious, not angry. Gary gathered up the blood soaked rags, which Marianne took away, before he answered.

'Our guard was attacked and knocked out while the dogs were distracted by the second intruder. They obviously tried to avoid your military guards outside our gates, and they appear to have used the side or back walls to enter.' Gary glanced sharply at Joseph. 'You should have a doctor see to that arm. You need a couple of stitches, Sir, and possibly a tetanus shot. You don't know how clean that blade was.'

It looked like Joseph was about to argue, but Prince Kahlee got in first. 'Of course Major, I'll see to it. I'm afraid, though, that it has brought the party to an end. The Police will be here shortly.'

Crystal stepped forward. 'I just hope it doesn't give you a dislike for our Embassy, your Highness.'

'Not at all, Miss Greene,' The Prince inclined his head, 'I pray that the next time that we meet the entertainment is a little less action packed.'

What Just Happened?

There was the sound of a Police car outside, and it wasn't long before a very competent Inspector Lowe entered the Embassy and took calm control of the situation. Most of the guests were soon permitted to leave, the intruders were thrown into the back of a Police car and the Prince escorted Joseph to the hospital to get medical attention. Soon all that was left was a stunned Embassy staff, the Inspector promising to visit in the morning to finalize any details.

Con mercilessly bombarded Sarah with questions barely giving her time to answer any of them as she tried to clean up the mess she had made when she had dropped the tray of food. 'Had she seen something out of the window? Was she in league with the intruders? Had she organized this as some sort of entertainment?' As Sarah answered, 'No,' to each of these accusations, she was beginning to get upset. Kevin smacked Con across the back of his head and told him to shut up. Marianne was trying to get Sarah to take a little more brandy, but she didn't want it. She ignored their chatter and speculation going on around her as she looked anxiously up at Gary.

'Jeb and Ash, are they all right? Also the guard, was he badly hurt?'

Gary shook his head. 'A lump on the back of his head, that's all. I've told him to have it checked out by a doctor. The dogs are fine; they thought it a good bit of exercise. I gave them a couple of doggy treats as a reward before dragging the second intruder in here.'

Satisfied, Sarah tuned back into the conversation going on with the other diplomats. 'Oh Marianne, please don't fuss! Con, I don't know why I had a premonition of danger. I suppose I just heard the dogs barking before anyone else did.'

Gary glanced down at his watch, 'It's time we all headed home.' He placed his hand under Sarah's elbow and assisted her to her feet. Crystal took one of Sarah's hands between her own.

'Will you be all right? I can sleep over tonight if you don't want to be alone? Or you can stay here.'

'Thank you Crystal, but I'm fine.' Sarah smiled in appreciation of her offer. 'Good night everyone.'

What Are Big Brothers For?

They were nearly to Sarah's home when Gary's mobile phone rang. He didn't have his earpiece to make it hands free, so he gave the phone to Sarah to answer.

'Major Winter's phone.'

There was a brief pause before a query, 'Sarah? Is that you?' A shiver of concern ran though Sarah as she recognized Colonel Nasseur's voice.

'Yes Colonel, Gary's driving me home and didn't want to pull over to answer the phone. How's your arm?'

'That's partly why I'm calling. I've had stitches and been sent home. No major damage done. Ask Gary if he can see me tomorrow morning please? I want to discuss tonight's events.'

Sarah repeated the question and Gary agreed.

'His place or the Embassy?' added Gary.

'The Embassy,' Joseph replied to Sarah. 'Try not to have nightmares over tonight Sarah. The Prince is alive because of you and is very grateful. Good night.'

Sarah glanced at Gary to see if he wanted to add anything, but he merely shook his head.

'Good night, Colonel.' Sarah switched off the phone, and placed it back into the holder that was attached to the dashboard.

When she sighed deeply, Gary glanced across at her, but it was too dark to discern her expression. 'Why so sad?'

'I'm just not as optimistic as Joseph that this relationship is going to work out. Also I feel guilty about burdening you with my secrets when you have enough on your plate.'

'Don't be silly.' Gary took one hand off the steering wheel to place over hers. 'What are big brothers for any way?'

Sarah smiled. 'Thank you Gary. You really are a softy under that muscular exterior.' She wasn't the only one to think that.

Another Téte A Téte

Pouring a large Scotch for her father, Crystal sank wearily onto the couch beside him.

'What is it my jewel?' James kissed the top of Crystal's head as he undid his tie.

'A little unrest I was prepared for Dad, but not for it to be brought to our door step.'

'Do you want out, baby? If it gets too hot, you only have to say and I'll have you on the next plane back to Australia.'

Crystal shook her head, 'No, not yet. I don't know what to make of Gary. When he ran out this evening I had no doubt that he would deal with any number of intruders. Then his dealings with Sarah are totally opposite. He was so gentle, kind and considerate.'

'Is that a spark of interest, Crystal?' James eyebrows rose in surprise and amusement.

She looked suitably horrified, 'Dad! I'm only just divorced! I'm hardly going to jump into another relationship.'

James hastily apologized before shooing his daughter off to bed. A smile lingered on his lips, though, for he knew Crystal and she was more interested in the Major than she wished to admit. Time would tell.

FRIDAY

Shell Shocked

Quite understandably Crystal didn't sleep well that night. Intruders haunted her dreams with knives and guns, and more than once, she got up to peer out the window into the star lit night outside. After such a restless night, James left orders that his daughter wasn't to be disturbed in the morning until she was ready. So it was nearly 10 a.m. when a weary Crystal finally emerged from her room. She wanted nothing but coffee for breakfast but Yisi, with her quiet persistence, urged her to eat a little toast as well. After a shower, Crystal was feeling a little more human and crossing the compound to the main building she hoped that every day wasn't going to be as exciting or dangerous.

Abu paused in his instructions to the native gardener to bid Crystal good morning and as she returned his greeting, the normalcy of another working day calmed some of her fears. Crystal trotted up the stairs and let herself into the secure area. Sarah was at her desk, her hands on the keyboard of her computer as she queried a certain passage on a piece of paper with Gary who stood behind her. They both looked up as the security door opened and smiled in pleasure to see Crystal. Gary put the papers down and came out from behind Sarah's desk.

'How are you feeling?' he asked. 'James told us you hadn't slept well. The first time you're exposed to violence like that can be very un-nerving.'

'I even turned the light on half a dozen times to make sure there was no one in the room.' Crystal smiled sheepishly.

Sarah nodded in understanding. 'After my first experience, I slept with the light on for a fortnight.'

'Fear is only natural,' Gary added.

Crystal looked at him in surprise. 'I can't believe you have ever been afraid!'

'Many times!' he admitted, a tightness entering his voice which told both women that they should not pursue that line of conversation.

I Want To Help You

The phone linking Sarah to Abu rang, interrupting their discussion. 'Yes Abu?'

'Mr. Fredericks wishes to see you. He says he wants to resign.'

'Oh dear! Yes I see. Tell Freddy, I'll come across to the Residency to see him.'

'What's Freddy done now?' Gary demanded in exasperation as Sarah replaced the phone.

'He wants to leave.' Sarah sighed. 'Last night was too much for his artistic temperament.'

'Do you want me to deal with him?'

Sarah shook her head as she pulled a face. 'No, you're too masculine for him. Apparently he gets turned on when you're angry with him.'

'Oh my God!' Gary exclaimed in horror.

'Is there anything I can do?' Asked Crystal as Sarah rose to her feet.

'It might be a good thing for you to learn how to deal with Freddy for the future.'

'Good, then I can discuss with you some of the changes that I want to make at the Residency.'

The two women headed towards the security door, but the Major stopped them, having heard Crystal's words. 'These changes, are they anything I should know about?' he asked.

'I don't know,' Crystal admitted. 'I want to make the Residency battle ready. That is if it was necessary for all the staff to move in to the Residency on a more permanent basis, that it could be done without too much fuss or discomfort. At the moment there are only three bedrooms set up for use and although Dad has started work on clearing the junk stored in the other bedrooms so that they can be used as bedrooms; to rush it now might raise questions.'

Gary nodded. 'We managed fairly well the week after Lucas' death when we were all forced to remain at the Residency. To start you might look into replacing the sofas. They were so uncomfortable to sleep on it was necessary to share the only beds. Give me a yell if you're going to move any furniture.' They agreed before trotting down the stairs and across to the Residency.

Crystal couldn't help herself; she just had to ask Sarah, 'So who did Gary end up sharing a bed with?'

Sarah blushed slightly, 'Me. Marianne shared with Peggy, Lucas' widow until she flew home with Lucas' body. Con was supposed to share with Kevin but he snores.' Crystal laughed as Sarah looked embarrassed. 'That's a well known secret that isn't spoken about,' the Secretary hastened to add.

'Understood. How did you end up with Gary?'

'Both Marianne and Peggy wanted to be certain that Con didn't attempt to sneak into bed with me. Gary's a very efficient deterrent.'

Crystal paused on the verandah, 'I understand that Con's a bit of a toad but isn't that being just a little over protective? How could they be certain that Gary would keep his hands to himself?'

'Neither of us have any feelings like that for each other.' Sarah's blush deepened, 'Gary really is like a brother. Besides which he already knew…' She broke off to prevent herself from revealing too much. That just whet Crystal's curiosity all the more.

'What? Oh come on! Is Gary actually your half-brother? Is he gay? Ooh! He knows you're a virgin? No I think he'd be a gentle, kind and generous lover. Gary knows you like someone, or that someone else likes you?'

'Yes!' Sarah held up her hands to slow the flood of words.

'Which one?' Crystal demanded despite the other's obvious embarrassment.

Sarah uttered a shaky laugh. 'The last one. And no I'm not going to tell you his… or her name. So no more questions please.'

Shaking her head, Crystal replied, 'Oh I like that "his or her name". Sweetie, I know you're not gay. So that halves the number of prospects. Well I do like a challenge.'

Sarah grasped hold of Crystal's arm, her features were deadly serious. 'Please Crystal, this is not a game! This secret could destroy more than one career, or make me an even bigger target for the Rebels.' Seeing the look of realization in Crystal's eyes, Sarah knew she had now said way too much.

'That really narrows the field!' laughing Crystal patted her hand, 'Don't panic sweetie, I already know who he is.'

Sarah hesitated in case it was a trick to get her to blurt out a name, 'How?'

'Last night I saw Gary escort you to meet someone. Don't worry I wasn't spying on you. Part of the double sided tape that is supposed to stop my dress revealing too much needed replacing. No one at the party would have witnessed who you met. I know who wasn't at the party when I returned. But I do know how to keep my mouth shut.'

'Crystal…' Sarah was prepared to beg but the Ambassador's daughter cut her off.

'I just want to help you. It's time true love was given a helping hand.'

Exhaling slowly, Sarah had to admit even with assistance from Crystal, this romance was impossible.

Dealing With Freddy

An anxious Yisi met them as they entered. She and the other Residency staff had been listening to Mr. Fredericks, the chef, complain all morning about the events last night, and Yisi feared that the other staff would also leave if Mr. Fredericks did. She enjoyed her work at the Australian Embassy but she didn't want to be left alone.

'Mr. Frederick is in the kitchen, Miss Trent.'

'Thank you Yisi.' Sarah smiled reassuringly at the frightened servant. 'Could you ask Freddy to come to the dining room please?'

'Yes Miss Trent.' As Yisi headed for the kitchen, Sarah and Crystal sat down at the dining table.

'Why not go to him in the kitchen?' queried Crystal.

Sarah's smile became a little mischievous. 'He's Master of that domain. By taking him away from his comfort zone, there is a shift in power. He's immediately at a disadvantage.' Her expression changed to one of concern as Jean Fredericks made a dramatic entrance. Yisi hovered nervously behind the temperamental chef.

'Can I get you anything Miss Trent, Miss Greene?' Yisi asked.

'Not for me thank you, Yisi.' Sarah shook her head. 'Crystal?'

Bemused by how professional and cool Sarah sounded, Crystal could only shake her head. Yisi quickly disappeared, if there was going to be a big argument she didn't want to be in the firing line.

Mr. Fredericks stood indignantly in front of the two girls, towering over them, as they were seated. Sarah indicated a chair adjacent to her.

'Please sit down Freddy,' she offered with a gentle smile. The Chef didn't immediately sit, but Sarah made it obvious by her silence that she wasn't going to continue until he did. Without acknowledging that she had won that round, Fredericks sat with as much dignity as he could muster. He cleared his throat, but Sarah spoke first.

'I understand that last night's activities have distressed you. Understandable, Freddy, I don't think any of us slept well, so you want to leave us?' Her tone was gentle, encouraging, with no hint of accusation. Freddy's prepared speech dried up on his tongue.

'Not want, Mademoiselle Trent, never that! But I must think of my family… What would happen to them if something was to occur to me?'

Sarah suddenly changed tactic. 'Do you really think you're in danger, Freddy? Apart from a jealous chef, who would want to kill you?'

Freddy preened at her compliment. 'These Rebels, they don't care who they kill.'

'Do you plan to leave Pangani?'

He hadn't obviously thought this far ahead. 'I have not considered that possibility.'

Frowning in concern, Sarah said, 'You'd be no safer if you found another job in Pangani. As a foreigner, you still could be a target.' There was no argument for this and Freddy remained silent. He hadn't been prepared for this counter attack. Sarah sighed deeply. 'We understand yours is a high pressure job. If you feel that you can't deal with the danger then we must allow you to leave.'

Freddy stared at her in disbelief. *I had expected her to beg me to stay, to reconsider my decision. That they can't do without me.* Crystal was just as surprised but she tried to keep it from reflecting upon her face.

Absently Sarah rubbed one of her temple with the fingers of her wounded hand as she sighed again, this time a little deeper. 'We won't expect you to give two weeks' notice, Freddy. Understandably you'll have to start looking for work elsewhere immediately or packing up your family to leave Kathou.'

Freddy found his voice, 'But surely you can't replace me so quickly here?'

Crystal was struck by a brilliant idea and said, 'Oh don't worry about us. I can cook for Dad and me.'

'Any functions we can get catered. It'll be a little more expensive, but we're keeping our functions simple during this crisis,' added Sarah and Freddy stared at them with his mouth open. Sarah continued, 'I can arrange to have your holiday pay as well as other entitlements to be added to this week's cheque if that is what you want.'

'I must think about this!' He spluttered.

Sarah looked at him with great concern. 'Isn't that what you wanted, Freddy? You'll be greatly missed but we wouldn't think of keeping you here if you feel unsafe.'

Freddy rose abruptly to his feet. 'Excuse me, please; there is something on the stove I must check on.'

'Of course.' Even as Sarah spoke, he was already at the door.

Freddy's Dramatic Gesture

Placing her hand over her mouth, Crystal tried to stifle a giggle, 'Oh My God! That was brilliant! I really thought we would have a right royal argument, but you turned it right around.'

Sarah smiled slightly. 'I like to study people, what makes them tick, what do they think is important, and what will they respond to.' She closed her eyes and this time when she rubbed her temples it was for real. 'Before we continue, I have to know if you're happy with Freddy.'

Puzzled, Crystal nodded. 'He's a magnificent chef. It would be a shame to lose him.'

Opening her eyes, Sarah sighed, she felt so tired. 'Then I need you to play along with what I'm about to do.'

Crystal didn't understand what that meant, but before she could speak, Sarah had started crying. At first it was just tears running down her face but as Crystal's expression turned from surprise to concern, Sarah uttered a sob and buried her head in her hands. Crystal immediately changed seats and placed her arms around Sarah. 'Sarah, what is it? What's wrong?'

Sarah sniffed and used one hand to wipe away her tears, but they continued to fall. 'I just wish that it was so easy for me to escape. I don't know how much more of this I can take!' She hiccupped and raised her hands to cover her face again as she sobbed harder. Crystal pulled Sarah's hands away and gently rocked her in her arms. 'What with finding Lucas' body, the attack outside the Palace and Con pestering me, last night was the final straw. That intruder intended to kill me before seeing the Prince changed his mind. What have I done to deserve such hatred?'

Crystal didn't know what to say, she didn't have the answers Sarah sought. Mr. Fredericks burst back into the room. He had returned in time to hear the majority of Sarah's words and once again his prepared speech vanished. His heart broke to see Sarah so unhappy, and he bent down beside her, taking one of her hands between his own.

'Oh Mademoiselle, what a selfish man I am! Here I am imagining possible attacks when you have already been the victim of these Rebels! Your courage is an inspiration to me. I cannot run away when you need me so!'

'Oh but we couldn't expect you to stay when you feel so threatened, Freddy.' Sarah raised her face to look at him through her tears.

He raised her hand to his lips. 'Always you think of others. If you stay, so will I! They will not drive us away from the work we both love.'

'But Freddy…'

'No, no!' The chef wouldn't allow her to finish. 'I have made my decision. I cannot only think of myself, you will have one less worry knowing that Freddy is in charge of your kitchens.' He removed his handkerchief and tenderly wiped her tears away.

'Oh Freddy!'

He wiggled his finger at her. 'No, not another word Mademoiselle, go and wash your face and compose yourself.'

Sarah meekly rose to her feet and headed up the passageway to the bathroom.

With her gone, Freddy pulled up the chair beside Crystal, who still looked stunned.

'Mademoiselle is under a considerable amount of stress. I shouldn't have thought only of myself. It is obvious that we must assist her in dealing with the additional pressure she is feeling.'

Crystal nodded in agreement. 'I intend to assist in the Embassy, but it would be a relief to know that everything here was under your control.'

'You may count on me, Mademoiselle.' Freddy's chest swelled with pride. With an elegant bow, he swept off back to his kitchen. Still shaken by what had just occurred, it was several minutes before Crystal went to see if Sarah had regained command of herself.

Emotions Are Draining

Knocking on the bathroom door, Crystal waited until she had Sarah's permission before she entered. Her jaw dropped in surprise as Sarah was sitting on the bathroom floor, leaning against the wall. Her arms and face were wet and her shoes were laying discarded, opposite.

'Oh my God! Sarah! Should I go and get help?' Crystal would've run out but Sarah took her hand.

'It's not as bad as it looks. Come and sit down, it's marvellously cool against the tiles.'

'Sarah!'

'Calm down Crystal. I'm just very, very tired.' The Secretary tugged on her hand and drew her down to the floor. 'I find expressing emotion in public very physically draining. I often appear cool, calm and collected in most situations, but once I'm alone, I let go of the emotions. To cry like that in front of others is more nerve racking to me than the situation that caused it.'

Crystal slipped off her own shoes and had to admit the tiles were cool against her skin. 'That scene, in the dining room, was that real or make believe?' she demanded.

'A little of both.' Sarah sighed, leaning her head back against the wall and closed her eyes, 'By revealing my fears to Freddy, was the sealing point to get him to stay. He now has a noble purpose in remaining to ease me of one less worry as I appear to be buckling under the pressure.'

'You are remarkable!' Crystal could not help laughing. 'Is duplicity a part of diplomacy?'

'Very much so. Sort of like poker, you have to know when to bluff and when to hold a hand.'

'And when to fold?'

Sarah managed to smile. 'Oh yes, definitely, when to fold.'

Gary's Concern

Abruptly the shape of Gary Winters appeared in the bathroom doorway, his chest rising and falling fast as he had been running. 'Crystal? Sarah? What is it? Freddy sent me an urgent message that Sarah had collapsed!'

Sarah opened her eyes to look up at the agitated Major. 'It's all right, Gary. After an emotional outburst with Freddy, I'm feeling a little tired.'

Gary glanced sceptically from one girl to the other. 'And the bathroom floor looked like a good place to take a nap?'

Sarah shook her head, 'No, but it is wonderfully cool and my head's throbbing fit to burst.'

'I'll get you something for your headache.' Crystal rose, left the room and upon returning several minutes later, Crystal found Gary squatting down in front of Sarah, his hand tenderly brushing wisps of hair away from her face. She handed Sarah a glass of water and a couple of tablets. She stared down at them hesitantly but took them meekly enough when Crystal said that they were only Panadol.

Gary made certain that she had actually taken the tablets before straightening and saying quietly to Crystal, 'We should get her to bed to sleep for a couple of hours.'

'I'm all right. No need to fuss.' Sarah held up the empty glass. 'I've been asked to go to the Zoo hospital where they think I might be able to help an injured Caracal.'

Gary frowned down at her. 'I don't think you should go today.'

Tears began to well in her eyes, and Crystal realized that this time it wasn't forced. 'Oh please, Gary, I need some distraction from the nightmare we currently living in.' Sarah broke off as a lump started to constrict in her throat.

Before he could veto the excursion, Crystal said, 'I'll go with Sarah this afternoon and if it gets too much for her, I'll drag her home.'

Thinking about this, Gary ignored Sarah's complaint about being treated like a child.

'All right then,' Gary finally agreed. 'But if Sarah's not looking a little better this afternoon, she won't be going! And I suppose I'd better take you or you'd get into trouble!'

'You enjoy being bossy, don't you?' Sarah struggled to her feet.

Gary reached out to support her as Sarah started to collapse. Holding her steady in his arms, he looked down at her with grim satisfaction. 'No, just being right!'

You Don't Have To Pretend

Sarah was surprised when Colonel Nasseur met them at the Zoo. Joseph politely greeted Crystal, as he asked how she was coping after the intrusion at the cocktail party. Crystal smiled as he focused his attention fully on her.

'A bit of a restless night, Colonel, but you don't need to be so guarded around me, I'm aware of you and Sarah.' Joseph shot an accusing glance at Gary, but Crystal added, 'Don't blame Gary. I'm just too observant. You have nothing to fear from me.'

Sarah wasn't happy about the Colonel's presence with the Australians at the Zoo. 'It's far too risky for us to be seen in public together, Colonel, even if Gary and Crystal are with us!'

Joseph smiled disarmingly, causing Sarah's will to withstand his pursuit to waver significantly. 'Ah but I am here at the express orders of my nephews who insist that all my resources are needed to ensure the recovery of the Caracal!' There was a twinkle of laughter in his eyes that caused Sarah's heart to skip a beat.

'Of course, I see now! All orders from the young Princes must be obeyed,' before she could stop herself Sarah was smiling shyly back at him.

'Well only when they give me a ready excuse to be with you. The Colonel's words were intimate, like a kiss, and Sarah was left extremely breathless.

'How long have you known?' Gary looked puzzled at Crystal.

Laughing, Crystal shook her head. 'As soon as I saw them together while we were in the pool on the day that I arrived. Don't worry, you're not obvious, I just pick up vibes.'

The Endangered Caracal

'Speaking of gifts,' said Joseph, 'it is actually Sarah's gift with animals that we need right now.'

'What is this about?' Sarah looked interested.

'Last week, whilst the riots and protesting were most active, a group of Rebels broke into the zoo and attempted to set the animals free to cause mayhem in the streets. Security caught up with them before they could succeed but not before they had set fire to several of the enclosures.'

Crystal gasped in horror. 'Oh no! How barbaric! The animals had no means of escape!'

Joseph shook his head reassuringly. 'No animals died, the zoo staff was very efficient in putting out the fires and the animals have been treated mainly for minor burns and distress.' When he paused, they all knew that there was more to come; only none of them were sure that they wanted to hear it.

'But?' Sarah finally prompted.

He took a deep breath and continued, 'You may, or may not know that the Caracal is the native Lynx cat in this country but due to development and de-forestation, its numbers are dwindling. So the Emir organized a few years ago, a breeding program at the zoo. They are bred with very little human contact and when their numbers had sufficiently increased, some were released into the wild,' pausing, Joseph smiled ruefully, 'Sorry, I didn't mean this to turn into a lecture.'

Crystal waved away his apology. 'It sounds fascinating. But what's Sarah's part in all this?'

'During the fire a mother and her cub were burnt, mainly superficial. They will be fine, but because it has been essential to keep human contact to a minimum to enable them to return to the wild, treating them now has been hard. The mother will be all right, but they cannot guarantee that the cub will pull through. I know you are not a vet, Sarah, but you worked wonders with Simon and the professionals are stumped.'

Sarah glanced at her colleagues before saying, 'How can I refuse?'

'Shall we go then?' Joseph knocked on the door of the Zoo hospital.

Feeding Dilemma

Inside the staff greeted the Australians politely but with a little scepticism. It hadn't been the Colonel who had recommended Sarah, but the vet who had treated Simon and was involved with the zoo's hospital as well. Their group was led through the behind scenes of the zoo, passing recovery cages and treatment rooms. The surgery was as well set up and as sterile as any human hospital and Crystal was very impressed by the state of the art equipment.

There was a hushed silence as they entered a room where a small cub lay listlessly on a floor cushion. His paws were covered with little socks to keep the bandages on to help heal his burns. Crystal just wanted to pick him up and cuddle him, but knew that he was not a harmless kitten. Out of one window a staff member pointed to where they could overlook the mother who was in a small enclosed area outside. No bigger than a medium sized dog, the Caracal was a slender animal, reddish brown in colour with rather large ears, edged in black and long tufts of black hair at the tips. There were no spots as Crystal had expected, as other Lynx she had seen in books had been spotted. The adult Caracal also had socks on and areas of fur on her body were missing.

The vet was explaining to Sarah all the difficulties they'd been having with treating Sheza and her cub Aziz. Due to their traumatic experience Sheza had stopped producing milk, and anyway it had been necessary to keep them apart while they tried to treat them. Now that the burns were slowly beginning to heal, the staff wanted to re-unite mother and son as soon as possible. Aziz, though, couldn't keep down any of the formulas they gave him. Either it went straight through him, or he brought it back up. If they sent Aziz back to Sheza sick, she might reject him or even kill him.

It was feeding time, and an assistant brought a warm baby's bottle. Sarah surprised them by asking to taste the formula. Although the assistant hesitated, she poured a small amount of the milky substance into a glass and handed it to Sarah, who took a sip. Immediately she pulled a pained face as she put the glass back on the table.

'That's terrible! No wonder he's rejecting it! I'm sorry, I don't mean to offend you, but did you ever taste this?'

The zoo staff stared at her stunned and Crystal could almost see them thinking, *Actually taste animal food?*

'This is a highly recommended formula, Miss Trent,' the vet explained.

Sarah shook her head. 'Maybe, but it is part of your problem. You need something sweet and heavier than normal milk to line his stomach. Then slowly introduce him to diluted Llamas milk or try goat's milk.' Sarah handed an assistant a can of evaporated milk.

The vet looked surprised. 'Surely you don't recommend sweetened milk?'

'Actually I do. As a baby, one of my cousins was unable to process his mother's milk or any formula available, so the evaporated milk was recommended by the doctor as a last resort,' explained Sarah.

As the assistant opened the can Sarah added, 'Only half fill his bottle and top up with a little water. Previously boiled water if possible but not hot.'

Sarah went to sit down beside the cub on the floor. He looked up at her with suspicion. *What is another human going to do to me?* He thought. With no intention of harming him, or even moving him for the moment, Sarah spoke softly to him, tickling him behind the ears. An idea came to her causing Sarah to ask, 'How do you hold him when you feed him?'

The vet looked bemused. 'Like a baby.'

'A human baby? On his back?'

'Of course,'

'Is he any trouble?'

'He fights like a spitfire!'

Sarah sighed as she nodded, 'It's not a natural position for him to feed in. A cat will only ever lie on its back when it feels completely comfortable and relaxed. Aziz is used to feeding while lying on his stomach, his feet on the ground. Not feeling safe won't have aided his digestion.'

Sarah looked back down at Aziz as she had found a particularly itchy spot and as she scratched it, his back paw came up and twitched in time to her fingers. No one else had managed to touch Aziz without him trying to scratch or bite them. His almost ready acceptance of Sarah was remarkable.

When she was handed the bottle, Sarah lay on her side on the floor, positioned so that Aziz was facing her stomach. All the while talking to him, Sarah offered Aziz the bottle. Probably associating the bottle with the previous formula, Aziz at first refused to drink. Sarah, not prepared to give up so easily, squirted a little of the milk into his mouth and waited until he had tasted the new milk before offering the bottle once more. This time he took it, and a huge sigh of relief went round the room as Aziz closed his eyes and began to suckle greedily upon the bottle.

It wasn't long before the bottle was empty, but when one of the staff went to refill it, Sarah stopped them. 'Only a small amount at first as his digestive system has to adjust to the new milk. Probably feed him again in another 30 minutes.'

Sarah remained on the ground, absently rubbing Aziz's tummy as his paws clumsily tried to play with the end of Sarah's plait that lay within his reach. Gary was frowning as he watched a bond forming between human and wild animal. He foresaw a problem.

'With the kind of care Aziz and his mother are going to need with their burns, will they be able to return to the outside world?'

The vet shook his head. 'No, they'll have to remain in the zoo. They haven't known true wilderness so there won't be any stress, but they will have to become more used to human handling. That would make release difficult.'

'Why?' Crystal didn't understand the reasoning.

The vet shrugged his shoulders. 'In here, they learn eventually to trust us. We mean them no harm. Once outside, they cannot understand why they can't trust other humans, until it is too late. At our breeding complex we have very little contact with them, they catch their own food, and they rely upon us for nothing except protection from predators via an electric fence.'

A cushion was found and placed under Sarah's head to make her more comfortable as she played with Aziz. Although the cub still seemed to tire quickly, there wasn't the air of despair that he had previously. Aziz's bonding with Sarah seemed to make him more tolerant of other humans as one of the vet assistants bent down to adjust one of Aziz's socks, and didn't receive the usual growl or attempt to bite them. Satisfied that Sarah wasn't about to get hurt by the Caracal, Gary wandered off to look at some of the other animals that were in the zoo hospital for treatment or general examination. An attendant followed him to answer any questions that Gary might have. It wasn't that they didn't trust Gary; the zoo was always very appreciative for the support that the Australians gave their organization.

Stirrings Of Desire

With Sarah's attention focused upon Aziz, Crystal and Joseph moved back to lean against an operating table to be more comfortable as they watched. Sarah made a strange little noise, emulating Aziz, a cross between a purr and a trill coming from the back of the throat. The noise sent a shiver down the Colonel's spine and an image suddenly flashed into his brain of them making slow, tender, but passionate love. His face must have briefly reflected his thoughts because Crystal chuckled in amusement. Immediately recalled to their present surroundings, Joseph's expression went deadpan as he glanced swiftly across at Crystal.

'That touched you didn't it?' She smiled mischievously up at him. 'That purr, it went straight through you, struck something deep inside, something primeval!'

'Did it affect you that way?' he asked, trying to keep his thought away from the image that seemed to be burnt into the back of his eyes. *I know it is pointless to try and argue with her true interpretation of my reaction.*

'Hum? Oh yes! It brought back memories of the first time Allan, my ex-husband and I made love. It was so new, so precious, so much animal need and yet essential that it was also tender.'

Joseph shifted uncomfortably, not liking where this conversation was heading, or the effect that it was having upon him. Sarah was completely oblivious to the effect she was having upon her friends as she played and talked to Aziz. Looking unintentionally alluring lying on the floor, her full length skirt tight against her curves, and positioned as they were above her, they were able to catch a glimpse of her ample breasts straining against the cotton material of her shirt.

A deep shudder ran through Joseph and he straightened to his feet. 'You're a very wicked girl!' he whispered to Crystal as he reached for his mobile phone. The sound had been turned off, but it was vibrating now and Joseph strode outside as he took the call. Gary passed Joseph on his way back in and went straight over to Crystal. He was wearing a worried frown.

Unleashing Passion

'What on earth have you been saying to Colonel Nasseur? He looked like he'd been hit by a bolt of lightning!'

Crystal gave a weary smile. Joseph wasn't the only one affected by the imagery that purr had conjured. *What I would give to drag Gary onto this operating table and satisfy the urges I've stirred up inside myself but I'm struggling to remember that as the Ambassador's daughter, I need to be a little more discreet than that.* Giggling, Crystal wondered, *if I can drag Gary out to the car, would that be discreet enough?* Gary looked at her in concern, wondering if she'd gone mad.

Laughing, Crystal leant forward and whispered in Gary's ear. 'I'm afraid we were both swept away on an erotic fantasy. You don't know of a handy broom cupboard do you?'

Gary was startled. He looked around the room but the zoo hospital attendants were all focused upon Sarah and Aziz.

'You can't be serious! You hardly know me, or will I simply be a tool to satisfy the burning desire you ignited with your sex talk?'

Crystal shook her head. 'Actually I probably know you better than you know yourself. If I only wanted to satisfy myself, then I could do that alone. The truth is I want to break through this barrier you place around yourself, and get to the real you.'

Gary stared at her hard for a full minute, then he strode away to one of the zoo staff. He asked them a question which seemed to be directions, before he came back to Crystal's side. He took her by the elbow and headed her towards the door.

'What on earth did you ask that man?' Crystal demanded. Excited thoughts of a broom cupboard sprung up suddenly.

'I told him you need to use the toilet, but was too shy to ask. I think you need to soak your head, as you're obviously not thinking straight.'

'Why?' Crystal demanded angrily. She felt like she was being treated like a child; a very naughty one at that. 'You're so afraid of anyone getting close, aren't you? What are you scared of that someone might find? Is everything in your life so damn serious?'

With something akin to a snarl, Gary threw open the door to the toilets and dragged her inside. He locked the door and thrust Crystal hard up against the wall. His body pressed against hers and his eyes gleamed dangerously.

'Yes damn you! Every day I'm dealing with death! Trying to prevent it, seeking it out, plotting to control it and sometimes even meeting it! That's my job! And doing that job is sometimes 24 hours a day, seven days a week. Until I met you I was satisfied with that life, but now you're slipping into my thoughts when I least expect it. You've only been here two days and already you're inside my head causing a distraction. You want to know what I'm hiding. Well I'll tell you. It's the fear that I'm exactly like Con! That this burning need inside of me, for sex would rampage out of control if I ever let my guard down. That my need for it would control me, taking away my reasoning and my pride.'

There was barely suppressed anger in his voice and Crystal was moved by the passion in his words. *I really like the feel of his hard body pressed against mine but I must try to put that distraction out of my head. For the moment anyway.*

'It doesn't have to be that way Gary. Not enough of something can be as harmful as too much! There should be a healthy balance.'

Gary shook his head. 'And this would be construed as being healthy?' He indicated how he had her pinned up against the wall.

'What's unhealthy is bottling it up inside like you do. One day you'll just go berserk from the pressure.'

Gary uttered a harsh laugh. 'You mean like now?' He didn't give Crystal the chance to reply as he sealed her mouth with his in a kiss that was forceful, demanding and all consuming. There was no malice or savagery in the kiss and she didn't feel afraid of him. Instead she melted against him, freeing her hands so that she could wrap them around his neck. She matched his passion for passion as his hands hungrily explored her body. Gary almost tore up Crystal's blouse as he lifted her to wrap her legs around his waist. His hands cupped her backside to help him support her against the wall. His mouth left hers to nibble upon her neck and Crystal exposed more of her throat to Gary's onslaught. She reached down between their bodies to try and undo the buckle of his trouser belt.

This action seemed to bring the Major to his senses causing him to suddenly release Crystal's backside and disentangle himself from her.

'No, I'm sorry, this isn't right! I can't use you like this. I can't sink to Con's level.' Gary adjusted his belt as Crystal pulled her shirt back down into place. She wasn't angry, only concerned for his change of mind.

'I think you're wrong. Well only partly wrong. Here and now is perhaps wrong, but not the people. I can't deny that I'm strongly attracted to you, but I'm at a loss to understand how you can compare yourself with Con Zuco.' She tucked her blouse back into her jeans and checked her reflection in the mirror to see if her hair or make up needed touching up.

'Sex is a distraction I don't need right now.' Gary ran a hand through his hair. *I don't understand why I don't just walk away from this conversation.*

Crystal's eyebrows rose as she looked at him via the mirror. 'But it is distracting you, whether you're having sex or not.'

Gary was floundering. *I honestly don't know why I am reacting this way. I hadn't really thought much about sex before Crystal's arrival. Although I've met plenty of attractive women, I'd never given them another thought. My work had been all that I had needed. Now Crystal invades my thoughts regularly and I had come so close to giving in to the burning desire to accept the offer that she had presented me. My confidence in my own judgment is shaken. I have to get my mind back onto business and away from the delectable creature beside me.*

'Perhaps we should return to the others now?' A wall had suddenly come up around him, indicating that Gary wasn't prepared to discuss this any longer. Crystal opened her mouth to argue, but decided against it and closed her mouth again, and just nodded. Gary turned and unlocked the door, leading the way silently out of the toilet. Crystal, though, wasn't prepared to allow Gary to continue to deny his natural desires. *In time, I hope to convince him that having an interest in sex needn't affect his efficiency in his work.*

Prepare For Trouble

In the surgery, Joseph was squatting down beside Sarah and coaxing Aziz to chase a piece of cord. The Colonel laughed in delight as Aziz pounced on the cord and tried to wrestle it awkwardly out of his hand. At Gary's and Crystal's return, Joseph rose to his feet, letting the Caracal cub have the cord. It wasn't embarrassment, though, that made him get up.

'I'm afraid I have to leave you Major, developments have arisen that I must attend to immediately.'

'Of course, Colonel Nasseur, we completely understand. Duty must always come first!' Crystal smiled at this subtle dig at her but Joseph studied them both closely with a slight frown.

'There could be trouble tonight,' warned the Colonel. 'Stick close to the Embassy, all of you.' He made no mention of the tension between Gary and Crystal, as he asked the zoo staff to look after the Australians before he departed.

Sitting up, Sarah glanced from her colleagues, but Gary refused to meet her eyes.

'So what happens now?' Crystal asked the room in general.

It was the vet who answered her, 'Miss Trent has offered us some welcome advice about how to soon re-unite Aziz with his mother. If this new milk works, that could be in a day or two.'

'As for us, we'd all better take Colonel Nasseur's advice and head for home,' Gary added.

Bunking Down

As night began to fall, the Capital city of Pangani, Kathou braced itself for an unusual onslaught. Shops closed early and boarded up their windows. Even more Police and Army personnel were on the streets, ready for trouble. Being kept completely up to date with what was happening; Gary was one of the first people to know about the attempt to blow up

Kathou's central train station. With the exception of Con, who said nothing got in the way of sex, all the Embassy staff gathered in the living room of the Residency to watch the live news broadcast. Even though they were prepared for it, they were still stunned into silence when the television returned to its usual program. Simon lay stretched out on Gary's lap enjoying a tummy rub, he was the only one oblivious to the tension. Crystal rose to her feet, went over to the drinks bar and refilled her father's Scotch before turning to Gary.

'All right Gary. This is your domain. Do we bunker down here, is it safe for everyone to go home, or should we check into a hotel away from the city?'

Scratching Simon's belly, it was a moment before Gary answered, 'The compound's the safest option. I just wish Con hadn't been stupid and gone out.'

'I'd better warn Freddy that we'll all be eating here tonight. I suppose he'll fly into a passion.' Marianne rose gracefully and straightened her skirt.

Sarah nodded. 'Yes, but honestly he enjoys the challenge, he just won't ever admit it!' Marianne laughed, hurrying out to confront Freddy in his lair.

Gary strode over to the telephone and picking up the receiver quickly dialled a mobile phone number. 'I'm just trying to get hold of Con to see if he's coming back to the Embassy,' Gary explained. As he spoke, his own mobile began to ring. 'Damn!'

Sarah hurried across and took the land line receiver from Gary. 'I'll deal with Con. Your phone call is probably more important.'

He thanked her, heading outside to answer his call and when he came back into the room, he was wearing a worried frown.

'Well?' he demanded as Sarah was just putting the receiver down. She shrugged her shoulders and smiled slightly.

'Con said that if the option is to sleep with Kevin again, he'd rather be...' Sarah broke off unable to use the 'f' word as Con had done. 'Rather be sleeping with the woman he's currently with.'

Gary's eyebrows rose. 'If he doesn't wake up one day because his throat has been cut, it will be his own fault. I've got no time to worry about him now.' There was an edge to his voice that they all caught.

'What is it Gary?' James asked.

The Major hesitated, not immediately answering, 'Colonel Nasseur just called. Although most of the action these past two weeks has been centred in the north of Kathou, now a major riot has started in the centre of the city and several Embassies are under siege. There have been no injuries or damage yet, but the mob is bloody angry. The Colonel is sending over several soldiers to boost our security.'

More Drama From Freddy

Entering a silenced room, Marianne looked around puzzled but before she could ask what had been going on, Freddy burst into the room after her. He was highly excited and waving his hands around dramatically.

'I do not complain. I put up with a lot, but is it too much to ask that I am given some warning when the covers change from 2 to 10?'

'Six actually,' corrected Crystal before she could help herself. Freddy shot her a pained look.

'No one appreciates the time it takes to create a Fredericks masterpiece. I cannot just slap a meal together in a minute.'

Crystal wondered, *why not because millions of mothers do it all the time and usually with less notice and more stress in their lives?* She didn't say any of this as it would only add more fuel to the fire. Gary looked frustrated enough to bounce Freddy's head off the wall, but Sarah held her hands out sympathetically to Freddy and he took them into his own.

'We obviously expect too much from you Freddy. We've no right to put this much pressure on to you. Forget dinner, I'll whip up an omelette and salad. I don't think anyone is terribly hungry anyway. You should go home to your family.'

There followed a silence that caused Crystal to bite down on her bottom lip, desperately trying hard to not break it by giggling. Freddy pulled himself up straighter. 'No, no Mademoiselle Trent! You're not up to slaving over a hot stove. Depend upon Freddy. I'll present you with a meal that will tempt the meagerest appetite.' Freddy gallantly raised her hands to his lips before returning with his head held high to his kitchen.

'How do you do that?' Gary shook his head in disbelief.

Sarah shrugged. 'Reverse psychology isn't it? I'd better feed the dogs.' As she headed for the front door, Gary joined her.

'I'll come with you,' he stated. 'Come on Simon, dinner.' Sarah didn't even attempt to argue with him, she knew it was pointless. Simon got up and stretched before happily limping after them out onto the verandah.

Do You Think They're Involved?

Watching them leave, Kevin had a peculiar expression on his face. 'Gary's awfully protective of Sarah. Do you think they're involved?' he asked, sipping his drink.

'No, they're not!' Crystal answered quickly; too quickly because everyone looked at her in surprise. 'Oh please!' She added, trying to quickly cover her mistake. 'It's obvious to me that Marianne is a substitute mother, and Gary a substitute brother. Anyway if they were involved, Gary would've knocked Con's head off before now for harassing Sarah.'

'That's true,' Marianne nodded. 'Besides which I think Sarah secretly has a crush on Prince Kahlee. You saw, James, how she became inarticulate when he arrived at your first function.'

James agreed, staring meditatively into his glass. 'Yes, but I thought it was Colonel Nasseur who was friendlier with Sarah.'

Crystal held her breath as Marianne shook her head, 'Only because the Embassy sees more of the Colonel than any other Pangani official. After all Joseph and Gary are close friends, so he's quite often here to see Gary.' The conversation was turned and when it didn't return to either Sarah's or Gary's relationships Crystal breathed a sigh of relief.

Is It Wrong To Be Afraid?

Outside on the verandah, Gary and Sarah sat quietly staring out into the darkening garden as the three dogs heartily ate their dinner. *What would happen if an angry mob stormed the compound?* She wondered.

What is the viability of using the bomb shelter that is a part of the basement of the main Embassy building? Contemplated Gary. *It hasn't been used in years except as housing for the backup generator. I suppose I should've looked into that during the day while it had still been light, instead of being distracted by Crystal.* So deep in thought was he that Gary actually jumped when Sarah placed her hand in his.

'Is it cowardly to feel scared?' Her voice sounded young and vulnerable as it quivered slightly.

'Only a fool knows no fear at all.' Gary placed his arm around her shoulders. 'Being scared is natural. It shows you still have so much to live for. That makes you fight all the harder to stay alive.' He shook his head. 'I'm probably only scaring you more. Sorry!'

'No, actually it makes sense. The more you want something, the harder you'll try anything to keep it.'

'And what do you want that you're prepared to fight tooth and nail for?'

'A happily ever after with my Prince Charming would be nice; impossible but nice. What about you?'

A sudden noise reached the Major's ears at the same time as Jeb and Ash looked up quickly from their food bowls. It was coming from the front gate. The two older German Shepherds raced off to investigate and Gary springing to his feet grabbed Simon by his collar to stop him following the other dogs.

'At the moment, to see another day,' Gary said, in answer to Sarah's question. 'Go inside and take Simon with you.' He ran off without waiting for an answer from Sarah; just as well really as his first statement had stunned her mute. Leading a reluctant puppy inside, Sarah wondered *if any of us will be allowed to see another day?*.

Do You Ever Pray?

The dogs were barking madly when the Major arrived at the gate, but immediately quietened down when he ordered them to return to his side. True to his word, Colonel Nasseur had posted additional soldiers at the Embassy gate. Even so, they were well and truly outnumbered by protesters, waving burning torches and shouting, 'Foreigners go home!'. Gary stood between the dogs, watching the mass of people being kept back by armed soldiers on the other side of the gate. He didn't even wince or move when a projectile flew over the gate and struck him, causing a slight gash along one cheek. The crowd were working themselves up to a fever pitch.

Gary wasn't helping by not running away but calmly facing their anger. He stood silently, his arms crossed over his chest as he watched them as if they were performing animals. There was a movement behind him, and he swung around, his gun out of its holster and aimed at the intruder. Colonel Nasseur chuckled as he continued to approach.

'I did not think I could sneak up on an old war horse like you.' Joseph joined Gary who immediately lowered his weapon.

'I could've shot your head off!' Gary exclaimed.

'No, I think not.' Joseph shook his head. 'You had not taken the safety catch off your gun because the dogs had not reacted to my presence as if I was a stranger.'

Gary couldn't help laughing. 'So that's why I felt no tingle of fear!'

For a moment Joseph Nasseur contemplated the angry mob outside before he spoke, 'Do you ever pray Gary?'

Surprised by the question, Gary nodded. 'Actually yes, I do.'

'Do you think God ever answers prayers?'

'Sometimes, but not always in the way we want or expect Him to.' Gary sighed.

'Tonight God will answer many prayers.' Slowly Joseph smiled.

Gary didn't immediately follow where Joseph was going with this, but then he felt it. It was like a teardrop against his cheek. Just one at first and then another. That one drop quickly became several more, and as if someone had turned on a tap, water suddenly poured profusely out of the sky. With so little warning, rain absolutely bucketed down. The fire torches went out and the mob quickly dispersed to seek shelter from the rain. Their rally cry died as rain drove them from their purpose and many homeward bound. For once it started raining in Kathou, it could be over again in minutes or it could last for days.

Laughing, Gary followed Joseph, Jeb and Ash back to the verandah of the Residency. The dogs were not happy in the rain and were glad to seek shelter and finish their dinner. The front door was flung open and the Embassy staff poured out of the Residency at the sound of rain thundering against the roof. There was rejoicing at the sight of rain. It would certainly cool down the heated passions of the angry people. They had averted a volatile scene and were prepared to celebrate that minor victory. Joseph was dragged inside to join their dinner, and for a while, they could all breathe a sigh of relief. The war was not yet won, but a major battle had been avoided or at least postponed.

SATURDAY

You Talk In Your Sleep

Rain continued to fall as daylight struggled to filter into the bedroom through the dark clouds. There was a feeling of surrealness about the previous evening so that Crystal could hardly believe that any of it had actually happened. Even though it was Saturday, Sarah was already up and as Crystal wandered into the dining room, she discovered so was everyone else.

Kevin stood in front of the television in the lounge room, chomping on a piece of toast as he watched the latest local news report. The camera shot returned to the newsreader who was happy to report that very little damage had occurred during the night, and one man's attempt to create havoc in the hospital was quickly subdued by their security guards. The rain looked to continue for at least another twenty-four hours, bringing welcome relief to some of the farming communities and momentarily dampening the people's anger.

The mood at the dining table in the Residency was rather subdued. No one was really talking unless it was necessary. Sort of like after a really heavy night of drinking, only they didn't have the hangover to go with it. Sarah came into the room from the front door. She'd just fed the dogs and she smiled as she looked mischievously around the room.

'It looks like a day one should apologize for breathing too loudly.' She selected toast as well as several different types of fruit and sat down beside Crystal.

James looked around and laughed. 'We do look like we've been through the wringer. What are you so chirpy about?'

'We've lived to see another day. Last night, before it began to rain, I honestly had doubts that we would all see morning. We have, therefore, I rejoice,' Sarah's words did little to brighten the mood. She cast a sideways glance at Crystal and said quietly, 'Did you know you talk in your sleep?'

Crystal choked on her coffee. 'Good God! Do I really? Did I say anything interesting?'

Sarah grinned, the tips of her ears turning quite red as she lowered her voice further. 'It was quite erotic. I honestly thought at one stage that I'd be safer with Marianne.'

Crystal couldn't stop laughing. Half way through the night Sarah had crept into Crystal's bed as Marianne, whom she had been sharing with, had been tossing and turning and occasionally throwing her arms around, making sleep impossible.

With breakfast over, they each went their own ways. Sarah and Marianne were going home; while Kevin was going to try and get through to his wife in Paris to let her know he was still alive. Crystal was dragging her father out to shop for new sofas. Gary had received a call from Colonel Nasseur and was joining him at his office to analyse the situation. The atmosphere was subdued on the streets. People went out in the rain, only when it was absolutely necessary. Mother Nature had momentarily taken the situation off the boil. The question they were all asking themselves was how long would it last?

A Girl's Night In

By late afternoon, it didn't appear as if the rain was about to let up too soon. Even so, it was an excited Crystal who turned up on Sarah's doorstep with several shopping bags. The Secretary was surprised to see her; but warmly welcomed her inside, assisting Crystal with her burden. Simon frisked around them happily feeling that there might just be something good in those bags for him. He wasn't to be disappointed as Crystal pulled out a squeaky ball and he eagerly chased it around the house. Sarah put the kettle on as Crystal collapsed wearily into a chair at the kitchen table.

'I hope you don't mind me dropping in on you Sarah, but Dad received an urgent message from Canberra and Marianne was asked to the Residency to help him deal with the contents. They didn't need me under their feet so I thought about livening up your evening.'

Laughing Sarah shook her head. 'Of course, I don't mind, but I must ask, what on earth have you brought with you?'

'I thought it was time we re-discovered what it was like to be irresponsible teenagers.' Crystal grinned mischievously. 'So we're going to have a slumber party!' She pulled out of one bag a sexy silk nightie.

The other bags were full of junk food, soft drinks and everything you needed for a manicure, a facial and a makeover. Sarah stared at Crystal for a stunned minute and then started laughing. She turned off the kettle, as irresponsible teens did not drink sensible boring things like tea or coffee. Sarah showed Crystal the spare room where she could change and emerged from her own room several minutes later in a cotton tee shirt nightie with a pair of black leggings and her hair pulled up into two pigtails.

Already emptying the bags Crystal couldn't help laughing as Sarah entered the kitchen. She looked ten years younger already. Cool drink was placed into the fridge and chips, chocolate and nibbles were put into bowls. The food and the other goodies were carried into the lounge room, where Sarah put the stereo on low as background noise. Simon looked at them a little puzzled as they were dressed for sleep already and he couldn't understand why he wasn't being sent out to his bed in the laundry. Seeing his confusion, Sarah called him to her and hugged him. This he could understand and his doubts eased as Crystal tossed him a chip. It might be weird but Simon decided he could live with that.

As they gave each other manicures and pedicures, they talked about what life had been like for them as teenagers. The boys they had kissed, the parties they had attended, the good old days of 'blue light discos' and the bands no one knew of now. Crystal had been far more outgoing than Sarah had, but their experiences evened out, as a lot of Crystal's spare time had been spent either dancing or training as she had been a ballroom dancer. All other exciting events of being a teen had to be squeezed in around that.

They painted their nails bright colours and experimented with different hair styles. All the while stuffing their faces with the sorts of food that were usually only an occasional treat. Despite all this, they were hungry at 6 p.m., so they cooked up some hot dogs and with a tall glass of coke with ice; they turned off the stereo, and put on a DVD.

It was an Australian movie called 'Hercules Returns' and was about a theatre that gets the Italian sound track instead of the English, so the owners of the theatre provide their own sound effects and voices. It was absolutely hilarious, having both the girls almost rolling around on the floor in laughter. They were making so much noise, cheering and laughing that the guard thought it best to check up on them. Crystal invited him to join them, but he declined as he was on duty.

Cadem's Make Over

One person who didn't refuse their offer was Cadem who had simply stopped by to see if they were all right. He was a little startled at first by their appearance. By the time he arrived, the girls had started their facial with a green mask.

They dragged him inside and couldn't stop giggling as they gave a protesting Lieutenant a facial before starting on his manicure. He could've easily over powered them both but strangely enough he didn't want to. Cadem got caught up in the movie as well. So much so that he wasn't aware of Sarah painting his fingernails a pretty pink. It was time for the girls to wash off their face masks and this ended up as a water fight in the bathroom leaving them both more than a little damp.

Normally that wouldn't be a problem, but it made their sleep wear cling rather revealingly to their curves. Cadem's eyes nearly popped out of his head as they came back into the lounge room and he didn't know where to look. Crystal started a tickle fight, which graduated into a pillow fight when Cadem grabbed a cushion to protect himself. It wasn't long before they were all laying on the floor exhausted, Cadem the obvious winner in that battle.

The movie had ended and the girls had got their second wind. Sarah picked up their dirty plates and glasses and left them in the sink to wash later. Crystal was sorting through her makeup case trying to decide what colours to experiment with upon Sarah. Cadem was permitted to finally wash his facial mask off and returning from the bathroom, he found Crystal outlining Sarah's lip with a lip pencil. For a while, the Lieutenant watched as Crystal used her professional knowledge to make up Sarah's face but he really wanted to watch the movie all the way through. So he started the DVD player, *I hope that I won't be a guinea pig in their game of makeup. I am determined to draw the line there.* The girls, though, seemed to respect that line and after Crystal had done Sarah's make up, she did her own and then experimented with a few sophisticated hairstyles on Sarah.

The results took Cadem's breath away. Gone was the usual single plait, and instead a third of Sarah's hair was pulled up into a bun on top of her head, out of which looped several small braids and finished off with the remainder of her hair streaming down her back. Always a pretty girl, Sarah now looked absolutely stunning. Crystal dragged her off to the bathroom so that Sarah could see in the larger mirror. Sarah was just as dumbfounded that this was her looking back out of the mirror.

Don't You Have Anything Sexy?

Simon had fallen asleep a long time ago, exhausted by their madness. He lay stretched out on the lounge; the humans were using cushions on the floor, with his new toy held securely under a paw. Crystal could be heard rummaging through Sarah's wardrobe looking for something sexy to dress Sarah in. By the sounds of her frustrated mutterings, Cadem assumed that Crystal wasn't having much luck.

'For goodness sake, Sarah, don't you have anything alluring in here?'

Lieutenant Cadem chuckled, as he already knew the answer to that. Sarah had always maintained a strict code of dress so as to never offend the Panganian people. Cadem rose to his feet and walked down the passage, pausing outside Sarah's bedroom. The door wasn't completely closed, but even so Cadem knocked and called out.

'Miss Trent? Are you dressed?'

The two girls giggled and Sarah said, 'You can come in, Cadem.' He pushed open the door and hesitantly entered the room. The sight before him made his knees buckle. Crystal had bullied Sarah into what looked like a red satin petticoat to Cadem.

'I'm sorry, Miss, you should have told be you were in your underwear!' Cadem started to back out of the room.

Crystal laughed. 'Actually, that is a dress, Cadem.'

'But it's so revealing!' He stared at them in disbelief.

Indeed it clung to Sarah like a second skin, leaving absolutely nothing to the imagination. Cadem wondered, *what will the Colonel say about his intended being so scantily clad? What will he say if he knew that I had actually seen her so scantily clad?*

Seeing that he was gob-smacked, Sarah shoved him out of the room. 'It's all right Cadem; we're only playing dress up. I would hardly appear like this in public.'

'But you should!' Crystal protested, 'You have a good figure Sarah, you shouldn't hide it.'

The two girls continued to argue about this as Cadem retreated to the lounge room again. When the girls finally rejoined him, Sarah was once more attired in a loose tee shirt nightie and leggings. Cadem found this easier to cope with than the revealing dress.

Report Of Strange Noises

A knock on the front door caused them all to jump startled. Cadem removed his side arm as he went to open the front door. The girls remained silent, Crystal taking Sarah's hand, but she wasn't as worried as the guard would have alerted them to danger. Simon jumped off the lounge and trotted after Cadem. The Lieutenant checked through the spy hole, before he actually opened the door and stood back to allow the visitors inside.

Simon eagerly wagged his tail until it seemed it would fall off as he frisked around Colonel Nasseur and Major Winters. Both men had to bend down to greet Simon before the puppy would allow them any further into the house. Cadem shut the front door and locked it before leading the way into the lounge room.

Both soldiers blinked in surprise to see Sarah and Crystal with their hair and faces made up, but in their nighties.

Neither of them, though, had the courage to ask why. Cadem had a question though, 'Is there anything wrong Sir?'

Gary tried to suppress a grin. 'An interesting report came through to headquarters from your guard about strange goings on here, so Joseph and I thought we'd better pop in and see if everything was all right.'

'It's called therapy,' Crystal giggled. 'A slumber party to help Sarah de-stress.'

Joseph's eyebrows rose as they all sat down. 'It sounded more like an argument from outside!'

'That was his fault.' Lightly Crystal punched Cadem's arm 'Cadem brought up a controversial subject.'

Joseph scrutinized his Lieutenant closely. 'You surprise me Miss Greene, and the Lieutenant looking so pretty this evening,' He softly drawled.

Cadem followed his boss' gaze down to his bright pink nails and flushed in embarrassment.

Sarah took pity on him, directing him to the bathroom. 'Try the mirrored cupboard for nail polish remover and cotton balls.' She suggested as Cadem scurried out of the room.

Gary shook his head. 'I'm surprised you didn't try to put make up on him as well.'

The girls exchanged a conspiring glance and Crystal said, 'We did think about it, but we thought Cadem might actually shoot us if we tried.'

'He probably would too,' mused Joseph thoughtfully. They could hear Cadem in the kitchen frantically scrubbing his nails to remove the pink polish.

Time For Bed

'Anyway,' said Gary with authority. 'I think it's time you girls were in bed. Is the spare bed made up?'

Sarah groaned. 'No. I was going to do it earlier but got distracted.' She got up to remedy this but Crystal grabbed her hand.

'I probably couldn't sleep in a strange room on my own. You don't mind sharing do you?'

Sarah wiggled a finger at her. 'You start having those dreams again like last night and I'll be moving to the lounge.'

Crystal laughed. 'I'll try and behave,' she promised.

'Go and wash that stuff off your faces then,' ordered Gary. 'Don't forget to brush your teeth.'

Sarah immediately headed for the bathroom but Crystal looked at him with her hands on her hips.

'You're such a bossy brother!'

'And you're such a disobedient little girl!' Gary gave her a slap across the bottom. 'Go on before I decide to discipline you the way you deserve!'

'You wouldn't dare!' Crystal's eyes blazed at him.

A wicked smile spread across Gary's features. 'Oh, I'd more than dare to discipline you, missy!'

You're Falling In Love

With a squeal of protest Crystal ran out of the room. Joseph glanced thoughtfully across at his friend. 'You enjoyed that, didn't you?'

Gary grinned sheepishly, 'I did actually.'

'You do realize you're falling in love with her, don't you?'

'How do you figure that?' Gary was surprised.

Joseph smiled gently. 'I have never seen you so animated before. Besides which something occurred at the zoo didn't it?'

'How did you know?' Gary was even more surprised.

'Miss Greene may have reapplied her lipstick, but you did not remove the trace from your mouth.' Gary groaned in disbelief. 'It's all right. It was not noticeable to anyone else.' Joseph added.

'How do you do it? How do you stop them turning your mind into mush?'

The Colonel considered this, 'Firstly you are not a paragon of virtue, so don't try to be one. Secondly, the more you try to not think about her, the more you will. With Miss Greene try to remember that having just been divorced, she may be vulnerable and not interested in a relationship but just having some fun.'

Sighing, Gary scratched his head. 'Yeah, but...'

Joseph interrupted, laying his hand on Gary's shoulder, 'Carpe diem Gary! Seize the day! We could all be dead tomorrow or the next day. Plan to leave without any regrets.'

'Now I'm really depressed!'

Joseph shook his head. 'See if you can distract Miss Greene for five minutes.' They headed into the passage, Gary was a little confused by the Colonel's request until he saw him head for Sarah's bedroom. Chuckling, Gary continued down to the bathroom to stall Crystal.

A Moment Of Passion

With her face scrubbed clean Sarah sat upon her bed undoing the bun and plaits in her hair when Joseph walked into the bedroom. She smiled shyly as he picked up a hair brush and sitting down behind her on the bed, began to brush out her hair. This contact wasn't enough for Joseph and he eventually lifted up her curtain of hair to press his lips against the nape of her neck. Sarah leant back against him, closing her eyes blissfully as Joseph whispered words of love while raining kisses against her neck, her jaw and earlobe.

At the zoo, Crystal had been right. Joseph desired Sarah so much that it almost hurt to have to limit their time together. She turned her head so that their lips met and Joseph felt all his resolutions to wait for a better time melt away. Her mouth was willing beneath his and her body soft, fragrant and desirable against him. *I know that if I asked Gary to make up the spare bed for Crystal so that I can spend the night with Sarah, the Major would immediately do it. The problem is if I stay the night, our relationship would be exposed. We all know that Pangani isn't ready for such a revelation.*

It was just such a temptation as Sarah lay down on the bed, drawing him down with her, their mouths locked together in a kiss that seemed to drain all the fight out of Joseph. *Just to give in for a moment is dangerous. One kiss, one caress will never be enough, I will always want more.* His hand trembled slightly as it slowly travelled down her body over her nightie. When Joseph's fingers lingered over her breasts, caressing them through the material, Sarah made that purring noise that snapped clean through his self-control.

Joseph slid his hand under her nightie so that he could caress her flesh and not her clothes, enjoying the shocked pleasure he was bringing her as his fingers teased her nipples. She was embarrassed and yet excited by his exploration. *I know we should stop, but oh how I do not want him to cease his actions.*

Interruption

'I really don't understand you Gary. One minute you're threatening punishment if we don't go the bed, now you're trying to stall me,' said Crystal as she opened the door and entered the bedroom. She stopped suddenly at the sight of the entwined couple, causing Gary to cannon into the back of her. Joseph hastily rearranged Sarah's nightie and rose quickly to his feet.

'Oh guys, I'm so sorry,' apologized Crystal before turning to slap Gary's arm. 'Why didn't you just tell me, idiot?'

Gary shrugged his shoulders helplessly. 'I didn't know what to say,' he admitted.

'Gary and I'll make up the spare bed,' Crystal tried to push Gary out of the room, but Joseph stopped them.

'No, no! It is all right. It is not possible for me to stay. I only wish it was! I had not meant a good night kiss to lead to… well where it did. I must leave soon.'

Crystal was angry. 'Damn it all, why must you? I mean what does it really signify if you and Sarah are in love? Why is it such a catastrophic big deal?'

The two men looked at each other, surprised that it needed explaining. It wasn't one of them, though that answered Crystal, it was Sarah. 'Joseph's family is a very powerful and influential one in Pangani. As well as this, being Prince Kahlee's brother-in-law and Joseph's position as Head of Security all mean that he has to be seen to be the model Panganian. I still believe it could seriously damage Joseph's career if we were to be married. Fresh foreigner hatred could break out if a non-Panganian snags such a matrimonial prize.'

'Bullocks!' exclaimed Crystal angrily. 'The people may surprise you and welcome your union.'

Gary shook his head. 'The fanatics would create chaos.'

'I doubt it!' Crystal shrugged. 'Are you sure you don't want to stay Joseph?'

Smiling lovingly down at Sarah, he brushed his hand against her cheek. 'It's not that I don't want to, but I have to go. To protect Sarah's reputation,' Joseph lowered his head to briefly kiss her.

Stop Treating Me Like A Child!

Sighing, Crystal pulled back the bed covers beside Sarah, 'Men! You can all be so pig-headed! There has to be a way for you to be together without it becoming public knowledge?' She climbed into bed and pulled the sheet up.

'Just being in the same room is dangerous.' Gary shook his head. 'Now stop arguing and go to sleep.'

'Make me!' Looking mutinous, Crystal folded her arms across her chest.

Gary's eyes nearly popped out of his head, 'you what?'

'I'm sick and tired of you thinking that you can boss me around like some child! Sarah might like having a bossy over-protective brother, but I don't! So either start treating me like an adult with a right to my own opinions, or be prepared for a battle.'

There was a deafening silence. Sarah and Joseph glanced at each other as they waited for Gary's response. When it came, they were all stunned.

'What sort of battle?' demanded Gary.

Sarah gasped in surprise and Joseph placed his hand over his mouth to hide a smile. They both looked at Crystal for her reaction. The Colonel wondered, *is there time to grab Sarah and flee from the room before the explosion?*

Crystal spoke very quietly, 'Are you trying to tell me that you think I'm childish?'

This was worse than an explosion. Joseph took Sarah's hand in his and dragging her off the bed, headed for the door. They were on the other side of the door and seeking safety before Gary had answered.

'No,' he started tentatively. 'You are neither childish, immature, juvenile nor an idiot. You may see Sarah and Joseph's situation a little simply, but you're new here and perhaps you don't realize how essential Joseph is to the security of this country.' He swallowed hard and took a deep breath. 'It's easier for me to think and act like you're a child so that I don't have to think or act like you're a woman. A very desirable woman who has just been divorced from her cheating husband and I don't want to be just a rebound.'

Crystal sat silently watching him. She let several minutes pass before she finally spoke, 'You really are an idiot! Why didn't you say all this before? I rebounded with Allan's best friend, Graeme. He knew the score, it would never amount to anything and we would remain friends afterwards.'

'And it would piss Allan off?' asked Gary, despite himself he was amused.

Crystal grinned. 'And it would totally piss Allan off! I don't expect you to go down on one knee and ask me to marry you this minute. I just want to have a little fun with someone I find very attractive. If something serious comes of it later, hey great, but I'm not looking too far forward at the present. I know we haven't known each other long, but I felt that something sparked between us almost immediately. If that's not the case for you, I'll back right off. In fact if I'm too much of a distraction during this trying time, I'll leave Pangani.'

'Why would you do that?' Gary frowned.

Crystal rolled her eyes. 'I could never forgive myself if you got killed because you were distracted by me.'

Deep in thought, Gary sat down on the edge of the bed by Crystal's feet. She waited patiently for him to put into words what was bothering him.

'There's still one problem,' he admitted.

Crystal nodded wisely, reaching across to take his hand. 'This Con complex you have? I think the problem is that you've been without sex for so long. Once you start having regular sex I believe you won't be so obsessed by it. I'll become a pleasant interlude rather than a distraction.'

'And you're happy with that?'

Shrugging Crystal smiled mischievously. 'Hey if you're any good, I get something out of it too!'

Gary laughed. 'Well you'll just have to wait and see if I'm any good!' He rose to his feet but Crystal didn't release his hand.

'You know you talked your way out of that rather cleverly, don't you? I was ready to tear you into strips.'

He raised her hand to his lips. 'Yes I know, it was a close thing, but all I had to do was tell you the truth.'

'Is there anything else I should know?'

'What? You want all my deep dark secrets?'

Releasing him, she shook her head. 'No, the horrors you have seen would give me nightmares. I want to know more about Gary Winters the man. Not all at once, but in time.'

Gary leaned over so that he spoke against Crystal's ear, 'Then I must tell you that the lingerie you're wearing makes me think of very wicked and naughty thoughts.'

She reached out to grab him, but he moved swiftly out of her reach. He laughed at her look of annoyance and before she could speak, Gary bent over the bed to kiss her. He kept his hands cupped either side of her face. *If I touch that delectable body I know I wouldn't be able to limit myself to a kiss.* It was with reluctance that Gary drew away. *If I don't leave now, I never will! Besides which I was supposed to be a moral support for Joseph. I haven't done so well so far.* Gary made it to the bedroom door, and with great resolution he didn't look back as he left. The mere sight of Crystal was too much for his will power.

My Apologises

Once they were safely out of Crystal's line of fire, Joseph and Sarah headed into the kitchen where they found Cadem doing the dishes. He looked up surprised at their presence, but it didn't take the Colonel long to explain the approach of battle in the bedroom. Cadem bit down on his bottom lip to stop from smiling, but couldn't contain it and started laughing.

Sarah went into the lounge to tidy up what was left of their slumber party. Joseph walked so quietly that when he entered the room and put his arms around her from behind, Sarah jumped in surprise. He pressed a tender kiss against her hair.

'I'm sorry.'

She turned in his arms and linked her hands behind his neck, 'What for?' Sarah rose on tippy toes to kiss him on the cheek.

'For starting something I could not finish.' He placed a kiss on her forehead, not trusting himself to kiss her lips.

'One day we won't have to think about anyone or anything else,' promised Sarah.

Joseph couldn't contain a groan. 'I just hope that day comes soon!' *Just standing this close, fully clothed is a strain. The feel of her hair flowing freely through my fingers, her ample breasts pressed against my chest and basically everything I want so close and yet I can't have it.* It was just as well for the Colonel's self-control that Gary emerged at that moment from the bedroom.

Joseph reluctantly slid his arms away from Sarah. 'We should be going,' There was no enthusiasm in his voice. Sarah smiled sympathetically. Gary looked rather sheepish as he entered the lounge room.

'Still in one piece?' Sarah asked.

Gary grinned, 'Only just!' He kissed Sarah on the cheek before strolling out again to join Cadem in the kitchen.

Sarah sighed deeply, she suddenly felt very tired. 'One day, Joseph, we'll be able to laugh about this,' she promised.

'Hum! So long as it's soon, my love,' Joseph kissed her just once, a lingering kiss full of passion but under control. It was Sarah who broke the kiss and linking her arm through his, saw all three men to the front door. Two of them, especially, had to get out of there before their control broke. There was only so much that they could be expected to withstand.

Turning off the lights, Sarah joined Crystal in her bed. They had a great deal to discuss before they finally fell asleep.

A Different Courtship

Having dealt with the orders from Canberra, James and Marianne shared a nice glass of wine over dinner and they talked about subjects other than the current crisis. They discussed their children, the various antics they used to get up to, and still did.

James wondered, *is it harder for Marianne to be separated from her children even though they are grown up? Perhaps that is why she has such a close relationship with Sarah?* Thinking about Sarah led to another thought. One that James shared with Marianne. 'What would happen if Sarah was in love with Prince Kahlee, and he with her?'

'Where on earth did that come from?' Marianne stared at him in disbelief.

James shrugged his shoulders. 'Something Kevin said yesterday. Would a relationship bring the community together or explode it?'

Marianne shook her head. 'It's hardly the opportune time to take another wife. To take a Western wife too, that would certainly turn the Fundamentalists against him.'

'So it's not a good idea?' James refilled Marianne's wine glass.

'No, if they were involved it would have to be kept secret.'

James suddenly changed the topic slightly. 'Is Crystal right that Gary has only brotherly interest in Sarah? I mean there's no obvious lady in his life. Then again there's no obvious gent in your life either and that does surprise me.'

'Gary has never shown any sexual feeling towards Sarah.' Marianne sipped her wine. 'He's always seemed to be too busy to worry about a personal life. He works very hard. I don't see why you're surprised that I have no gent. Besides, what has that to do with anything?'

'What about you and Gary? Any possibilities of a romance there?'

Marianne started laughing. 'He's a boy!'

His eyebrows went up. 'There's only ten years between you.'

'Yes, with me being on the plus side! My God, it'd be like having a toy boy.'

James smiled, 'Hardly that. So is there anyone in your life at the moment?'

'No, but I don't see where you're going with all of this? You're not going to suggest I marry the Prince are you?' she took another sip of her wine.

He chuckled, 'No, purely selfish reasons.' James picked up the wine bottle and would have topped up Marianne's glass but she put her hand over it.

'No more or I won't be able to drive home.'

He moved her hand out of the way. 'Well then I'd better top your glass up.'

Stunned, Marianne stared at him. She doubted that she had heard him correctly. 'Are you trying to get me drunk Mr. Ambassador?'

James couldn't hide his look of guilt. 'Well at least to get you relaxed.'

'Why?' She was becoming suspicious.

'So that I might get away with this,' James leaned across and kissed her. He sat back again and waited a little apprehensively for Marianne's reaction.

'You didn't have to get me drunk to try that,' she said.

James breathed a sigh of relief but it was a trifle premature.

'I need to know about the way you tease Sarah,' demanded Marianne.

He choked in disbelief. 'Now you're talking about cradle snatching! She's a sweet kid, but my youngest child is older than her!'

Marianne smiled, satisfied. She finished her glass of wine and held it out to James. 'How about some more wine then?'

James readily reached for the bottle and topped up her glass. 'So,' He refilled his own glass before raising it towards Marianne. 'How drunk do we intend to get?'

'So long as it doesn't affect your performance!' Marianne raised her glass and clinked it against his.

James accidentally spilt some of his wine on the tablecloth in his surprise, 'My performance?'

'Yes James.' Marianne smiled as she sipped her wine. 'If this isn't leading to the bedroom, I'll be seriously disappointed.'

He was a little un-nerved by her forthrightness. 'Aren't we moving a little fast?'

She sighed wistfully. 'If we don't take what we can get at our age, it might just pass us by.'

James smiled. 'You mean while we totter along with our walking frames?'

'Exactly! Oh I will understand if you're not up to the challenge. I believe it's sometimes hard to become aroused, as you get older. It's nothing to be ashamed about!'

James laid down his glass. 'I have no trouble being aroused, as you're about to find out!' He dragged Marianne to her feet and into his arms. This time when he kissed her it was not a tame peck on the lips, but a passionate onslaught that left her gasping for breath. With a fiery look in his eyes, James took Marianne by the hand and led her down the passage to his bedroom. He locked the door behind him, determined to prove that he had no trouble what so ever in the sex department.

SUNDAY

The Morning After

When James woke that morning, rain continued to pitter-patter against the window and he was alone in bed. He felt acute disappointment as the previous evening; he had enjoyed getting to intimately know Marianne and to take them both more than once to complete fulfilment. Sitting up and pulling on a dressing gown, the Ambassador wondered gloomily how Marianne intended to keep last night a secret. *The night guard will know that she hadn't left the compound and Yisi will know that no other bed has been slept in.*

Rising and heading for the bathroom, James considered when she may have left him; perhaps she had slept in Crystal's bed to avert suspicion. The euphoria of the night was quickly being replaced by depression. *How is this going to affect our working relationship?* Wandering listlessly into the dining room, his jaw nearly dropped to the floor for sitting at the table wearing the top of his pyjamas and eating toast was Marianne.

Looking up from the newspaper spread out in front of her, she smiled and rose to her feet to pour strong coffee into a cup and brought it to him. Marianne kissed him on the mouth before returning to her seat.

'Sorry I didn't wait for you to wake, James, but I woke up absolutely starving. I suppose it was all that exercise last night,' she said mischievously, through bites of toast.

161

James put his cup on the table before sitting down beside her. 'When I woke up, I honestly thought you'd fled in regret,' He blurted out.

'Why on earth would you think that?' She looked at him in surprise. 'My God! It was the best sex I've had in years! If I hadn't been so hungry this morning I might have woken you for another round.'

Completely embarrassed, James was grateful for Yisi's arrival and he ordered a substantial breakfast. Indeed he felt quite hungry, but as Marianne ran her hand along his thigh discretely under the table, James wasn't exactly sure for what he was hungrier.

Marianne left him to eat his breakfast in peace as she went to shower and dress. James wondered, *Will she then leave and should I ask her to stay? Am I pushing my luck?* Still deep in thought, having finished his meal, without thinking what he was doing, he walked straight into the bathroom, which was unlocked. Marianne was still in the shower and James snapping out of his daze hastily apologized, trying to retreat. She laughed, stepping out of the shower only long enough to tear off his dressing gown and pull him into the shower with her. After she had completely soaped him over, James was left in no doubt as to what plans Marianne had for the morning and they definitely included him.

Do You Ever Just Relax?

Crystal wasn't surprised when she woke up alone in Sarah's bed. As she stretched and yawned she wondered if the secretary ever just relaxed. When the smell of coffee and toast wafted down the corridor to her, she already knew the answer and hurried to get up as she was famished. Placing a rack of toast on the table Sarah smiled as Crystal dropped into a seat breathing in deeply the aromas of breakfast. Sarah had already showered and dressed, her hair pulled back into a plait which suggested to

Crystal that Sarah would be working. Taking a big bite of hot buttery toast, Crystal frowned as she tried to study the calendar on the fridge door.

'My fridge's not about to attack is it?' Sarah looked at her amused.

Crystal nearly snorted up her coffee as she laughed, 'No, I was wondering if I had slept through Sunday as you seem to be ready for work.'

Sarah gave a delightful gurgle of laughter. 'Oh it's still Sunday but I do have work to do.' She sat down opposite Crystal and poured cereal into a bowl. 'Once a month I would go with Peggy Lucas, the Ambassador's widow, to assist women rescued from the slave trade and other atrocities.'

Crystal put her coffee cup down a little absently so the cup rocked in its saucer. 'Hang on; I thought slavery was abolished in the 1800's?'

'1830's in the British Empire.' Sarah reached over to stop Crystal's cup emptying its contents. 'In Pangani there was no serious law enforcement until the present Emir came to the throne. Prince Kahlee's mother Queen Tabina founded an organisation to assist the women and children rescued from slavery and abuse and Peggy Lucas was a serious sponsor. She would go every week to help out.'

'Doing what?' Crystal was a little incoherent through a mouthful of toast.

'Teaching them how to survive without needing a man to support them. Sometimes it is necessary for them to leave Pangani as they're in danger from their husband or his family.'

'Oh wow! So what do you teach them?' Crystal took the last piece of toast.

'Secretarial skills, using a computer, cooking western food.'

Crystal choked on her toast. 'Why western cooking?'

Sarah rose quickly to give her a firm pat on the back. 'Some of our nationals here live in a gated community. They are often looking for housekeepers or nannies and are happy to have the women bring their children with them.'

'Cool! Any chance for some more toast before I hit the shower?' Crystal had already eaten four slices.

Sarah chuckled, 'There's more bread on the bench, help yourself. I can drop you back at the Residency if you don't want to accompany me today.'

'Oh I'm not missing out on this!' Crystal popped two pieces of bread into the toaster. 'Do you expect Marianne to come with us?'

Sarah slowly shook her head. 'She usually does but today she might be tied up with Embassy issues with James. Is that a problem?'

'Not at all, I just wondered if they'd managed to sort everything out yesterday.' Crystal flung the hot toast onto her plate and lavished them in butter. Watching Crystal for a moment, Sarah wondered, *Is Crystal referring to the current crisis or something a little more personal?*

The Refuge

When Cadem arrived to escort them, Simon insisted on accompanying the women. The Lieutenant would remain with the Aussie girls but in respect to the abused women, he would stay outside on guard duty. To all their surprise Simon decided to stay with Cadem. The refuge was an old backpackers hotel done up for their requirements. Individual rooms for a woman alone or slightly bigger rooms with bunk beds for women who managed to regain possession of their children. Sometimes only the girls as their fathers weren't prepared to give up any sons without a fight. It depended on whether those responsible could be sent to prison and the children separated from the rest of the family.

There was a large communal kitchen, dining and lounge area. The woman who ran the refuge, Yasmina, was once a victim of an abusive husband whose idea of discipline was to beat her almost but not quite to death. He was now in prison but Yasmina could never have any more children due to the damage he had inflicted.

It was Yasmina who showed Crystal around the refuge as Sarah was mobbed by all the children the second she entered the common area. Sarah barely had enough time to introduce Crystal to the refuge manager before more than a dozen little hands were pulling her away from the adults.

The Wise King Solomon

'Sarah! Sarah! Tell us a story! Tell us a story!' The children chanted as they dragged her to sit on the carpet and they sat around her. In the excitement, Sarah's scarf fell from her head but there was no shock as it was possible when there was no men present for women to be unveiled.

'Now have I told you the story about the koala, the kangaroo and the possum?'

'Yes!' they sang back at her.

'Hum, well how about the gumnut babies?'

'Yes!'

'Well I know I haven't told you the story about...' Sarah broke off as a pained scream came from a puppy that two of the children were fighting over. They had both grabbed a leg and tried to pull him away from the other child. Jumping to her feet Sarah caught the frightened puppy as he struggled to get away from the children. She calmed him down as she checked to make certain that no serious damage had been done. He was trembling all over and the other children shouting at the pair wasn't helping.

'Silence!' Sarah didn't raise her voice but did speak with authority. She waited until all the children quietened and returned their attention to her. 'Now sit down, please, all of you,' Sarah waited until they obeyed before continuing, 'So why were you fighting over this poor puppy? Did you mean to cause him pain?'

'No, oh no, Miss Sarah! He is my puppy!' protested the first child.

'No he isn't! He's mine!' the second child thumped the first, who cried and went to pull the other's hair but Sarah interceded.

'Enough! I'm not sure that either of you deserve to have this puppy!' Sarah sat down again in front of the children on the floor, the puppy hid in her lap, too afraid to leave her protection. 'I think the story you need today is about a wise King who lived many years ago!' She immediately had all the children's complete attention.

'Was he a Muslim Miss Sarah?'

She shook her head. 'No he was a Jew.' There was a general gasp but looking up at the women who stood around them, Sarah smiled. 'It's all right, this isn't about religion.' She returned her attention to the children, 'This King's name was Solomon and all his people came from far and wide to him to judge their disputes. One day two women came before King Solomon each claiming to be the mother of the same baby boy.'

'A baby cannot have two mothers!' protested one child.

'They can in America!' retorted another.

'But they are all heathens!'

'Shh! I want to hear Miss Sarah's story.'

'Well King Solomon heard each woman's story, then that of their witnesses. The King asked for the baby to be brought to him. The baby was placed upon the King's knee; he was a very happy and beautiful baby.'

There was absolute silence as the children waited breathlessly for Sarah to reveal the baby's fate. Dredging up long forgotten Sunday school lessons, Crystal was the only other person who knew what was coming next.

'Solomon said, "I have decided the only fair solution is to cut the baby in half so that both of you may have equal possession."'

The children cried out in horror and it took Sarah a moment to reassure them before she could continue, 'The King reached for his sword and one woman fell to her knees crying, "Oh please your Majesty, give her the baby! Just don't harm him!" Solomon handed the unharmed boy to the woman in her knees. "You are truly his mother. Rather than see him die you would give up your own happiness for his wellbeing."'

'He wouldn't have really cut the baby in half would he?' asked one child.

Smiling Sarah shook her head. 'No, he understood people and Solomon knew the special bond that exists between a mother and her child.'

The two children who had been fighting over the puppy looked nervously at each other.

'You're not going to cut our puppy in half are you Miss Sarah?'

Sarah laughed, 'definitely not, but in this case I am appointing you both to be mothers of the puppy. Not just the fun times but also the responsibility of feeding and cleaning up after him. Right now you must be his protectors and ensure that no one, including you mistreat him. One day he will be big and strong and because of your love he will protect you in return.'

'We will never fight over puppy again Miss Sarah,' the children promised and Sarah handed the calmer puppy back to them.

'You will have to win back his trust of you. He can't understand why you hurt him just that you did.'

The Family Siege

The front door burst open and a gasp of horror rose amongst the women and children as Cadem entered abruptly. The women sprang for their head scarves but the Lieutenant only had eyes for Sarah.

'I have to get you and Miss Greene out of here now Miss Trent. There is an angry husband and his family outside. They want his wife and children returned.'

The women hurried to the curtain to see whose husband was now banging on the door. One woman screamed in terror and grabbing her children, ran down the hall to lock themselves into their bedroom. Cadem was trying unsuccessfully to drag Sarah and Crystal to the back door but he was hampered by Simon wriggling frantically in his arms. Simon thought it was time to play with the other children. Sarah retrieved her head scarf and put it back on.

'Yasmina, take all the women and children into the panic room. Leave Leila and her children where they are. She won't be able to listen to logic until they have gone away outside.' Sarah started towards the front door causing Crystal to swear.

'What the hell do you think you're doing?'

Sarah glanced back at Crystal, 'Stay here!' she ordered calmly.

'Call the police!' suggested Yasmina as she shepherded her scared tenants out of the room.

As Cadem thrust Simon into Crystal's arms, she said, 'No Cadem, call your boss and go after her!' He nodded and was on Sarah's heels as she walked out of the door. Close enough that Sarah couldn't shut the door in his face but not close enough to pull her back into the refuge.

The crowd was shouting in Arabic but they didn't attempt to break down the door and enter the refuge. When they caught sight of Sarah, their shouting grew louder, more specifically aimed at her.

'Please Miss Trent, go back inside. You should not be here,' begged Cadem. Sarah, though, wasn't paying attention to him as she walked calmly down the steps towards the crowd. 'Miss, it is not safe here for you.' Cadem tried to turn Sarah away, but she refused to listen. The crowd fell back a little, surprised at Sarah's actions. She stared silently at the mob. She was a curious sight as she was not a tall woman, most men towered over her.

'How dare you!' She spoke quietly in Arabic, but everyone could hear her, as they had become reticent. 'So you think I don't understand what you say when you swear at me in Arabic? What do you know of me, to have the right to call me a whore? You make assumptions and over generalizations about people you don't even know.'

'All women are whores! Any excuse they get they have their legs open! They are the devil's servants!' was the defiant shout from the irate husband, Tareek.

Sarah shook her head. 'You are a very, very bitter little man. Is that why you set your wife on fire? Was she unfaithful?'

'No!' He spat out.

'Did she disobey you?'

'No!'

'Not show you the proper respect?'

'No!'

'Did she display herself inappropriately?'

'No!'

'Did she fail in her duty as a mother to care for your children?'

'No!'

'Did she refuse you access to her bed?'

Tareek exploded, 'No! I have the right to discipline my wife!'

Sarah sighed, 'Discipline, Sir, but not attempted murder. You've just admitted before your whole family that there was no reason for you to discipline Leila, let alone throw kerosene over her and lighting her on fire. You are a disgrace as a man and as a Muslim! You've corrupted the teachings of the prophet Mohammad. You'll be going to prison and it will be a long time before you see your sons again!'

Leila's husband roared as he rushed at Sarah, tearing off her head scarf before attempting to grab her. He managed to rip away one of Sarah's long sleeves before Cadem was standing in front of her, his gun pressed against Tareek's nose.

'Step away from the lady or I will blow your face off!' Cadem spoke quietly, calmly and in complete control. Tareek didn't move, his eyes locked with the Lieutenant's.

'You would stand with a woman; a western woman, against one of your own?'

'This woman; in a heartbeat! Stand back or I will shoot you!' Cadem deliberately cocked his gun and waited; his hand as steady as a rock. Sarah stepped out from behind Cadem but didn't get in his line of fire.

'Do you really want a faceless corpse to be the last memory your sons will have of their father?'

Tareek's eyes flicked back to where his young sons stood with the rest of his family. Swallowing hard he took a step back but Cadem didn't lower his weapon. He was just one man against a mob of ten or more, and both Sarah and Cadem gave a sigh of relief as a military vehicle sped towards them through the crowd. Three armed guards and Colonel Nasseur jumped out of the car and swiftly joined Sarah and Cadem in front of the mob.

In The Nick Of Time

The Colonel's eyebrows rose quizzically as he looked calmly down at Sarah. The soldiers reacted to a gesture of his hand, and although they didn't raise their rifles at the crowd, they did remain completely alert for trouble.

'My dear Miss Trent, you must indeed be overwrought by Ambassador Lucas' death, why else would you thoughtlessly put yourself into such danger?' Joseph took Sarah's arm in a firm grip. 'How could you be so crazy, Sarah?' he demanded in an undertone.

'I'm sorry Joseph, but I can't take any more of this!' There were tears in her eyes as she looked beseechingly up at him. 'Surrounded everyday by hatred. Knowing that when we can do so much to help people, a real need, it isn't appreciated. To be called names, spat upon, and ridiculed because we're different. Then to discover Ambassador Lucas murdered because he was trying to help sick children. Here we have women being attacked by the very men the Koran states are supposed to protect them! I've just had enough!' Sarah began to sob uncontrollably and Joseph took her into his arms to comfort her before addressing the family.

'Go home or back to work my friends. You have no business being here. Any attempt to attack the refuge again and you will all be arrested. Do you want to lose your sons as well as your wife and daughters?'

The crowd slowly began to leave the area. Only a few remained, determined to make a point, but with the three armed soldiers at the main door, they soon moved on. Realization of the stupidity of her actions in walking out to confront an angry mob had set in and Sarah found that she had lost the use of her legs as they were shaking so much. It was only Joseph's arm around her waist that kept her upright. Her feet refused to ascend the front steps, so Joseph easily scooped her up into his arms and carried her inside. Cadem led them into the common area. Joseph laid Sarah down on one of the lounges and kept her there with a hand lying gently on her shoulder when she tried to get up.

When Yasmina rushed over to place a pillow beneath Sarah's head, Joseph straightened to address her, 'My apologies, Madame Yasmina, for intruding upon you like this. We will remove our male presence from your refuge as soon as Miss Trent can be moved. I will leave the guards outside to prevent further attacks.'

'You're always welcome Colonel.' Yasmina adjusted her scarf. 'We don't fear your presence amongst us.'

'Thank you Madame. Are your tenants all right?'

'Yes thank you Colonel.'

Sarah struggled to sit up and Crystal pressed a glass of water into her hand. She took a deep breath and let it out slowly before even attempting to speak. 'I'm so sorry Yasmina. It wasn't my intention to make matters worse for the refuge. It just made me so angry that Tareek would dare come here and demand the return of his wife after all that he did to her.'

Yasmina chuckled, 'I think being told by a westerner and a woman that he was abusing the teachings of Mohammad really was the highlight for me.'

Crystal shook her head, 'I was impressed with Cadem, how quickly he had his gun in that's guy's face when he ripped off Sarah's scarf.'

The Lieutenant turned red and Sarah put the glass down so that she could get to her feet. 'If it's safe to leave, then I suggest we do so before the Lieutenant is further embarrassed,' Sarah suggested.

Without thinking Joseph put his arm around Sarah's waist and briefly pressed a kiss against her forehead. Not by so much as a flicker of an eyelash did Yasmina reveal that she had witnessed anything unusual. Joseph escorted Crystal, Simon and Sarah to the back door as Cadem paused beside Yasmina but before he could speak she shook her head.

'I saw nothing Lieutenant!'

Cadem nodded, 'Thank you Madame,' he followed his Commanding Officer out to his car, thankful that no shots had needed to be fired.

A Leisurely Afternoon

As the rain petered out so did James' and Marianne's energy. They spent the afternoon leisurely exercising Jeb and Ash around the compound, also checking the garden and buildings to see if the storm had done any damage. They held hands, threw balls for the dogs to chase, talked and laughed. It was idyllic so long as they didn't think about the mayhem and instability the country was in. With extreme reluctance, Marianne finally went home before it became dark. She had ironing to do and James had to attend a meeting with the other Ambassadors to discuss their future in Pangani. Personal moments could only be fleeting but they both hoped that this one wouldn't be the conclusion of their relationship, merely the beginning.

The Intruder

It was with a feeling of great relief that Sarah stepped into a hot soothing bubble bath that evening. It had been a gruelling couple of weeks. Her fair skin was still bruised all over. Her wounded hand hung over the side of the bath so that the book she held didn't get wet. The water had just started to get cool and Sarah was considering getting out when she heard a noise in the kitchen. Simon, who was lying on the floor beside the bath, also looked up alert. Sarah lay very still, waiting breathlessly hoping that it had just been her imagination. Just as she started to relax again, the sound repeated. Quietly she rose up out of the bath, wrapping herself in a towelling robe and padded her way softly to the door and stepped warily into the passageway.

She shut the puppy in the bathroom, so that he wouldn't get hurt.

The house was again silent but Sarah wasn't prepared to risk the chance. Heading towards the kitchen, she picked up a ceramic figurine to use as a weapon. The kitchen was empty as she entered but Sarah didn't immediately lower her guard. The door behind her slammed shut. She was grasped from behind. Her elbow rammed back into her assailant's stomach freeing one of her hands. She reached back and grabbed his hair, yanking as hard as she could. Her attacker cried out as he released her. Sarah sprang away from him. He was tall, his face barely visible due to the lack of light. She didn't care. She swung her statue and cracked him across his head. As he tried to grab her again, she kicked him in the groin. A final whack across the head saw him drop to his knees. She pushed him down to the ground.

As he rolled professionally onto his back, Sarah gasped in surprise as she finally saw his face. 'Joseph!' Her guard was immediately dropped. He used her surprise to his advantage, hooking her legs from behind with his own and rolled her to the ground. He knelt over her as his hands pinned down her arms.

'You must never lose concentration, Sarah!' He ordered, breathing slightly faster. Sarah tried to get up but found that she couldn't compete against the Colonel's strength.

'Joseph, what are you doing here?'

'I wanted to see how you were after this morning's excitement as well as the opportunity to finally talk to you alone,' the glance that he cast down her robe-covered body was far from his usual professional manner. 'I was just thinking that perhaps I should surprise you more often!' He raised one hand to feel the back of his head. 'The headache is more than worth it for such a view.'

Sarah glanced down to find that the top of her robe was gaping to reveal the naked swell of her breasts beneath. Hastily she drew the robe together and hoped that her face wasn't as scarlet as it felt. 'Joseph!'

There's Something I Want To Ask You

He didn't immediately answer, picking Sarah up so that they were both standing. One arm surrounded her waist as his other hand cupped her face. He lowered his head towards hers but Sarah wouldn't allow the kiss to develop into anything serious. She felt self-conscious in only a bathrobe.

'I'll just throw some clothes on and let Simon out of the bathroom.' As she disappeared into her bedroom, Colonel Nasseur sat down at the kitchen table and checked if his skull was actually bleeding. *I am quite happily but painfully pleased with how well Sarah defended herself. It was only her surprise at the end that had been her undoing; aside from the fact I had been pulling my punches. If I had been in earnest, Sarah would never have hurt me, let alone been able to land a single blow.*

Sarah made a cup of tea and found an ice pack for Joseph's head where she had hit him with the statue, before they sat down in her cosy lounge room. She was more appropriately dressed in a light cotton maxi dress. Sarah sipped thoughtfully on her tea. Joseph placed his cup and the ice pack on the coffee table and leant forward to take her cup away before grasping her hands between his own and going down on one knee.

'Sarah, I want you to marry me. Tomorrow we'll go down to the registry office and make it official!'

She stared at him dumbfounded; his close proximity made it hard for her to focus on the real issues at stake. She fought hard to keep her thoughts on track and not on the desirable body so close to her. Seeing that she was stunned, Joseph continued, 'I do not expect you to convert to Islam. I would like our children to be brought up Muslim.'

'We've discussed this before and never resolved the problems our relationship would create!' Sarah looked at him in total amazement.

He shook his head. 'I am sick and tired of worrying about what other people will think or say. For once I want to consider my and your needs first!'

'Oh Joseph, please don't do anything you'll regret for the rest of your life! If you satisfy your mother by marrying one of the brides she wants then perhaps she mightn't raise an objection to us.'

Joseph Nasseur laughed. 'My darling, you are my one and only love! It will be you or no one! Any further objections?'

'I had best not; you seem to have all the answers!' Sarah managed a mischievous smile, allowing herself to be drawn into his embrace upon the sofa. Joseph removed from his pocket a ring box and opening it, presented it to Sarah. With shaking hands, he removed the ring and slid it onto her finger. It was extremely beautiful as the diamonds sparkled in the light. She drew him into a kiss that could have easily lasted all night.

More Intruders

Simon suddenly barked. Someone was at the back of the house, trying to enter.

'Are you expecting someone?' Joseph looked suspiciously at Sarah.

She shook her head as they both rose to their feet. 'I was planning a night in the bath with a book.'

'Stay here, I'll go and look,' ordered Joseph, cautiously leaving the room and heading down the hall. Three men were as surprised to see the Colonel as he was to see them. He managed to knock two down without the least bit of trouble. Then Ahkman Amed was sent flying onto his back from a single high kick and his brothers were back on their feet and rushed into the scuffle. As the Amed brothers were knocked down once more, Ahkman pulled out a gun and shot Joseph. Not once, but several times. Koyad and Saladin Amed stared at their brother in disbelief. Joseph fell to the floor, blood pouring from his chest and leg.

Hearing the fighting start and realising that her mobile phone was in her bedroom, Sarah ran to the telephone and dialled Gary's mobile number. She didn't hear Ahkman race up the passage after the shots had been fired. He hit her over the head with the butt of his gun and she collapsed to the floor, dropping the telephone receiver. Ahkman placed it back into the cradle. Simon jumped out from under the sofa and attacked the Embassy security guard, biting him around the ankles. Ahkman kicked Simon until finally the pup yelped in pain and ran to hide under Sarah's bed.

'You never said anything about anyone getting hurt Ahkman! You said that she would be alone!' protested Koyad as his other brother Saladin slung Sarah's unconscious body over his shoulder.

'Desperate times call for desperate measures! Now hurry before someone comes to investigate those shots!' Ahkman led them out of the house. On arrival they had knocked out Hamid, the guard. Ahkman and his brothers disappeared into the night. The very essence of life drained from the Colonel's body as he was dragged out of the house by Ahkman and Koyad. They threw their victims into the back of a van. Their plans had gone awry but they weren't going to give up now.

I'm Too Late

Parking behind the Colonel's car outside Sarah's house, Lieutenant Cadem got out of his vehicle, filled with apprehension and he called out to the security guard. Receiving no answer, a chill raced down his spine. He had tried to contact

Colonel Nasseur by both mobile and Sarah's landline. Neither attempt had been answered, which was why he was now there.

A rustle and a groan came from a bush to his right. He immediately pounced upon the sound, discovering Hamid, the guard. Cadem couldn't get any sense out of him. So Cadem left Hamid to recover as he headed cautiously into the house with his gun drawn. Seeing the passageway covered in blood caused a cold fury to rush up in the young Lieutenant. He made certain that no one was still in the house to take him by surprise before he whipped out his mobile and called Inspector Lowe and then Gary Winters.

We Have To Stop The Bleeding

'Miss Trent! Wake up please Miss Trent!' Sarah came back to consciousness in a very painful and uncomfortable position. She cautiously opened her eyes as she seemed to be bouncing around in some kind of noisy sardine can.

'Miss Trent! Please I need your help!' The desperation of the plea snapped the Secretary back into full awareness. The bouncing mechanical chamber turned out to be the back of a clapped out old van. Koyad Amed was kneeling over the unconscious and bleeding body of Joseph Nasseur, as he struggled to plug up the bullet holes that were draining away Joseph's life force.

'Joseph! What've you done to him?' Sarah tried to steady herself as she rose to her knees. Pushing Koyad's hands aside she ripped open the Colonel's shirt to reveal his chest wounds. 'Do you have any bandages, anything sterile?'

Koyad handed over the first aid kit he had been using. 'The leg wound was the more fatal so I started there. Here, take this and put as much pressure as you can on the shoulder wound.' Koyad placed a sterile pad in Sarah's hands as he opened his last bandage. Koyad was an orderly at the main hospital and knew what he was doing. The bandage was barely enough to hold the pad in place and there were other wounds to still deal with. Sarah grabbed hold of the hem of her dress in her bloodied hands and began to tear her dress into one long strip. Koyad used the last of the sterile solution to cleanse the bullet wound through Joseph's forearm before pressing a dressing over it. He picked up the end of Sarah's strip of dress and began to wrap Joseph's arm.

'We have to get him to the hospital!' Sarah used the tiny scissors in the kit to cut off the end of her dress just above the knees. There was an awkward silence as Sarah cradled Joseph's head in her lap. 'Well? What on earth is going on? Ahkman, why were you and your brothers at my home? Why aren't we heading towards the hospital?' Ahkman was in the driver's seat. Saladin, in the front seat beside him, was constantly checking the side mirror for anyone following them.

'You were supposed to be alone! No one should have got hurt!' Ahkman explained.

'Well someone did get hurt! Take us to the hospital and I'll arrange for Inspector Lowe to drop all charges for firearms and abduction.' Sarah glanced down at Joseph, who was sweating and moaning but not conscious. 'Ahkman please, end this now! Let it continue and it's going to become very messy! Joseph's people will hunt you down,' Sarah used a scrap from her dress to wipe Joseph's brow.

'Koyad...' Ahkman's voice caused Sarah to hope that he had listened, 'Tape her mouth and secure her hands.'

Sarah screamed in disbelief but with an injured man between them she couldn't fight off being bound and gagged. Koyad glanced at the back of his brother's head but didn't question his older brother's authority. Sarah's eyes pleaded with him in the dim light but Koyad dared not disobey.

I Should Have Stayed With Her

Gary arrived at Sarah's home to find a forensic team already at work. Cadem was standing on the verandah looking rather grim as he talked to Inspector Lowe. The Major, turning quite white, sprinted the short distance to the house.

'What the hell's going on? I got a call from Sarah's phone but it was cut off before I could answer it. Is Sarah all right?'

Inspector Lowe headed inside to supervise his forensic team as Cadem led Gary towards a couple of chairs on the verandah.

'Major, it's not good,' Cadem said gently.

'Oh God! Oh God, No!'

Cadem urged him to sit down. 'When the Colonel did not answer his phone I came to investigate. I found Hamid knocked unconscious and the Colonel and Miss Trent missing.'

'Oh my God! I should have stayed! Damn it all. Why didn't I stay to protect her?'

Cadem shook his head. 'Then you would be the one perhaps bleeding to death. Berating yourself won't help, Major.'

'Con! I bet that toad has something to do with all of this!' Gary jumped to his feet.

'Not personally, anyway, as we have had him shadowed. At this moment he is paralytic in the Pink Pagoda Lounge. He was not one of the men who did this.'

Gary looked at Cadem in surprise. 'How do you know there was more than one man?'

'It would have taken more than one man to overpower Colonel Nasseur. The bullet holes in the walls suggest that one of them at least had a gun.'

'Bloody hell!' Major Winters groaned, 'What a nightmare! What about Simon? Is he all right?'

Cadem looked a little guilty. 'I'm sorry; I have not looked for him.'

'Do you think they'll let us in to find him?' Gary glanced through the window at the forensic officers clad in their sterile plastic overalls.

This question was answered by the return of Inspector Lowe. 'Sorry to interrupt, but one of my people has found a dog under a bed. It won't come out for him, and I wondered if a familiar voice might coax him out.'

Gary nodded. 'I'll come and get him.' He followed the Inspector inside, being careful to walk where the Inspector did so as to not destroy any possible evidence. Gary knelt down to peer under the bed and seeing Simon huddled up against the wall, he felt like killing someone for terrifying the puppy. Hearing Gary's reassuring voice, Simon slowly crawled out. He whimpered as Gary lifted him up but a quick examination couldn't determine any major damage, just some very sore ribs. One thing Gary did find was a piece of material caught on one of Simon's teeth. Carefully removing it, Gary placed it into an evidence bag that Inspector Lowe had ready. Glancing at it closely, the Inspector's eyes gleamed.

'Unless the pup has bled, we may have the blood of one of the attackers.'

Gary carried Simon and followed Lowe back to the front door. 'That'll be great if the attacker has a previous record,' said the Major.

'Have faith Major Winters.' The Inspector frowned at him. 'I thought Christians were supposed to believe in miracles?'

Gary grunted. 'I'll believe in miracles when I see both Sarah and Joseph alive!' He gently laid Simon on the back seat of his car before turning to Cadem. 'Let me know the second you hear anything. It doesn't matter about what time it is. What a mess!'

Cadem nodded. There was going to have to be a lot of faith if they were to get through this nightmare.

The Cottage

Allowing Koyad to assist her out of the van, Sarah looked around for any signs to indicate where the Amed brothers had taken them. They were no longer in the city; the road behind them seemed little more than a dirt track. The only lights were the headlights of the van, a lantern inside the cottage and the multitude of stars above them. Saladin and Ahkman came round the back of the van to assist Koyad lift an unconscious Joseph out. Ahkman saw Sarah looking around and roughly grabbed her arm.

'If you run, we will kill him!'

Sarah looked at him in surprise, she was certainly not thinking of going anywhere without Joseph. Not that she could say anything as she still had tape over her mouth. Lifting Joseph between them, Koyad and Saladin carried him into the cottage with Ahkman and Sarah following. The cottage was a fairly basic wooden structure with four rooms, consisting of two bedrooms, a bathroom and a kitchen/lounge area. Jaeda, Saladin's wife, turned away from the stove as the group entered and let out an exclamation of disbelief.

'Silence your woman Sal! Put him in the smaller bedroom, while we sort this out,' ordered Ahkman. Ignoring Jaeda's explosion of indignation, the brothers placed Joseph on the mattress on the floor of the second bedroom before thrusting Sarah in and locking the door.

Despite the closed door, Sarah could easily hear Jaeda screaming in their native tongue at the men, 'are you out of your minds? You've brought not only a death sentence down upon us but our entire family!'

Sarah sank down onto the mattress and wiped the sweat from Joseph's brow. Koyad had tied her hands in front so that she was able to rip off the tape from her mouth. Not that there was any point screaming, she had already seen that there was no one close by to rescue them. As the screaming match continued in the next room, Sarah took a moment to scope out the possibilities of escape. That didn't take long. There was only the internal door, and one window which had a bar down the middle. Even if they could remove the bar, Sarah didn't know how far she could get with Joseph in his current state. The bleeding may have stopped but he seriously needed medical assistance.

Glancing down at the engagement ring on her finger, Sarah twisted it nervously as she contemplated having to use it to barter for basic necessities for the Colonel. Taking a deep breath Sarah hoped that her next actions were going to be the right ones. She knocked on the door. Not banging, not timidly, but firmly enough to be heard over the argument. The voices ceased and Sarah was relieved that it was Jaeda who opened the door.

'Please Miss Trent; do not make this more difficult for all of us!'

Sarah reached out for Jaeda's hands as she was about to close the door again. 'I'm not trying to be difficult but I need to use the bathroom.'

Jaeda glanced back briefly at the men but opened the door for Sarah to pass through. Ahkman ordered Jaeda to go into the bathroom with Sarah as she untied her hands, but she refused, locking the door instead. Sarah didn't desperately need to use the bathroom but it gave her a chance to clean off the Colonel's blood from her hands and face. The main reason was she wanted to begin developing a relationship with Jaeda which might assist in getting medical attention for Joseph. Jaeda brought a clean towel for Sarah to dry her hands.

'Jaeda, could I please have a blanket for Joseph? It'll get cold soon, also a bowl of water so that I can try to bring his temperature down?'

'Of course Miss Trent.'

Sarah didn't resist as Jaeda led her back in to the smaller bedroom. *I want to ask for so much more but I have to build up Jaeda's trust.* Almost immediately Jaeda returned with a couple of blankets, a pillow and a bowl of water with clean rags. Sarah took them looking Jaeda briefly in the eyes as she thanked her.

'Jaeda, if they won't take Joseph to the hospital then I'll need to be able to take care of him. If he dies, then it'll be so much harder for any of us to get out of this alive.' Sarah glanced down at the ring on her finger. Jaeda followed her glance and took Sarah's hands into her own to stare at the sparkling diamonds. 'I'll give you that ring if you can get medical supplies for me,' Sarah offered.

Jaeda shook her head, 'You are his woman?'

Sarah's expression softened as she glanced back at Joseph. 'He asked me to marry him tonight.'

'And you said yes?'

Glancing briefly at the ring, Sarah nodded, unable to stop the tears welling up in her eyes. Jaeda pressed her fingers before releasing her hands. 'I will help you!'

Sarah caught back a sob in her throat as tears fell. 'Thank you!' As Jaeda left the room and the lock clicked, Sarah didn't feel that this situation was completely hopeless.

Grim Report

Less than half an hour later, Gary had gathered Kevin, Marianne, James and Crystal together at the Residency. The first thing Gary did upon entering the Residency was to place Simon gently on one of the lounges before helping himself to a large scotch. He downed it in one gulp. *I know I shouldn't do it as I really need all my faculties, but I suppose I'm in shock.* He had called Kevin and Marianne as he had driven to the Embassy, so their arrival hadn't been too long after his. Against his better judgment, Gary had called Con but only getting his voice mail, he left a brief message about Sarah being kidnapped.

When the other diplomats had assembled, as calmly as possible, Gary explained all that he knew, but left out any mention of Colonel Nasseur being with Sarah. Crystal gasped in shock and immediately changed seats to put her arm around Marianne, who looked stunned.

'This can't be happening,' Marianne managed to say, in deep shock. 'Not Sarah! What has she ever done to harm anyone?'

'It was probably her innocence that made them choose her.' Gary sighed.

James rose to his feet and wandered over to a window to open it and allow a cool breeze to blow through the room. 'So what do they want in return?'

Gary would have preferred to not answer that question in front of Crystal and Marianne. 'If they had only wanted to make a statement, they would've simply killed Sarah as they had Lucas. The most likely options are ransom for money, for political influence or a swap for one of their own that may be imprisoned. The fifth option is highly unlikely.'

James turned around, his eyebrows raised. 'What is the unlikely fifth option?'

Gary sighed, 'The slave trade.'

'But that's illegal!' stated Crystal in surprise.

Gary nodded. 'Very! There are underground networks throughout the country.'

Turning back to stare at the night sky, James said, 'We may lose, no matter which option the kidnappers chose. If it's money they want, we have nothing to bargain with. The Australian Government will not pay a ransom demand.'

That prospect silenced them to reflect upon the difficulties of their situation. There wasn't time, though, to pause for long. James had to contact Canberra. Gary tried to call Cadem to get an update before he drove Marianne home. Crystal had suggested that the older woman stay at the Residency, but Marianne wanted some time alone. So Crystal checked Simon over and finding only bruises, she fed him before bringing his basket into her room. No one got much sleep that night. One of their people was in serious danger and there would be no peace of mind until she was returned to them.

Please Stay Still

Although the shouting was now all over, Sarah still didn't know what exactly the Amed brothers wanted. *The vehicle has driven away and the resulting silence is even more disturbing than the arguing had been. I am beginning to worry about Joseph. He has regained consciousness at least half a dozen times but never for any great length of time or to comprehend what had happened. I hope that this isn't permanent as I fear that I'm not able to do this alone.* She was just dozing as she sat by his side when Joseph groaned and opened his eyes.

'Sarah?'

'Don't try and move Joseph, if you start bleeding again I'll not be able to stop it.'

There was a definite silence as the Colonel's eyes adjusted to the limited light afforded by the full moon streaming in through the undressed window. 'No matter how I analyse that statement I do not see how I can take comfort from it!'

Sarah chuckled, briefly pressing her lips against his forehead. 'Sorry but I really can't afford for you to jump up and be in attack mode!'

'So apart from feeling like I was run over by a tank how bad is it?' Joseph used his undamaged hand to push back the blanket to determine the extent of his injuries.

'I'm afraid the head ache was probably when I smacked you with a statue when I thought you were a burglar.'

'Mea culpa,' He reached out to lace his fingers through hers.

'Well as for bullet holes, there's one in your right arm, one in your right shoulder and one in your left leg. Koyad did what he could to stop you bleeding to death. I would be happier if they'd taken you to the hospital.'

'You know your attackers?' Joseph's fingers tightened momentarily in surprise.

Sarah nodded, 'Ahkman is the daytime Embassy Security Guard, and the other two are his brothers Koyad and Saladin.'

'Damnation! Aside from Con Zuco I did not think you were in any danger from within the Embassy! Do you have any idea what they want? Do we have anything to negotiate with?'

'They haven't told me what they want. I've some money put aside and a few nice pieces of jewellery but nothing worth all of this.'

Joseph shook his head and then wished he hadn't. 'They'll be after something bigger.'

A shiver ran through Sarah. 'Well I don't know what it can be as the Australian Government doesn't pay ransom demands.'

Hearing a note of fear in her voice, the Colonel changed the subject, 'We will worry about that later. I need your help to get up. I need to use the... facilities.'

'Only if it can't be avoided.' Sarah rose to her feet, 'They have supplied us with a bucket in the corner but if it's only fluid then Jaeda gave me a plastic bottle. She seems to understand that we need to keep you as still as possible until we have better medical supplies.'

Joseph tried to raise himself up on one elbow and found it took an incredible effort to not pass out. Sarah didn't even try to translate the oath he uttered in his native language.

'Just the bottle,' Joseph managed when he was able to speak at all. Sarah felt across the other side of the room and brought back a two litre empty plastic bottle.

'Do you need my help?' She knelt back down beside him. 'It's just that I've never done anything like this before and to be frank I'm a little nervous.'

Despite the pain he was in, Joseph managed to smile, 'If you could undo my belt and trousers that would be a great help.'

'One of the Ameds took your belt. I suppose they thought you could use it as a weapon or something.' When completed Sarah placed the bottle into his hand and rising again to her feet, moved away to the window. Staring out into the night, she softly hummed until he asked her to take the bottle away again.

As Joseph lay flat on his back once more, Sarah rearranged the blanket over him. His fingers brushed against the torn hem of her dress and his body went rigid in anger.

'Sarah, what happened to your dress? Did they touch you? Have they...'

She interrupted, 'It was nothing like that! Koyad only had a very basic first aid kit in the van so I tore off the bottom of my dress for bandages.'

The rigidity left him as he sighed in relief. 'What can you tell me about where we are? Is there any possibility of you getting away to raise the alarm?'

'Ahkman warned me that if I tried to escape they would immediately kill you. I think it took about 45 to 60 minutes to get here and even though it was dark, I didn't see any other houses around us.'

'It does not matter. You must be exhausted. Help me to move a little so that we can both fit on the mattress.'

Sarah tried to protest but she couldn't deny that she was very tired. Sliding onto the mattress beside Joseph, she laid her blanket over the top of them both. He put his good arm around her shoulders and drew her closer to his side.

'I don't want to hurt you!' she momentarily resisted.

Joseph chuckled, 'You won't. Go to sleep.'

'Joseph?'

'Yes?'

'I'm afraid!'

'That is only natural.'

'Not for myself. You've lost so much blood and should be in a hospital.'

'Sarah, go to sleep. We will deal with that tomorrow.'

'If you're not actually dying, do you think we can pretend you are so we can bluff them into letting us go sooner?'

He chuckled, 'Yes, my heart, now go to sleep!' Although they were silent, he could feel her shaking. About to say something Joseph realised that Sarah was actually laughing and smiling, he closed his eyes to try and sleep. He too was relieved that they were both still alive and together.

MONDAY

Ransom Demand

Arriving at the Embassy compound, Gary's attention was momentarily distracted and he didn't immediately react when a child ran up to the gate and threw a rock at his car. It hit the roof and bounced off. Gary stamped on the brakes and jumped out of the car. Ahkman had been standing by the open gate and ran out into the street after the lad, but young legs and stamina was no match for the guard to compete with. Gary picked up the rock and untied the envelope that was attached to it with string. Ahkman came back to the Major, puffing for breath.

'I'm sorry Sir, I could not catch him.'

Absently Gary nodded. 'That's all right Ahkman.' He went back to his car and parked it before heading into the Residency.

James looked up, surprised when Gary entered unceremoniously. When asked what was wrong, the Major only grunted as he pulled out his mobile phone, 'Ransom Demand,' was all Gary would say. The phone number he dialled was immediately answered. 'Sorry to disturb you so early Inspector Lowe. The ransom demand has just arrived and I thought you'd want to see it.'

There was a pause before the Inspector answered, 'Have you opened the envelope yet?'

'No, I've only touched the envelope. I thought you'd fingerprint the letter.'

'I will be with you immediately. If your Ambassador insists on opening the letter, use protective gloves.' The Inspector hung up and James finally gained Gary's attention.

Briefly Gary described the method of delivering the letter and poured himself a cup of coffee as he sat down to await the policeman's arrival. James left him to brood and went back to his bedroom to finish dressing for work. Gary was on his second cup of coffee and Simon had jumped up onto his lap when Crystal entered the dining room, wrapped in a silky dressing gown. She looked him over rather carefully and she sighed sadly.

'You're not going to help Sarah by beating yourself up over her abduction. It wasn't your fault!' Crystal laid a reassuring hand on his shoulder.

'I should never have left her!'

'You're not Superman, Gary. Could you have fought off three or four armed guys? They didn't care who they hurt.'

Gary shook his head. 'You don't understand. I couldn't tell you last night as I don't yet have permission to reveal their relationship to the others, but Joseph was with Sarah. One of them was badly wounded. There was a massive pool of blood in the hall.'

In disbelief, Crystal sank into a chair beside him, 'Oh no! No! Not that!'

Easing Simon to the floor and rising to his feet, Gary refilled his coffee cup. 'Cadem promised to keep me informed of the results of the blood tests. That should at least tell us who was injured.' They sat together in silence until the older dogs informed them that a car had pulled into the compound.

Bathroom Privileges

'Damnation!'

This curse woke Sarah abruptly and before she could fully comprehend what was going on, she was on her feet ready to defend Joseph.

'Sorry Sarah, I was just trying to get up.' He was perched on his good hand as he leant against the wall for support. Sarah wiped her hand across her face.

'Okay. Bottle, bucket or do I bang on the door?'

'Door.'

'Good, I want that option too.' Sarah knocked on the door before returning to Joseph's side to assist him to rise.

'I would love to be a gentleman and allow you to go first but...'

Sarah slipped his good arm over her shoulder as she supported his weight and headed for the door.

'That's all right. I'm going to be selfish and ask Jaeda for a shower. You'll have to settle for a sponge bath.'

'I look forward to it.'

Saladin opened the door and took the other side of the wounded man. They helped him into the bathroom and Sarah left Saladin to assist Joseph.

Jaeda didn't force Sarah back into the spare room but offered her a cup of tea and a chair at the kitchen table. 'Koyad will be dropping off some medical supplies once his shift is over this morning Miss Trent.'

'Thank you Jaeda.' Sarah sipped her tea. 'Could I beg a shower and clean clothes?'

'Of course Miss Trent,' Jaeda checked that her husband was still busy in the bathroom, 'if the Colonel is fit enough to be moved, I will help you escape this afternoon.'

Sarah stared at Jaeda in surprise. 'You'd defy your husband?'

'I tried to persuade Sal and his brothers that this was wrong but apparently I know nothing as I am only a mere woman. I have three young children and an elderly mother to consider. I will do anything to protect them.'

Sarah looked across at the external door as a vehicle pulled up outside. 'Okay, thank you Jaeda.'

As Koyad entered the cottage with a large backpack, which he threw onto the kitchen table, Saladin opened the bathroom door and struggled to support Joseph out of the room. Koyad hurried forward to take the Colonel's other arm. Sarah cast a quick glance over her fiancé to make sure that moving him had not started any major bleeding again. He wasn't so Sarah nipped into the bathroom. Laying Joseph back onto the mattress Koyad pulled Saladin out of the room.

'These people aren't house guests!' Koyad protested.

'Jaeda's right,' Saladin pulled his arm away. 'Ahkman should never have forced us into this ridiculous position.'

Koyad shook his head. 'Disobey Ahkman and he'll make us all suffer. Just keep strong. I'm going to bed.'

'Aren't you going at help Miss Trent with the Colonel's wounds?' demanded Jaeda, putting breakfast for Saladin on the table.

'We had three car accidents, a shot gun victim and a breech birth in Emergency last night. I'm exhausted.' Koyad didn't wait for their response as he left them.

Coming out of the bathroom, Sarah finished her tea before addressing Jaeda, 'Thank you, I appreciate your kindness. Could I please ask for a bowl of warm water and a sponge to wash Joseph while I change his dressings?'

'Of course Miss Trent.'

Saladin looked at Jaeda in disbelief but she ignored him as she prepared what Sarah needed. Entering the spare room, Sarah left the door open to allow Jaeda to easily carry in the water.

Saladin looked at the open door but Jaeda threw a wet sponge at his head.

'I want to come out of this madness untainted by your brother's stupidity!' Jaeda slammed the door shut behind her as she entered the spare room, with the backpack of medical supplies over her shoulder. Sarah was attempting to remove Joseph's trousers but he was refusing to let her undo them. Kneeling down Jaeda cut away the section of trouser surrounding the leg wound instead. Working together the women removed the makeshift bandages, sponged him clean, sterilised the wounds and redressed them with the supplies from the backpack. Sarah was happier about the cleanliness of Joseph's wounds but still would rather he was in a hospital. Jaeda collected up all the used bandages and dressings as she rose to her feet.

'I'll just get you a towel and something to wear so that you may shower Miss Trent.' Jaeda stepped out of the room locking it again.

'Why don't you offer a chocolate on their pillow?'

'Don't start with me Sal! I'm thinking of our children!' Jaeda slammed the main bedroom door as she entered that room. Returning with a towel and a cotton dress, Jaeda let Sarah out, glaring defiantly at her husband, daring him to say anything else. Sarah thanked Jaeda as she slipped into the bathroom, hoping that this tension wouldn't hamper their escape plan.

Analysing The Ransom Note

Inspector Lowe strode smartly into the Residency. He greeted Gary respectfully, but a glint entered his eyes as he glanced at Crystal.

'Good morning Miss Greene. Another wonderful ensemble you are wearing today.'

Crystal glanced down to find that her dressing gown was lying open to reveal a sexy, silk negligee. Laughing she drew her robe around her.

'Thank you Inspector, but I don't think you're here to admire my nightie. I suppose you'll want Dad present when you open the envelope. I'll go and get him.' Crystal rose to her feet and would have put her words into action, when James entered the room. 'I'll go and dress so that I'm not a distraction to the poor Inspector.'

The Inspector bowed as she left, her lively wit was something he could appreciate. *With our nerves all on end, we need something to lighten the tension.*

Pulling on a pair of latex gloves, Inspector Lowe took the envelope that Gary held out. He carefully examined the envelope, a cheap quality paper, which appeared to be second hand. The flap had been stuck down with sticky tape. The Inspector slid a penknife into the flap and slit it open. He laid it on the table before opening the letter and read it aloud.

'If you want to see Miss Sarah Trent alive we want one million Australian dollars. The money is to be deposited in the Pangani bank account 4579 6004 3578 by next Monday's close of business.'

'Can you trace the abductors through the bank account?' James grunted.

Lowe shrugged his shoulders. 'We will try, but if they have any brains it will be a dummy account. As soon as the money is deposited into it, they would siphon it off into a dozen different accounts.'

Inspector Lowe's attention returned to the letter, and he held it up to the light. 'Hum! This paper is neither A4 nor foolscap. It is of excellent quality, not matching the envelope. It has a watermark. The letters are cut out from the 'Pangani Times'.'

Gary frowned. 'Could I have a look?'

The Inspector handed him a pair of gloves to put on before passing over the letter. Gary also held it up to the light before rising and striding out of the room to the writing desk in the study. He removed a sheet of Embassy headed paper and compared them.

'That's why it's not standard size,' explained Gary as he re-entered the dining room. 'We received a box full of headed paper that had too many mistakes for Ambassador Lucas to tolerate. Instead of wasting the lot, Sarah cut off the letter head and it was used as note paper.'

James' eyes nearly popped out of his head. 'Then the ransom note came from someone working in this Embassy?'

Gary shook his head. 'Only one problem, Sarah gave a ream of paper to the children at the hospital and another ream to the local orphanage. Sarah also gave some of the paper to the native staff at the Embassy. So I'm afraid that opens up the field slightly.'

Inspector Lowe pulled out his notebook. 'I'll start with the staff at the Embassy and once they are cleared we can widen the search.'

'I'll get a list of names and addresses if you'll come up to my office.' Gary handed the letter back to the Inspector, who slipped the letter and envelope into an evidence bag before following Gary out of the Residency and across the compound. The local staff would be allowed to remain but Inspector Lowe would place a man of his own in the Embassy to keep an eye on them.

Con Freaks Out

Con was still on cloud nine as his car approached the Embassy. *I'd had the perfect weekend even with all the rain. The Friday night pick up ended up continuing over the weekend in two days and three nights of freaky, wild and reckless sex. If it wasn't for the fact her husband was due home this morning, I'd probably still be there.* The attention focused on the Embassy with the added security and the media crews finally sunk into Con's narcissistic brain that something was going on. Jeb and Ash barked angrily as Con drove through the gate.

Gary was escorting Inspector Lowe out of the Embassy and back to his car as Con pulled up beside them. The German Shepherds continued to bark at Con until the Major said quietly, 'Sit!' The dogs immediately stopped barking and sat, waiting for Gary's next command. Inspector Lowe hid a smile as he half expected the Public Affairs Officer to also sit as commanded.

'What the hell is going on Gary?' Con got out of his car, excitement flooded through his veins at the thought of how many drinks this might be worth for him amongst the other newsmen in Kathou. 'Has something happened to our new Ambassador?'

Gary frowned at Con's obvious enthusiasm. 'No!' He turned his back on Con to shake hands with Inspector Lowe. 'Please let me know the instant there are any developments.'

The Inspector smiled, 'Of course Major Winters,' His eyes flicked briefly to Con before adding to Gary, 'Good Luck!'

Con immediately began to bombard Gary with questions but the Major refused to answer until the policeman had driven out of the compound. Gary picked up a tennis ball and threw it for the dogs before he attempted to answer Con's questions.

'Lighten up Gary! Nothing can be that bad!' Con followed him up the steps of the main building. Looking back at Con, Gary swallowed hard on the lump that was trying to choke him.

'You'd know what was going on if you ever checked your bloody phone!' Gary managed to master his temper before he continued, 'Sarah was abducted last night from her home.'

The grin evaporated from Con's face as he stared unblinkingly at Gary. The Major wondered if he was going to remain frozen for a long time. Turning away to continue inside,

Gary was momentarily taken by surprise as Con suddenly punched him in the face.

Before he could stop himself Gary had grabbed Con by his arms and lifted him off his feet. It took every bit of his training to calm down enough so that he didn't kill Con.

'I'll let that one slide, but do it again and I will break your arm!' Gary slowly released the Public Affairs Officer so that his feet touched the ground again.

'What the fuck were you doing? Why weren't you protecting her? If you hadn't been fooling around with the boss' daughter you mighta been able to do your fucking job properly!' Con shouted into Gary's face. The Major let him get it out of his system and only spoke when Con finally stopped.

'Have you finished?' Gary's tone was a monotone.

Con dragged in a haggard breath. 'Yes!'

'Good!' Gary swiftly bent to grab Con by the knees and lifted him over his shoulder in a fireman's lift. He ignored Con's protests as he carried him across the compound and dropped him into the pool.

'When you've cooled off, I'll explain what's happened.' Gary turned and strode back to the main building. *As if I haven't been beating myself up ever since I had arrived at Sarah's cottage the previous night and had seen the pool of blood in her hallway. I don't need Con's accusations or being slugged in the face for that matter. Under any other circumstances I would've knocked Con into next week but if he hadn't seen any of the text messages I had sent; then my announcement had been a complete shock. Desperately I want a double scotch but that isn't going to help anyone, so I will settle for a very strong black coffee. I hope that when the time came for my talk with Con, we are both calm enough to avoid a fight. The scandal of putting Con into hospital would be too much for the Embassy to withstand as well as abduction and someone had lost an awful amount of blood, perhaps even a murder.*

Cadem's Update

It was less than half an hour later when Major Winters escorted Cadem into the Ambassador's office. The Lieutenant was as tidy as ever in his uniform but he looked as if he hadn't slept all night. Crystal was helping out with some typing and filing, and was in her father's office when Cadem entered. She looked from Gary to Cadem and collected up her notebook.

'Do you want me to leave?' she asked.

Cadem shook his head, 'No, Miss Greene, but could you ask Mrs. Davis and Mr. Shaw to join us?'

'Of course.' Crystal hurried out.

Not until they had all gathered in the Ambassador's office did Cadem speak again. 'What Major Winters told you about last night's events at Miss Trent's house was not all the truth. I am now permitted to inform you the whole story. Last night Colonel Nasseur decided to drop in to ensure Miss Trent was all right. We have now verified that the blood we found at Miss Trent's home was the Colonel's. He was shot, we believe, at least three times. With the passing of every hour without medical assistance, the less likely it is that the Colonel will be found alive.' Crystal burst into tears. Everyone but the military men looked at her bewildered.

'Crystal, what has Colonel Nasseur to do with Sarah?' asked James.

His daughter couldn't stop crying enough to make herself coherent. Gary answered instead, 'Joseph and Sarah are in a relationship. Once the current crisis had quietened down, he had every intention of asking Sarah to marry him.'

There were gasps of surprise and Cadem withdrew an empty ring box from his pocket. 'Colonel Nasseur planned to ask Miss Trent to marry him last night. This box was found on the coffee table. Either the ring is on Miss Trent's finger, or the abductors took it.'

Gary sighed. 'So he actually found the courage to ask her and now it might be too late. God help the abductors if I ever get my hands on them!'

Cadem looked at him sharply. 'Do not attempt to search for Miss Trent on you own. Either Inspector Lowe or myself will keep you informed about the situation.'

'Is that an order, Lieutenant?' Gary's eyes twinkled dangerously.

Cadem nodded. 'Yes Major, it comes straight from Prince Kahlee.'

'Very well,' Gary capitulated, 'but I shall not wait for long,' he warned.

The Major escorted Cadem down to his car as he had some questions he wished to ask without being overheard. 'Has any demands been made yet for the Colonel's release?'

The Lieutenant shook his head. 'No Sir. Inspector Lowe has an officer with Mrs Nasseur and the Princess in case a ransom demand is delivered to either of them.'

Gary was frowning. 'Don't you think that is a little odd that we've heard nothing about Joseph?'

Cadem shrugged. 'If Miss Trent was the intended victim, they may have had their ransom note ready. The Colonel is collateral damage and the new note may take time to prepare.'

'They've had 12 hours to arrange one and he is the more logical target for a demand for money.'

'Why do you say that sir?'

Gary stroked his chin. 'If they had really done their homework then they'd already know that our government doesn't pay ransoms. Whereas it is more feasible that the Nasseur family could raise a million dollar ransom, certainly Prince Kahlee could raise that sum for the release of his best friend. It just feels like we've dealing with amateurs.'

'Why do you make it sound like a bad thing Major?'

'Because there's no way of knowing what they will do next. They don't know what they are doing and that makes them dangerous. Anything could happen.'

Cadem hesitated before he spoke. 'There is another reason they might not have sent a ransom demand to the Colonel's family. That is if he is not…'

Gary wouldn't let him finish. 'Don't even think that Cadem!'

'That was a lot of blood at Miss Trent's home, Major!'

'Until we know anything different they are still alive and together!'

'Sir, you are not being realistic!'

'To hell with realistic! That's my sister!'

Cadem was stunned into silence for a moment. 'Literally?'

Gary uttered a short laugh. 'No, sorry I didn't mean to snap but by God Sarah really does feel like my sister.'

Lieutenant Cadem squeezed Gary's arm reassuringly. 'We will bring them home Sir… both of them. I am prepared to do anything to see that we do succeed!'

The Search Begins

Marianne took Crystal across to the Residency to try and calm her down. *I can hardly believe that Sarah had managed to keep such a secret from me. I understand the need for secrecy, but I had thought that I was trustworthy.* Crystal explained everything to Marianne. How she'd discovered the truth by accident. Marianne was slightly mollified but Gary was very unhappy about having his hands tied. He wanted desperately to be involved with the search for Sarah. By doing something, by being actively involved was much better than having to sit back and wait.

Inspector Lowe and Cadem both understood this, so when the Police began to search the home of every Embassy employee, the Inspector picked Gary up and took him with them. Their searching was thorough and professional. The people in the homes, if there were any, were treated correctly. There was so little to go on and so little time left for the investigations.

Con's Discovery

Con sat in his office staring angrily at his mobile phone. He had accused Gary of not calling when Sarah had been abducted but his mobile showed that Gary had actually called twice and sent over a dozen text messages. He had been so caught up in his own affairs that he was 12 hours behind the police in the search for Sarah. *Where do I even start to look?* Con fumed. The room was starting to feel stifling and Con longed for a cigarette.

Hunting through his top drawer and coming up with an empty packet, he went to his reserve packet hidden in the bottom drawer of the vertical file. *To find out what the police already know I'll have to apologise to Gary for yelling at him and hitting him, but the last one had felt so good.* Con grabbed a Berocca and his cigarettes and ran down the stairs to clear his head. *I am going to need to concentrate if I'm going to rescue Sarah first.*

Two cigarettes later, Con felt ready to tackle Gary but as he was about to re-enter the Embassy, the Security Guard, Ahkman met him on the front steps.

'Could I have a word with you Mr Zuco?'

Con often shared a cigarette with Ahkman so he automatically offered him the packet. 'Hey Ahkman, I bet you're glad the abduction didn't happen here on your watch?'

'Indeed Sir, I hope the guard, Hamid will not lose his job over this?'

Con shrugged his shoulders, as he had never thought about anyone other than himself. 'Probably not, unless it proves that he was a part of it.'

Ahkman took a cigarette and lit it as they moved back to his post by the gate. 'He wasn't!'

'How could you know that?' Con was finally paying attention.

Ahkman looked surprised. 'It was not part of your plan Mr Zuco.'

'My plan?' Con's voice rose an octave. He glanced quickly around to see if anyone was watching them. 'What the fuck are you talking about? I never told you to kidnap Sarah!'

Ahkman shook his head. 'But Sir it was all you have been able to talk about since the incident at the palace. How you would finally win Miss Trent's love by rescuing her from a fatal situation. You went over several different scenarios and I chose the one most likely to succeed.'

'Oh my God! How could you have taken me seriously? How the fuck do we get out of this alive?' Con paced up and down the driveway, his fingers tearing through his hair. 'I'll have to tell Gary and maybe he'll be able to pass it off as some sort of practical joke.'

'I don't understand, Sir, I thought this is what you wanted? You get to be a hero, we get the money and Miss Trent falls in love with you.' Ahkman scratched his head in thought, 'But I am still puzzled as to how Colonel Nasseur fits into your kidnap scenario.'

Con stopped pacing and turned to stare at Ahkman in surprise. 'What does he have to do with any of this? He was never part of the plan!' He shook his head, 'What am I saying? There wasn't a plan! This is crazy!'

'Well I did wonder if you wanted to show Miss Trent that the Colonel is a mere mortal and not worthy of her love. So we made him a victim as well.'

'But what was he doing with her? Why was he at her home?'

'According to my brother's wife, they are betrothed.'

'No! That's impossible!'

'Yes so I thought.' Ahkman sneered. 'That a foreigner would dare to think they are worthy to enter one of our most prestigious families?'

'Hey! You make it sound like Sarah is a gold digging slut!'

Ahkman bowed his head. 'She is not one of us!'

'Well that's all wonderful but what the fuck are we supposed to do now? Did you keep your identity a secret from Sarah when you took them?'

'No, should we have?'

Con groaned, 'Did you at least wear gloves?'

'No,'

'Oh My God! The police could be on to you at any minute! Even after Sarah is released she'll be able to identify you as her kidnappers! We're completely screwed!' Con sank to the ground with his head in his hands.

'So how do we proceed now Mr Zuco? When will the Australian Government send our ransom money?'

'Never, Ahkman; our government doesn't pay out for hostages!'

The security guard squatted down beside Con. 'That can't be true Sir; I remember a news report about hostages being released as the money was delivered.'

Con looked up, and shook his head. 'Not by the government. I think it was Dick Smith, a private citizen who came up with the money in the end. And I'm not certain but I think it was only because the hostages were in considerable ill health after many years of imprisonment. Anyway I'm going to talk to Gary and see if we can make this a joke. In the meantime tell your family to get ready to escape the country.' Con rose to his feet and dusted off his trousers as Ahkman also straightened up.

'You really have no plan for rescuing Miss Trent do you?'

Con shook his head. 'Not a bloody clue!' He stormed back up into the Embassy to salvage the impossible position he had unwittingly created.

A Ministerial Visit

By lunch time, Sarah's abduction had become a worldwide news item. Phone calls, emails, text messages and facsimiles from friends and family of Sarah's inundated the Australian Embassy. Crystal did what she could to help out but it was still pretty hectic. To make matters worse, Minister Amwar Beodan waltzed into the Ambassador's office.

'Ambassador Greene! Such a tragic event to happen to such a lovely young lady! It is to be hoped that the kidnappers do not deal too harshly with Miss Trent, but I fear that she may well share Lucas' fate.'

Marianne Davis entered the office to hear the last part of the Minister's words. 'What a comfort you are to us Minister Beodan in this time of crisis!' Marianne's sarcasm was lost on the Minister, but brought a smile to James' lips.

'Indeed, Mrs. Davis,' The Minister bowed formally to her, his eyes holding a lecherous gleam. 'Is it true what I have heard about Miss Trent and Colonel Nasseur? That they were having an affair? If this rumour took hold, imagine the damage it would do to his career if it was known that he was fucking a foreigner!'

'How dare you!' Marianne's eyes blazed as her cheeks flushed with the indignation of such a slur upon Sarah's honour. 'How dare you use such language in front of me and about such an innocent child as Sarah Trent? I'll have you know that there was absolutely nothing dishonourable in the actions of either Sarah or Joseph Nasseur! You have a mind of a gutter rat, Minister Beodan, which I feel is insulting to the rat! You will have me to answer to if you dare spread one single rumour about either person and so help me I'll ruin you and your career!'

James stared at Marianne in amazement. *I've never seen her so angry and I am only now realizing how close she had been to Sarah.* In full support of her, James rose to his feet.

'I think Marianne has accurately expressed the opinion of this Embassy. We don't need or want your rumours or your false compassion. If that's all that you have to say, then I must now ask you to leave! Good day Minister!' When the Ambassador pressed the intercom buzzer on his desk, Crystal entered the room in answer to it.

'Yes Dad?'

'Ask Abu to escort the Minister down to his car please. He is leaving!'

'Of course!' Crystal held the door open and looked expectantly at Minister Beodan who stormed out of the room without bidding the Ambassador farewell.

Onto a small couch in the Ambassador's room, James urged Marianne to sit down before getting her a glass of water.

'How dare he slander that dear girl? How dare he place his sleazy thoughts and deeds upon such an honourable man as Joseph Nasseur?' Her tears were unstoppable as she worked herself up into a towering rage. There was a polite knock at the door but neither James nor Marianne heard it. Gary entered the room, his countenance rather grim.

'Did you just have Minister Beodan here, Ambassador?'

James looked up surprised and nodded. 'That's right. Is there a problem?'

'Do you mind if I ask what he said? It was a request from Prince Kahlee that all Embassies in Kathou keep a record of all conversations with Pangani ministers.'

James briefly detailed their conversation. 'How long has that been going on for?' Although James knew of the practice, he hadn't known the reason behind it.

'About three years, since the Rebellion had escalated. Prince Kahlee was certain that several ministers were not only sympathetic to the Rebel cause but also funding or supporting them. They hoped that the overthrow of the Emir would bring them to power as heads of a new democratic government. The actions and words of suspected ministers were watched and recorded.'

James was interested and momentarily forgot Marianne's agitation. 'And did they uncover any conspiracies with the ministers?'

A nod from Gary was quite curt. 'Five ministers were caught, tried and found guilty of treason and disloyalty to the state. The Prince fears that disloyalty still exists in the ministry.'

The look of despair that Marianne cast upon him made Gary realize that he had said too much.

'These people have Sarah imprisoned! My God! What will they do to her?'

Sitting down beside Marianne, James placed his arm around her shoulders, embarrassed at having forgotten her presence.

'We don't know that it is the Rebels who have Sarah.' James tried to reassure Marianne, but he failed. 'Since they have demanded money and not political influence or the release of a comrade, it might very well not be Rebels.'

'So someone desperate to make a quick buck has Sarah? Do you think that makes it any easier to accept what has happened or ease the worry for her safety?'

Gary looked guilty at her accusation. 'Please excuse me; I have an appointment with Lieutenant Cadem and Inspector Lowe.'

James grasped hold of Marianne's hand to prevent her from leaving also. 'Marianne, I don't want you to go to an empty house tonight!'

A look of surprise crossed her face, 'Yes of course, all Embassy staff should remain at the Residency until this crisis is over.'

'That's not exactly what I meant.' It was James' turn to look surprised.

Marianne managed to conceal a mischievous smile, 'Well what did you mean Mr. Ambassador? Were you trying to seduce me?'

James laughed, 'I don't know, would it have worked?'

Smiling Marianne headed for the door, 'You've been doing well so far, so maybe…'

James opened the door for her before heading back to his desk. Too soon his smile disappeared as the Embassy tried to carry on without its efficient secretary.

Con Seeks Advice

It wasn't until Gary had returned from the house searches with Lieutenant Cadem that Con managed to speak to him. By that time Con was such a nervous wreck that he had gone through a whole packet of cigarettes. He was just lighting his last one as Gary headed up the Embassy front steps.

'Hey Gary, you got a sec?'

The Major paused, his eyebrows rose in surprise as he looked down at Con sitting on the top step. 'What's up?'

'This kidnapping thing, how serious is it?'

'What do you mean?' Con now had Gary's complete attention.

'Well, what if it's not what it seems? You know someone's idea of a practical joke but it sorta got outta hand. Would there be any way of putting it right without making it a big deal?'

Gary squatted down until he was eye to eye with Con. 'Do you know something about Sarah's abduction, Con? Did you have anything to do with it?'

'What me?' Con blustered, 'No, no way! I'm just saying… you know…'

Gary straightened up. 'A man has been wounded, maybe fatally! This is as serious as it gets.'

Dragging on his cigarette Con suddenly frowned. 'What was he doing at Sarah's house anyway? What's all this rubbish about them being engaged?'

It was Gary's turn to frown. *Con wasn't present when Cadem revealed to the other Embassy staff about Joseph asking Sarah to marry him, so how had he learnt about it?* 'Just before they were abducted Sarah had agreed to marry Joseph.'

Con screwed up his face. 'That's disgusting! He must be at least twenty years older than her!'

'Actually he is only nine years older. You didn't really think you'd ever get Sarah to go out with you, did you?'

'What does she want to go and marry one of them for? She should have stuck to her own kind!' Con finally came to the end of his cigarette and flicked it into the bushes beside him.

'Racism like that will see you kicked out of the diplomatic corp,' warned Gary.

'Actually I'm surprised you didn't end up with Sarah. I mean the week we were all forced to bunker down at the Residency you were sleeping with her right?'

Gary shook his head, 'Sleeping in the same bed, not sleeping with her. A definite difference!'

'Why? Was Sarah even then involved with Nasseur? Don't you find her attractive?'

Gary sighed, 'No, Sarah wasn't involved with the Colonel then, but I was aware of his feelings for her. Yes Sarah is attractive but I don't feel sexually attracted to her.'

Con snorted in derision. 'Oh please! Are you trying to tell me that if she had turned to you one night and said, "Take me in your arms, you big strong Major man, and make me feel like a woman!", that you'd have said, "No!"?'

Gary continued up the steps. 'Sarah didn't ask, she wouldn't have asked but in the improbability that she ever would, the answer would have been "No!". Satisfied?'

Con shook his head. 'You're weird!'

'No Con, I'm a gentleman!'

Only waiting long enough for the Major to enter the Embassy, Con ran down to the main gate where Ahkman stood.

'Get the hell outta Kathou! Forget the money, you won't get it! Tell Saladin to just leave Sarah and the Colonel there and flee the country.'

'And what will you do Mr Zuco?'

Con scratched his head. 'In a couple of hours I'll turn up at Saladin's to rescue them.'

Ahkman wasn't at all pleased. 'You get what you want; Sir, but we get nothing!'

Con uttered a maniacal laugh. 'I'm offering you a chance to get out with your lives! If you're caught, you're dead men!' He glanced back at the Embassy to ensure that no one was watching them. 'Just save yourselves and your families. That is all I can offer you.' Con turned back to the building, intending on a cool swim to calm down and a chance to think through his next move.

Nurse Sarah

There wasn't much they could do but wait until Jaeda found an opportune time for them to escape. Waiting, though, wasn't something Colonel Nasseur did easily. He was filled with restless need for action but every slight movement was like being stabbed with a thousand knives. For Sarah's sake, he tried to hide his pain and lie as still as possible but she wasn't fooled. Earlier Sarah had emptied the medical supplies out of the backpack and had found several vials of morphine, a hypodermic needle and a packet of pain killers. She had hoped to have to use the morphine as a last resort but the tablets were not controlling his pain at all.

Sarah slipped out from under his good arm and carefully stepping over Joseph, she knelt beside the backpack to prepare an injection.

'Sarah, it's not that bad. I don't want to be doped out! I need to be able to think clearly.'

Sarah continued removing the hypodermic from its packaging.

'Sarah!' There was an edge to his voice but instead of answering, she reached over and gently lay her hand over his which was attached to his injured arm. She didn't touch the wound itself but that small gesture caused Joseph to groan involuntarily.

'This is such a low dose that it shouldn't affect your mind. By taking the edge off your pain, it might make you think more clearly.'

Joseph exhaled slowly. 'Do you know what you are doing?' He watched as Sarah plunged the tip of the needle into the top of the vial and drew up the small amount of liquid.

'Oh yes, once you have all the liquid out of the vial, you remove the needle and turn the syringe so the needle points upwards.' She continued to explain as she went, 'now you gently squeeze the syringe to remove any air bubbles. Tear open a sterile swab for the injection site. You don't need to find a vein, thank goodness; the injection goes straight into the muscle, preferably as close to the source of pain as possible. Needle goes in, press the syringe, withdraw and dispose of the needle responsibly.'

Joseph chuckled. 'Thank you Nurse Sarah.'

She wrapped the needle back in its packaging. 'Unfortunately we only have the one needle so I can't dispose of it yet.' Once Sarah had packed away the medical supplies again,

Joseph reached out his good hand and drew her back down onto the mattress beside him.

'Where did you learn to do that? Did you train as a nurse?'

Sarah snuggled carefully against him. 'No, I keep my first aid certificate up to date but mainly because my grandmother has to deal with chronic pain all the time. There are the occasional days when the meds she takes aren't enough and one of us needs to give her an injection of morphine and send her to bed until it's manageable again.'

'I'm sorry; it must be hard to see her like that.'

'Yes, but when she is well we have so much fun together. I suppose I compensate how much I miss my real family by creating a pseudo one with Marianne and Gary.'

'Do you think I should have asked your father for his blessing before asking you to marry me?'

'No...' There was a great deal of hesitance in her voice.

'Are you still having doubts?'

'No, it's not that. It's just I would've liked my parents to have heard it from me first and not through the media.' She sighed deeply. 'Do you know what I would really like?'

'To be married in Australia?'

'Not quite. If it's not too hard to organise or too expensive, a wedding ceremony here with your family and our friends, and a reception back in Perth before we honeymoon in Australia for a couple of months.'

'That sounds very nice.' Joseph caressed his hand down her hair. 'I would like to meet your family and see Australia. We'll have to discuss if you want to keep working at the Embassy after we are married.'

'I think we need to solve a few more important problems before we can live happily ever after.'

'Like our current predicament?' he suggested.

'Actually I'm not referring to that.' Sarah sighed. 'Your family's objections to me, your people's objections to me, the fundamentalists wanting to take over the country.'

'Oh is that all?' Joseph could feel his pain finally easing.

'Yes, that is all! Perhaps once you've taken care of all that, you can tackle world peace!'

Escape Attempt

Sarah sat up and placed a finger over Joseph's lips. She had heard a car pull up. Saladin was back for lunch and if Jaeda was able to distract her husband, this might be their chance to escape. Hoping this was the case; Sarah assisted Joseph to sit up and was ready to get him to his feet when Jaeda quietly unlocked their door.

'Quietly now, Saladin is in the yard for prayers.' She came to the other side of Joseph to help him walk out to the car. Jaeda produced the car keys and helped Joseph into the passenger seat while Sarah ran round to get in behind the wheel. Her trembling fingers managed to insert the key in the ignition without dropping it but turning the key, the car only made a spluttering noise.

By the second attempt Saladin was standing beside the driver's door. 'I disabled the car. Ahkman thought Jaeda might try something like this. Back inside now.'

Sarah hesitated, glancing across at Joseph who looked awfully pale from having been moved. Saladin produced Ahkman's gun and pointed it at Joseph, 'Now Miss Trent! Or he will have another hole to contend with.'

Sarah handed the bunch of keys to Saladin. With Jaeda's help, Sarah assisted Joseph back into their temporary bedroom.

'I'm so sorry Miss Trent.' Jaeda whispered as she headed for the door again.

'Don't be Jaeda; we appreciate you trying to help us.' Sarah sank back onto the mattress beside Joseph and wiped the sweat from his brow as the argument began on the other side of the door.

The Search Continues

Gary Winters' meeting with Cadem took place outside a central park. Gary pulled up into a parking spot, turned off his engine and waited. Almost immediately Lieutenant Cadem slipped into the passenger seat. The Major was slightly surprised as he had been looking out of Cadem and had not seen him approach.

'Drive Sir, I have some bad news.' Cadem waited until they had pulled away from the kerb and back into the traffic before he spoke again, briefly giving directions before getting to the heart of the matter. 'The Embassy link was our strongest lead and I still feel that it is part of the solution. We have searched the houses of all the Embassy staff, Panganian and Australian, and drawn a blank. Now we will widen the search to other family members of the staff. The element of surprise, though, has gone. They will know that we are coming and they may have the opportunity to spirit them away.' Cadem sighed and actually let down his usual guard and reserve, an indication to how he was so tired.

'So how do we catch them out if they are prepared for us?'

Cadem ran a hand over his eyes, a hand that wasn't quite steady. 'I had an odd feeling about a couple of places we visited. These homes will be watched. For definite proof we may have to wait for forensics to finish their tests of the crime scene. Would you like to join us again on our searches?'

The Major's eyes lit up in eagerness; at last he felt he could do something useful. 'Yes please!'

Time To Flee

Ahkman descended upon the cottage like a mini hurricane taking them all by surprise. He didn't call them after Con's warning to get out of there before the police arrived, but had called someone else who could possibly help them now. Someone who could give them the money they needed to leave the country but at a price.

'The police are on to us! We have to leave now!' Ahkman unlocked the spare bedroom door and dragged Sarah out of the room. 'Leave him! Get your children and get out of the city!' he added, in too much hurry to even speak in English.

Jaeda grasped hold of Sarah's other arm to prevent Ahkman from dragging her out to his vehicle. 'What's going on? Where are you taking Miss Trent?'

'There won't be any ransom money, but I can still get something for this little package!'

Jaeda refused to release Sarah's arm. 'Please Ahkman, if we have to run, leave Miss Trent with the Colonel so that they can be rescued together!'

Ahkman half lifted Sarah up under his arm, tearing her out of Jaeda's grip, 'No! She's still worth her weight in gold!'

Although Sarah fought against Ahkman, his threat to immediately put a bullet through Joseph's head subdued her actions. Throwing the Secretary onto the back seat Ahkman quickly bound her hands together and placed a gag in her mouth.

'Sal, are you going to just let him kidnap her again?' Jaeda confronted her husband who was hunting through a kitchen drawer.

'Get in the van Jaeda! We've got to get the children before the police come!' Saladin had found the part he had removed to disable the van and was already heading out the door to fix it. Jaeda glanced across to where Joseph was struggling to rise to his feet. They heard Ahkman start his car and tear off down the dirt road and Jaeda heard a sound that tore apart her heart as the Colonel roared in despair as he struggled to the doorway of the bedroom.

'Jaeda! Come on!' Saladin commanded as he slammed down the bonnet of the van. Jaeda ran out of the house, pulling open the back door of the van and slammed it shut behind her. Joseph had barely managed to drag his injured leg to the outer doorway of the cottage as the van also disappeared down the track.

Roaring again in anger, Joseph smashed his fist into the door, sending it flying off its hinges. It didn't solve his problem and it had hurt his hand but it had felt good to do something physical to let off steam. He struggled to turn as a slight noise behind him suggested that he wasn't in fact alone.

'Please sit down Colonel,' said Jaeda, 'You don't want to make your wounds worse.' She stepped towards Joseph offering her arm for him to lean upon.

'I heard you leave,' he accepted her help to the kitchen table and a chair.

'I jumped into the back of Saladin's van for his mobile phone and out again before he drove away. There is no land line phone here. I must protect my family, Colonel Nasseur, as you must protect Miss Trent from what awaits her.' Jaeda placed a mobile on the table in front of him. 'Call your people to come and take you to the hospital. I'll tell you anything I can to help get Miss Trent back.'

Briefly Joseph laid his hand over hers. 'Thank you! I won't forget your help.' He quickly punched in Cadem's number and raising it to his ear, waited for it to connect.

Results At Last!

Still in Major Winter's car, when Cadem's mobile phone rang he answered it monosyllabic. 'Speak!'

'Inspector Lowe here, the forensics has come back about the fingerprints and bloody scrap found in the puppy's mouth.'

'Yes?'

'Both match Ahkman Amed.'

'Good work Inspector.'

'Our search of Ahkman's home came up empty.'

'Start with his family. Get a warrant for his arrest.'

'Yes sir.'

Hanging up the call Cadem checked on the phone a list of Ahkman's family members.

'Where do you want to start?' Gary finally asked.

Cadem scrolled down the list until he chose one, 'This one.' Cadem held the phone up so that Gary could read the screen.

'Not a problem.' The Major altered their direction and for good measure put his foot down on the accelerator.

The Lieutenant's phone rang once more. 'Speak!'

'I cannot express how gratifying it is to hear your voice.'

There was a momentary pause before Cadem asked, 'Colonel Nasseur?'

'What's left of him. I need you to come and get me. I'm... where exactly am I?' The Colonel's voice faded and as Cadem tried to get a response another voice answered.

'Eh, sir, I need to give you our directions.' A female voice startled Cadem.

'Miss Trent?'

'Oh no sir, I am Jaeda Amed. My brother-in-law Ahkman has taken her away again. Oh please come the Colonel is bleeding again!' Jaeda gave Cadem the directions for the cottage before hanging up. Cadem stared at his phone stunned.

'Well?' Gary's demand snapped Cadem back to the present.

'Sorry, it's where we are already heading.' Cadem contacted first Inspector Lowe and then an ambulance to meet them there. Disconnecting the last call, the phone dropped out of Cadem's hand to the floor of the car but he didn't immediately attempt to pick it up. He was trying to hold on as the car sped dangerously through the streets. His desire to get to the cottage was as great as Major Winters' but Cadem was forced to protest as they seemed likely to cause an accident. Gary slowed slightly as he grinned at his passenger.

'Sorry, I've done some rally driving in the bush back home and usually the only things we had to really worry about hitting were trees and kangaroos.'

Cadem's knuckles were white as he clung to the hand support above the door, 'I'm as anxious to rescue Colonel Nasseur and Miss Trent as you but I would prefer to arrive there in one piece!' Gary laughed but obliged by slowing down further.

Leaving The Cottage

By the time they finally drew up outside the cottage, Cadem was wondering, *Are my fingers going to leave a permanent imprint in the hand support above the window?* Gary pulled up before reaching the building so that the forensics team could get a cast of any tyre impressions. If they knew what vehicle Ahkman was driving it might be easier to track him down. There was no other vehicle in sight; even so both the Major and the Lieutenant had their guns drawn as they cautiously entered the simple dwelling.

Colonel Nasseur was slumped in the chair at the kitchen table as Jaeda tried to get him to drink some coffee. She had reinforced the bandages to stop the bleeding but Joseph was looking rather wan. Cadem immediately returned his weapon to its holster as he knelt down to check on his Commanding Officer. Gary, though, kept his gun drawn as he checked each room for anyone else. As Cadem placed Joseph's good arm around his neck and dragged him to his feet, the Colonel revived slightly, 'Sarah?'

Gary put away his own gun and grabbed hold of the other side of his friend, 'We'll find her Joseph! Be strong! We will bring her back to you.' He promised. Joseph managed to nod before he collapsed unconscious against them.

By the time Cadem and Gary had chair lifted Joseph to the doorway, the Ambulance and Inspector Lowe with his forensic team had arrived. The paramedics placed the Colonel on a stretcher as Inspector Lowe directed the forensics to start work. When Jaeda came out of the cottage, the Inspector immediately slapped the handcuffs on her. Joseph struggled to raise himself on one elbow, fighting to stay conscious this time.

'No Inspector, she helped us.'

Reluctantly Lowe released her as he demanded, 'Where is Miss Trent?'

'I don't know Sir.' Jaeda nervously shook her head. 'Ahkman burst in, said there would be no ransom money. The police would be here soon and that we had to flee. Ahkman said he could still get paid for Miss Trent. That she was worth her weight in gold.'

The Colonel added, 'She's telling the truth.'

'Shall I arrange for all the Ameds to be arrested Sir?' asked Lowe.

'Oh no please!' Jaeda desperately grabbed hold of Lowe's arm, 'No one else in our family is involved, just Ahkman, Koyad and Saladin. I was brought into it to protect Miss Trent's reputation. Ahkman said that although she was a westerner, Miss Trent was a true lady.'

The paramedics were trying to get Joseph Nasseur to lie down but he wanted his orders to be clear. 'Just arrest the three Amed brothers! As well as whomever Ahkman took Sarah to for money. Jaeda, do you have any idea where he would take her?'

Sadly Jaeda shook her head, 'no, I'm sorry. Ahkman may have told his brothers but I am just a woman.' She was fearful that the Colonel would withdraw his protection.

'Inspector, protect Mrs Amed until her husband and his brothers are arrested and then take her home to her children,' ordered Joseph, finally allowing the medics to lay him down flat on the stretcher. Jaeda ran forward to press his hand.

'Oh thank you! Thank you!'

Joseph squeezed her hand. 'No, thank you! I won't forget what you did for us.' The stretcher was placed in the ambulance and a nervous Jaeda turned to the Inspector as it drove away. Cadem was staring angrily down at the ground but it was Gary who had an idea.

'You need to subpoena Ahkman's telephone records. As well as what type of vehicles he has access to. It could be the quickest way to discover where he has taken Sarah.'

The Inspector nodded. 'I'll organise that immediately.'

Cadem headed back to Gary's car, 'when you have arrested the Ameds or have those records, call me.'

'Where will you be?' asked the Inspector as Gary followed Cadem, who answered,

'For now the hospital.'

Gary paused with his driver's door open and glanced back at Jaeda who was looking small, scared and shaking. 'Mrs Amed, why don't you come with us until we can allow you to go home?'

Jaeda hurried towards them and got into the back of the car as Cadem raised an eyebrow but Gary simply shrugged.

'She looked after them mate, she doesn't deserve to be scared out of her wits.'

Cadem got into the car. 'All right, but I'm not going easy on the brothers when I get hold of them!'

Jaeda surprised them by saying, 'I hope you don't Sir! What they did was despicable!'

Gary slipped behind the wheel and automatically put on his seat belt, 'Right! Well now I've heard everything!'

Foiled Again

Furious, frustrated and fuming Con Zuco watched from a distance as Gary drove away. He had arrived at the cottage too late to rescue Sarah and it looked like she still wasn't safe yet. *Ahkman hadn't mentioned he was taking Sarah anywhere else. Why had he deviated from the plan?* Con smacked the steering wheel of his car with the palm of his hand. He had to stop this idea that he had been instrumental in Sarah's abduction, although he could still be the one to find her. *I just have to remember all I'd ever learnt about Ahkman. Who would be wealthy enough to want to buy a beautiful blonde woman?* A chill of fear ran through Con as he couldn't stomach the thought of another man touching Sarah. *I just have to find her first before something happened that I couldn't possible live with.*

Medical Care

The doctors were amazed at how well Sarah had managed to keep Joseph's wounds clean and from bleeding to death. Even so they insisted that the Colonel was admitted into the hospital for observation once they had extracted the bullets from his body. He was placed on a drip along with a course of antibiotics. Joseph wasn't happy about being stuck in a hospital bed but until he got his strength back there was nothing he could do about rescuing Sarah.

Girl Talk

Later that afternoon Marianne went home to pack a few essential things so that she could spend at least a couple of days at the Residency without having to return home for anything. She discarded any perishable goods, put the rubbish out and made sure that all the windows and doors were securely locked. Her guard would remain on duty to ensure that vandalism and theft didn't occur while she wasn't there. *That is a comfort but I'm a little sad at leaving my home. I know it isn't permanent, but I had made the place into my own oasis of escape, where I felt free from worry and stress.* Loading up her car, she tried to shake off the feeling that she was never going to see her house again. *I need to remain optimistic and positive, for Sarah's sake and Crystal's. I need to be the calm, supportive mother and I need to be strong.*

Crystal helped to move Marianne's belongings into the spare bedroom.

'That's just for the moment,' Marianne reassured. 'You never know when things will change.'

Crystal brightened up at that; *I like Marianne, and think she would do dad the world of good. I'm all for their relationship. I only wish I understood my own feelings for Gary.*

A Second Escape Attempt

Sarah managed to sit up on the back seat of Ahkman's car, her hands uncomfortably tied behind her but Ahkman hadn't tied her feet. She didn't try anything until the car was once more travelling through the city. Slightly slouched, Sarah tried to stay out of the vision of the rear view mirror as she attempted to manipulate the door handle from behind her back. She was guaranteed to get spectators' attention as she was shoeless and wore only Jaeda's simple cotton dress. Her blonde hair was uncovered as were her legs below the knees. *Never in a million years would I consider disrespecting the local culture and religious constraints but I have to take every chance offered to escape. At least I'm not naked; I couldn't go ahead with escaping if I had been that exposed.*

Once they were in the city central, Sarah grasped the door handle and when Ahkman pulled up at traffic lights, she pushed against the door with her shoulder as she turned the handle. The door didn't open, Sarah hurt her shoulder and she screamed in frustration (muffled by the tape over her mouth) as Ahkman laughed at her.

'Child safety locks,' he admitted, 'door can only be opened from the outside.' Ahkman leant over the front seat and hit Sarah so hard that she was already unconscious before her head hit the cushioned back of the seat. He paused only long enough to ensure that Sarah was still breathing before slamming his foot on the accelerator. He tore through the traffic in his anger to get rid of her once and for all.

I Trust You To Get The Job Done

Ahkman, Koyad and Saladin Amed were soon apprehended but Sarah wasn't with Ahkman when he had finally been tracked down by Inspector Lowe. Ahkman's phone records weren't of any use either as he hadn't used his home telephone, his mobile or any pay phone in a close proximity to the Embassy or his home to a number not already connected to the case. The forensics team hadn't yet been able to identify how Ahkman had contacted a potential buyer, or who could possibly be that buyer.

When the news of their lack of success was relayed to Lieutenant Cadem at the hospital, the only immediate indication to his agitation was the snapping of the pencil he had been using. He paced the Colonel's hospital room; his face set in a mask of stone. The soldier, who had brought the news, disappeared before the approaching storm. Joseph wearily watched Cadem pace for several minutes before he attempted to speak.

'Cadem, you aren't to blame yourself for this set back. You will succeed in finding Sarah, but it must be done our way. My orders are for you and you alone. Do what you must to find Sarah and that does include using your initiative.'

The Lieutenant stared at his superior in disbelief. 'I am prepared to torture the Amed brothers to get them to talk!'

'I know Cadem.' Colonel Nasseur inclined his head in acknowledgment. 'I hope that it won't come to that, but if it does, I don't want you to hesitate. Sarah's life may very well depend upon how quickly you succeed in breaking them.'

Cadem snapped to attention and saluted. 'You can depend upon me, Colonel!' He whirled around and marched out of the hospital ward.

Colonel Nasseur closed his eyes and sighed, 'I do, Cadem, completely!'

Where Am I Now?

With a groan, Sarah tentatively opened her eyes. Her head ached, her jaw throbbed where Ahkman had hit her and she shifted her position to get back feeling in her hands which were pinned beneath her. The bedroom was in semi-darkness and as Sarah looked around her, she wondered, *where am I this time and why wasn't Joseph brought with me? Have the Ameds just abandoned him to die alone in that remote cottage?* The door suddenly opened and the light was turned on as a large, buxom Panganian woman entered the room but she halted when she saw that Sarah was awake. The placid look on her face changed to pity as she approached the bed on which Sarah lay.

'Poor child! How do you feel?' The woman spoke in Arabic as she removed Sarah's gag and untied her hands so that she was able to sit up properly and massage her aching wrists.

'Where am I?' Sarah replied in the same language.

The other woman sat down on a chair beside the bed as she administered to Sarah a couple of painkillers. 'You're in the house of Hashim Benzaar. You're here to be added to his collection of women.'

'This isn't right! Where is my fiancé, Joseph Nasseur? What's happened to him?'

'I don't know the answers to these questions, my dear. Try and sleep, if you have any problems, just call out to me. I'm in the next room. I am Fatima, the housekeeper.'

Sarah struggled to her feet. 'Please don't leave me here!'

Fatima patted Sarah's hand reassuringly. 'You're perfectly safe tonight. The master is with his new wife.'

'That's not what I meant. Can I at least use the bathroom?'

Fatima chuckled, 'Of course my dear. I'll have to lock you in and that window is too small to escape through.' She led Sarah out of the room and down a short corridor. Sarah thanked her as she hurried into the bathroom. When Fatima returned from the kitchen with a hot meal for the prisoner, she was surprised that Sarah was quietly waiting.

Back in the bedroom Sarah sat down on the bed as she scanned the room for exits. Fatima, placing the bowl of chicken and rice on a table beside the bed, had followed Sarah's gaze towards the window.

'I know that there are no bars but don't try it my dear. Bruno will tear you apart before you get to the gate.'

Sarah transferred her gaze to Fatima; 'Bruno?' *Could this be a guard who could possibly be bribed?*

Fatima opened the window and called out, 'Bruno!' and an angry, savage bark answered her and a large Doberman appeared at the window. Sarah refused to flinch at the salivating jaws. Fatima gently patted Sarah on the shoulder.

'Never mind, you might even enjoy yourself with the master.'

Sarah shuddered at the idea of any other man than Joseph touching her. Fatima locked the door as she left the room confident that Sarah would still be there in the morning.

Yet Another Escape Attempt

Picking up the fork beside the bowl, Sarah ran it through the rice as she thought seriously about her next move. She drank some of the water left for her as she pulled out the chicken pieces and placed them onto the plate that had been under the bowl. Sarah didn't know if she could win over a savage guard dog. It had been different with Simon as he had only been an injured puppy who needed the right diagnosis and treatment to make him sociable.

Sarah took the plate and the bowl to the open window and taking a deep breath, she knelt down. She didn't have to call very loudly for the dog to return snarling to the window. Sarah kept her hands safely out of the way and tilted her head slightly to one side as she spoke kindly to Bruno.

'Oh poor baby, I bet no one has been feeding you properly. How about some chicken?' Sarah tossed a piece of chicken to the ground close to the Doberman and waited, continuing to talk to him. The delicious smell of the chicken finally stopped the dog growling until he had finished that piece and then he returned his aggression back to Sarah. She tilted her head the other way. 'Was that nice Bruno? Do you like chicken? I'm sorry it's not a big juicy steak. Would you like some more?'

Sarah threw another bit of chicken beside Bruno. This time he was less hesitant to eat it so Sarah continued to place food beside him until he finally reached up and took a piece of chicken straight out of her hand. The growling had stopped but Sarah was still cautious offering food to the dog and continued to speak gently to him. When all the chicken was gone, Sarah leant out the window so that she could place the bowl of rice on the ground. Bruno sniffed at it but decided it was better than nothing and woofed it down.

Sarah waited to see if Bruno would return to being savage now the food was all gone. He looked up at her to see if Sarah had anything else to eat. She showed him her empty hands, her fingers trembling slightly as he licked them.

'Sorry Bruno, I've nothing else. I suppose that means an end to our friendship.' Sarah leant back from the window and Bruno barked as he placed his huge front paws on the window ledge. It wasn't an angry bark and Bruno whimpered happily as he began to mimic Sarah's tilting head action.

'Well this might just be possible,' Cautiously Sarah began to ease herself out of the window and as Bruno only danced excitedly around her, she stepped out of the house. Hugging Bruno, Sarah looked around the garden in the darkness illuminated only by the full moon. *If Bruno and I can get to the gate there is a chance we could get to safety.* Bruno thought it was play time with his new friend and it wasn't easy to convince him that he had to be quiet as they made their way unchallenged to the gate. As Sarah opened the unlocked gate she began to think that, *apart from the trouble it took to befriend Bruno, this is way too easy.* Bruno happily followed Sarah through the gate, prepared to follow where ever she went.

A blinding spot light startled them and Bruno placed himself in front of Sarah to protect her and began to growl.

'Had I not seen it myself, I would never have believed it possible!' Hashim Benzaar approached with several guards with hand guns drawn.

'Please I just want to go home,' Sarah begged, placing her hand on Bruno's head to calm him as he barked at his owner.

'No I don't think so my dear. I'm glad Ahkman hadn't broken your spirit. I'm looking forward to taming you myself.' Turning to his armed guards, Hashim Benzaar added, 'Take her back to her room and handcuff her to the bed railing.'

One of the guards moved forward to obey but Bruno was not prepared to let anyone touch his new friend. Bruno latched onto a guard's arm and refused to release him even though he screamed in agony. Any order Hashim gave the Doberman,

Bruno ignored. Sarah tried to get Bruno to let go but he was set on protecting her.

'Kill him! He's no use to me now!' ordered Hashim.

Sarah didn't know if he meant the guard or the dog but she didn't like either option and she screamed in protest, 'No! Please don't!' She tried to get between the other guard and Bruno but the injured guard still had his gun in his other hand. He fired twice and Bruno whimpered as he slumped to the ground. Tears were streaming down her cheeks as Sarah screamed in disbelief and grief. She felt responsible for the dog's death and was mortified. Sarah fell to her knees and cradled Bruno, her fingers entangled in his blood drenched fur as she sobbed her heart out.

'Get her inside before someone sees or hears her,' ordered Hashim, turning and striding back into the house, disgusted by the scene before him. It took both guards to remove Sarah from Bruno and carry her sobbing and screaming back to her bedroom. They threw her onto the bed and handcuffed her to the metal bed head. Locking the door behind them, they were finally able to tend to the guard's injured arm.

Sarah attempted a couple of times to get the handcuff off the bed post but the knob on the top refused to budge an inch. Exhausted, covered in Bruno's blood and sobbing uncontrollably Sarah finally fell asleep. She had no more fight to escape that evening; she was consumed with grief and despair. *My chances of being reunited with Joseph Nasseur seem to becoming less and less possible.*

Peace Destroyed

That evening, Kathou's streets erupted in violence once more. Protesters stormed against the palace gates, demanding the release of the Ameds. The force of guards, human and canine, who stood behind the locked gate watched with disinterest as futile attempts were made to break the palace's impregnable security. In the streets, the Police were out in force to keep down the rioting and looting by the rioters. They were managing, and it wasn't necessary for the army to return from their campaign in the north. Yet. The Emir and Prince Kahlee watched the riot being broadcasted on the television, causing the Emir to sigh and shake his head.

'We could have lost Joseph! General Farouk Nasseur was my closest friend. His son became my son's best friend. The Ameds won't walk away from this insult! This division between our people has gone on long enough, Kahlee. I want it brought to an end.'

Kahlee studied his father, thoughtfully, 'Peacefully, father?'

The Emir shook his head. 'Any way that you see fit, my son!'

Kahlee rose and bowed. 'As you wish father,' with that he left the room and via a secret passage, departed from the palace and its grounds before disappearing into the night.

I Have Kept My Promise

At about this time, Cadem attended a gathering at the Australian Ambassador's residence. All the diplomatic staff was present and their obvious topic of discussion was Sarah's whereabouts now that the Ameds had been arrested and Colonel Nasseur safe in hospital. When Cadem entered the room, a silence fell over those assembled. Before he could speak, Marianne approached Cadem, pulling out a handkerchief from her cardigan pocket.

'You have blood on your cheek, Lieutenant. Have you hurt yourself?' She offered him the hanky as he absently brushed his fingers against his face. Cadem took the handkerchief, wiped his wet fingers before wiping away the remainder of the blood from his cheek.

'It is not my blood, Mrs. Davis, but I thank you for your concern.' Cadem's hard, cold eyes found Gary's. 'I have kept my promise to you,' he added.

The Major rose swiftly to his feet. 'Then you know who has Sarah?'

Cadem shook his head. 'Not yet. But we are not far off an answer. The Amed brothers have all confessed to their involvement with Sarah's abduction but as yet we have been able to eliminate only two brothers from knowing her present whereabouts.'

'And the third?' This came from the Ambassador.

'He knows but is trying to protect someone. He is resisting at the moment but we hope to have broken him before morning.'

Kevin could see a multitude of international repercussions of what Cadem was saying. 'Are your interrogations ethical Lieutenant?'

A ghost of a smile appeared and then disappeared. 'Do you want a positive and quick result Mr. Shaw?'

Kevin stiffened in indignation, 'Of course! But...'

'But nothing!' Cadem cut him off sharply, 'A young woman's life may depend upon how quickly we find her! My methods may offend you, but I can promise to deliver a living girl and not a corpse!' Cadem transferred his attention back to Gary. 'One of my men will temporarily take over Embassy security until a suitable replacement can be found. If you have any problems you know how to get in touch with me.' He bowed his head to the assembled group before departing.

Almost immediately Kevin turned on the Ambassador. 'Do you mean to condone such behaviour, James?'

The Ambassador's eyebrows rose in surprise as he glanced at the others, all waiting for his reply. 'Do you really need to ask?'

Kevin smiled. 'Then you'll be reporting Lieutenant Cadem to the appropriate authorities?'

Marianne gasped in disbelief but didn't speak. Crystal shook her head at the stupidity of his question.

'Now why would I do something as idiotic as that?' demanded the Ambassador, 'This young man could be our saving grace! If he can get Sarah back to us safe and sound, then I don't care if he makes a pact with the devil, himself! You will not hinder the Lieutenant. If we interfere, we could very well end up with her returning chopped up in a box like Ambassador Lucas!'

'Oh James, no!' Marianne cried and reached for Crystal's hand, pressing it for support.

'It'll be all right, Marianne. Lieutenant Cadem will bring Sarah back to us,' Gary promised. 'Joseph needs to keep that dream alive!'

TUESDAY

Secret Meeting

In the grey light of pre-dawn, an important meeting was taking place. In a simple wooden structure, in Pangani's north, Prince Kahlee was shown into the home of Caracal, the leader of the Commune. Kahlee was unarmed and unescorted, which goes without saying. Caracal had pure snow-white hair even though he was not yet 40 years old. His features were tanned and rugged, not exactly handsome, but there was a presence about the man, almost a holy aura seemed to surround him. He wore only a white robe and sandals.

When Caracal looked up and across at Kahlee, there was a cold hardness in his eyes and the Prince found it hard to believe that this was the laughing friend who had always been there for Joseph and himself as they grew up.

'What's happened to you, Trevane?' Kahlee's words in their native tongue were touched with sadness. Caracal stiffened, his eyes darting to the two men that stood beside Kahlee and with a jerk of his head, he silently dismissed them.

'I've renounced that name and my birth right.' Leading Kahlee into an adjoining room, Caracal added, 'One hero in our family was enough. It's funny, I never wanted to follow in the footsteps of the great General Nasseur but was forced to and yet Joseph went willingly. He could've been anything that he wanted. Trevane had to be what father wanted!' His lips

232

thinned as his mind travelled back to a time that he would rather forget.

Recalling his thoughts, Caracal gestured towards one of the two cushions upon the wooden floor as he lowered himself upon the second. Kahlee waited until they were settled before he spoke.

'We can't continue the way we are. Something must give and peace must be achieved.'

Caracal nodded. 'True. But there will have to be some sacrifices!' He too wanted peace but on his own terms.

'It's not as easy as that.' sighed Kahlee, 'To begin with the bloodshed must stop. Meet us at a negotiating table with the Fundamentalists. Those causing unrest in our country must be stopped. The people think they are supporting a bid for democracy. They don't realize that they're being manipulated by corrupt doctrine.'

There was a moment of silence as Caracal stared at the wall before saying, 'I'll not stand in your way while you deal with the rebels. I ask that the Ameds are tried so that they spend the maximum time in prison and not the death penalty.'

'Trevane!' Kahlee gasped in disbelief, 'They almost killed your brother! They may still have killed Miss Trent! Don't you wish them to be punished for these crimes? This is Joseph we're talking about!'

Caracal closed his eyes and exhaled slowly. 'My brother was the only one who understood the fire that burned within me.' He opened his eyes; again they appeared hard and cold. 'But that was my old life. I turned my back on that life when I decided to answer the calling that consumed my soul. The Ameds can't be allowed to escape justice so easily. I want them to suffer every single day for the rest of their lives for what they have done. They will wish that they had been allowed a quick death!'

A frown settled upon Kahlee's brow and he didn't immediately speak. 'If I arrange that, will you come to the negotiating table?'

Caracal inclined his head in agreement. 'There's something else though, isn't there?'

'The Fundamentalists, have agreed to meet with the Emir and to cease all protesting so that we can eradicate the rioting and take back our streets from the Rebels.'

'Of course! If any of our people are protesting, I'll get them to stand down. Will you be asking the leaders of the Rebels to also join us in negotiations?'

'No! We will not negotiate with terrorists!'

'Anything else?'

Kahlee hesitated before adding, 'Sarah Trent! We want her returned alive and well.'

'I'll make enquiries and will contact you when I find out where Miss Trent is.' Caracal rose to his feet, signalling that their meeting was over. Kahlee stood and held his hand out to his once friend, Caracal looked at it for a moment before taking Kahlee's hand between his own.

'You were very brave to come here alone, Kahlee!'

The Prince smiled, 'No, my friend, only desperate!'

I'd Hoped It Had Been A Nightmare

Sunlight dancing across her face finally woke Sarah. Her arm was sore and reddened from being handcuffed to the bed post and the dog's blood had dried and stiffened on her dress. Her heart was heavy with memories of the previous night but she felt all cried out. Fatima entered following a timid knock on the door. The older woman smiled sadly as Sarah greeted her.

'Good morning Fatima. I'd hoped that this was only a nightmare, but if it is, I don't know how to wake up.'

'Unfortunately, my dear, this is all too real.' Fatima's smile disappeared as she unlocked the handcuffs. 'Come, we have prepared a bath for you and some new clothes. After breakfast you shall be formally presented to the Master.'

Fear entered Sarah's eyes as she followed Fatima out of the room and down a short corridor. The housekeeper sighed, hesitating upon entering a bathroom as she added, 'If you please the Master, you'll do well here.'

'And if I don't?' Sarah had to know.

Again Fatima sighed. 'He will make your life Hell!'

Sarah's Faux Pas

Entering the bathroom, Sarah was confronted by a sea of marble and a young Panganian woman about 15. Glancing at her reflection in one of the many mirrors, Sarah stated, 'He can't possibly want someone who is black and blue with bruises.' The fact that Sarah had lapsed into English meant that Fatima had to translate for the teenager. Closing the door behind her, Fatima helped Sarah to undress and step into the fragrant bath. The women oohed and ahhed over the bruises and abrasions that covered Sarah and were as careful as they could be with her damaged body.

The assistance embarrassed Sarah as one woman washed her hair and another scrubbed her down. Fatima explained the girl's fascination was due to the fact that although Hashim Benzaar had a fetish for blonde western women, he'd never until now actually brought one to the house, his desires normally being satisfied elsewhere. This didn't reassure Sarah but this wasn't the moment to try and rectify the situation.

The girl remained silent, obviously uncomfortable about putting herself forward and Sarah smiled in a friendly manner at her.

'You must be Hashim's daughter.' Sarah looked at Fatima for an explanation when the girl burst into tears.

The Housekeeper glanced pityingly at the girl. 'Meelia is the Master's latest wife.'

Sarah's face showed her horror, 'The poor child! To lose her childhood like that!'

Fatima shook her head. 'You're a woman of the West. You will have more difficulties adjusting to this way of life.'

Sarah rose out of the water and stepping out of the bath, she thanked Fatima as she wrapped a towel around her. A smaller towel was wrapped around her hair, turban style. Not until this was done did Sarah speak.

'That won't be necessary! I'm not staying! My fiancé won't allow this to continue!' A significant look was cast between the Pangani women.

'After the Master has finished with you, your fiancé won't want you back!'

Sarah swallowed hard to keep the bile from rising into her mouth, accepting Fatima's explanation. She obediently followed Fatima back to her room where the housekeeper assisted her to dress in fresh clothes before they headed down to breakfast. *I can't wait upon being rescued but will have to escape on my own; somehow.* Sarah plotted her break for freedom.

A Delay In The Search

Prince Kahlee entered Colonel Nasseur's office (which was temporarily Cadem's) without knocking. Cadem rose immediately to his feet and stood at attention. Kahlee waved the Lieutenant back into his chair as he sat down opposite.

'How goes your interrogation?' asked the Prince.

'I now have information to Miss Trent's whereabouts.'

Prince Kahlee nodded. 'About that, I want you to wait at least 24 hours before you take any action.'

Cadem was moved to protest. 'Is that an order, your Highness?'

'Yes! I haven't gone mad, I assure you. I've a good reason for holding off as I have a plan that must remain top secret.' Kahlee wrote upon a pad of paper on the desk before handing it to Cadem.

The Lieutenant glanced at the message and as he ripped off the top two sheets of paper, he said, 'I understand, your Highness. I only hope that Miss Trent isn't made to suffer further for this delay.' He crumbled the two pieces of paper and dropped them into an ashtray that stood on the desk. Then removing a lighter from his pocket, Cadem set the paper alight.

'I'm just as concerned for Miss Trent's well-being, but there's much more at stake here.' Both men rose to their feet and Cadem saluted.

'I understand perfectly, your Highness!'

'Good!' Kahlee nodded his approval. 'Then perhaps one day you can explain it to me! No need to see me out, you have much work to do.' And upon these words the Prince left the room. Cadem sank back into his chair and picking up the telephone receiver, he dialled up a number and relayed the Prince's orders.

Disobedience Will Be Punished

Once fed, Fatima took Sarah to a cheery, sunny room that was obviously used for reading as books lined two walls from ceiling to floor. The room was unoccupied and Fatima left Sarah with a parting warning not to anger the Master. Alone, Sarah opened the large French doors that led out to a pretty courtyard. She stood in the doorway to admire the exquisite beauty of the gardens that lay before her. She was all too aware of the guard standing outside the doors and she stepped back into the room as she contemplated her next move.

'It's as expensive as it is exquisite,' stated a sarcastic voice from behind Sarah. She turned around, startled, as a man moved swiftly towards her. It hadn't been possible for Sarah to see Hashim Benzaar properly in the moonlight. She found herself faced with a forty-year-old copy of Laurence Olivier, and would have considered him handsome had his eyes not been hard and his lips curled in a sneer.

'I'm Hashim Benzaar. You will address me as Master or Sir. Is that understood?'

For a moment rebellion sparked in Sarah's eyes but she calmly said, 'Yes Sir!'

Hashim grasped Sarah by the shoulders and turned her so that her face was highlighted by the sunshine and he could take in every detail of her face and figure.

'You are indeed a very attractive young woman. Ahkman didn't exaggerate the perfections of your beauty. It is a pity though that you've tarnished such beautiful skin with bruises. Behave well and you may prosper.' Hashim ran a finger across Sarah's cheek and she tried to not shudder at his touch. 'Perhaps it'll be better for you to forget your life before now.' He released her and closing the French doors, added, 'I have a phone call to make, so present yourself in my bedroom in an hour's time.'

'No Sir!' Sarah's words were quietly yet defiantly spoken. Hashim's response was sudden and violent, striking her across the face, the force sending her reeling back against the wall.

'Fatima has obviously not impressed enough upon you the rules of the house. My word is law and disobedience is severely punished! This is your last warning, Sarah, you'll not be so lucky again.' She pressed her hand against her stinging cheek as Hashim smiled. 'Remember that and we shall deal well together. One hour then.' He didn't wait for her to answer.

Why Didn't You Listen To Me?

A few minutes later, Fatima cautiously entered the room. Her searching eyes instantly found the red hand mark on Sarah's cheek and she shook her head.

'Oh Miss Trent! Why didn't you heed my warning? The Master can't stand to have his will crossed. We'll all pay now for his displeasure.'

Sarah sank into a chair. 'I'm sorry if I've caused trouble, but this is not over yet! I will never submit! I'll get myself free, I'm meant to be with Joseph!' She sighed deeply and Fatima patted her shoulder reassuringly.

'Be patient, Miss Trent. Someone is looking for you. It can only be a matter of time before the trail will lead them here.'

'But then again it might not.'

Trap Set

Prince Kahlee stood quietly as he surveyed the men gathered in the Palace's main meeting room. The suddenness in which he called this meeting of all the Ministers was the main topic of discussion around the assembled tables. On Kahlee's left sat the Emir and on his right, Lieutenant Cadem. Kahlee's silent observation continued until all Ministers had stopped talking.

'Gentlemen, we're entering a new era of evolution in Pangani. Negotiations are under way to settle our differences with the Commune and the Fundamentalists. It is with high hopes that we may see a resolution before the New Year.' Kahlee paused as murmurs of surprise and conjecture flew around the room.

It was several minutes before the Prince attempted to speak again, 'As a first step in these negotiations, I have agreed to Caracal's demands that the Amed brothers are immediately executed.' Again Kahlee paused, not prepared to even try to make himself heard over the angry voices that resulted.

Only when the Ministers had quietened down again did Kahlee continue, 'In return for this show of faith, Caracal will discover the whereabouts of Miss Trent. Tomorrow morning we'll begin the process of reconciliation and although your attendance isn't compulsory, it would be advisable for all to attend. Be assured that all involved with Miss Trent's abduction or with the rebels will be disciplined. These discussions will hopefully bring a new peaceful era for Pangani. Please consider this future carefully and let us all contribute to making it possible. Thank you!'

As the Emir rose to his feet, so did Cadem and the Ministers. They bowed formally to the Emir and remained standing as the Emir, Kahlee and Cadem left the room. Once they had left, the Ministers would leap into speech about the Prince's revelations. *I know and expect this and I'm not particularly worried about what they might say to each other,* mused Kahlee. *I am concerned, though, about what they might do* and with this in mind, Kahlee led Cadem off to his own office. Cadem politely refused the Prince's offer of a cigarette as they sat down and Kahlee apologized as he lit a cigarette for himself.

'Relanna won't let me smoke because of the baby but at the moment I need a stress reliever,' Kahlee paused, giving Cadem the chance to reply, but the Lieutenant thought it more politically correct not to comment.

'I just hope they don't think too long and hard about Trevane, a pacifist, wanting the death penalty! I need them scared enough for their own lives. They mustn't question our ruse.' After a long drag on the cigarette, the Prince continued, 'Tell me Captain, are your men prepared as I requested?'

A moment of surprise flickered in Cadem's eyes but he quickly concealed it. 'As agreed, each Minister as he leaves the Palace will have an unobserved shadow. There is also a tap placed upon their landline and mobile phones. If any of them attempt to contact Hashim Benzaar of his impending arrest, then we'll immediately know about it. Also, your Highness, I'm a Lieutenant and not a Captain,' Cadem quietly corrected. Kahlee stubbed out his cigarette and laughed.

'Not any more, Captain Cadem. In due course I'd like you to take over from Joseph. I foresee that he may well turn to politics and become Minister of Security.'

Cadem was visibly shaken and tried to protest but Kahlee waved aside his attempt to deny the truth.

'I want the Ameds to suffer for what they have done to Joseph. Right now he should have been enjoying congratulations for his engagement to a beautiful and intelligent young woman and not languishing in a hospital wondering if he's ever going to see her again.'

Cadem was surprised. 'You knew this too?'

Kahlee smiled. 'What gave you the impression that I was blind as well as stupid?'

'Your Highness!' protested Cadem but Kahlee only laughed.

'Relax Captain; you'll have to become accustomed to my strange sense of humour. Keep me informed upon Joseph's condition and when your people report in.' Cadem rose to his feet, understanding that the interview was over. He saluted and marched out of the room.

What Do They Really Want?

Crystal and Gary sat on the verandah of the Residency after lunch and the noise of the protesters at the front gate didn't immediately disturb their conversation. It was the sound of Jeb and Ash barking that finally attracted Crystal's attention, and she rose to cross to the railing. A couple of protesters had attempted to climb over the wall and the dogs took exception to this, so did the military guards who roughly hauled them off the wall.

Running her fingers through her auburn curls, Crystal sighed. This caused Gary to look up in concern.

'What is it Crystal?'

She looked back at him, as she sat down on the railing. 'This might be a really stupid question, but what exactly are they protesting for?'

Gary shrugged, 'Communism? Anti-foreigners? Supporters of the Islamic State?' Absently he scratched Simon's ear as the puppy lay across his lap.

'But what's behind it? I can see how the Fundamentalists would benefit from the chaos. It could lead to stricter, harsher controls being implemented, but the people, in general, don't want that, do they? So who is pushing the hysteria?'

Gary leant back in his chair as he considered her question. 'The Fundamentalists and the Commune want opposite changes but are happy enough to keep the Emir as head of the country.'

'What do the Rebels want? Their demands seem to be the most extreme.'

Gary nodded. 'Removing the Emir as ruler of Pangani will not bring about a democratic government as the military would step in and create Marshall Law.'

'Then what? I mean how would that benefit the Rebels?'

'They would have to then destroy the military to seize power for themselves.'

'But that could mean the deaths of hundreds if not thousands of their own people! That is insane!' Crystal stared at him.

Gary calmly agreed. 'Yes, but they are driven by their desire for a pure Islamic State with no foreigners.'

'Why can't the people see that they're being manipulated?' Crystal turned back to look out of the window again.

'Racism is very emotive. Most people feel it to some degree, no matter how well they try to deny the fact. Some can control it better than others.'

Have You Heard The News?

A gasp escaped from Crystal as Con drove into the compound at a reckless pace and stopped in a spray of gravel in front of them. He was out of the car and up the steps in a state of panic. Gary immediately rose and caught Con as he collapsed against the front door.

'Oh my God! Gary, they're dead! They're all dead!' Con screamed.

The excessive noise Con was making saw a half dressed Ambassador rip open the door. Con Zuco burst into the living room, in an agitated state. Gary and Crystal followed by Simon staying close to Gary's heels; he still didn't like Con.

'He's done it! He actually went and did it!' exclaimed Con, breathless.

James Greene shook his head in confusion, 'Who?' He demanded. By this stage Con had noticed the Ambassador's state of undress, as he wore only trousers.

'Isn't it a little late to be getting up, James?' asked Con.

Gary glared at his lack of diplomacy. 'That isn't important Con! I've been listening to the radio. The Amed brothers have been executed. Caracal had demanded it. Apparently he was displeased that not only was his brother nearly killed but also that he has lost a sister-in-law.'

'James? What is it? Is it Sarah?' Marianne appeared from the Ambassador's bedroom, fully dressed but without her shoes. Con Zuco's eyebrows rose into his hairline but a warning stab in the kidneys from Crystal meant that he was to keep his tongue between his teeth. James briefly filled Marianne in on what Con had told him.

'When do they find Sarah?'

'Prince Kahlee and Lieutenant Cadem are doing all they can to locate Sarah.' James pressed her hand reassuringly.

Gary nodded. 'The major problem is that all along the abductors have known every move made to rescue Sarah, almost as soon as we do. Caracal has permission to deal with anyone else that has been involved with Sarah's abduction. They may not get the severity of judgment that the Ameds received but I don't envy them.'

Although Con had gone quite pale, no one paid any notice to him as Marianne gave a cry of despair. 'I don't care if Caracal roasts them alive! When will they return poor Sarah to us?'

'We all want her back, Marianne,' James placed a comforting arm around her shoulders, 'but Lieutenant Cadem wants to get all the people involved with Sarah's kidnapping. We must trust him to deliver Sarah safely to us as soon as he can.'

Gary agreed with the Ambassador, but he had one correction to make, 'Lieutenant Cadem has been promoted to Captain.'

James paced back and forth; a frown marred his brow as his colleagues waited silently for him to speak. The Ambassador paused and shot a penetrating look at Gary. 'This just waiting is killing us! Is there nothing we can do to speed up the search?'

'I'm barely allowed to assist!' Gary said as he shook his head. 'The best you can do is keep the Embassy running and the staff out of trouble. I've got some enquires I wish to make.' He glanced across at Con, who was also frowning in thought. 'I think I'll go and check on Colonel Nasseur. Do you want a lift?' The Major's question startled Con but he managed to answer.

'No thanks. I've got some business that needs sorting.' Con turned and simply walked out, leaving the Ambassador to raise a questioning eyebrow at Gary, who only shook his head.

'Who knows what goes on in that mind of Con's? I'm sorry we disturbed you.' Gary laid a comforting hand on Marianne's shoulder and added, 'Sarah should be back with us tomorrow.'

'She'd better be, Gary!' Fire returned to Marianne's eyes as she rose regally to her feet. 'I want to see some action before anyone else gets seriously hurt.'

James nodded his agreement. 'We all want that, but all those guilty must be brought to justice,' He transferred his gaze to Gary. 'Keep us informed of any new developments.'

The Major nodded and escaped to follow his own lead of enquiry, hopeful that James would be able to calm Marianne down.

I Am Not A Possession!

Fatima reluctantly led Sarah to Hashim's bedroom. The Housekeeper begged Sarah not to anger the Master any further, but she would only promise that no one else would suffer because of her. This didn't reassure Fatima, in fact it gave her more cause for concern but there was little she could do to change Sarah's mind. The Housekeeper checked her watch to ensure that it was exactly one hour before knocking on the door.

'Come!'

'Please Miss Trent, you got off lightly before. The Master has a sadistic streak in him and he would enjoy making you suffer if you defy him again,' Fatima pleaded.

Sarah shook her head. 'Don't worry; he won't take me unaware again.' She opened the door and entered the room, closing the door confidently behind her.

The room was dominated by a large elaborately decorated queen sized bed, which Sarah tried to ignore, keeping her eyes firmly fixed upon Hashim Benzaar as he reclined in a comfortable chair by the window. His eyes ran down her body, mentally stripping Sarah of her clothes. Despite this, she kept her chin up and was determined not to be afraid of what lay before her.

'Come here!'

Sarah momentarily thought about immediately rebelling but stepping forward she decided that she would wait for the appropriate time to challenge Hashim. He smiled at Sarah's apparent docility as he rose to his feet and drew her into his arms. Sarah stiffened but didn't resist, keeping her head raised as her eyes sparkled in defiance.

'I am glad to see that you have heeded my warning, Sarah. I admit that I would've enjoyed breaking your spirit, but you shall find me a generous master if you choose to please me.' Hashim's hold on Sarah was not restrictive and she easily pulled away from him.

'But I don't choose to, Hashim Benzaar! I'm not a possession and won't be treated like one! Nor will you punish others for my rebellion. This is solely between you and me.'

A sneer marred Hashim's features. 'I completely agree. You're a foolish girl; no one defies me in my own home. You shall learn the wisdom of keeping your tongue between your teeth.' As Hashim approached her, Sarah stepped back to give herself room. Hashim saw her retreat as a sign of weakness and continued to advance.

'Your tyranny ends here and now, Benzaar. You have no power over me and shall return me to where I rightly belong.'

'Oh honey, that man won't even acknowledge your existence once I've finished with you!' Hashim grabbed Sarah but she wasn't going to give in without a fight. She hadn't had any self-defence lessons from Joseph or Gary but Sarah had grown up with three older siblings. Despite her injuries she kicked and scratched and punched Hashim like a wild animal until one punch connected with his nose.

Blood poured down his face and Hashim roared in pain. Taking advantage of his distraction, Sarah kicked him in the groin. The noise of the fight brought several of his guards running to his assistance and it took two men to pull Sarah away as she tried to continue fighting. Hashim held a handkerchief to his bleeding nose.

'Get her out of here! Send her to the trader, Draken; he might be able to make some money from her!' The guards dragged Sarah out of the bedroom, for the moment the winner of that round.

I Want Some Answers

The guard stationed outside of Colonel Nasseur's room in the hospital was taken by surprise as Gary Winters walked purposefully towards him and without a second glance, entered the secured area. The guard, raising his rifle, ordered the Major to halt and desist. With fire in his eyes, Gary easily relieved the guard of his weapon and threw it on to a nearby empty bed.

'Go away son! I'm not in the mood for party games!'

The guard reached for his side arm but a commanding voice from within the room, stilled his attempt to remove Gary.

'That will be all, Corporal. Major Winters is no threat.' Captain Cadem came forward to stand beside Gary. The guard saluted, retrieving his rifle before retreating. A ghost of a smile lingered about the Captain's mouth.

'You like to live dangerously, Major. If the Corporal had been quicker off the mark, you would now be dead.'

Gary uttered a harsh laugh. 'Why haven't you rescued Sarah yet?'

A significant glance was exchanged between Cadem and Colonel Nasseur, who was sitting up in his bed. He was no longer connected to half a dozen machines but still looked very weak and tired.

Gary sat down opposite Nasseur as Cadem moved to stand by the Colonel's right hand.

'We can go in and get Miss Trent at any time.' The newly appointed Captain shook his head. 'But it is essential that all involved are caught. Every member of the Ministry has a shadow. We will know immediately if any of them attempt to contact the man who has Sarah.'

The Major frowned as he thought this through. 'But what if it isn't one of the Ministers who are involved?'

Cadem's face registered his surprise. 'Who else, apart from the Rebels, would have anything to gain from Miss Trent's abduction?'

'Con!' Gary supplied. *It is clear now why the execution of the Ameds had so affected Con Zuco.*

A silence followed as both men looked to the Colonel for an answer, 'I want you positioned outside of Benzaar's house as of five minutes ago!' Cadem saluted and dragged Gary to his feet and out the door. They had no time to waste.

How Do You Know About Me?

Hashim Benzaar was not in a very receptive mood when he entered his study to find Con Zuco making himself at home. Fatima had managed to stop Hashim's nose bleeding but it was rather swollen and already both his eyes were starting to go black with bruising. Hashim was in considerable pain which meant his temper was shorter than usual.

'I don't know how you found out about me, but I thought we were supposed to have nothing to do with each other. Didn't you deal with this in your plan?'

'There was no plan!' Con snapped, 'I never actually thought Ahkman would kidnap Sarah. Why didn't he leave her at the cottage to be rescued?'

'He wanted money to get out of Kathou. How did you find me?' Hashim sat down behind his desk.

Con dismissed that question as being insignificant. 'Ahkman used to boast about his wealthy cousin and his... fetishes shall we call them? That's not important, where is Sarah?'

Hashim grunted. 'The bitch is more of a fighter than I was prepared to put up with. She's disfigured me!'

Jumping to his feet Con paced up and down the room. 'You'll live, damn you! Four to six weeks and you'll be as good as new. Where is she? Did you... you didn't actually... you know...' He didn't want to actually say the words in case it brought up images that couldn't be erased from his mind.

'No, I barely touched her. I wonder if I gave up too soon. It would certainly be rewarding to break her. She'd have to be subdued somehow though.'

'If she isn't here then where the fuck is she?' In his frustration Con thrust his fingers through his hair.

'Gone. In a fit of pique I sent her to a trader,' Hashim went to press his hand against his face but it was still too painful to touch.

'What sort of trader?' Con stopped pacing to stare at Hashim in disbelief. 'Who the fuck buys women?'

Hashim raised a sardonic eyebrow. 'You mean apart from people like me?' Con mumbled an apology that he didn't feel. 'I sent her to a slave trader I know. He supplies me sometimes when I have a specific need.'

'Where can I find him? I have to get Sarah back?'

Hashim shook his head as he smiled. 'You'll have to join the others at the auction. She will be a prime article apart from her bruises. Every man will want to make her his sex toy.'

'For fuck's sake man, don't say that! I must save her!' Con went deathly pale in horror.

'Why not? It is after all what you only wanted her for isn't it?' Laughing Hashim flipped through a pile of business cards before finally selecting one and tossed it across to Con. 'It's only a telephone number. I suggest you attend the auction if you ever want to see her again.' He rose to his feet, clearly indicating that this conversation was at an end. Con shoved the business card into his breast pocket as he stormed out of the house.

I'll Kill Him!

Cadem and Gary were parked on the opposite side of the street and a few houses down from Hashim's house. They'd been there half an hour when they observed Con Zuco's car pull into the driveway. Gary was obviously shocked when he recognized his colleague. Cadem was more composed as he reported in to Colonel Nasseur.

'So he really was behind all this! I'll kill him! That spineless bastard has known all this time where Sarah was! If she has been made to suffer, I'll kill him!'

Cadem wasn't seriously disturbed by Gary's threats. 'Five seconds of justice is not worth it, Major. There are difficulties, though, serious difficulties. Con Zuco can never be tried in this country unless his diplomatic immunity is revoked by Canberra.'

Gary's face showed his anger. 'You can't expect me to stand by as a criminal gets away?'

Cadem shook his head, a look of steel in his eyes. 'As you know the Colonel doesn't always play by the rules and in this instance, if you keep a cool head and follow orders, we may be able to apply our own justice.'

'What do you want me to do?' Gary's eyes brightened in determination.

They watched as Con came back outside alone and Cadem placed a restraining hand on Gary's shoulder as he was about to get out of the car to tackle Con.

'Not yet! I want somewhere more private to deal with Con Zuco. Trust me!'

You Blood Sucking Maggot!

Con returned to his car, completely unaware that he was being watched, even though he did look up and down the street before backing out of the driveway. Cadem started his car and they followed Con at a safe distance, sitting well back in the traffic but never letting him out of their sight. Con drove back into the city, barely able to consider any road rules as he frantically tried to think how to raise a large sum of money in a very short period of time. *The real trouble is that Sarah will be expensive; perhaps more than any amount I could raise in the limited time I have available.*

Con pulled into an alley behind the bar he usually frequented and parked. The bar manager owed him some money from a poker game, not enough to buy Sarah outright but enough perhaps for a down payment. He had barely stepped out of his vehicle when Cadem's car came abruptly around the corner and stopped millimetres from hitting Con.

'What the fuck are you doing?' Con's protest was the only sound he could make before Gary had leapt out of the car and had his hand clasped around Con's throat.

'You worthless blood sucking maggot! You were behind Sarah's abduction this whole time? If that man has laid a finger on Sarah I'll be chopping yours off one by one!'

Con couldn't answer as he could barely breathe; Cadem, appearing on the other side of Con, had one objection.

'Not to dampen your justifiable rage, Major, but maggots eat rotting flesh, leeches suck blood.'

Gary transferred his gaze away from Con but the grip on his throat didn't lessen, 'Really? Leeches huh? Thanks.' Con was starting to go blue and Cadem reluctantly pointed this out to Gary. With even greater reluctance the Major loosened his grip.

'Is Sarah still in Benzaar's house? Has he touched her?' Gary demanded as Con gasped gratefully for breath.

'She fought like a wild cat so he was unable to get near her. I swear it Gary. Benzaar sent her to some slave trader.' Con struggled to pull out the business card from his breast pocket and pressed it into Cadem's hand. 'There's a sale on this evening at a warehouse. The address I wrote it on the back. Ease up

Gary! Fucking hell!' Although Con was no longer blue, he was still struggling to breathe. Gary released Con's throat but cuffed him over the back of the head.

'Shut up Con! Cadem, can you trace this man?' Gary motioned to the card in Cadem's hand.

Before the Captain could answer, Con interjected, 'There's no point, he said on the phone that the girls were kept at a secret location that only he knows about. I tried to buy Sarah on the quiet but Draken said she was his draw card for a big sale.'

A look of revulsion swept over Gary's face as he sprang upon Con, both hands reaching for his throat, 'you loathsome, repulsive toad! This world would be a better place if I removed you from it!'

With lightning reactions Cadem pulled Gary away before he could choke the life out of Con. 'No Major! We don't have time for that! We must report to Colonel Nasseur and make our plans to rescue Miss Trent.' It was several minutes before Gary had enough control over his rage to allow Cadem to release him.

'I will deal with you later Con. Don't think you'll escape punishment!' Gary got back into the car beside Cadem, so consumed with fury that he didn't speak as they headed back to the hospital.

How Do You Want To Handle This?

Although the Colonel's eyes were closed, he wasn't asleep as he was listening to the report from Gary and Cadem.

'How do you want to tackle this Cadem?'

The Captain was surprised that Joseph was handing the rescue over to him. 'Don't you want to run this operation yourself Sir?'

As Joseph opened his eyes, the pain in them was hard to ignore. 'At the moment the drugs to relieve pain also mean that my brain feels like cotton wool.'

Gary fought hard to keep his features from reflecting his pity for his friend.

'I do have an idea,' Cadem rushed into speech also struggling to contain his emotions, 'hit the warehouse with overwhelming force. Not guns blazing but seal off every exit with enough armed men to make them realise that any resistance is not an option they want to make.'

His two senior officers thought over his plan. Joseph finally glanced over at Gary, 'I see one problem, but I'm not certain it is the only one. Gary, what do you think?'

The Major slowly ran a hand over his jaw as he tried to find the right words. 'Fundamentally, it could work. An amazing show of force could make them shit themselves and just surrender.'

'Please Sir just give me the one or more 'buts' that are coming.' Cadem sighed.

Gary chuckled. 'Okay, that much man power would mean pulling all personnel away from the fight against the rebels. Even for Joseph I don't think you'll get ministry approval.'

'That was my fear.' Joseph nodded.

'There is another,' Gary added, 'going in like that, Draken could use the women as a shield and refuse to give them up. If it came to a fire fight, you may have them out gunned but you can't guarantee that the women won't be injured or killed.' Gary settled down into his seat and put his fingers together as he struggled to think of an alternative.

'What you want is to capture not just Draken but everyone also involved in the trade,' the Colonel suggested.

'The only way to achieve that, Sir,' answered Cadem, 'would be to go in as a buyer.'

'That's what Con had planned if he could raise the capital,' added Gary.

Something akin to a growl emanated from Joseph. 'I don't want that man anywhere near Sarah!'

Gary was worried that his friend would rip out the tubes leading into his arm in frustration. 'Stay calm Joseph. We'll get Sarah back and deal with Con Zuco!'

Cadem had another concern, 'That sort of money, sir, well it's beyond my pay scale.' The Captain didn't want to bring up the sensitive subject of money. He had no idea how much money his superior officer made or what the Nasseur family were actually worth.

'Would Prince Kahlee consider a temporary loan as once the traders are arrested, he'll get the money back,' suggested Gary.

Joseph smiled, 'I don't think getting the money will be a problem.'

Cadem wasn't certain that the Colonel understood how much they would actually require to succeed, 'Being fair and western, Miss Trent could go as high as half a million dollars.'

Joseph Nasseur nodded, 'Do you want me to organise a banker's cheque or a briefcase of cash?'

Cadem choked slightly. 'Are you joking sir?'

'Not at all. Cash will give you more bargaining power.' Despite the pain Joseph was in, there was a twinkle in his eyes. 'If you can get me some paper and pen for me, I'll write to the bank for you.' He left both his colleagues speechless, not really certain if Colonel Nasseur was serious or not.

Princess Relanna's Protest

Later that day, Princess Relanna did something forbidden by entering her husband's office without being summoned or prior permission being granted. Kahlee looked up; the anger in his eyes dying almost as quickly as it had risen when he perceived that Relanna was looking very tired. The Prince hurried to his feet to ease his pregnant wife into a chair.

'Relanna…' Kahlee's protest was cut short by a wave of the Princess' hand.

'Kahlee, it is time!'

The devoted husband knelt down beside her, his hands resting affectionately upon her extended stomach. 'I'll have an ambulance sent for immediately.'

'No, Kah!' Relanna smiled slightly as she shook her head. 'It is time that you bring this charade to an end. Allah will see that all guilty will be punished, but right now a young woman's life is in danger. It stops here, Kahlee, no more political games!'

'Well said sister!' The drawl from the doorway surprised them both. Kahlee rose to his feet and instinctively stood protectively in front of his wife.

'Have you forgotten how to knock, Trevane?' demanded the Prince, relaxing slightly.

The Commune leader smiled, 'One of the privileges of being an outcast, Kahlee.' Caracal shook his head before continuing, 'Where is he?'

Prince Kahlee looked at him with a blank expression, 'Joseph? He is in Pangani General Hospital.'

Caracal sighed and cast his brother in law a weary look. 'No more games! I want Con Zuco! He will face our justice as the Ameds will.'

Relanna uttered a protest but Kahlee shook his head. 'I can't do that. The Australian Public Affairs officer is, for the moment, beyond our justice.'

'Is that all you men can think about?' Relanna's demand came as a surprise. 'I can see how Marianne Davis becomes frustrated with your politics. Getting Sarah back should be your priority; not who has the right to punish the criminals. Captain Cadem is the only one actually doing something about rescuing Sarah. Even so, you both manage to hamper his efforts from succeeding! Please, just stop all this nonsense and end this madness.'

Both men were momentarily shamed but Caracal eventually shook his head as he said, 'It's not that easy Relanna. But I'll leave the fine print to Kahlee. I basically came to inform you that I've made a few enquires through contacts in the black market. It would appear that it's now a race between Cadem and myself to whom brings home the results.'

'This is not a game, Trevane!' Relanna threw her hands up in disgust.

The only answer she received was a deep throaty laugh as Caracal left as mysteriously as he had arrived. To infuriate Relanna further, Kahlee, who was thoughtfully stroking his chin, stated, 'My money's on Cadem.' Relanna screamed in disbelief and told her husband exactly what she thought of his cavalier attitude.

The Warehouse

When Sarah finally became conscious that evening, her head throbbed from the drug Benzaar's men had given her. When she tried to raise her hands, she found that they were bound together by rope, as were her feet. Glancing around, Sarah discovered that she was lying on the floor of a medium sized room filled with at least a dozen women of varying nationalities. *With no windows and a door that looks like we would need a tank to break it open; I realize the futility of even contemplating escape.* Yet struggling to sit up, she was surprised to be addressed in English. A tall, handsome woman with long brown, curly hair and the features and attire of a gypsy, rose to her feet and approached Sarah. As the woman knelt down beside Sarah, she produced a small, sharp knife from under her belt and although she smiled, Sarah shrank away from her.

'I mean you no harm, Sarah Trent! The fact that you've made it this far, alive, is testimony to your bravery.' The woman cut the ropes that bound Sarah's hands and feet.

'You know who I am?' Sarah asked.

'The whole world has heard of Sarah Trent.' The gypsy girl laughed. 'Your abduction made front-page news worldwide. Your escape from this ordeal may be a little more difficult.'

As she considered their options, Sarah rubbed her wrists, being careful of the injured one. Although there was a low murmur of voices in the room, the other women were basically silent, as the petite Secretary may just be their only ticket to freedom. Sarah finally looked up at the gypsy.

'Do you have a basic understanding of the layout of Kathou?'

The gypsy nodded. 'If we get out of here, I can get you back to the Australian Embassy.'

Sarah shook her head. 'I'm sorry; I haven't even asked you your name.'

'I've been called many things in my life time, but my mother named me Chandelle.' The gypsy smiled.

'Describe to me the building that we are in please, Chandelle.'

There was a moment's pause before the gypsy answered, 'It's a manufacturing warehouse, about 20 miles south from Kathou. From what I saw on the way in, there are at least three rooms underground and we're in the middle one. Escape from this room is impossible but it won't be any easier once we're taken upstairs.'

'There are guards?'

Chandelle nodded.

'Dogs?'

'No.'

'Damn! Are we taken out one at a time or all together?'

Chandelle frowned in thought. 'Probably all together so that the buyers can see over the menu!' The gypsy's humour caused several of the women to shudder in horror. They all wore just their usually clothing having been stripped of their hijab.

'You, though, they'll sell first, a sort of piece de resistance! The bidding will be highest for you.'

Sarah tried to ignore the feeling of revulsion that swept over her. 'Can you handle a gun?'

'Naturally!' Chandelle inclined her head as she smiled mischievously.

Sarah glanced at each of the women. 'Then this is what we're going to do.' They gathered around her, grasping at what might just be their one chance for freedom.

Don't Sugar Coat It!

Crystal looked up in surprise as Gary's car drew up outside the Residency in a spray of gravel. She hadn't seen or heard from him since Con had burst in at lunchtime to announce that the Ameds had been executed. She was sitting on the verandah with Simon, Ash and Jeb. As the Major slammed the car door, Crystal started to become alarmed.

'Gary, what is it? What's happened? Are you any closer to finding Sarah?' She rose to her feet as he leapt up the steps.

'Has Con been back here?' demanded Gary.

'No, should he return? Is Con responsible for all this madness?' Crystal tried to keep up with him as he strode into the Residency. Gary stopped abruptly and turning as she ploughed into him, he reached out to steady her.

'Why do you ask that? What do you know Crystal?'

'I don't know anything Gary.' She was shocked by how fierce he looked. 'Con's been acting peculiar ever since Sarah went missing. He seemed about to wet himself when he revealed that the Ameds were executed. Is he involved?'

'Yes, he's involved!' Letting go of her, Gary continued towards the liquor cabinet to pour a large whiskey, 'He claims Ahkman misunderstood his whinging about Sarah as a request to abduct her.'

'Misunderstood?' Crystal took his glass once he had tossed its contents down and refilled it for him. 'Where's Sarah now? When is she coming back?'

'She was sold to a slave trader,' Gary groaned, 'There's a sale tonight.'

Collapsing into a chair, Crystal went deathly pale, 'Oh my God! Gary, you've got to get Sarah back! Please, please tell me you've got a plan!'

Hesitating raising his glass back to his mouth, Gary changed his mind and pressed it against Crystal's lips. 'Drink!' he ordered, tipping the liquor down her throat. As Crystal spluttered and choked, colour came back to her cheeks. Gary gently patted her on the back until the coughing stopped.

'There is a plan but anything we do try is going to be risky.' He poured out another drink for himself. 'We're going in blind. No idea of the warehouse's layout, or the number of people we'll have to deal with. We can't take any guns in with us and there will be other women in danger apart from Sarah.'

'You can tell it to me straight Gary, don't sugar coat the situation for my sensibilities.' Crystal drew Gary down onto the sofa beside her.

Gary burst into laughter, 'Oh Crystal, thank you! Was I being over melodramatic?'

'Just a tad darling! Is Joseph starting to crack too under the stress of it all?' Crystal wrapped her arms around him to offer comfort.

'I seriously think Joseph would much rather be back with Sarah in that cottage than being separated from her. Not knowing what's happening to her right now is pure torture for him. Con reckons the first guy she was sold to didn't get a chance to touch her but we've no idea what the new guy could be doing.'

Crystal shuddered in horror. 'Oh God, Gary, if that's the way you try to cheer the Colonel up, he's probably homicidal by now! You can't give up hope. Whatever they have done to her, we'll get her back and together we'll get her through the nightmares.'

'Cling to that dream, Crystal, somehow in a couple of hours, we're going to try and make it a reality.' He buried his face for a moment in Crystal's hair.

I'm Going To De-Stress You

She brought his cheek down to rest against her breasts. 'What do you need to do before you and Cadem ride in with the Calvary?'

Gary groaned, 'There's nothing I can do until Cadem picks me up in about four hours.' He really liked the way she felt in his arms.

'When did you last eat something? I don't remember you actually eating at lunchtime.'

'Breakfast, I think.' Gary was surprised that he couldn't really remember eating the past two days. Getting to her feet, Crystal dragged him up as well.

'Come on, I'm going to de-stress you and then I'm going to feed you.'

'Okay, then what are you going to do?'

Crystal smiled, 'Then I'm going to de-stress you again.'

'Let me get this straight...'

Crystal gave him a shove in the back. 'Just get in the bedroom before I strip you here!'

As he followed Crystal towards her bedroom, he did have one last question, 'Where is...?'

'Dad and Marianne are over at the Embassy.' Crystal was already pulling off her t-shirt. 'Here, put this on the outer door knob, it should be enough of a hint not to enter.' Crystal handed Gary her bra and he stared at her in disbelief. In less than a minute she had stripped naked.

'My God, you're so beautiful!' He seemed to be frozen so Crystal placed her bra on the door knob, made certain it was locked before she started to undress Gary. *I hope that he isn't going to be frozen for too long as I don't want to do all the work.*

The Sale

When the guards came for the women, although they were naturally scared about what was to take place, they held some hope in their breasts that they would survive the ordeal. Sarah remained sitting as the other women rose reluctantly to their feet. One guard came forward and dragged her up and Chandelle pushed him away as Sarah cried out.

'For goodness sake! Can't you see that she's incapable of standing on her own?' Chandelle made a show of helping an obviously unsteady Sarah out of the room. The other women followed silently behind them, through a small cramped corridor and up a dozen steps to the empty warehouse. In the open work area before them were nearly a hundred men of varying nationalities and ages, and the sight of so many searching, leering eyes caused Sarah's courage to falter.

'Holy Mother grant me strength!' she whispered.

'In unity there will be strength, Sarah, but for unity we must have a strong leader.' Chandelle tightened her grip upon Sarah's arm. 'Consider the fate of us all if we fail!' She took a deep breath and nodded.

The women were lined up across a make-shift stage so that they were all visible to their potential buyers. Sarah found her knees were shaking and was grateful for Chandelle's supporting hand. A middle aged, obese and sweating man waddled up the line of women on the stage, leering at each woman as he went passed. Most of the women lowered their eyes away from his lustful gaze; only Chandelle met his gaze with an arrogance that was a part of her blood. He was the one to first break eye contact with the gypsy as he hurriedly turned to address the assembly.

'Gentlemen! Welcome to Draken's warehouse sale. All intending bidders must have a numbered card; otherwise bids will not be accepted. Please ensure that you have sufficient credit as disclaimers are dealt with very harshly. I would like to remind all newcomers that armed guards man every exit. Trouble makers will also be harshly dealt with. Now that the preliminaries have been dealt with, we shall begin the auction with the little item that many of you are here expressly to bid upon.'

Con turned up the collar of his jacket as he moved through the other buyers, trying to get closer to the stage. *I don't have the money to compete against this crowd and looking at the guards Draken has positioned around the warehouse, a "grab her and run for it" scenario is virtually a suicide mission. I have no idea what I am going to do, I had hoped an opportunity would present itself in due course. I still have dreams of rescuing Sarah in a blaze of glory but I have to face the fact that I just mightn't have the balls to carry it off.* Looking around, Con half expected to see either Cadem or Gary in the crowd but either they hadn't arrived yet or perhaps were so well disguised that Con couldn't distinguish them from the rest of the pariah around him.

Draken turned and grabbing Sarah by the arm dragged her forward. Mindful of the role she had to play, Sarah swayed and as Draken released her, she elegantly collapsed to the floor. A couple of men closest to the stage stepped forward to assist Sarah, but the sound of the armed guards slotting back the bolts of their rifles made them step warily back. Draken looked back at Chandelle.

'Pick her up!'

Chandelle moved forward to obey, managing to hide her smile as their plan was working perfectly.

'Such beauty, such refinement, so western and such blonde hair,' crooned Draken, 'who will start the bidding with a thousand US dollars?'

This bid was accepted and the bidding quickly escalated by a thousand dollars each new bid. Sarah's obvious western attributes were an essential key to her popularity, even with all her bruises. When the bidding rose to a quarter of a million dollars, Chandelle removed her sharp little knife and holding Sarah in a crushing grip, placed her knife against Sarah's throat.

Another Escape Attempt

A hush fell over the warehouse so that it wasn't necessary for Chandelle to raise her voice to be heard. 'If such a pretty little package is worth so much money, then my freedom for her life is a small price to pay. Now if you want to be really generous you will pay for the release us all, and I won't hurt the western woman!'

There was a low murmur and much shaking of heads in the crowd. Draken tried to silently signal his guards but Chandelle held Sarah so that her body sheltered the gypsy from possible assassination.

'Don't even think about it!' Chandelle warned. One man moved through the crowd, his eyes meeting and holding Chandelle's in a way that she found disturbing. He was a tall man, a native Panganian with snow-white hair, although he wasn't very old. When he stood in front of the stage, he calmly spoke, 'You're lying! You are incapable of injuring Miss Trent.'

Chandelle laughed, 'Do I have to carve up this pretty girl's face to prove that I am serious?'

Sarah closed her eyes and remained perfectly still as Chandelle slowly ran her blade across the side of her throat. Chandelle was careful to avoid major veins and arteries, but the blood that spurted forth made a spectacular display. The white haired man held out his hand. 'Enough! I will purchase all of you for a million dollars and your freedom and that of the others will be assured!'

Chandelle hesitated. 'Why should I trust you?'

'Miss Trent's hand in marriage to my Master will be your guarantee of safety for all the women.' He had jumped up onto the stage. Whispers flew around the warehouse at this latest revelation.

Chandelle still hesitated, her eyes never wavering from the man's face.

'It's all right Chandelle,' Sarah spoke calmly, 'if it means you and the other women can go free, I'll do this.' *I know every step we take now is one more step away from Joseph and safety. My only hope is if I can reason with my 'husband' to let me go before anything happens.* Slowly, the gypsy relaxed her hold upon Sarah and handed him the knife. The whole room waited, breathlessly as the buyer wiped the blade before placing it into his trouser pocket. Chandelle pulled out a clean handkerchief and pressed it firmly against Sarah's bleeding throat.

'Understand this, if you double cross me, I'll hunt you down and kill you!' promised Chandelle.

'What would stop me from killing you here and now?' He smiled, amused at being threatened.

Chandelle laughed, 'You have just given your word in front of all these witnesses that you will guarantee our safety!'

'Excellent!' The gentleman laughed in delight. 'My master shall enjoy debating with you.'

Draken threw a first aid kit at Chandelle, ordering her to patch up Sarah while he did business with the buyer. The rest of the buyers were told to clear out until the next auction. Con tried to move forward against the sea of men who were exiting the warehouse in the opposite direction. He looked back helplessly as Draken led the buyer into the office to finalise the deal and the other women were escorted out the back door.

They were loaded into a mini bus as Chandelle placed a dressing on Sarah's throat.

'Please don't leave me!' begged Sarah as the guards came to collect them and Chandelle squeezed her hand.

'I'll never leave you!' she promised as they were dragged into the office.

A Wedding

Sarah was beginning to feel light headed and stumbled for real against Chandelle for support. *I haven't eaten since breakfast and I may have lost more blood than we had anticipated with our foiled escape plan.* When one of the guards reached out to take Sarah's arm, Chandelle snarled at him like a savage dog. He shrunk back in surprise and Sarah tried to smile reassuringly up at him but she found it increasingly hard to control any facial movements. She clung tighter to the gypsy's arm, afraid she was about to pass out.

In the office apart from Draken and the buyer, was a Qazi, an official who performed Muslim marriages. *It looks like the marriage is going to be difficult to dispute as being legal. An annulment will be the best option that I can hope for. How can I possible talk my way out of a stranger's bed who literally owns me is going to take more strength than I possess at the moment,* Sarah mused.

The brief ceremony passed over Sarah in a blur of faces and words. She barely heard as the Qazi asked, 'Do you wish to accept this man as your husband?'

Sarah was surprised to hear she said, 'Yes,' without hesitation *but I know I have to agree for the other women.* She fought to keep her eyes open but everything appeared to be shrouded in smoke. *What is the Qazi saying now?*

'God's blessing to be with the couple in their lives together.' *It sounds so hollow; it should be for two people deeply in love. It should be me and Joseph. It will never be me and Joseph now!* Tears streamed down her face and Sarah didn't even feel the little gold band that was slipped onto her bare finger. Draken had taken Joseph's engagement ring so as this new ring slid into its place, Sarah felt as if the last link to Joseph had been severed forever. With a heart breaking sob Sarah gave into the fog enclosing around her, barely aware of the taste of honey on her tongue or someone placing her hand in something sticky and then it was gone again. There was a pen in her hand and instinctively she signed the paper placed in front of her. *It is finally over! My dream of marriage to the man I love will now never happen! I can't fight any more! I can't see! I can't breathe!* Sarah welcomed the darkness as it came to take her by the hand and led her to oblivion and she fainted backwards into the buyer's arms.

Con Faces A Harsh Reality

Once again Con watched from his car as events were taken out of his control. The other women had been loaded into a mini bus and the driver, with his cap pulled down over his dark sunglasses, guarded the door with a semi-automatic machine gun. The bus driver had a briefcase handcuffed to his wrist, which the buyer came outside to unlock and take back inside with him. The driver of the limousine parked beside the minibus also had his cap pulled down low over his dark sunglasses. Both drivers held formidable weapons. Con scratched his head as he tried to rationalise what was going on. *It's 10 at night. Why the hell are these dudes wearing shades? Who would bring a bus to an auction unless they're absolutely certain they're going to walk away with the lot? Why is there something so familiar about the chiselled jaw of the mini bus driver?*

Con was distracted from this chain of thought as the back door of the warehouse opened again. Chandelle led the way as the buyer carried a limp Sarah outside. Con swore and jumped out of his car. He wanted to run over and grab Sarah's unconscious body but they were surrounded by Draken's armed guards. The buyer didn't approach the mini bus but headed for the black limousine next to it. The driver immediately opened the door of the limousine. Con opened his mouth to scream in protest but no noise came out.

As the buyer gently laid Sarah along the back seat, Con was frozen in his own cowardice. *All that grand talk and wishful thinking about rescuing Sarah was just that, talk and an empty promise.* Chandelle entered the limo after the buyer and they were driving away. The mini bus followed the limo; driving away from the warehouse. Driving away from where Con stood watching helpless to stop them. *There's still time*, he thought, *there's still time to follow, to see where they take Sarah; to still be able to save Sarah.* Con wanted so much to make that happen but his body knew that this wasn't true. His body, still frozen, knew he was deluding himself. *I'm no hero! I never will be! I'm just standing here and watching them drive away, taking Sarah to a place where I will never find her again.*

I Shouldn't Be Here

Sarah felt Joseph slipping further and further away and no matter how much she struggled, she was going to lose him forever. 'Joseph!' The cry was torn from her throat as Sarah jerked awake. Although she could feel a very comfortable bed beneath her, the room was in complete darkness and she didn't know where she was, or if Chandelle still protected her, 'Chandelle? Are you there Chandelle?' Sarah whispered as she reached out to search the bed beside her. She gave a gasp of surprise as one of her hands brushed against a bare wall of a muscular chest. There was no way that was Chandelle and Sarah's hand recoiled in horror.

Sitting up, she shrank away from the man sleeping beside her. She frantically tried to piece together the various snatches of conversation from the auction. The buyer had referred to "his Master" so it might be a complete stranger.

'Are you... are you my-y husband?' she stammered, her heart pounding wildly as she hoped to God that nothing had happened while she had been unconscious. *Why isn't Chandelle here? She promised to never leave me!* Someone had undressed her and she now wore only her knickers and a large man's t-shirt. Her throat had been bandaged.

'Only technically. It's all right Sarah, you are safe now. Chandelle is only in the next room.' A sleepy, deep and masculine voice stated. Self-consciously Sarah drew up the sheet to cover her.

'Y-You shouldn't be here! Or I – I shouldn't be here. I'm not sure which.'

A gentle laugh answered her, 'Calm down Sarah. Damnation! I cannot reach the bedside lamp. There is another switch your side of the bed.'

Sarah eagerly reached for the light as his curse sounded so familiar but she wasn't going to get her hopes raised if she turned out to be wrong. *There are only two reasons that Chandelle would leave me alone with my "husband"; one would be if she was forced to go or two if we are truly safe. And the only person I would feel safe with is...*

'Joseph!' Sarah's trembling fingers found the lamp and as light filled the bedroom, she turned quickly back, praying she wasn't wrong. Her breath caught in her throat and as she stared unbelievingly at Joseph Nasseur lying beside her, Sarah continued to hold her breath. Her trembling fingers reached out to touch his cheek to make sure that he wasn't a mirage. Her vision became blurred again as tears of joy streamed down her face.

'Sarah, my heart, if you do not start breathing again, you are going to pass out.' She let out her breath in a shaky laugh as she collapsed onto Joseph's chest.

He allowed her to cry uncontrollably in relief that it was finally over. Or thought it was. He continued to stroke her hair, whispering words of comfort until she could cry no more.

Raising her face Joseph tenderly kissed her tears away and was about to kiss her properly but she drew back from him to sit up. For a brief second he thought Sarah was rejecting him but as she reached over him for a box of tissues, Joseph's fears were eased. She turned slightly away from him to wipe away her tears and blow her nose. As Sarah looked around the room for a bin, Joseph laughed.

'Just throw them on the floor.'

Sarah looked at him in disbelief. 'I can't do that!' He continued to chuckle as she laid a clean tissue on the bedside table and put the dirty tissues upon it.

'All right now?' The Colonel held out his good hand towards her and Sarah willingly slipped back into his embrace.

'This is real isn't it? I'm not still dreaming about you?'

'This is really happening.' Joseph liked the way she fitted against him as she snuggled in his arms, her hand trembling nervously against his bare chest. 'You are finally safe. No one can hurt you now.'

Sarah inhaled sharply and let her breath out slowly. 'I'm not going to cry again!'

I wonder if she is trying to convince me or herself? 'It is a natural reaction, Sarah, but it is over. After you and the other women left the warehouse, Hashim Benzaar, Draken and his guards as well as the Qazi were taken into custody.'

'The other women? Are they all right?'

Joseph wasn't surprised at his fiancée's, sorry, bride's compassion for the welfare of others. 'They are under my protection until I can hand them over to Madame Yasmina.'

Sarah swallowed hard before she asked her next question, 'and what about us?' She held up her hand so that the gold band of her new wedding ring gleamed in the light. 'I mean, is this legal? Is this real? Or just make believe?' Her voice shook in deep emotion.

'He was a real Qazi.' The Colonel caressed his hand across her hair. 'The wedding was legal. For now you are my wife.'

An Important Question

Sarah caught the tightness in his voice and found herself trembling, 'For now? Are you having doubts about me Joseph? Benzaar never touched me apart from a slap to the face and Chandelle wouldn't let Draken's people near me,' Sarah tried valiantly to keep the tears back.

'I know, Sarah that is not what I meant. When you say "yes" before a Qazi with me, I want it to be because you love me and not in fear for your life or that of a dozen other women.'

Sarah gave a choked laugh. 'Nearly all I could think about was how to convince my new "husband" to let me return to the only man I've ever loved! Even if he wouldn't want me as a wife any more,' Sarah couldn't stop the tears again but Joseph only chuckled.

'Why wouldn't I want you, my love?'

'If the... if the marriage couldn't be annulled because he had...' Sarah couldn't finish her sentence even if Joseph hadn't placed his hand over her mouth to stop her.

'Don't even think about that Sarah! Chandelle assured me that she would not have let even your legal "husband" touch you. She was going to return you to me in mint condition.' He held out a couple of tissues to her as she started to laugh and blush.

'Oh you have no idea how true that is!'

Before Joseph could ask what Sarah meant, Chandelle appeared in the doorway. She made no apology for eavesdropping.

'What exactly does that mean?' demanded Chandelle approaching to sit down on the bed beside them.

Sarah blushed a beetroot red which was enough of an answer for the other two. 'Please we are so not having this conversation, here and now!' She sat up, hugging her knees to her chest.

'No, it is not important,' agreed Joseph.

Chandelle shook her head, 'Actually Colonel, it is very important,' She took a deep breath before continuing, 'No disrespect, Sir, but your mother will do anything to dissolve this marriage. She would rather an annulment than a divorce. So she'd be happy to prove you didn't consummate this marriage. Unless you can prove that you did.'

Joseph held up his hand to silence her. 'Enough! I will not sacrifice Sarah. This is not how I envisioned our wedding night to be.'

Chandelle nodded. 'I do understand, Sir, in your current predicament you can't be in complete control. You're an Alpha male; it hurts you more to rely on others than the wounds under those bandages.'

'Then you understand that what you are suggesting is not going to happen,' Joseph demanded.

The gypsy shook her head. 'No Sir, it's why it must happen. For Sarah's sake.'

Sarah looked startled. 'What do I have to do with this?' When they both looked at her in surprise, she sighed, 'Apart from that! Why does it have to be here and now? Why not wait until Joseph has recovered?'

'Before you were abducted, you were what did Minister Beodan call you? A mouse?' Chandelle reached over to take Sarah's hand.

'Yes,' agreed Sarah.

'After the two of you were abducted, what did she become Colonel?'

'A tigress.' He smiled at the memory of Sarah fighting to protect him.

Chandelle nodded, 'Yes and she continued to fight all the way. Benzaar will be scarred for life, and Draken was already folding to our demands when your man stepped forward to buy all of us. Her plan! Her risk of me slipping when I cut her throat! Her sacrifice to marry the buyer to save us!'

'Yeah I'm a real heroine!' An embarrassed Sarah interjected, 'Can you get to the point really soon? What has that to do with when we consummate our marriage?'

'Simply put then, if you wait for the Colonel to be the dominant partner you face the possibility that his family will pressure him into an annulment. If Sarah takes charge it is because she wants this to be a real marriage. That she can once again put the fear of the unknown behind her and be the master of it. She needs to continue to be a tigress if you both are going to survive what the opposition will throw at you over your marriage.'

Sarah Makes A Stand

Joseph kept silent, allowing Sarah time to process what Chandelle had said. It had to be her decision. When he held out his good hand to Sarah, she smiled as she took it and raised it to her cheek.

'No!' The single word quietly spoken stunned both her companions. Sarah smiled, 'What? I'm sorry; did you want the short answer?'

Joseph Nasseur laughed so hard that he was forced to release Sarah's hand and press it against his injured shoulder. Sarah took a clean tissue and wiped the sweat from his brow.

'Sorry but that proves my point. Anything, even the slightest physical activity, is going to hurt Joseph. Also his family might see it as me seducing Joseph when he's in a state that he can't defend himself.'

'Hardly defenceless, my love, but definitely in a weakened condition,' The Colonel chuckled, 'Do you really think I could not stop you if I wanted to?'

'Probably quite easily but that would also cause you pain.' Sarah kissed Joseph's cheek before addressing Chandelle, 'I don't think reverting to a mouse is exactly a bad thing. The tigress is still there, waiting whenever I should need her; to protect my husband, our... our children and our future. But it isn't necessary that she is present all the time. There are going to be times when I would rather defer to my... my husband's greater experience or knowledge especially as I learn something new.'

Chandelle stared at Sarah, deep in thought as the Colonel raised his bride's hand to his lips. 'Why don't I believe you?' she asked.

'I'm sorry?' Sarah looked up startled.

Chandelle shook her head, 'No one's that sweet! Are you actually frozen inside or... or are you scared that it will hurt?'

'I thought we've already covered that I don't want Joseph to be in any more pain because of me?' Sarah looked puzzled from one to the other.

Chandelle laughed, 'That's not what I meant and you know it! You're afraid that it might be painful for you!'

Sarah took a deep breath, 'No, I'm not afraid that it might hurt because I know that it will hurt! Do you need me to say it? Yes, Chandelle, I am a virgin. Virgo Intacta! Chaste! Untouched by any man! Is that what you wanted me to admit?' Tears welled up in her eyes once more but Sarah fought to keep them back. 'The first time you're supposed to remember for the rest of your life. I want it to be with the only man I've ever loved and with his complete ability to ensure that it is memorable for all the right reasons. Not to force his family to accept me. Not to make a forced marriage legit. I would rather Joseph obtained an annulment so that we are both free to say "yes" the next time.'

'Are you certain that there will be a next time?' asked Chandelle.

Smiling, Sarah glanced down at Joseph, 'I'm certain about the man who has my heart. Doctor Said told me to have faith in God and my man. If it is meant to be then we will make it happen.'

Joseph laughed, 'So not everything will be left up to my greater expertise and knowledge?'

Do I Need To Separate You?

In answer, Sarah leant over and kissed Joseph. Not a timid or nervous kiss but the same soul searching, knee buckling kiss that Joseph had given Sarah the first time he had kissed her. When Joseph reached up with his good hand to hold her tighter against him, she gently drew away again. 'Well teacher? That was our first lesson wasn't it? Outside Crystal's welcoming party,' Sarah smiled as she watched Joseph as he searched his memory for that night. A slow smile spread across his features and his eyes began to twinkle.

'Yes it was. So how about lesson two?'

Sarah looked at him a little sceptically, 'Do you mean what was lesson two or what will be lesson two?'

Joseph didn't hesitate, 'Was! Crystal's slumber party on Saturday.'

'All right children, I think it's time you both got some sleep.' Chandelle rose from the bed, 'You'll have to review your lessons some other time as tomorrow you'll have to deal with the fall out from your abduction, your injuries and your unconventional wedding. Now do I need to separate you?' A secretive smile was exchanged between the newlyweds.

'We will be all right,' reassured Joseph but when Chandelle reached out to turn off the lamp, Sarah stopped her.

'Please leave it on. The complete darkness reminds me of...'

Chandelle didn't need Sarah to finish as she understood. The darkness of their prison still haunted her as well. She had reached the doorway before she turned to face them, 'I'm sorry but I have to ask... you were getting rather cute and that could lead to something more intimate. I know you said you were going to wait but I think it's important that you have proof that...' Chandelle found this harder to say than she thought.

Joseph's eyebrows rose but it was a blushing Sarah who asked, 'Proof of what? That I am a virgin?'

'Yes, exactly.' Chandelle nodded, 'The Koran states that there is nothing wrong with a Muslim man marrying a Christian or Jewish woman so long as she is chaste. It would have to be proven before the wedding night.'

Joseph smiled, 'I do not think we would let it go that far, but you doubt our restraint? Do you wish to verify for yourself or separate us?'

'Do I get a say in this?' Sarah shifted uncomfortably.

Chandelle looked at her with her piercing gaze, 'You will have to be examined by a doctor before you are re-married to the Colonel especially if you want an annulment.'

Joseph shook his head, 'One minute you are telling us to consummate the marriage, the next you want us to behave ourselves. You are a very confusing woman.'

'Sorry, but if you promise to behave I won't separate you. I just want to protect Sarah's reputation.'

'Well I can honestly say I won't be trying anything tonight.' A twinkle was back in the Colonel's eyes.

'Sorry, but I'm so very tired.' Sarah was attempting to smother a yawn.

Chandelle smiled at her, 'Go to sleep Sarah. I'll be nearby if either of you needs me.' She left the door between the bedrooms open as Sarah settled down back into her husband's arms.

'Are you actually tired or was that just to get out of inspection?' asked Joseph, tenderly kissing the top of her head.

'Exhausted actually. You'll just have to wait and see what I've learnt from lesson two,' Sarah covered another yawn.

Joseph chuckled as her hand danced lightly across his naked chest. 'And what about lesson three?' He captured her hand and raised the palm to his lips.

'Oh no, not lesson three!' Sarah yawned once more.

'Why not?' Joseph was trying to remember what the third lesson had been to cause her to veto it like that.

'Not until you're fully recovered any way, Mystery Intruder!' Sarah sighed, allowing sleep to claim her as she lay safe in the arms of her man. Grinning at the memory of Sarah clobbering him over the head with a statue, Joseph marvelled how far they had come from that encounter. *We still have much more to face, but at least now we will do it together.*

WEDNESDAY

I Need You!

Joseph felt, despite the pain, a sense of peace and contentment. *I had slept well with Sarah safe once more in my arms and there is nothing I won't do to make certain it stayed that way.* So he wasn't completely awake before he realised that Sarah was no longer curled into his side. His eyes flew open as his good hand searched the bed for her presence.

'Sarah? Sarah, where are you?' There was desperation in his voice as he dragged himself up into a sitting position. *That hurt like hell. But not anywhere near the pain I'm suffering at the thought that Sarah has been taken from me again.* Sarah ran out of the bathroom, still damp, a towel hastily wrapped around her and another in her hands to dry her wet hair. She used one hand to keep her towel in place as she sat down on the bed beside her husband and used the other towel to mop the sweat from Joseph's brow.

'I was only in the bathroom Joseph. You were sleeping so peacefully that I didn't want to disturb you.' As Sarah leant over to ease him back down, he breathed in deep the intoxicating scent of soap and shampoo. *I have never known that anything so ordinary can be so erotic or perhaps it is just the body it is attached to?*

Joseph reached up to tangle his fingers into the damp curtain of hair that cascaded down onto the bed. Gently he brought Sarah's head down so that their lips met. *This isn't the time for tenderness as my momentary fear means I need to stake my claim on the prize that is to be mine alone.* As he took possession of Sarah's

277

mouth, his hand slipped down to cover hers holding her towel in place for her modesty. Reluctantly Joseph released her lips.

'Take it off!' He demanded, his voice so low and filled with such passion that it surprised even him.

'You're not up to this.' Sarah shook her head, refusing to submit to the insistence of his hand as it slid across the towel to caress her breasts.

Joseph growled, 'Damnation! Do you think I don't know that? I want to see you! If that is all I can have just now don't deny me that. Please!'

Sarah didn't like the frustration in his voice and knew that just looking wouldn't be enough for him. 'Joseph, I'm black and blue and damaged all over. I don't want you to see me like that.' She couldn't contain the gasp that arose as Joseph's hand found a way under the towel and cupped one of her breasts.

'Show me,' he undid the towel from underneath and tugged it loose. Blushing, Sarah slowly stood up and as Joseph held onto one corner of the towel, it dropped away from her. Not knowing what to do, Sarah stood stock still, her arms trembling by her sides as Joseph slowly scanned her from head to toe.

'Turn around,' he ordered, unable to take his eyes off her as she obeyed. Sarah moved her curtain of hair so that he could see the naked damaged body hidden beneath it. As she turned back to face Joseph again, he drew her back down onto the bed.

'I will never let anyone hurt you ever again!' He kissed the palm of her hand before laying it over his heart. 'I promise you!'

Sarah brought her lips back to his in a kiss to show she understood his need to protect what was his.

'I need you!' Joseph moaned against Sarah's lips.

'You need to shower and dress if you intend to join Prince Kahlee at the meeting with the Commune and the Fundamentalists.' Sighing, Sarah drew back a little to look deep into his eyes.

'Always the practical diplomat!' He moaned, 'I'd rather remain here and make love with my bride.'

Laughing Sarah pulled the towel out of Joseph's grasp. 'So would I but there are things we need to take care of before we can do that.' She wrapped the towel around herself and rising from the bed she rang the bell that would summon Joseph's servant. Before she could return to the bathroom, her husband lightly grasped her hand.

'You won't leave this house until after I return will you?'

Sarah smiled, 'Gary brought me some clothes first thing this morning. He intends to bring Marianne and Crystal to see me later. I don't need to go anywhere until you want me to go.'

'Then you will never leave here my love!' Joseph declared.

Meet Abdul, My Servant.

Sarah held the towel tighter around her as the buyer and Cadem entered the room. She gave a gasp of horror as the slave trade auction came flooding back to her. Joseph tightened his hold on her hand.

'It is all right Sarah, this is Abdul my butler. We thought that Cadem, Gary or myself entering as a buyer last night would risk your life further.'

Sarah swallowed hard. 'Yes I see.' She ran into the bathroom and grabbing her clothes, she disappeared into Chandelle's room to dress.

'I am most sorry Colonel Nasseur.' Abdul bowed humbly before Joseph. 'I should have realised my presence would upset Madame.' The servant spoke in their native language.

'It is all right Abdul,' the two men assisted Joseph to rise to his feet. 'Remind me to organise counselling for Sarah very soon.'

'Certainly Colonel.'

Some time was needed to assist Joseph to wash, shave and dress. Some more time was needed for him to recover enough to think about breakfast. When this too was completed, Cadem was about to drive his superior officer to the Palace when a worried Abdul stepped into the dining room.

'My apology for disturbing you Colonel, but your mother is here to see you.'

Sarah looked more frightened than she had during the whole abduction. Reassuringly Chandelle moved closer to her as Joseph checked his watch.

'Well it would appear we are going to have to deal with that problem sooner rather than later.' He sounded more confident than he felt and leaning on Cadem's arm and a walking stick, Joseph led Sarah and Chandelle into the living room to meet his mother.

Joseph's Mother

Mrs Caliana Nasseur didn't stand up as her son entered the room with his entourage as she was outraged at the two women being brought into her presence. She refused to speak in English.

'I'd hoped to speak to you alone Joseph. This infatuation of yours has to stop. You're making our family a laughing stock with your pursuit of a foreigner!'

Colonel Nasseur bowed slightly to his mother before Cadem assisted him onto a comfortable lounge. 'You will have to forgive me, mother, for not greeting you properly but it is only with assistance that I am able to be on my feet at all!' Joseph deliberately spoke in English to exert his dominance in his own home. He gestured for the others to be seated also, but drew Sarah down onto the lounge beside him.

'You shouldn't have left the hospital Joseph! There was no need for you to further endanger your health! You should've left the rescue of this woman to the appropriate authorities!'

Joseph shook his head. 'If it hadn't been for Sarah's care I would have died from the gunshot wounds.'

'If you hadn't been pursuing her, you wouldn't have been there in the first place!' Mrs Nasseur's lips curled.

'I love Sarah, mother, and I intend to marry her.' The Colonel took Sarah's trembling hand into his own.

'What has love to do with marriage? Marry one of the fine young women I have selected for you and you may keep this one as a mistress. I'll even acknowledge any bastards she bears you.' Sarah's gasp of shock brought Mrs Nasseur's gaze to meet hers properly for the first time. 'Don't play the innocent with me! I know what you westerners are like! Sex before marriage! Children out of wedlock, many different fathers! Displaying yourselves so all men can see what is meant only for your husband! You may have talked your way into my son's bed, but he will never marry you!'

Never taking his eyes from his mother's face, Joseph slowly raised Sarah's left hand until the gleam of the gold band caught the older woman's attention. The oath that erupted from the matriarch brought a blush to not just Sarah's cheeks. She sat like a rock as Mrs Nasseur called her every derogatory name under the sun. Cadem's hands clenched into angry fists; *if she wasn't the Colonel's mother, I would slap her.*

'Enough! There is so much that you still do not know.' Mrs Nasseur was struck silent as her son had never before spoken like that to her.

'You sound just like your father!' Caliana spat out at him. Cadem knew that was a low blow as the Colonel was nothing like his tyrannical father.

'Insult me all you like but I will not allow you to abuse Sarah! Now just be quiet and listen!' Joseph detailed the events starting with their abduction and concluding with the slave sale.

'So the marriage can be annulled! Technically she was forced into it! Have you slept with her?' demanded Mrs Nasseur becoming excited. 'You don't have to be tied to a mistake Joseph.'

Cadem took a deep breath as he saw the muscle in the Colonel's cheek spasm.

'Stop talking now or I will forget you are my mother!' Joseph took a moment to compose himself before he continued, 'We did not consummate the marriage. We do intend to get an annulment,' He held up a finger to silence his mother's outburst of relief. 'I have not finished! As soon as Sarah will allow, we will be officially and freely married.'

'No! Don't throw your life away Joseph!'

Chandelle couldn't keep quiet any longer. 'What on earth is wrong with you? You've already lost one son and his family; do you seriously want to lose another?' Mrs Nasseur was actually silenced for a moment as Chandelle continued, 'Doing what mummy says just doesn't cut it anymore! The Colonel is a grown man. It's time to let him make his own decisions. Make his own mistakes. If you want to see your grandchildren then it's time to shut the hell up!'

Mrs Nasseur eyed Chandelle in hostility before addressing her son, 'Did you marry this one as well?'

'No.' The Colonel checked his watch. 'I don't have time for this. I need to be at the palace. No matter what you say or do, mother, I will be spending the rest of my life with Sarah as my wife. If that means having to leave Pangani then so be it.' Ignoring his mother's shocked gasp, Joseph struggled to his feet with the aid of Sarah and Cadem.

'You love Pangani!' protested Caliana Nasseur, but she couldn't ignore the look of pure love as Joseph looked down at Sarah.

'I love Sarah more!' He briefly pressed his lips against Sarah's palm. 'Stay inside, my heart, you will be safe here until I return.'

'Do you really have to attend this meeting? You really should be back in bed.' Sarah's concern for him showed in her eyes.

'Is that an invitation?' A slow sexy smile appeared.

Laughing Sarah couldn't stop blushing. 'Not until you've recovered.'

'I look forward to it,' Joseph sighed as Cadem silently tapped his watch. 'Goodbye mother. We will let you know when the wedding will be held.' He allowed Cadem to assist him out to his waiting car. Joseph would've preferred to not leave Sarah with his mother still there but he had some traitors to deal with first.

A Traitor Is Revealed

Promptly at 9 o'clock Caracal and one of his men, entered the main palace meeting room with a palace guard. A contingency from the Fundamentalist group was already there. A sigh of relief swept over the room as it hadn't been certain that all the parties would appear. As the Commune leader took his place beside Prince Kahlee the negotiations began.

The discussions were not going at all well, so when the door opened and Cadem entered, Kahlee looked justifiably annoyed.

'I ordered that we weren't to be disturbed, Captain. This had better be important!'

Cadem bowed in respect to the Emir before resting his eyes upon Kahlee. 'This is very important, your Highness.' Cadem stepped aside as Colonel Joseph Nasseur, dressed in his full military uniform, entered the room; still using a walking stick. A murmur of wonderment swept through the room as Joseph bowed, with a little difficulty, to the Emir. Visibly shaken, Caracal rose to his feet, his eyes never leaving his brother's face, but it was the Emir who moved forward to embrace Joseph.

'I had truly felt that I'd lost you, my son and although you look paler and thinner, I'm glad to see you all the same. Come, we need your assistance to bring order to this business.'

'As you wish, your Majesty.' The Colonel inclined his head in agreement. 'Unfortunately I bring bad news,' He hesitated until he was assured that he had everyone's complete attention before continuing, 'when it seemed that the abductors had inside knowledge of our every move, we first thought that it was someone in the ministry. That perhaps the abduction was a political attack on the Emir. Prince Kahlee informed the ministry that the Amed brothers had been executed and that anyone found to be involved with them would meet the same fate. Then ministers' calls and movements were monitored to see if they attempted to contact the man holding Miss Trent hostage.'

A murmur of disbelief and astonishment raced through the room.

'This is an absolute abuse of official power, Colonel!' demanded Minister Beodan.

Joseph removed, with a little difficulty, from his inside pocket, a folded sheet of paper. 'I assure you that every step taken by either Inspector Lowe or Captain Cadem has been properly authorized by the Emir!' Joseph Nasseur continued, 'When we learnt that Con Zuco, the Australian Public Affairs Officer, was responsible for the information leak there shouldn't have been any unusual telephone activity from the ministry. The Prince also informed the ministry that the Fundamentalists were ceasing their demonstrations to allow our forces to concentrate on eradicating the rebels. Straight after these two announcements, calls were made from a particular minister not to the abductor of Miss Trent but to a suspected contact of the Rebels.' He swayed on his feet, reaching out for the table to steady himself. Caracal sprang up to support his brother.

'Thank you,' said the Colonel as he was assisted to a chair.

'What does this mean?' demanded Minister Mudin. 'Is the Colonel trying to suggest that one of us isn't to be trusted?' There was a murmur of conjecture throughout the room and the Emir held up his hand for silence.

'We will hear what Colonel Nasseur has to say. I'm sure that he will supply us with proof before casting any aspersions.'

Minister Mudin rose to his feet. 'I'll not remain here to be falsely accused of criminal activities!'

As he headed towards the door, the Emir nodded to Cadem. 'Captain, if Mudin steps outside that door, shoot him!'

'You wouldn't dare!' Mudin turned around to stare at Cadem.

In answer, the soldier removed his side arm and took off the safety catch. 'I follow orders, Minister; I suggest that you do the same.' Mudin looked from Cadem to the Emir before resuming his seat. Joseph removed a CD and held it up.

'Do we really need to go to all the trouble of playing back to you your betrayal of the Emir and our country Minister Beodan?' He said quietly.

All eyes in the meeting room rested upon Minister Beodan, who had begun to rise but feeling the muzzle of Cadem's gun pressed lightly against his neck, was forced him to resume his seat. Beodan turned to the Emir in appeal.

'Surely you're not going to believe this nonsense, Your Majesty? I've always been your loyal servant. Why would I risk my career and my life for rebels?'

The Emir looked at Beodan long and hard. 'Captain, remove Minister Beodan to surroundings that will be more suitable to his future status.'

Cadem bowed to the Emir before leading the reluctant Minister to the door. Before exiting, Beodan turned to address the room. 'Be warned, I shall return!'

'I very much doubt that!' Prince Kahlee said as he shook his head.

'Gentlemen,' The Emir rose to his feet to gain the attention of all in the room. 'We all agree that partition is not the way to peace. History has shown us with Ireland, India and Israel, that partition not only divides a country, but also tears it apart. I believe that Caracal, the Fundamentalists and I don't wish to do this to Pangani. If peace is to be achieved, then we must find a compromise to satisfy all parties. I truly believe that this compromise can be met by creating a democratic government in Pangani. Although I can't approve of your deviation from our Faith, Caracal, I'm more than prepared to be tolerant of your beliefs if it can bring about peace.'

A silence fell over the room as they all waited for Caracal to reply.

'My people will no longer be persecuted?'

The Emir agreed.

'We will have a voice in this government?'

Again the Emir agreed.

'Harsher penalties will be brought against those involved with the rebels?'

Again the Emir agreed.

'I have one final request, your Majesty. I wish to attend my brother's official wedding.'

The Emir's eyebrows rose in surprise. 'You had no doubt that Miss Trent was already married to Joseph?'

Caracal smiled and glanced across at Joseph. 'If Sarah Trent was married to another, Seph wouldn't have let that man live long enough to consummate that union. Well brother?'

Joseph matched his older brother's smile. 'I think a wedding invitation can be easily arranged.'

Let Me Explain

Even though Sarah was extremely nervous about being left alone with Joseph's mother, Chandelle thought that she was handling it quite well.

'Would you like a cup of tea?' offered Sarah as she sank back down onto the lounge.

Mrs Nasseur opened her mouth to say something acid but looking at Sarah it suddenly vanished from the tip of her tongue. *There are dark shadows beneath my daughter-in-law's eyes as well as a worried expression that suggests Sarah's thoughts are still on Joseph who we both believe shouldn't be attending meetings but in bed. There are bruises on her face from being hit several times by different people, the dressing on Sarah's throat where Chandelle had cut her, and there were friction burns on her wrists and ankles from being bound with rope and handcuffs.* Joseph's mother swallowed hard and finally said, 'Actually, yes I would.'

'I'll organise that.' Chandelle was already heading for the door. 'No fighting while I'm gone.'

Mrs Nasseur waited until Chandelle was out of hearing before asking, 'If she isn't married to Joseph, then who is she?'

'Chandelle was one of the women in the slave trade auction,' Sarah explained as she smiled, 'We planned an escape plot together which was working before Joseph's man stepped in. I begged Chandelle to not leave me even though I willingly agreed to marry the buyer to free the other women. She stayed with me, all night, determined to protect my reputation. Why, you'll have to ask her.'

The older woman nodded, 'Probably monetary reasons.'

'I don't think so.' Sarah laughed lightly, 'We couldn't guarantee that anyone was coming to save us, so the plan to escape meant that there was an element of real risk on my part. Chandelle assured me that she could cut my throat in such a way that it was an impressive show of blood without doing any serious damage. Once I passed out, Chandelle refused to leave me.'

'You lost more blood than I had counted on.' Chandelle admitted as she re-entered the room, 'Once I learnt it was Colonel Nasseur behind the purchase I would have rejoined the other women but he asked me to stay with the two of them. I cleaned up Sarah's wound and redressed her in one of the Colonel's t-shirts. He insisted on protecting Sarah's reputation. I did try to talk them into consummating their marriage but Sarah wouldn't have it.'

'I don't believe you!' Mrs Nasseur looked from one to the other. 'The conception of an heir could have forced me to accept her!'

'I want to wait until Joseph has recovered and we are officially married.' Sarah as blushing as she explained. 'How many people do I have to have this conversation with?'

'There won't be a wedding, official or otherwise!' retorted Mrs Nasseur, 'Don't make Joseph choose between his country and you. It would destroy him to leave here. This infatuation will be over soon but his pride won't allow him to return in shame.'

Sighing Sarah rubbed her least damaged hand against her weary eyes. 'I'm sorry; I've had this conversation with Princess Relanna and Joseph. I tried to convince him that such a relationship was impossible, impractical and illogical but Joseph wouldn't take "no" for an answer.'

'Are you telling me that you tried to discourage my son?' Disbelief was written all over Mrs Nasseur's features. 'That he was chasing you? That you actually said "no"?'

Sarah smiled, she was aware of the irony. 'Yes, the little Aussie mouse said "no" to the dashing and handsome Prince Charming! Several times!'

'Does that mean that you don't love Joseph?' demanded his mother, clinging to a fragile hope.

Laughing Sarah shook her head. 'That would make it so much easier for you wouldn't it? I told Joseph I loved him too much to make him choose between me and his people, his religion, his country.'

'Then why didn't you just leave Pangani?'

'I couldn't do that to our new Ambassador. He had a hard enough job to step into without me adding to it. Also,' Sarah couldn't help blushing at her next words, 'Joseph said if I left the country that he would follow.'

When Abdul brought in the tea tray, Sarah showed no revulsion to his presence and managed to smile up at him. 'Thank you Abdul, I think a cup of tea is exactly what I need right now.'

'You are very welcome Mrs Nasseur,' Abdul bowed to Sarah. Caliana Nasseur looked up at him in surprise as he wasn't looking at her but at Sarah. Chandelle grinned in pleasure as a disapproving look fell over the older woman's face.

Sarah hastened to speak, 'Perhaps it should be "Miss Trent" for now Abdul,'

'Legally Madame you have the right...' The servant bowed once more.

Sarah cut him off, 'Please Abdul, there's already enough fuel on this fire.'

'Yes Madame! I will be nearby if you should need me.' He left the room; Chandelle could have sworn that Abdul was laughing.

Sarah didn't say anything until she had a sip of tea. Sighing, she closed her eyes as she exhaled slowly. 'I needed that!'

Grudgingly Mrs Nasseur also sipped her tea, black and unsweetened. 'Miss Trent! You need to go home and pack your bags. There is no way you can remain in Kathou now you have caused such a scandal.'

Sarah shook her head, opening her eyes once more, 'Joseph told me to wait for him here. When he tells me to leave, I will go. Until then I'll follow his orders and no one else's.'

Looking at the stubborn set to Sarah's jaw, Mrs Nasseur realised that nothing she could say or do would change Sarah's mind but it wasn't going to stop her trying. 'Now see here Miss Trent...'

Sarah waited for the barrage to start but something about that weary, battered and bruised young woman melted a mother's heart.

'I'll be completely honest with you Mrs Nasseur,' Sarah chose her next words very carefully as she didn't want to be misunderstood, 'When Joseph returns from his meeting, you may speak to him in private and if you manage to convince him that I have to go away then I will go. I didn't make it my mission to force Joseph to fall in love with me. I tried to deny I had feelings for him to make it easier for him to walk away. I would never have initiated anything beyond the professional relationship that already existed. I thought I could keep on arguing against a relationship until Joseph came to his senses but... but then something happened...'

Mrs Nasseur groaned in despair, 'So he has slept with you? Are you pregnant?'

Sarah wished that she hadn't such a fair complexion as she felt her face flame red again in embarrassment. 'No! No to either question. Please just let me finish, expressing my deepest emotions is especially difficult for me.' Sarah took a deep breath and put down her tea cup to hide how her hands were shaking.

'Go on then.'

Sarah let her breath out just as slowly, 'I thought I could keep saying "no" but then Joseph kissed me...'

'Let me guess, like you'd never been kissed before?' Mrs Nasseur's interruptions were starting to annoy even Chandelle.

'For goodness sake, will you just let the girl tell her story? I think I already know where she is heading and you should listen.' Chandelle put her tea cup back onto the tray before she was tempted to use it as a missile.

Caliana Nasseur looked up at the gypsy with resentment, 'All right! So what happened when my son kissed you?'

Expressing My Emotions

Is Hard For Me

Sarah took a deep breath and let it out slowly before she attempted to explain, 'I need to go back a little and tell you something about myself but it will make it so much harder for you to understand if you keep interrupting me. So please just let me get my story out in full and then you can ask any questions.'

Mrs Nasseur looked at the determined petite package in front of her with new eyes and began to see what attracted her son. 'All right then,' she noticed a pen and a pad of paper on the coffee table and pulled them towards her. 'If I have any questions I will write them down to ask at the end.'

Chandelle was surprised when Sarah smiled in relief and said, 'Thank you. Five years ago when I signed up, the diplomatic corps was concerned that being so far from home, I might easily miss my close knit family. It probably explains why I created a pseudo family with my colleagues Gary and Marianne. So just over three weeks ago my life was as close to perfect as I wanted it to be. I loved my job. I loved the people I worked with; with one exception. Because romance and sex had never been a part of my life, it wasn't something I missed.' Sarah saw Mrs Nasseur's jaw drop open and a question trembling on her lips but she quickly added, 'Yes that does mean what it sounds like but please let me continue.'

Mrs Nasseur nodded, stunned.

'But then the world exploded. Not literally of course but it made me realise that I don't like change. I mean before I came to Pangani, I learnt the language, about the culture and the people. I was prepared for different. I was prepared for being a minority in a country where the local people mightn't even give you the time of day, but was pleasantly surprised that so many do. What I wasn't prepared for was... was...' Sarah fought against her throat closing up upon the words. Chandelle leant forward and placed her hand over Sarah's.

'It's all right, Sarah, you don't have to say it, we know what you've had to go through the past three weeks.'

'I don't think you do.' Sarah took a sip of her tea to soothe her constricting throat. 'You see I'd never actually seen a dead body before, let alone one that as one policeman described as being "sliced and diced". I've never before been in what some might call a war zone. I've never thought that I'd ever need a body guard to simply walk down the street. I never thought that in the 21st century I would still have to deal with sexual harassment in the workplace.'

Sarah dragged in a deep shuddering breath to control her emotions. 'Before Joseph kissed me, I disagreed with him each time we met about getting involved. Not because I didn't love him but I just could not take any more stress in my life. I didn't need any further hostility aimed at me.'

'And after the Colonel had kissed you?' Chandelle smiled sympathetically.

A wistful look appeared, sweeping away some of the stress that Sarah felt when expressing her emotions. 'It was like I was free, that I no longer had to keep my feelings bottled up. That I didn't have to deal with all the stress alone. There was someone prepared to lift the burden from my shoulders and protect me from the approaching storm.'

Mrs Nasseur nodded solemnly. 'Yes it must have been a relief to have Joseph to look after you when you were abducted.'

Sarah looked at her, surprised but couldn't bring herself to dispel that image. Chandelle, laughing, had no qualms about telling Sarah's story for her.

'Colonel Nasseur wasn't exaggerating when he told you Sarah's care of him saved his life. If it wasn't for Koyad Amed and Sarah, the Colonel would have bled to death. The doctors at the hospital can't believe that he didn't get some kind of infection before he finally received real medical attention. The Colonel was helpless to defend himself or Sarah. She had to negotiate with their abductors for water and medical supplies to keep him alive.'

A shiver of horror ran through Sarah as the gypsy's words took her back to a time not so long ago that she would not be forgetting any time soon. 'Please Chandelle, stop. I can't relive those memories right now. It doesn't matter what Mrs Nasseur chooses to believe about me, or what did or didn't happen. I don't have the strength to argue and nothing either of us says will change how unsuitable she believes I am for her son.' Sarah rose hastily to her feet; the vague notion of escaping interrogation to seek solitude was fleeting and she paced restlessly instead.

'Is it true?' quietly demanded Mrs Nasseur, her eyes resting upon her own hands in her lap.

'What? That I am unworthy of Joseph?'

Mrs Nasseur raised her eyes to meet Sarah's, 'No, my dear, that you fought to save Joseph's life?'

Sarah stopped pacing. 'I never stopped fighting; first to protect him, then when we were separated, to get back to him.' She broke off as her voice caught in a sob. 'I'm sorry you don't approve of me, Mrs Nasseur, but in the end it will be Joseph's decision if I stay... or if I go.'

'What do you want Miss Trent?'

Sarah rubbed a shaking hand against the back of her neck, 'Right now I'd settle for an ice pack and a couple of Panadol!' At the puzzled look on their faces Sarah hastened to add, 'Sorry Panadol is a brand of pain killer in Australia.'

'I thought it might be one of those cocktails I understand westerners like so much.' Mrs Nasseur said as she shook her head.

Sarah smiled; calm enough to sit down again. 'No I don't drink.' She had managed to surprise her mother-in-law.

'You don't drink alcohol and you've never had sex? You're like no westerner I have ever met.'

'There's a problem with alcoholism in our extended family and I'd never met a man I actually wanted to be that intimate with; until now.' Sarah blushed uncomfortable that the conversation was once more very personal. 'Is there anything else you would like to know about me? Now would be a good time to ask.' Sarah's tone was quite friendly even though she dreaded being interrogated about herself.

'Actually yes there is one more thing I would like to know Sarah.'

The Secretary's eyes widened in surprise, it was the first time Mrs Nasseur had used her first name.

'Yes?'

'Do you intend to drag Joseph off to Australia?'

'For holidays, most definitely, I would like our children to be able to spend time with both families. Permanently, only if we could no longer make this our home.'

Mrs Nasseur's eyes lit up, 'Children?'

'Yes,' Sarah nodded, 'Joseph and I haven't had time to talk about children but I would like at least one of each. Probably first name will be Panganian, middle name Aussie and if they have a nickname that will depend upon the type of child they are. They'll be brought up Muslim but have an understanding of their Christian heritage. Whether or not I'll convert I just don't know yet. All this I want to discuss with Joseph when he is stronger. Right now we need to convince him that he isn't indestructible or irreplaceable and needs time to heal properly.'

For the first time Mrs Nasseur smiled, 'Yes we do Sarah. I want him to be without that walking stick at the official wedding.'

'I'm not certain Joseph is prepared to wait that long.' Sarah smiled.

'Then he'd better heal quickly.' Caliana Nasseur said as she reached over to take Sarah's hand.

Chandelle let out a sigh of relief, 'Is it safe to leave you two alone now?'

'Yes, thank you Chandelle.' Mrs Nasseur smiled at her, 'In a day or two when Sarah has had time to recover, we can start planning the wedding. We'll need to consult with Marianne Davies.'

'Good,' Chandelle rose to her feet, 'If we leave Sarah now she should call her parents in Western Australia. They are probably completely freaked out about the abduction by now.'

Sarah laughed, 'I called them earlier this morning when Gary brought me some clothing. He also brought my mobile so I could call home.'

'Joseph won't have minded if you had used his phone, after all you are his wife.' Mrs Nasseur also rose to her feet.

Sarah exchanged an amused glance with Chandelle, only just managing to keep from laughing as she replied, 'Thank you, but a lengthy long distance call is the last thing Joseph would want to see when he gets his next telephone bill.'

Abdul saw the two women out of the house as Sarah collapsed backwards into the couch. *I got through that meeting much better than I had ever hoped and I pray that it is a good sign for the future.*

Reunion

Marianne could barely contain herself as Gary led her and Crystal into the Colonel's home. Abdul had just opened the door into the living room when Marianne moved impatiently around him and dragged Sarah up off the lounge and into her arms.

'Oh my dear girl! Dear, dear girl! I thought we'd lost you forever!' Marianne chocked back a sob but tears fell regardless.

'Don't cry Marianne. Your mascara will run,' laughed Sarah, managing to loosen the diplomat's hold upon her.

Crystal smiled, 'Sorry Sarah but I'm going to hug you too!' She managed to do it without crushing Sarah and her place was soon replaced by Gary. She was surprised that he was actually shaking.

'The other women told me how you risked your life in your plan to escape. Did you really think that we wouldn't be hunting for you?' His voice was muffled against Sarah's hair.

'I couldn't be certain.' A lump formed in Sarah's throat as she hugged him back and started to cry. 'I didn't know if you'd be in time...'

Gary shushed her. 'We were never far from you!' Marianne wasn't the only one having to deal with tears. They were tears of joy and relief, but so long as the Major didn't join the women, he could handle it.

Sarah managed to pull herself together enough to ask them all to sit down. 'I never had a chance this morning to talk to you Gary. What happens now to the other women? Yasmina can't handle any more refugees at the moment. I feel responsible for their well-being. We have to keep them safe.'

The Welfare Of Others

Before Gary could reply, an answer came from the open doorway, 'Always thinking of others! You are indeed the perfect diplomat!' Joseph Nasseur stood mostly with the aid of his walking stick. Crystal half expected Sarah to jump up and run into his arms but instead she rose in a dignified manner and moved towards her husband to assist him onto the lounge.

'Thank you but I feel far from perfect. I should've done something about Con long before this blew up on us. I just didn't think he'd do anything so crazy.' Sarah rubbed a weary hand over her eyes as she sank back down beside Joseph.

'If Yasmina's place is full,' asked Crystal, 'what will happen to those women you rescued?'

Joseph took Sarah's hand between his. 'My sister was so moved by their story that Relanna is putting them up temporarily at a five star hotel. Queen Tabina is looking at purchasing another backpackers hostel for Yasmina to renovate.'

Punishments Expected

Ambassador James Greene cautiously stuck his head around the door. 'Did someone call a meeting and didn't inform me?' His eyes softened into a tender smile as his gaze rested on Sarah. Entering the room, James cast a brief glance and a wink at Marianne. 'You had us worried, young lady! You've been extremely difficult to keep up with!' He bent down to kiss Sarah's cheek but paused to look at Joseph, 'With your permission Colonel?'

'I'll only object when that is a real wedding ring on Sarah's finger.' Joseph smiled.

James' kiss on Sarah's cheek was brief and even before he had straightened, he was once more serious. 'I've just been in contact with Canberra. Con Zuco's diplomatic immunity has been revoked and Inspector Lowe is hunting for him now.'

'What about these other men, Benzaar and Draken?' asked Crystal, 'will they be executed like the Amed brothers?'

'The Ameds are still very much alive and well,' Joseph laughed, 'That was Kahlee's attempt to scare anyone else involved in our abduction to panic and reveal themselves.'

Con's Capture

At that moment there was a knock at the door and Abdul announced Inspector Lowe to the gathering. It wasn't his presence that stunned all of them in the parlour; it was the wreck of a man that the Inspector hauled inside with him. Con Zuco fell to his hands and knees with his hair standing up on end and his clothes dishevelled. Frantically Con glanced around the room, desperately seeking an ally.

'You can't do this to me! I've diplomatic immunity!' Con blustered with fake bravado as he raised himself to his feet.

'Canberra has revoked your immunity Con,' said Ambassador Greene as he shook his head. 'You'll pay for what you have done!'

Inspector Lowe immediately added, "Now that you have heard it from your own Ambassador, I will read you your rights once more.' He began to read the memoranda but Con cut him off.

'Don't bother, I heard it the first three times you said it.'

'It is for your benefit Mr Zuco.' Inspector Lowe frowned in disapproval. 'You are facing some very serious charges.'

Con ran his hands wildly through his hair. 'No! It was never meant to happen at all!' He caught sight of Sarah and hastily stepped towards her. 'Oh my God! Sarah! How did you manage to escape from the buyer?' Con's progress was impeded by Joseph's walking cane rising to poke him in the stomach to keep him at a distance from Sarah.

'Stay away from my wife!' Joseph's words barely concealed his disgust.

Con looked from one to the other, his lower jaw was dragging on the floor. 'What the fuck is going on? He was the buyer? My God! Please tell me you haven't let him touch you!' The loathing in his voice caused Sarah to blush as she sprang to her feet.

'Don't' you dare talk to Joseph like that! You have no right to say anything about my life! Joseph nearly died because you had some insane desire to play the hero! I was sold as a slave because of you! I could have been raped by several different men over the last four days! So what happened to my great saviour? Why did you let a stranger just drive away from the warehouse with me and not follow?'

Con's eyes widened in surprise as he demanded, 'How do you know that I didn't follow the limo? How did you know I was at the warehouse?'

It was Gary who answered, 'I was there Con. Cadem was the limo driver and I drove the mini bus. I saw you in the parking lot and I know you did not follow us.'

'So that's why I thought the driver looked familiar.'

Marianne was stunned as she watched a mouse turn into a tigress.

'So why didn't you follow me Con? Why didn't you try to rescue me? Wasn't that your big plan? Or did it just become too hard and couldn't be bothered? Did it suddenly become too real for you? Was it just so much easier to walk away Con?'

Con baulked at the passionate being in front of him and he tried to defend his actions. 'No! I wanted to follow, I wanted to save you. It's just that... I never wanted any of this!'

Sarah poked her finger into his chest. 'You must have wanted it Con! Ahkman didn't come up with the idea on his own. For over a week you were droning into his ear about how you wanted to be a hero. Again wanting something you could not have! There is nothing on this earth that you could do that would ever make me love you. Nothing!'

'But if I saved you...'

Sarah looked at him contemptuously, 'but you didn't save me! You didn't even try! You had no idea where the buyer was taking me! You obviously didn't care what the buyer was going to do with me! You obviously didn't care if I was alive or dead!' Sarah broke off in a sob and Marianne reached out to take her hand as she continued a little calmer, 'This wasn't some sort of harmless game Con! It wasn't "Cowboys and Indians" where everyone can die and then when mum calls for tea everyone can jump straight up again! This was real! People could have died! Joseph could have died! I could have been...' Sarah stopped, unable to say the word again.

'But **he** didn't die! And no one managed to touch you...' Gary had to restrain himself from hitting Con as Sarah exploded at the stupidity of Con's statement.

'Are you freaking kidding me? Does it look like I was untouched?' Sarah tore off the dressing at her throat and held out her bandaged hands and bruised arms. 'The only reason Benzaar didn't manage to rape me was because I fought back! I fought to get back to Joseph!'

Con reached out to take her hands and in revulsion Sarah tore free. Before Gary or Joseph could react, Sarah's clenched fist slammed into Con's face. There was a satisfying crunching sound as she broke his nose. As blood streamed forth, Con screamed a chorus of profanities, slightly muffled as he pressed a tissue against his bloodied nose.

Joseph eased Sarah back down onto the lounge beside him and placed his arm around her waist as he whispered calming words into her ear. This angered Con especially when the Colonel tenderly pressed a clean handkerchief against Sarah's neck as her knife wound had begun to bleed again. Gary had already risen to his feet and left the room in search of a first aid kit; for Sarah, not for Con.

Spitting blood out of his mouth Con snarled, 'get your hands off her you filthy Arab!'

'Watch your mouth lad!' Inspector Lowe's hand went immediately to his sidearm as he stiffened in indignation. 'You're in enough trouble as it is!'

Joseph held up his hand to calm the situation down. 'It's all right Inspector. Perhaps you should take Mr Zuco to the police station now.'

Lowe relaxed and bowed slightly to Joseph. 'Of course, Colonel, I thought as Mr Zuco would not believe me when I told him he had lost his immunity that he needed to hear it from his own Ambassador. Also...' the Inspector's eyes rested briefly upon Sarah.

'Yes Inspector?' Joseph prompted, his arm tightening around his bride.

Lowe smiled, 'I thought it would be therapeutic for Miss Trent... sorry... Mrs Nasseur to be able to face her tormentor and finally make Mr Zuco realise that he never had a chance with someone who is a true lady.'

'Thank you Inspector Lowe.' Sarah blushed.

Gary came back into the room and placed the first aid kit into Sarah's hands to hold as Marianne took away Joseph's handkerchief to redress Sarah's throat. Con continued to rage.

'I can't believe I was prepared to waste any time or energy on such a fucking slut! Who'd want her once she's been with one of them?'

Before Joseph could struggle to his feet, Gary had turned and hit Con so hard that the Public Affairs Officer was knocked flat onto his back.

'Sorry Joseph but I'm claiming a brother's privilege on that one! Take him away Inspector,' Gary said, 'I think I can safely say we are all sick of the sight and sound of him!'

'Of course Major, it will be my pleasure,' Inspector Lowe picked Con up off the floor but before he could drag the prisoner out, Sarah stopped them.

'There is something I want Con to know before he is thrown into a prison cell,' she paused as she took in a deep breath, 'I spent last night in my husband's arms!'

Con roared in disgust as the Inspector dragged him out of the room.

Time To Celebrate

Joseph pressed his lips against Sarah's hair. 'Why did you tell him that, my heart?' He was not angry, just curious.

Sarah smiled mischievously, 'Technically it was true, just not in the way that disgusting animal would mean it. I want Con to suffer, just a little bit for all the hell he has put me through since we met. I know I should have been stronger but nothing I ever said to him discouraged him in the slightest. I don't deal well with confrontations.'

Joseph gently stroked Sarah's hair. 'From now on I will be there to protect you from all confrontations.'

Sarah took a deep breath to steady her emotions before asking, 'So it's finally over?'

'Not quite,' Joseph retrieved from his pocket a jeweller's box from which he removed a diamond ring. Cadem had recovered it from Draken when he had arrested him. 'I am sorry I am not able to go down on one knee again Sarah but the question is the same. Will you marry me?' Crystal gave an excited coo and grabbed hold of Gary's arm. She'd never been a witness to a proposal before.

As Joseph slipped the ring on Sarah's finger, she said, 'Yes, Joseph I will." Briefly he kissed her as their visitors broke into a cheer.

There was a strange scratching noise at the door attracting all their attention. Defensively the Colonel's hand travelled to his side arm as the door opened. An excited bark relieved the tension as the puppy, Simon pushed passed Abdul and launched himself into Sarah's lap. Abdul placed a tray of glasses onto the coffee table and presented a bottle of champagne to the Colonel.

'We thought we might need to celebrate,' James admitted as he took the bottle to open it and begin pouring out the sparkling liquid. Joseph frowned in disapproval but Marianne got in first.

'It's all right Colonel, its non-alcoholic.'

'And as you are my pseudo mother-in-law, I think you should start calling me Joseph.'

Gary rose to his feet to help hand out the glasses before raising his glass to Sarah. 'Does that mean as your pseudo brother-in-law I can promise to kick your butt if you don't treat my sister with the respect she deserves?'

'I'd like to see you try!'

'Boys behave!' Marianne sighed. 'Honestly we can't take you anywhere!'

James cleared his throat as he raised his glass. 'To Sarah Trent, a true survivor!'

All glasses were raised, 'To Sarah!'

With her cheeks touched with colour from all this attention Sarah glanced up shyly at Joseph and smiled, 'To our future!'

ABOUT THE AUTHOR

Anne-Marie Price was born and raised in Perth, Western Australia. She lives with her parents Margaret and Laurence and has two cats, Mickey and Jackson.

She has been a member of the Society of Women Writers WA since 2009 and has been their secretary since 2011.

Anne-Marie has had articles and flash fiction stories published in the SWW In Print Magazine as well as The Readers World Magazine. Although this is not the first novel she has written it is the first to be published.

In 1997, she obtained a Degree– Library And Information Studies, in 1998 a Diploma of Comprehensive Writing and in 2009 a Cert IV Training and Assessment to assist her ability to teach others the craft of writing.

Writing is in the blood of the Price family with Anne-Marie being the fourth generation of writers. Anne-Marie has been writing fiction since the age of ten and still uses pen and paper as a preference for a first draft.

www.ingramcontent.com/pod-product-compliance
Lightning Source LLC
Chambersburg PA
CBHW071109250626
47159CB00002B/670